FROM ALTAR TO CHIMNEY-PIECE

RECOVERED CLASSICS

From Altar to Chimney-piece

Selected Stories

Mary Butts

Preface by John Ashbery

McPHERSON & COMPANY

Library of Congress Cataloging-in-Publication Data

Butts, Mary, 1892-1937.
   From altar to chimney-piece : selected stories / Mary Butts : preface by John Ashbery
      p. cm.
   ISBN 0-929701-19-4 (cloth)—ISBN 0-929701-20-8 (paper)
   I. Title.
PR6003.U7A6 1992b
823'.912—dc20   91-32692

Printed on pH neutral paper.

Manufactured in the United States of America.
1 3 5 7 9 10 8 6 4 2   1992 1993 1994 1995

CONTENTS

CONTENTS

PREFACE

I first heard of Mary Butts in the summer of 1949 when, after graduating from Harvard, I had moved to New York and taken a summer job at the Brooklyn Public Library. It was a time when I was looking for contemporary writers, especially fiction writers, who had somehow escaped classification in what is now called "the canon." Only a couple of months earlier my friend Frank O'Hara had introduced me to the then-unknown Jean Rhys, Ronald Firbank, Flann O'Brien and Samuel Beckett (this was in pre-*Godot* days), and I had stumbled on Ivy Compton-Burnett, Laura Riding and Henry Green. All of whom began to persuade me that there was a lot more to twentieth-century literature than Harvard was then letting on.

My immediate superior at the Brooklyn Library was a man in his forties named Richard Elliott who, rather unexpectedly, turned out to be an expert guide to the esoterica I was interested in, and was himself a talented author of strange short stories of which only a few, as far as I know, were published, in obscure little magazines. Of the many writers he suggested I look into, two in particular have remained favorites: Jane Bowles and Mary Butts.

Except for Mary Butts, all the writers I've mentioned so far will doubtless be known to most readers of twentieth-century literature; doubtless she will not be. However, that is about to change. As Patricia Beer wrote in the *London Review of Books* recently: "She is one of the current victims of the fashionable drive to exhume 'forgotten women writers.' The category is dreary. Mary Butts is not."

Yet as recently as 1988, Humphrey Carpenter in *Geniuses Together,* his survey of the 1920s expatriate Montparnasse milieu in which Mary Butts moved, referred to her in passing as "a woman named Mary Butts." Still, she was admired and encouraged by Pound and Eliot; Ford Madox Ford published her in his *Transatlantic Review* (she also appeared in the American review *Hound and Horn*); she was a friend of Cocteau (who drew her portrait and illustrations for two of her books, and is the model for the character André in her story "The House-party"); had a close relationship with Virgil Thomson (who reportedly once proposed marriage to her); and seems to have frequented Gertrude Stein's salon. Of course, these credentials wouldn't matter if she were a negligible talent—the pages of 'twenties little magazines like *transition* and *The Little Review* are crammed with forgotten names that will doubtless remain so. Butts was an extraordinary original who deserves to be remembered on the strength of her work alone—one of those *femmes maudites* like Jean Rhys or Djuna Barnes, shadowy presences on the fringes of the Lost Generation in Paris. Until recently, despite the efforts of a few stubborn fans (the American poets Robert Duncan, Robert Kelly and Ken Irby among them), none was more spectral than Mary Butts. Then in 1988 her memoir of childhood, *The Crystal Cabinet,* was reprinted in England (Carcanet Press) and America (Beacon Press).

It was not, however, an ideal vehicle to launch a Mary Butts revival, since it will interest mainly those already won over to her fiction. It rambles occasionally when she sets out her ideas on the education of children and Freudian psychology, and tells us almost nothing of her certainly tumultuous adult years in London and Paris. Fortunately, there is now this collection of stories, as well as an omnibus edition of the novels *Armed with Madness* and *Death of Felicity Taverner* with a preface by Paul West (also published by McPherson & Company). The world can now decide whether it wants reprints of her first novel, *Ashe of Rings*—actually quite different from the others, in an "expressionist" style rather like that of the extraordinary novella "In Bayswater," reprinted here—and of her two historical novels, *The Macedonian* and *Scenes from the Life of Cleopatra,* as well as the still unreprinted stories and the uncollected and virtually unknown poems.

A biography of Mary Butts is said to be on the way, but until it materializes, our knowledge of the person behind the fictions will remain tantalizingly slight. The charms of *The Crystal Cabinet* lie mainly in her evocation of memories of early childhood and of the Dorset landscape which recurs constantly as a setting, a character really, in the novels and the stories. Family relationships are not dealt with in depth. Her brother Tony, obviously an important person in her life, barely appears, and though she speaks fondly of him, Virginia Woolf reported he told her that he had always hated Mary. (Tony was the companion of the writer William Plomer, and committed suicide in 1941.) Hence, it's difficult to know whether to look for traces of Tony in Felix, the heroine's sympathetic gay brother in the *Taverner* novels—

he sounds more like Felicity's cruel and capricious brother Adrian in the latter one, just as Adrian's mother and several scheming dowagers in the stories resemble, given certain of her traits set down in *The Crystal Cabinet,* Mary's mother.

We know that Mary Butts was born December 13, 1890, at Salterns, the family estate near the Dorset coast. The pleasantly eccentric house was notable chiefly for its collection of William Blake paintings (the phrase, "the crystal cabinet," is taken from Blake). They were acquired by her great-grandfather Thomas Butts, Blake's enthusiastic patron. She was educated at St. Andrews school in Scotland, went to live in London before World War I, and married the poet and translator John Rodker, by whom she had her only child, Camilla, in 1920. She seems to have lived mostly in Paris in the 1920s, with occasional revivifying visits to Dorset. Divorced from Rodker, she married the painter Gabriel Aitken (who designed the jacket of her book *Several Occasions*); they too were later divorced. She spent the last years of her life in Sennen, Cornwall, where she died in 1937, aged forty-six.

Paul West mentions her disjointed, dislocated style, and indeed she can be a difficult writer to "follow." Her fondness for double and even triple negatives ("Nothing upstairs makes me believe anything but that you are all mad, but she is too young to tell nothing but lies"; "It is getting more and more inopportune to suppose women have no secrets unconnected with sex"); her occasional carelessness in indicating who is saying what, to the point where we don't always know who is still in the room; a lapidary terseness that verges on mannerism and is sometimes merely mannered: these traits abound in her stories, which nevertheless succeed oftener than the novels. Perhaps she was aware of this, since in *Death of Felicity Taverner* she tries harder than elsewhere to construct a plot (in this case one rather like that of a detective novel), but it sags under the weight of too many stylistic *trouvailles,* often beautiful in themselves.

I seem to be building a case against her; that is by no means my intention, but since I've begun I should perhaps point to her other flaws before going on to her virtues. It will be noticed that the same character-types appear throughout her fiction, sometimes with the same names: the gay brother (her brother Tony?); the taciturn painter-husband (Aitken?); the selfish dominating mother; the Russian gigolo-in-Paris, Boris, who is sometimes *méchant* (to lapse into French, *à la* Butts), sometimes (as in *Felicity Taverner*) a perverse savior; and the central female character, sometimes called Scylla, who must confront Charybdises of her own, through whose eyes we see everything and who is Butts herself. The supporting cast includes a number of sharply etched expatriate Americans, sometimes heroic and almost as smart as the Europeans (like Carston, another savior, in *Armed with Madness*); sometimes victims of European corruptors (Paul in "The House-party"), sometimes victim-tormentors (Cherry in "From Altar to Chimney-piece"). Indeed, her take on Americans is fresh and unconventional, though it is hard to believe that the Stein-Toklas salon was a coven of satanist bolsheviks, as she seems to be suggesting in "From Altar to Chimney-piece."

The problem is that it isn't always possible to sympathize with these decadent darlings, so determined to put up a brave front in their reduced though hardly indigent circumstances, who have secret access to the earth's magic, who "know," as this passage from *Felicity Taverner* puts it rather too bluntly:

The Taverners were the kind of people who, if they have to choose, choose a boat and a library rather than a car and a club; cherry blossom before orchids, apples before tinned peaches, wine to whiskey, one dress from Chanel to six "from a shop." . . . They knew what in relation to Chardin has been called "all the splendour and glory of matter." Like him, they were in love.

This is atypical of the author. Usually she brings on her characters without explaining them, especially in the stories, where there is little room to do so. In the amazing one called "Brightness Falls," a character named Max tells the male narrator: "I feel I've got to tell someone, and it might as well be you. I won't ask you not to repeat it, because you won't be able to." This is in fact true of "Brightness Falls" and of her stories in general. They start just about anywhere. "This happened in the kind of house people live in who used not to live in that kind of house, who were taught to have very distinct opinions about the kind of people who lived in them" is the first line of "The Warning." They unfold, rather than unroll, with lacunae and bits of seemingly irrelevant information interrupting the flow, and then, having brought us somewhere, they leave us. Thus, at the end of "Brightness Falls," Max has just finished describing his wife's and her girl friend's hilarity after all three had passed through an episode that seems tinged with witchcraft:

"Anyhow, they got livelier and livelier; out of their clothes and into them again, telephones, taxis, dancing somewhere; more mischief—"
"Did you go out with them?"
"No, I would not do that."

End of story. But meanwhile we have been to some extraordinary places without leaving London: the enchantment scene takes place in Lincoln's Inn, where

The air was wild and mist-softened, moisture everywhere, but without shine. Like a picture that might easily become another picture, and has to be very good to stay put at all. It was all so dull, a London pool, and not deep enough.

Before that, when Parmys, Max's wife, is starting to explain the mystery, he says:

"I didn't want to listen, but I found myself attending to noises. In November the third week was still, you remember. A few leaves left to fall, and each one I thought was like a little word that you just couldn't catch. Light and brown and so few of them—whispers in the air. I used to stand at the window and watch, until I thought of coral and pearl and how red and white they are."

Where are we? Where have we come from? But the narrator has already warned us in the story's opening sentences: "There is no head or tail to this story, except that it happened. On the other hand, how does one know that anything happened? How does one know?"

Paul West likens Mary Butts to a hummingbird, and he is right: we admire hummingbirds because we can't quite see them; their erratic motion prevents that and is what we like about them. After reading Butts one is left with an impression of dazzle, of magic, but what made it is hard to pin down. Rereading after forty years her marvelous story "Friendship's Garland" (all the stories set in London as well as the London parts of *Ashe of Rings* have a haze of madness in them, the author being indeed "armed with madness"—a phrase, incidentally, that I would dearly love to trace), I found that the only thing I remembered from my first reading was a single metaphor. We are in rather sinister company at a café called the Craven.

JOHN ASHBERY

*Through the noise and the iron streets, even through the racing wind
the sun poured, roaring its heat through the wind at the huge buildings
and the crowd. Those are the hours when the city pays for being a city,
and is delivered over to the wind and the sun and their jackal the dust.
All the earth pays, but principally the city. On the other hand, inside the
Craven there is no nature at all. These things are not natural, marble
like cheese, red velvet, and plaster gilt.*

"Marble like cheese" was all I had retained, except for a sense
of the whole story as something evil, glittering, funny and, at the
end, surreally beautiful, as the narrator sees her face in a mirror
looking "half old, like a child's recovering from a sickness," and
later "like a child that has been dipped in dew." To remember
the stories, even just after finishing them, necessitates rereading
them; there is no other way to hang onto their breathless skitter-
ing as it evolves before us.

Though Mary Butts was not exactly unknown during her
lifetime, she became so almost immediately afterward. Only
now, after more than half a century, is the public discovering
her. The very features of her writing that taxed earlier readers—her startling ellipses, especially in conversations; her dras-
tic cutting in the cinematic sense; her technique of collaging bits
of poetry and popular song lyrics ("Lady Be Good" and "What'll
I Do") into the narratives—make her seem our contemporary.
So do the freewheeling and disordered lives of her characters,
who can be "wired" in a very 1990s way—the homosexual ones,
for instance, whom she treats with a sympathy and openness
astonishing for the England of her time. One keeps getting the
feeling that these stories were written yesterday.

"The old man belonged to the majority who do not approve—
say of cats or earrings or 'bus tickets," she writes in "In Bayswater." Today that majority is bigger than ever, but so is the minority that opposes it—the minority who approves. We need Mary
Butts now, to guide us, "armed with madness," through mazes
and forests to the pure sources of storytelling.

—JOHN ASHBERY

FROM ALTAR TO CHIMNEY-PIECE

The House

I

ONCE THERE WERE four friends who shared a house between them: a husband, a wife, and two sisters. The sisters' old nurse looked after them. They were poor, and the house was principally furnished with mirrors and pictures and books. When the things they had were dirty they washed them; when they were shabby they painted them. The house became a place where all their friends were equally glad to come, and where they could do anything or nothing, as they liked. There the four lived without a quarrel for three years.

At the end of that time they decided to go abroad for a spring and a summer, and inquired among their friends who would care to take the house and pay the rent and a little over while they were away. They could not find another family like themselves, but the husband and wife found a girl called Pippa to live in their part, and a young man called Arnold. They had known them a long time, and the arrangement seemed good.

One day the eldest sister said to the husband and wife who were called Julian and Anne:

"Our married sister—whom you don't know—and her husband and her babies and their nurse and their cook want to come to our part of the house for the summer. We could just get them in, and they always pay their rent." Julian, who was not listening, said, "All right," and Anne said, "That sounds all right." The old nurse said nothing at the time, but when Anne came down to the kitchen late in the evening for a cup of tea, she said to her:

"So Christina's coming when you're away, duckies?"

"So I've heard," said Anne. "Well, if she's anything like Charmian and Chloe, it will be all right." The old nurse tried out a fresh iron and said: "I shan't be here, I'm going to my brother's while you're away. I don't want to see her nosing about my kitchen."

"Does she nose, Nurse?"

"Always did, as a child, and always will. I don't care to see any of her servants washing up at my taps."

"Isn't she nice, Nurse?"

"I wouldn't care to say that, dearie. She's a lovely little housekeeper. But you'll see for yourselves. She'll be here for lunch to-morrow."

Anne went to look for Julian.

"There is a horrid woman coming," she said.

"How do you know? She is Charmian's sister."

"Nurse says she doesn't want her down in the basement with her cat. And Nurse was her nurse."

"Well, we shan't see her."

"Yes, we shall. She is coming to lunch to-morrow."

"Well, we can be out."

"No, I want to know the worst."

"Why hurry so? Anyhow, Pippa and Arnold will be in our rooms."

"I don't want the wrong sort of people in our house."

"What we want is the rent."

Next day Anne was late for lunch. The nurse was too busy carving to scold her, and there was a feeling of un-friendliness. She sat quiet, observing the woman who was Charmian's sister. She was not like either Charmian or Chloe. She was rounder and redder and not so quiet and not so gay; and she talked positively about babies and about books. She was very pleased that she was married, and wished to appear seriously intelligent and a woman of the world. Anne was thankful that Julian was out.

The husband amused Anne. He was little, and red-dish-dark, and there was no fat on him. He was restless

and genial, but every time he began to make her laugh
there was something in his voice that only allowed her half
a laugh. Each time she was ready, each time he checked
her. She thought he was like a hill pony, and understood
that she did not know the hills he came from. She sat back
in her chair and attended to Christina, his wife.

"I am convinced we shall go back to the matriarchate
again," she said. "I don't agree with Frazer there. He is
right about many things, but I feel that a partial return to
that phase of primitive life—"

Prunes and prisms, said Anne to herself—and it's not
her style, anyhow—and forgot her manners and answered
back: "I don't think he ever said what ought to happen.
Anyhow, a matriarchate, if there ever was one, sounds
unpleasant. Think of all the old women bullying the
young." Christina went on: "I'm sure that when descent is
traced through the mother, it has immense influence on
society. Think of the position of women in Homer."

"But," said Anne, "d'you think the people in Homer
wanted to be traced through their mothers? Think of all
the stories they invented to call themselves Zeus-born—"
and was out to argue to win. But Charmian got up from
the table, and took her sisters with her and the old nurse.

Anne had tea alone with Julian, and told him: "She's a
woman who has all the wrong points. She reads *The Golden
Bough* to keep her husband in order. She has married a
little black man from somewhere queer—"

"Horrid little man," said Julian. "Yes, I've seen him.
We passed the time of day on the stairs."

If Julian and Anne had had any sense, they would
have gone to Charmian and Chloe and told them that their
sister and her husband would not do. That, though they
would pay the rent and preserve the linen, they would
alter the house. Instead, Julian bought drinks and Anne
bought flowers, and they gave a party for their friends.
As they were arriving, Anne went upstairs and asked
Charmian and her sisters to come down. Taff and

Christina were not there. Charmian was making a cluster of grapes for Chloe's hair. She put them away, and said, "Yes, we're coming." Chloe threw her book away. She was so young that she still pretended not to care for parties, though she was the last to go to bed. Charmian, who was a Tuesday's child, stood up, folding her sewing away in a linen cloth, lit a cigarette and followed Anne lightly down the stairs.

It was a good party. They lit a bonfire in the garden, and threw the cat over it because it was the spring equinox. The cat did not care. Pippa and Arnold came, who were to live in Anne's part of the house. Pippa was more beautiful than Charmian or Chloe, or Anne, or any of their friends, but nobody minded. Arnold fell in love with Charmian.

When the bonfire was over, and they were sitting out on the round balcony, and some were drinking and some were singing, and some were looking at the sky, Taff and Christina came in and joined them. Pippa was running about, and Taff said to Charmian: "Who is that very pretty girl?" When Charmian introduced them, he said: "Delighted to meet you, Miss Arundel, delighted to meet you," and shook hands up and down. Christina looked at Arnold and said: "Who is that young man?" and Anne, who was watching, got up and said: "You will all know each other before long. You will be sharing the house while we are away." Christina said: "How I envy you all. But, you see, mine are only babies."

Anne knew that Julian was missing this, and saw Pippa attending with round eyes. They went down to the basement room to dance.

"Are they your friends, Mrs. Ker?" said Christina to Anne.

"Yes."

"Do they give many parties?"

"A great many parties."

"I only ask because of my babies, you know."

Anne thought: that is reasonable. "I will explain to them," she said, "that the parties must happen down here, where you won't hear them. It will be quite all right." But as they went downstairs together, she thought: It won't be. And I don't care what happens to these people at all.

The long room in the basement was full of young men and women. There was a brilliant fire, and the doors into the garden were open. There were glass panels on the walls, and the green floor was waxed like a sheet of dark water.

Anne was not at ease. She went to find Julian, but as she sat down beside him, he said: "I am going to bed," and Anne knew why.

He did not go, and Anne could not blame him, because his room was exactly over the party, and he would not have been able to sleep. He tried to talk to Taff and make him say what he thought about something, but Taff would not play. He enjoyed himself by pretending to be one of the party, but the fun lay, as someone said, "in only pretending to be a bee." All the time he talked a great deal, and now and again he looked at Pippa. Anne went and sat by Arnold, and they watched what was happening, very comfortably, with a box of chocolates between them.

First of all Pippa danced, and her round bright eyes looked at nothing. Taff's little eyes looked at her, and Christina looked too, not with attention but between her stitches, as if she were keeping a child in its place. Then she cried: "Really, how delightful. Will you show my babies how it's done? It must be so good for you. I believe in eurhythmics. Do you think of these dances all yourself?"

Pippa stood with her bare legs apart.

"Arnold and I make them up together, and when I do them on the stage, he produces me. Yes, I'll show your children, if they like. How old are they?"

"Only babies. Three and four. But Joan has some idea of dancing already, and I want her to express herself." Then she went on: "Now the fault I find in the Russian ballet is that they insist on technique for its own sake. —You see what I mean? —One is interested only in the wonderful way it is done."—Everybody listened, excepting Julian, on the floor between two mirrors, playing a very small game of bowls with some walnuts. He bowled once, much too far, and the kitten chased it. Christina went on: "You are not shown the emotions of the characters taking part, only their gestures."

"But don't you think that you get it all in with the gestures?" said Pippa. "I don't know; it seems to me all right. I wish I could dance like that. Anyhow, I can turn cart-wheels. I'm sure your kids would like that."

She turned cart-wheels across the floor to Arnold and Anne's corner, and laid herself down between them, very warm, her child's face turned to the ceiling.

Anne thought she heard Julian gnashing his teeth, but when she looked he was cracking nuts.

Later on, when Pippa was running about again, Taff came over to Anne and sat down by her and said: "Tell me, Mrs. Ker, who these people are."

She wanted to say: "They won't interest you. It would be much better to leave your acquaintance with them as it is, and then, please God, we may get through this summer in peace."

She was not brave enough. She tried to amuse him, and felt that if she amused him she would have to be disloyal. Then she said: "Charmian is the best story-teller I know. She knows everybody. Ask her."

She saw Charmian, looking like a woman in an old song, with her hair over her eyes in gold shells and a scarlet dress to her feet. She thought that Charmian would not be hurt, anyhow, and contrasted her choice words and conversation with her sister's streams of opinions it was impossible to cut short, examine, or in any way chasten. In fact, do anything but enjoy. Only she could not treat it as a play. She got up and caught Pippa, passing, by the hair.

"We'd better dance. Make us."

Arnold went to the piano. Taff and Christina danced once together and went to bed. Charmian followed them.

Some time later they were singing songs. There was a pause. Julian got up and said: "Sing this," and whistled. They heard it, and the room roared.

"Taffy was a Welshman.
Taffy was a thief,
Taffy came to my house and stole a piece of beef.
There I met a little man who wouldn't say his
    prayers.
I took him by the left leg and flung him down the
    stairs."

Anne thought: Where's Chloe? She was there, but she did not seem to mind.

Much later one of the men, who was a painter, said that he must see a picture that was in Charmian's sitting-room at the top of the house. Chloe told him the door, but in a few minutes he came back, embarrassed: "I say," he said, "I must have gone in at the wrong door, because before I turned the light on, a man's voice said, 'Good night, sir.'"

"I suppose," said Chloe, "that they missed their train, and you went into the room where they were asleep."

"But," said the painter, "why did he say good night to me like that? It was a mistake. I wasn't even drunk."

"That's how they do be talking," said Julian, surprising Anne by using one of the turns of Charmian's speech. Agreeable from her mouth, it sounded ridiculous in his. Or spiteful. The painter protested: "It sounds silly—I don't know why, but I feel embarrassed. Not as though I had blundered into your room, Anne's, in the middle of the night."

"He only wanted to go to sleep," said Chloe.

"How did he manage to make you feel a Don Juan

manqué?" said Arnold anxiously, who was in love with Charmian.

Next day Anne got up early, made some tea and woke Julian, and said: "What about that woman?"

"What about her?" said Julian.

"She won't play up, and our tenants are half across each other already."

"She plays her play. The common and ancient game, if you like it, of putting one's neighbours in the wrong."

"Envy," said Anne.

"Perhaps," said Julian.

"Patronage," said Anne.

"Principles," said Julian.

"What about the rights of man?"

"She has them too."

"She'll bitch up our good house."

"Probably," said Julian.

"Malice," said Anne.

"Position," said Julian. "I can't stand her husband at any price."

"Snobbery," said Anne.

"Certainly," said Julian.

"What has a woman like that got to be a snob about?"

"What are English people snobs about, anyhow?" said Julian, who was a Scot.

"What are we going to do about it?" said Anne, who was not.

"Nothing," said Julian, and went to sleep again. Anne sucked her thumb, but after tea she called on Christina again.

"I'm sorry if you were disturbed last night, it was a stupid mistake." she said.

"Of course," said Christina, "I understand. It was only an accident. I am sure we shall get on very well." Anne thought: Now that sounds kind. Charmian smiled. Her smile usually quieted Anne. Now, for the first time, she noticed that she was critical of Charmian's smile.

The three young ladies went downstairs.

II

Julian and Anne sat out in Paris in the sun and read a letter from Pippa which said:

"We have not got on badly, so far. One thing went wrong, but I think I put it right. It is light very early now and I came back from a dance with three boys. I went down to the kitchen to cook breakfast, or it wouldn't have happened. Cherry began to play Purcell in the room under their bedroom and they thumped on the floor. Cherry didn't mind, I mean he didn't stop, and the sausages took a long time.

"Next day I stopped Mr. Guest, you called Taffy, on the stairs and shook hands with him and told him I was very, very sorry. He said it was all right, and next day there was a box of cigarettes, with a message, 'from a disagreeable neighbour,' on it, and next day there were fireworks in the park, and he and I were alone in the house except for the children, and we watched them a little. They shot up over the trees. It sounded like air-raids and I was rather frightened. He told me at first it was guns.

"A vest of mine got mixed up in their wash. I don't know how. Or why. Do you? I think it is all right . . ."

"It might be much worse," said Anne.

"Or, you might say it has begun," said Julian.

It was a long way off, and they were happy. It was interesting to think of two kinds of life going on in the house, and wonder which would come off best. Anne said it would be all right, because if Pippa was naughty Taff and Christina knew the rules of behaviour for people who were not living under their own roof. There were going to be amusing stories. That was all.

After this Julian and Anne left Paris. A huge train took them out into the middle of Europe, and they went on, always through new countries, till they forgot that there was a house in England from which they came, to which they would go back. Julian would never have remembered. Anne only partly forgot; both would have been content to go on, she for a long time, he for ever.

In the middle of a black Silesian wood a letter found them. Anne read it aloud. It made a small tinkling noise that did not sound real:

"You know Charmian and Arnold like each other. They arranged that he should meet them for a time when he went away. A postcard came from her to him, and Taff and that woman Christina saw it. I know he took it upstairs to read and put it back. Arnold asked him for it. That didn't matter because Taff was in the wrong; but a little later there was more trouble about bedroom doors. Another friend went up to look at that picture and walked into the room where Christina's servants slept. They shrieked; I suppose they thought they were being ladies; but Taff wrote us a letter. He said it was the second occurrence, and he must mention it because a servant's feelings had been hurt. There were two and he didn't say which. Arnold apologised at once. They were all right about it. 'We know the young gentleman' sort of touch. It wasn't that anyone was drunk but there were lots of doors. Dear Anne, I am very sorry about it."

"That's that," they said, and forgot about it.

They went out into the black woods that go on for ever and ever. Anne made up a song called "Quiet in the Woods," about a tall, magic animal with cold, innocent eyes, walking between the trees when no one was there.

Anne wanted to turn east and follow the Danube, but Julian's mind went north always to the edge of the snow. They went to the Baltic and ran in and out of the water all day, and lay stretched on the beaches. The memory of

England was like an old top humming, turning slower and slower until it fell off sideways into the sea.

In September, when it began to get cold too soon, they turned south to meet Charmian and Chloe in Berlin. (Anne said: "In autumn it should rain, and there should be a warm wind. This wind comes from another place and I want more clothes.") They walked in the Tiergarten through a storm of leaves. Only Julian liked it. In a week they were going home. It was then that Anne remembered the two letters, and one day when they were at dinner she said: "Charmian, you have not been so far away. What has happened to the house?"

Charmian said, without moving an eyelash: "I think it has gone off as well as could be expected."

Anne wanted to go home. "Then there has been trouble?" she said.

"Tell us about it, Charmian," said Julian.

Chloe began:

"There was the fuss about a postcard Taff read. Do you know about that?"

"Yes, and about the maids' room."

"Well, when Arnold was away, I expect Pippa did what she liked. She is quite young enough to show Taff and Christina she didn't like them."

"All right, young Chloe," said Julian.

"There must have been a great deal too much noise," said Charmian. "I think you will find Taff and Christina were so far in the right."

"But what has actually happened?" said Julian.

"Nothing," said the sisters.

Anne thought: I don't believe you. I have never not believed anything you have said before, but I don't believe you now.

"I can tell you one thing," said Chloe, "the house has been sold. To an old man who lives up the road. Anne, we really don't know anything more. That news came in a letter from Nurse. Christina's cook told her."

But Anne was irritated and said: "Nurse said that your sister turns the gas off and keeps the fire down as though to have two saucepans boiling at once was the shortest cut to ruin."

"It sometimes is," said Charmian, in her light voice. "But those two never got on. Christina is used to authority, and so is Nurse. It is better to keep them away from each other."

"Anne," said Julian later, "Chloe and Charmian have nothing to do with whatever has happened. If you let houses to people like that, you take the consequences."

"Little squireens," said Anne.

"A managing woman, two ordinary servants, Pippa and Arnold—casual people —"

"—People like Taff and Christina dislike charm—"

"—Certainly they do."

"Never mind," said Anne. "I'll have them all out in a week."

A small grey letter came for Julian. He turned away, read it, put it in his pocket and looked at Anne. He went out, walked half the way down the Unter den Linden and turned back. He met Chloe and they went to drink beer and read it together:

> "How awful for you and Anne about the house. I take it that you will have to go, but that it will be all right for Charmian and Chloe."

Chloe shrugged her shoulders. "Julian, you know this may be nothing but gossip from the club."

"So I suppose, but I must tell Anne; and Anne loves the house. . . ."

Anne snatched the letter, read it, and backed away from them, staring.

"This is how it stands. The house is on a lease in my name. I have broken the lease. Apart from any lies the new landlord may have heard, I have sub-let. I have left the garden to be a paradise of dandelions, and people have hung out their washing on the balcony rails. God only knows what Pippa may have done. But the point is that Pippa does not know. I have a letter from her to-day about fun, and nothing else.

"I want to go home at once."

III

It surprised Anne that the house was still there. She stared over her shoulder as she kissed the old nurse, trying to see into her rooms that seemed hollow with dark, and colder than the October night. She worked till past midnight, setting her own room exactly, dragging out of her boxes colour that would cover the disorder, sleeping under a leopard-skin and a Polish shawl.

Next day they all worked at the house while the telephone bell rang, and their friends found out they were back, until they realised it themselves. Anne found two letters from a lawyer on her writing-table. They frightened her. They said the garden was full of weeds. Which it was. They said that there had been noises at night. Which no one tried to deny. They said that to sub-let to an unknown number of people made a break in the lease. Which it did.

But Julian said: "This is a new landlord asserting himself. What he minds is that the house is let so cheap. Order a gardener at once. Tell him to take out the dandelions and put in geraniums. I don't care if geraniums will grow now or not. You must do that, Anne. Send these letters to your lawyers. Tell them that you are allowed to sub-let, which you are, though you interpreted it freely. Say that your tenants were the children of bishops, and that there will be no more noise. Don't pay the rent. I tell you, it will be quite all right."

Anne left off polishing the surfaces of the house, the glass, the brass, the wood, and did what he told her. But she was full of fear and pain, and the realisation that something had been spoiled. Never before had she loved the house so much as now that its unity had gone, destroyed by Taff and Christina, not deliberately, but naturally. Her innocence was to suffer, and Charmian's and Julian's. But Charmian must have known.

She went to see her lawyer.

"He told me that I had done everything wrong, and that the landlord has a case. But I think he means that there is something which hasn't been said yet. I am going to see the landlord."

"Would you like me to see him?" said Julian.

"No. I have told him to come here. A woman had better see a man."

Pippa came at once. She said:

"Since the last row, when Arnold's friend got into the servant's room, I thought it was all right. There were a few parties, but they were downstairs and indoors. I don't think we ever saw each other. Not once in three days. I used to play with the children now and then, but even that stopped. Yes, I hung out chemises on the balcony railings to dry. I'm sorry about that. I saw an old man walking about the garden. I ran down the steps to him, and he said: 'I have bought the house,' and he looked at me and went away."

"Had you much on?"

"Everything, Anne, except my shoes and stockings."

"No one," said Julian, "is going to law about Pippa's bare feet."

"Who cares about the law?" said Anne, "when the house itself is broken up."

Anne went upstairs to see Charmian and Chloe, and found Taff there. He sprang up. She did not like to look at him, because she thought that it would be difficult for him to look at her. She gave Charmian back two books, borrowed another, and said:

"What did you tell the landlord, Mr. Guest?"

He began to talk at a pace, to a tune that made her

feel that it did not matter, and she was not there. It did not matter because he would never, unless it went with his plan, tell the truth. He always had a plan, and the plan did not matter because it had nothing to do with the truth. He said that he had never seen the landlord, it was his wife who had seen the landlord, and she was in the country, and that Charmian must write to her, and she would tell them about it. This was the truth, and the truth did not matter. Anne left them.

An hour later, the new landlord called on her.

"Mr. and Mrs. Guest—" he said.

"Of whom are you speaking? —Of Miss Trelawney's married sister and her husband? —Yes."

"People in their position—"

"In their position—?"

"Have been very seriously offended—"

"And by what?"

"By the conduct of other tenants who have lived here."

"What did the other tenants do?"

He looked out into the garden, where an old man was setting geraniums in a plump bed of dark soil.

"I had several conversations with Mrs. Guest— She has returned, I understand, to her country estate."

"She is out of town."

"She was naturally very much surprised—and that the neighbourhood should complain—"

"Of what did the neighbourhood complain?"

"Of noise, and of articles of dress hung out on the balcony to dry—"

"The clothes of Mrs. Guest's children—"

"Colonel Hicks, who lives next door, did not mention any children's clothes. There was a young woman, commonly referred to as Pippa—"

"Miss Arundel. Go on."

"And a young man, Mr. Copley—"

"Arnold," she said, to be sure that he was meant.

"—entertained their friends in a suspicious manner."

"Tell me what they did."

"Mrs. Guest had doubts of their relations."

Ho! thought Anne. More fool she.

"Their friends came here at night to sing and drink. The piano was played at all hours. They even found their way into the upstairs bedrooms. It was impossible to foresee what strange young man or woman would be found in the bathroom in the morning—"

"It was agreed that the bathroom should be shared."

"This Miss Arundel was seen in the bathroom with a man. She was seen by Mrs. Guest's nurse—"

"I do not think that the relations of landlord and tenant are affected by Mrs. Guest's nurse."

"Mrs. Ker, you must know what it is I wish to say."

"Say it, then."

"I can only remind you of the number of persons who were known to have slept in the long room downstairs. From that it seems plain to me that, for some months, this has been little better than a disorderly house."

"You mean a brothel?" An image of Christina as Bawd created itself in Anne's mind. Brothel. Arnold. That splendid child. "I think Mr. Guest is upstairs. He had better come down."

"I have not, up to now, become acquainted with Mr. Guest. You must understand that I am reluctant to offend them—"

(Can I say that Christina is a *divorcée,* trying to get up in the world again? Oh, my soul, how mean you are. Besides, that is the kind of lie that is found out. I must try dignity, whitewash, and truth. But what am I to say?) She heard herself saying: "Miss Arundel is young. Mr. Copley is an actor. Mrs. Guest is quite unknown to us. Young girls who are dancers do not understand that women like Mrs. Guest are specialists in impropriety." Julian came in. She heard him say to the landlord: "I'm sorry there have been difficulties, and that a lot of nonsense has been talked; but you realise that we have our lease and are now in possession. There is no need to discuss Mrs. Guest's misapprehensions."

"But," said the landlord, "I saw Miss Arundel run up the road in her nightdress to see a fire myself."

"I expect it was her practice dress. Anyhow, Mrs. Guest should have complained to us. From her point of view, it was our house—" She was surprised that the landlord had no more to say to Julian, and that when Julian saw him to the door, they left the house together. She went down into the kitchen, where the old nurse was ironing, and sat on the corner of the table and watched her. The nurse's cat rubbed her ankles.

"Glad to see us, Nurse?"

"Yes, dearie. Now you're back I don't want for anything." Anne kissed her. The warm smell of ironing was like peace, it was peace to be scolded a little for cigarette-ends left on the dresser, to bring frocks to be pressed before parties, to have rings found left about the house; all the things old nurses do.

"Tell me, did the cook next door tell you anything about what happened last summer?"

"Well, dearie, she said that there were rare larks going on, high old times, as you might say; and that Miss Pippa was a little love with her boys and her bare legs, and Mr. Arnold behaved quite like a gentleman when her cat had kittens in his portmanteau."

"You know that Taff and Christina tried to get us turned out?" The old nurse said nothing. Anne said: "I hate them."

"Well, precious, I know whom I like."

"Why did they try and hurt us? Hullo! there's Julian."

The night was wet. Julian shook the drops off his hair like a dog.

"Why did you take the landlord out?"

"To give him a drink and find out what it's all about; and I have. Taff and Christina were trying to buy the house off him. Between them they might have turned us out, and kept Charmian and Chloe. That, I suppose, was why it was worth while to suggest that Pippa was a harlot." Anne stared. The old nurse went on ironing. . . .

The next night Arnold came to dine with Charmian, but after dinner he came down to Anne's room, and Julian gave him a drink.

"This room is the same," he said. "It was my room when I was here. I had Taff Guest above me. I used to fancy he sat with his ear to the window to hear if I was talking to Pippa or not. He is still here; that was why I came down."

"Why should he?" said Julian.

"To tell Charmian who his friends were," said Anne.

"Have another drink," said Julian.

"I was asked here to-night to hear a letter," Arnold said. "After I'd heard it, I should have come away anyhow."

"Do you remember it?"

"It was written to be remembered. It was from Charmian's sister."

"Say it."

Arnold repeated: "'Of course one is not intolerant. But the children's maid made me understand what common women think of a type like Pippa. Especially one like ours who has worked in a rescue-home. She asked me if I thought it was safe to use the bath after her. Of course, I explained that it was not quite like that, but she recognised the type.'"

"Stop!" shouted Anne.

"Go on," said Julian. Arnold went on:

"'As for that unfortunate child, Pippa, when I think of what her life must be in ten years, I can only hope that she will suddenly fall down dead.' And Charmian said to me: 'It's a point of view, Arnold. So many people think like that.' So I came down here."

* * * * *

Julian shaved in the bathroom and talked to the old nurse. Anne came restlessly upstairs to join them.

"See what I've found," said the old nurse. "It isn't often they leave anything behind them. It's a bottle of something that'll come in handy for the dustbin. Mr. Taff's written something on it too." Julian took it from her and read: "*You may find this useful.*"

"Why?" said Anne.

"I think," said Julian, "it's the disinfectant for Pippa's bath. Yes, it must be that. The last word's with them. Don't tremble so, Anne. Remember, if you play any game, you must play it thoroughly and well. Even games like that—and not shy at details. Try and think of it like that, my dear; try and think of it like that."

"She said," said Anne, "she said: *'Mine are only babies.'*"

With and Without Buttons

I T IS NOT ONLY true, it is comforting, to say that incredulity is often no more than superstition turned inside
out. But there can be a faith of disbelief as inaccurate as its
excess, and in some ways more trying, for the right answers to it have not yet been thought up. It was only because Trenchard said at lunch that the mass was a drama-
tised wish-fulfilment that what came after ever happened.
At least I wish we did not think so. It was trying to get out
anyhow, but if he had not irritated us and made us want
to show off, we would not have made ourselves serviceable
to it. And it was we who came off lightly. To him it has
been something that he has not been able to shake off.
When it happened he behaved so well about it, but that
didn't save him. Now he cannot think what he used to
think, and he does not know what else there is that he
might think.

I am seeing him now, more vividly than I like. He was
our next-door neighbour in a remote village in Kent. A
nest of wasps had divided their attention between us, and
we had met after sunset to return their calls with cyanide
and squibs.

He was a sanguine man, positive and hearty, actually
emotional. He had known and done a great many things,
but when he came to give his account of them, all he had
to say was a set of pseudo-rationalisations, calling the bluff,
in inaccurate language, of God, the arts, the imagination,
the emotions. That is not even chic science for laymen
to-day. He might have thought that way as much as he
liked, but there was no reason, we said, to try and prove it
to us all one hot, sweet, blue-drawn summer, in a Kentish
orchard; to sweat for our conversion; to shame us into

agreement. Until the evening I told him to stop boring us with his wish-fulfilments, for they weren't ours, and saw his healthy skin start to sweat and a stare come into his eyes. That ought to have warned me, as it did my sister, of whom I am sometimes afraid. It did warn us, but it wound us up also. We went home through the orchard in the starlight and sat downstairs in the mid-summer night between lit candles, inviting in all that composed it, night hunting cries and scents of things that grow and ripen, cooled in the star-flow. A world visible, but not in terms of colour. With every door and every window open, the old house was no more than a frame, a set of screens to display night, mid-summer, perfume, the threaded stillness, the stars strung together, their spears glancing, penetrating an earth breathing silently, a female power asleep.

"All he hears is nature snoring," said my sister. "Let's give him a nightmare." It was a good idea.

"How?" I said.

"We'll find out to-morrow. I can feel one about." I got up to close the doors before we mounted with our candles. Through walls and glass, through open doors or shut, a tide poured in, not of air or any light or dark or scent or sound or heat or coolness. Tide. Without distinction from north or south or without or within; without flow or ebb, a Becoming; without stir or departure or stay: without radiance or pace. Star-tide. Has not Science had wind of rays poured in from interstellar space?

There is no kind of ill-doing more fascinating than one which has a moral object, a result in view which will justify the means without taking the fun out of them. All that is implied when one says that one will give someone something to cry about. It was that line which we took at breakfast.

"We'll try his simple faith," we said. "We'll scare him stiff and see how he stands the strain. We'll haunt him." And asked each other if either of us knew of a practising vampire in the neighbourhood or a were-cow.

MARY BUTTS

It was several days before we hit on a suitable technique, examining and rejecting every known variety of apparition, realising that apparatus must be reduced to a minimum, and that when nothing will bear scrutiny, there must be very little given to scrutinise. In fact, what we meant to do was to suggest him into an experience—the worse the better—wholly incompatible with the incredulities of his faith. That it would be easy to do, we guessed; that it would be dangerous to him—that appeared at the moment as part of the fun. Not because we did not like him, but because we wanted to have power over him, the power women sometimes want to have over men, the pure, not erotic power, whose point is that it shall have nothing to do with sex. We could have made him make love, to either or to both of us, any day of the week.

This is what we planned, understanding that, like a work of art, once it had started, its development could be left to look after itself.

"Suppose," said my sister, "that we have heard a ridiculous superstition in the village that there is Something Wrong with the house. We will tell him that, and when he has gone through his reaction exercises—it may take a day or so and will depend on our hints, and if we make the right ones, the battle's won—he will ask us what the story is."

"What is it to be?" I said, who can rarely attain to my sister's breadth of mind.

"That does not matter. Because before we begin we'll *do* something. Anything. A last year's leaf for a start, so long as it can go into a series—on his blotter or his pillow. We're always in and out. We'll put them there and get asked round for the evening and start when we see one, and that's where our village story begins. All that he has to get out of us is that there *is* a story, and that wet leaves or whatever it is we choose are found about. Signatures, you know. If he doesn't rise the first night, he'll find that leaf when he goes to bed. It depends on how well we do it—"

I recognised a master's direction, but it all seemed to depend on our choice of stimulants. Last year's leaves, delicate damp articulations; coloured pebbles, dead flies, scraps of torn paper with half a word decipherable.... A mixture of these or a selection?

"Keep it tangible," my sister said—"that's the way. Our only difficulty is the planting of them."

"Which," I asked, "are suitable to what?" It seemed to be necessary in laying our train to determine the kind of unpleasantness for which they were ominous. But I could not get my sister to attend.

"It's not that way round," she said at length—"dead bees, feathers, drops of candle-grease? Old kid gloves? With and Without Buttons. That will do."

I felt a trifle queer. "Well," I said, "they're the sort of things a man never has in his house, so that's sound so far. But women do. Not the sort óf things we wear, but he'd not know that. And how do we get hold of them?"

"There's a shoe box in the loft full of them, by the door into his place when these houses were one." (Our cottages were very old, side by side, with a common wall, our orchards divided by a hedge. We had rented ours from a friend who had recently bought it as it stood from a local family which had died out, and of which very little seemed known.) My sister said:

"Shiny black kid and brown, with little white glass buttons and cross stitching and braid. All one size, and I suppose for one pair of hands. Some have all the buttons and some have none and some have some—" I listened to this rune until I was not sure how many times my sister had said it.

"With and without buttons," I repeated, and could not remember how often I had said that.

After that we said nothing more about it, and it was three days later that he asked us to supper, and we walked round through the gap in the hedge in the pure daylight, and sat in his little verandah, whose wooden pillars spread

as they met the roof in fans of plaited green laths. Prim
fantasy, with its french windows behind it, knocked out of
walls of flint rubble three feet thick. Roses trailed up it. A
tidy little home, with something behind it of monstrous old
age one did as well to forget.

"By the way," he said. (As I have said before, his name
was Trenchard, and he had come back to his own part of
England to rest, after a long time spent in looking after
something in East Africa.) "By the way, have either of you
two lost a glove?"

So she's got busy already and didn't tell me, the spoil
sport, I thought.

"No," we said, "but one always does. What sort of a
glove?"

"A funny little thing of brown kid with no buttons. I
didn't think it could be yours. I found it on the top of the
loft stairs. Outside the door. Here it is." He went inside
and came out on to the verandah where we were having
supper, a moment later, puzzled.

"Here it is," he said. "I put it in the bureau, and the
odd thing is that when I went to look for it I found another. Not its pair either. This one's black."

Two little lady-like shiny kid gloves, the kind worn by
one's aunts when one was a child. I had not yet seen our
collection. The black had three of its buttons missing. We
told him that they were not the kind that women wore
now.

"My landlady bought the place furnished," he said.
"Must have come out of the things the old owners left
behind when they died." My sister gave a slight start, a
slight frown and bit her lip. I shook my head at her.

"What's up?" he asked, simply.

"Nothing," we said.

"I'm not going to be laughed at by you," said my sister.

"I'm not laughing," he said, his goodwill beaming at
us, prepared even to be tolerant.

"Oh, but you'd have the right to—"

After that, he wanted to know at once.

"It's playing into your hands," she said, "but don't you know that your half of the house is the Village Haunt? And that it's all about gloves? With and without buttons?"

It was ridiculously easy. He was amiable rather than irritated at her story, while I was still hurt that she had not first rehearsed it with me. She began to tell him a story about old Miss Blacken, who had lived here with her brother, a musty old maid in horrible clothes, but nice about her hands; and how there was something—no, not a ghost—but something which happened that was always preceded by gloves being found about. This we told him and he behaved very prettily about it, sparing us a lecture.

"But it's not quite fair," he said. "I mustn't be selfish. She must leave some at your place. Remember, in her day, it was all one house."

Then we talked about other things, but when we had gone home I found my sister a little pensive. I began on my grievance.

"Why didn't you tell me you had begun? Why didn't you coach me?" Then she said:

"To tell you the truth, I hadn't meant to begin. What I said I made up on the spot. All I'd done was that just before we left I ran up to the loft and snatched a glove from the box and left in on his bureau. That's the second one he found."

"Then what about the one he found outside the loft door?"

"It's that that's odd. That's why he never thought it was us. I haven't had a chance to get to that part of his house. I didn't put it there."

* * * * *

Well, now that the affair was launched, we felt it had better go on. Though I am not sure if we were quite so keen about it. It was as though—and we had known this to be possible before—it had already started itself. One sometimes feels this has happened. Anyhow, it was two days later before I thought it was my turn to lay a glove on his premises, and went up to our loft and took one out of the box. There was nothing in it but gloves. I took a white one, a little cracked, with only two buttons, and having made sure he was out, slipped through the hedge and dropped it at the foot of the stair. He startled me considerably by returning at that instant. I said I had come for a book. He saw the thing.

"Hullo," he said, "there's another. It's beginning. That makes four."

"Four?" I said. "There were only two the other night."

"I found one in my bedroom. A grey. Are we never going to get a pair?"

Then it occurred to me that he'd seen through us all along, and was getting in ahead with gloves. I took my book and returned to my sister.

"That won't do," she said, "he's sharp, but we didn't begin it. He found his first."

I said: "I'm beginning to wonder if it mightn't be a good thing to find out in the village if anything is known about Miss Blacken and her brother."

"You go," said my sister, still pensive.

I went to the pub when it opened and drew blank. I heard about diseases of bees and chickens and the neighbours. The Post Office was no good. I was returning by a detour, along a remote lane, when a voice said:

"You *were* asking about Miss Blacken along at Stone Cottages?"

It was only a keeper who had been in the pub, come up suddenly through a gate, out of a dark fir planting. "—Seeing as you have the uses of her furniture," said he. We passed into step. I learned that after fifty years' odd residence in the place there was nothing that you might have to tell about her and waited.

"—Now her brother, he was not what you might call ordinary." Again that stopped at that.

"—Regular old maid she was. If maid she'd ever been. Not that you could be saying regular old man for him, he wasn't either, if you take my meaning, Miss."

I did. Finally I learned—and I am not quite sure how I learned—it was certainly not all by direct statement—that Miss Blacken had been a little grey creature, who had never seemed naturally to be living or dying; whose clothes were little bits and pieces, as you might say. Anyhow, she'd dropped something—an excuse me, Miss, petticoat, his wife had said—on the green, and run away without stopping to pick it up, opening and shutting her mouth. It was then it had begun. If you could call *that* beginning. I was asking to know what that was? In a manner of speaking he couldn't rightly say. It was the women took it to heart. What became of the petticoat? That was the meaning of it. 'Twasn't rightly speaking a petticoat at all. There weren't no wind, and when they came to pick it up, it upped and sailed as if there were a gale of wind behind it, right out of sight along the sky. And one day it had come back; hung down from the top of an elm and waved at them, and the women had it there were holes in it, like a face. And no wonder, seeing it had passed half a winter blowing about in the tops of the trees. Did it never come down to earth? Not it they said. Nor old Miss Blacken start to look for it, except that it was then that people remembered her about at nights.

A little pensive now myself, I asked about gloves and was told no more than that "they say that she's left her gloves about."

I returned to my sister and we spent the evening doing a reconstruction of Miss Blacken out of victorian oddments. It was most amusing and not in the least convincing.

"To-morrow, shall we feed him a glove?" I said. It was

then that it came across our minds, like a full statement to that effect, that it was no longer necessary. The gloves would feed themselves.

"I know what it is we've done," said my sister, "we've wound it up."

"Wound up what?" I answered. "Ghost of a village eccentric, who was careful about her hands?"

"Oh no," said my sister. "I don't know. Oh no."

* * * * *

After another three days, I said:

"Nothing more has happened over there. I mean he's found no more gloves. Hadn't we better help things along a bit?"

"There was one yesterday in my room, unbuttoned," she said. "I didn't drop it."

I was seriously annoyed. This seemed to be going too far. And in what direction? What does one do when this sort of thing happens? I was looking as one does when one has heard one's best friend talking about oneself, when the shadow of a heavy man fell across our floor. It was Trenchard. My sister looked up and said quickly:

"We've found one now."

"Have you?" he said. "So have I." He hesitated. There was something very direct and somehow comforting in the way he was taking it, piece by piece as it happened, not as what he would think it ought to mean. It was then that we began to be ashamed of ourselves. He went on:

"You know my cat. She's her kittens hidden somewhere in the loft and I wanted to have a look at them. I went up softly not to scare her. You know it's dark on that top stair. I got there, and then I heard—well—a little thing falling off a step. Thought it was a kitten trying to explore. Peered and felt and picked up a glove."

He pulled it out of his pocket and held it up by a finger with slight distaste. A brown one this time.

"One button," he said. "The kittens aren't big enough

to have been playing with it and the cat wasn't about. There's no draught. Funny, isn't it? Reminded me of one of those humpty-dumpty toys we had, a little silk man with arms and legs and a painted face, and a loose marble inside him to make him turn over and fall about."

My sister said:

"We've found a box of loose gloves in our attic close to your bricked-up door."

His answer was that it was bricked up all right, and had we thought to count them in case either of our maids was up to some village trick. We hadn't, but I noticed that he mistrusted our maids as little as we did. Also that his behaviour was so reasonable because he had not yet thought that there was any cause for suspicion.

"Let's do it now," he said. "Put them all back, yours and mine. Count them and lock your door."

He went back and fetched his five, and together we went upstairs. They sat on a basket trunk while I emptied the box.

"Twenty-seven. Eleven pairs in all and one missing." I shovelled them back into the cardboard box, yellow with time and dust. I looked up at his broad straight nose and my sister's little one that turns up. Both were sniffing.

"There's a smell here," they said. There was. Not the dust-camphor-mouse-and-apple smell proper to lofts.

"I know what it is," Trenchard said, "smelt it in Africa in a damp place. Bad skins."

The loft went suddenly darker. We looked up. There was no window, but someone had cut the thatch and let in a sky-light. Something was covering it, had suddenly blown across it, though outside there was no wind. I took the iron handle with holes in it to stick through the pin in the frame, and threw it up. The piece of stuff slid backwards into the thatch. I put my arm out, caught hold of it and pulled it in. A piece of calico with a stiff waxy surface, once used for linings, again some time ago. It seemed to have no shape, but there were holes in it. Holes not tears.

"Nasty slummy rag," I said. "I suppose it was lying about in the thatch."

Our thatch was old and full of flowers. This thing went with dustbins and tin cans. One piece was clotted together. A large spider ran out of it. I dropped it on the floor beside the box and the gloves. I was surprised to see Trenchard look at it with disgust.

"Never could stand seeing things go bad," he said. We left the attic, locking the door, and went downstairs. We gave him the key. It seemed the decent thing to do.

Over a late and thoughtful tea, we talked of other things. We did not think it necessary to tell him what the keeper had said.

* * * * *

The evening was exquisite and the next day and the next night. Days refreshed with night-showers to draw out scent, and steady sun to ripen; a pattern on the world like the dry dew on a moth's wing, or the skin on a grape or a rose. And nothing more happened. The next evening Trenchard was to give a little party for his birthday, for some friends who would motor over; and my sister and I were to see that all was in order for it, flowers and fruit and wine and all the good cold things to eat. We had the delicate pleasant things to do; to slice the cucumbers and drench sprays of borage and balm-in-Gilead for the iced drinks. The almonds did not come, so we salted some ourselves, blanching them in the garden, getting hot in the kitchen over pans of burnt salt.

At about six o'clock we went back to dress. Trying, as was appropriate, to look like Paris, in compliment to Trenchard, but principally to the garden and to the weather and to the earth. There was a bump overhead from the attic.

"What's that?" said my sister, painting her face.

"I left the skylight open," I said. "It must have slipped.

Let's leave it. Am I in a state of dress or undress to go up there?"

She was ready before I was, and said that she was going across to Trenchard's to have one more look to see if all was in order there. Half of our day's work had been to keep him out of the way. We had just sent him up to the village after more strawberries and hoped that he would be back in time—and there was still plenty of time—for him to dress. As she went, I heard his step at his front door, and a few moments later, my dressing finished, I went downstairs and out across the orchard to join them. He had gone upstairs to change, but just as I reached the verandah, I heard a short cry which must have come from him. I ran in with my sister, who was also outside, building a last pyramid of strawberries on a dish shaped like a green leaf. He came out of the dining-room.

"Who's done this?" he said.

The supper-table was set with food to be fetched and eaten when people pleased. There were little bowls of cut-glass set with sweets and almonds. One of these had been sprinkled with buttons, little white buttons that had been torn off, still ragged with red-brown threads.

"I filled it," said my sister in a small weak voice, "with those sugar rose leaves, and a real one on top."

"Your servant—" I began, when he cried out again:

"What's that glove doing up the back of your dress?"

It was a little silver coat I had on to begin with. I pulled it off, and there fell off the collar, but with a tiny thud, another glove, a black one. It had no buttons on it and was open like a hand. Trenchard picked it up, and I thought I saw it collapse a little.

"No time to count them to-night," he said, and looked round. It was too hot for a fire, but they were laid in all the rooms. He put the glove down and struck a match. The huge chimney used to roar with its draught, but the fire would not catch. He went out to the lavatory with the glove and the dish.

"Go up and dress," we said when he came back; but instead he sniffed.

"It's what we smelt the other day," he said. "Up in the loft. Dead skin."

Outside, the air was hot and sweet and laced with coolness, but we noticed that here indoors it was cold, stale cold.

"Go up and dress," we said again, with the female instinct to keep the minutiae of things steady and in sequence.

"They won't be here till eight: there's plenty of time," he said, feeling not fear or even much curiosity, but that it was not the proper thing to leave us alone with the inexplicable unpleasant.

"Your servant," I began again.

"My servant's all right," he said. "Go out and wait in the verandah. I'll be down quickly."

So he went up. We took a chair and sat each side of the open glass doors where we could see into the house. We remembered that his maid as well as ours had gone back to her cottage to get ready for company. So there was no one in either house.

"He's taking it well," we said, and, "What is it?" And what we meant was: "What have we stirred up?" And (for my sister and I cannot lie to one another), "You did not do that with the buttons in the dish?" "Dear God, I did not."

"A dirty old woman," said my sister, "nice about her hands."

I said: "Dirty things done in a delicate way. There was that piece of stuff."

The house and the little orchard were backed with tall trees. There was a hint of evening, and high branches black against strong gold. Was there something hanging high up, very high, that looked like a square of stuff that had holes in it?

Upstairs, Trenchard must have gone to the bathroom first. Then we heard him, moving about in his bedroom, just above the verandah roof. Then we heard him shout again, a cry he tried to stop. We ran out across the grass and called up at his window. He answered: "No, don't come up." Of course we ran up, in and through the sitting-room and up the stairs. The dining-room door was still open, and with a corner of my eye I saw a candle, guttering hideously in the windless room.

"Let us in," we said at the door.

"Of all the filthy nonsense—" he was repeating: "— Look at my shirt."

On the top of the chest of drawers out of which he had taken it, his shirt was lying; and on its stiff white linen was what looked like a patch of grey jelly. Only it had spread out from a clot into five ribbons, like a hand or the fingers of a glove.

"Fine sort of beastliness," he said, "that won't let you dress for dinner." I heard myself saying:

"Are all your shirts like that?"

"No," he said grimly, "and if you don't mind waiting here till I've finished, we'll go downstairs and see what this is about."

He took another shirt and finished his dressing, wincing as he touched things; while we felt as if there were slugs about, the things of which we are most afraid; and that we must keep our long dresses tight about us.

We went down together into the dining-room, and there my sister screamed. On top of the centre strawberry pyramid, hanging over the berries like a cluster of slugs, was a glove, yellow-orange kid-skin, still and fat. A colour we had not seen in the box. The wrist and the fingers open and swollen. No buttons.

"What witches' trick is this?" he cried, and stared at us, for we were women. And like a wave moving towards us, rearing its head, came the knowledge that we were responsible for this; that our greed and vanity in devising this had evoked this: that we would now have to show courage, courage and intelligence to put an end to this, to lay this. And we had no idea how.

"The fire must burn," I said. "A great fire." He turned towards the outhouse.

"What's that lovely scent you wear?" he said to my sister. —"I want to smell it. Get that."

She ran away, and I stood still, aware of my shoulder-blades and the back of my neck, and all of my body that I couldn't *see*. Doors would not open easily. I heard him swearing and stumbling, the clang of a bucket tripped over and kicked away in the yard. My sister ran in, a scent-spray in her hand, crying:

"It's not scent any more. I tried it. It smells like the attic—"

She was squeezing the bulb and spraying us all violently; and I could not smell the dead smell of the loft, but the sweetness, like a lady-like animal, of old kid gloves.

Outside, the delicious evening was pouring in, to meet the original smell of the house; smell of flowers and tobacco, of polished furniture and wood-smoke and good things to eat. Trenchard had brought in a gallon jar of paraffin. He tipped and splashed it over the sitting-room fire.

"Get all the gloves," he said, looking at our helpless skirts: "I'll go across. I've got the loft key."

We peered again into the dining-room, that the kitchen opened out of. The candle guttered in fat dripping folds; a spider ran across a plate. My sister said:

"It's got only five fingers. Like a glove."

We waited. "Let's have the fire ready," we said, and I staggered with the can at arm's length to the sitting-room fire and drenched the piled wood. The ugly vulgar smell was sweet with reassurance. My sister threw in a match. A roar drowned the crackle of catching sticks.

"Now for it," we said, and tore open the bureau drawer for the gloves. I ran up for Trenchard's shirt, and when I came back, my sister, her hands full of strawberries, threw them, yellow glove and all, on the leaping pillars of fire. I shook the guttering candle out of its stick; my sister unscrewed her spray and emptied the precious stuff, that waved blue and white fingers at us out of the fierce, shrill yellow flames.

"So much for that," I said. "Where is he?" said my sister. We looked at each other.

"This is our fault," we said. —"We must go over. If it starts here again when we're gone, God knows what we're to do." Then she said:

"The loft's the place. It started there."

Outside, the orchard was full of bird-conversation. Inside, in half an hour we were to give a birthday party. We ran through the gap in the hedge and into our side of the house, which had become again part of one house.

Inside it we expected to find one large, troubled man, upstairs collecting things. Instead there was quiet, a kind of dead quiet that came to meet us down the steep stair. The loft door was open. On the flight that led up to it he was lying, feet down, his head upon the sill; his head invisible, wrapped up in what looked like a piece of dark green cotton, dirty and torn. We dragged it off.

"Burn. Burn," my sister said.

Some of it was in his mouth. We pulled it out. His tongue and mouth were stained. We slid him down to the foot of the flight and got water.

"Draw it fresh," she said. And, "Keep it tight in your hand," for I wanted to drop the cloth, to pull it away, as if it were trying to wrap itself round me, to stick to me.

We threw water on him. (Two shirts already; what an evening! thought a bit of me.) By this time I had hold of the cloth like grim death, for it felt as though it was straining away in a wind that wasn't there. "Gloves," she said. We went into the loft. The sky-light was open, and the cardboard box lay open and full. She put on the lid and put it under her arm, and we left him on the stairs and made off again, across the orchard to the fire. It was dying down. The room stifling, the wood sulky with oil-black. My sister flung in the box, drenched it with the oil, and stiff grey smoke poured out on us. She tossed a match on it, and there was the grunt of an explosion, and, as we jumped back, the fire poured up again. I felt a smart in my hand, as if the cloth was raw between my fingers.

"It mustn't fly up the chimney," she said. "If it does, it will come back all over again."

There was a box of cigars on the table. We turned them out, and thrust it in between the thin cedar boards and shut it up. Flung it into the fire wall and held it down. The box rose once or twice, bucked under the poker and the shovel.

Then we went back to Trenchard. He had come round, and was sitting at the foot of the loft stair.

"Everything's burned," we said. "Tell us what happened to you."

"God knows," he said. And then: "I was stooping to get the box, and something flapped against the sky-light. Blew in, I suppose, and the next thing I knew it had wrapped itself round my head and I couldn't get it off. I tore at it and I tried to get out. Then I couldn't bear it any more. It was winding itself tight. Then I must have passed out. But, oh God, it was the smell of it . . ."

In Bloomsbury

IN ABOUT 1850 there were once two brothers. The elder brother disliked the world in which he found himself and went away to India where he did not stay long; to Cochin China where even less was heard of him; to South Africa where he finally disappeared. The younger brother stayed in London and became a solicitor of repute. He had a son. The son became a barrister, took silk, and married a daughter of a famous man at the British Museum, who left her his magnificent collection of jade. They were a good and useful and delightful family, and lived in three houses between them, two in Bloomsbury and one in Hampstead, until the fathers died, and one house, in Bloomsbury, was enough. There were seven children in the third generation. The War accounted for the two eldest, leaving four boys and a girl almost grown up.

When something is known of two generations, the third is worth watching. Families like this are of the stuff of England, of the stuff of any distinct civilisation. They have moderate direct and great indirect power. They come naturally to high positions of trust, and their exceeding security often makes them generous and kind, even to their children. Having lost two sons they were quite determined that those who remained should enjoy themselves. In the best kind of way. And so they did.

There are no people who know less about the War or what life was like before it than the people who were just too young to play any part in it. And with their fathers and mothers it is a point of honour not to speak of it, not to try to explain. Nor did their children encourage them, but politely ignored the occurrence. Of this family, whose name was Curtin, the eldest was at the Museum; one wrote; one took it out in elaborate dissipation; the girl, Clarissa, painted; one had a fashionable taste in sex. All had received an admirable education, talked the current psychology, dressed in the admired disorder of their world; had a true and just, if rather *faisandé*, understanding of the arts. Each of them moved, without knowing it, in as rigid a convention as any other. Each of them cultivated an over life-size ego. No one had ever seen them enjoying themselves. None of them were in the least grateful for their blessings. None of them were fools. Not very long ago it was time for something to happen to them. In reality they had all been marking time, are still marking time, until something shall happen in the world; something sufficiently vital—that is to say, strange and oblique—to catch their whole attention, exercise them, use them. For when a pinch of credulity would have served them, they were taken in by nothing. Not sex or by the arts even. Secretly each one was ambitious, with nothing, that they acknowledged, to be ambitious about. Five steel blades used to cut butter—the best butter, the worst, any butter. In the low voices they took care should not sound harmonious they insisted on quality. It was their keynote. Quality in learning or lust or priggishness or the refinements of pride. In this they were infinitely correct. In their early thirties, though exasperating, they were sufferable.

While at that time, over the flank of a planet, the twin branch of that family had been growing, working, reproducing, dying, restating itself. The son of the grand-uncle had left three sons by two mothers, three men, their cousins, whom they had never seen, of whom they knew nothing, though two had served in the War in the East, and had come back to South Africa to find the youngest, their half-brother, a man.

It was by chance that I met them in Paris, the two elder come to Europe for the first time, on their way to England in search of the relations they had heard of and had equally never seen. They were in a café in the heart of Paris, set back opposite a bridge, outside which, in a wide space, the traffic flew, parting at the bridge-head to meet five other streams. In the open space their arcs swung and intersected freely, so that their flights were never interrupted, and sitting outside on the terrace one had the illusion of flying also.

I saw them lope in like powerful animals, a glint in their eyes, not a light. Not tranquil or steadfast, but aware. Wary, I thought, and what were they, with their tanned faces and great bones, their clothes new but practical, as if, once in the green woods outside Paris, there was a desert with wild beasts? For that was the landscape they carried with them, as each person carries his landscape; and at any moment they might step off into their own business. War and hunting business, without doubt. "Guerilla," "gorilla" said the subconscious in its helpful way. Then I knew I should meet them. Very soon after I did, for they sat next to me and my brother, and could not make the café understand what they wanted, and intended that their wants should be understood. We translated. They wanted cold chicken and whisky, and when the leg bones cracked under their knives it sounded like teeth. Then we talked. I was not sorry. One has one's Kipling side. "South Africa," the subconscious completed. They did not talk about it, or much about themselves—not as we talk about ourselves; and I do not know how it was done, not by words, the picture of them completed itself, image by image, as we sat. Picture, it was a cinema, an *actualité*, infinitely prosaic; and not until I had listened for some time with the minimum of polite interrogation and response, did I notice that it was creepy. Wary beasts were padding about in moonlight, identifying themselves with shadows and sand. To them the gracious amenities of Paris were no more than traps. I spoke in praise of it. They did not believe me. My brother was not amused.

But they were very helpless, and we were English. They asked shrewd questions, and gave up our directions in despair.

"Are you going to England?" I said, implying that they'd better. There was the shortest possible hesitation. Then they said that they might, that they supposed they should, that they had heard that they had relations there. In London, by name of Curtin, legal folk once. I saw a father and a mother, infinitely courteous and intelligent and formed. Five offspring, more intelligent, run into more extravagant moulds and hardly courteous at all. A critical extravaganza of five. I said boldly: "I know them." The two men backed like wild animals when a flare is thrust in front of their eyes. For an instant. Then they circled round. "Was that so?" I repeated it. "Well, we might meet there." And then (they were now used to the light), did I know their address? I gave it because I could not think of a reason not to give it. Then we said good night. From the step of our taxi I looked back, and saw them in conversation under an arc lamp.

The next day I ran into Julian Curtin on the Boulevard Saint Germain, and as we walked along the gay antique street I told him. "How *most* eccentric," he said; "they might be Great-Uncle Francis' progeny." I remembered where they were staying; and the next thing I saw was Julian and his sister Clarissa sitting outside the Deux Magots with the two men I had been calling the Wolves.

* * * * *

The next scene took place on the steps of the British Museum. I had been staring at the Easter Island enigma, turned away from it to look down the calm terrace, and saw the men from South Africa walking up the gravel drive from the gates. In the same belted raincoats and crêpe-soled shoes and bashed hats; on the same stride that might side-step at any moment. In they went. To see what,

I wondered. Culture to face their new relations? The night we had met I had seen that they were not nice people, but they had power. Not pleasant power. How was the power working? It was a raw, delicate thing, easily got out of gear. Had it been used yet for anything more than immediate ends? Did they know they had it? Had they? Or was I doped with talk about Empire builders?

Pigeons clattered down. In the mild gold air an antique charm was captured by that terrace and its courtyard and stabilised there. Chord of a classic circle dropped in London, a memory of that preoccupation of our race. Inside were the mysterious treasures of the world, separate, almost sterilised, but *there*. And all the books which have ever been written. What had they gone in to look at? They had entered like pirates who dare not swagger, who would loot if they could. Loot was their property and they'd collect it. Up-country? In war? Heartened by the thought of a smash-and-grab raid in the British Museum, I followed them inside.

They had not gone far. Down the narrow lit shaft of the Assyrian Room I saw them, looking at the lions arrow-pierced and stabbed. Their eyes were on the glance backwards. For what might be coming up behind? An animal or a man? One drew the attention of the other to points about lions. Neither was greatly interested. (Were the stone panels of the Assyrian Room a wall without ears?) There was nothing for the Museum authorities to fear. I left them and went to see if Julian and Clarissa Curtin were at their flat.

There I explained without pretence that I wanted to know what their cousins were really like.

"*Too* extraordinary." "*Most* peculiar," said the sister and the brother. "Clinton agrees with them best." Clinton was the one who took it out in stylised excess.

"But how d'you know they are your cousins?" I looked at the pale olive faces, the brown crystal eyes and cropped black heads. Clarissa answered: "Father is quite convinced.

Says that he has known *all* along about his great-uncle. He got out a series of daguerreotypes, and is quite positive. Altogether fascinating and obscenely like—"

"You say there's a third brother. Why didn't they all three come?" I wanted to know that.

Julian said: "That's the marvellous bit, and such a pity. The youngest was *quite* legitimate and *half* Bantu. And he's *just* dead."

"Careless of him to die now."

"The way they told us about it was charming," said Clarissa. "I don't think they would have told us if Father hadn't been so certain that there had been a second marriage, and that they were three. Then Clinton said to them: 'I suppose he was a native. Your father must have done *something* with his opportunities.' They gave a sort of snarl and glanced at each other. One could see Lewis telling Peter—that's their names—with his eyes to make the best of it. I suppose they thought we knew more than we did. But they actually showed us their stepmother's marriage-lines. Clinton said: 'What's that for?' And they said: 'It's genuine, I tell you.' And Julian said: 'Don't you think he'd have *better* been a bastard?' 'Maybe,' they said, 'but he wasn't.'"

The brother and sister said nothing more for a moment, and I knew that silence had fallen in Mrs. Curtin's long drawing-room also, where the jade was, and the Veronese, and the *petit point* chairs. I tried again: "How d'you get on with them?"

Julian answered: "*Each* member of *our* family seems to have a *different* point of view—"

That surprised me, for they usually formed a league, a tacit league, for offence and defence.

"Father and Mother" (they were usually Gillian and George to their children, so I judged the situation had reached full tribal significance) "seem quite disturbed. We had always assumed they must have known about some previous skeleton. But no. Mother went so far as to say that she was so sorry for the little nigger-boy who could not come. So were we all. *Most* intriguing. Father spends almost *all* his time with the jade and a *new* burglar alarm. Lewis has actually been in Asia with some *mongol* tribes whose business it is to find it and sell it to the Chinese to be carved."

Ghenghis Khan's men: out of Karakorum in High Asia: the Golden Horde. Jade hunters in Kurdistan: to Bloomsbury: to gentlefolk in an eighteenth-century house. How long a trail? Men to find, and men to love and make, and men to keep and love. The becoming, the *durée* of a work of art. Jade lasts: jade you cannot destroy or make or unmake. Jade is secure. Jade is loot.

Clarissa went on: "I found I couldn't possibly have an affair with one or both of them, as was suggested. When I'd seen them, I felt quite positive about civilisation—"

Good for Clarissa. Women invent good reasons for their sense.

"Fabian does not seem able to make up his mind which he likes best. He complains that once you know them well they're practically interchangeable. John says that he is quite afraid of them, and that he'll explain it all in a book he is writing—" (After the delicate classicism of Julian, Fabian, Clarissa, why had the Curtins run short on names and called their youngest John?) I was harassed that day with irrelevant speculations.

"Clinton takes them out on the most protracted parties. Down to the docks. He finds the places and they find the way back."

"Then you, Julian?" I said.

"I find that I spend as *much* of my time at the Museum as possible, and there I spend it trying to *make* up my mind. *Most* disturbing."

It was. I said: "Are they here for good?"

"They're not going back to *South* Africa. When they've

spent their money, they seem to be thinking of *South America*. They're staying in a *temperance* hotel, but we see them every day."

"They may be coming now," I said, and told them about the Museum and the lions. There was a light ring at the door. They came in, and were exceedingly restless and heavy in hand. Yet I saw them impose their weight, the weight of kinsfolk who, without help from God or man, have kept on their feet; whose hands have kept their heads; who are hardy, unencumbered, and, within their sequence, adaptable. Figures of stone and running water and wind-drawn trees. Of the forces, strong, subtle, delicate, and pure, which had shaped their english cousins, they had no conception. They were not awed by such things, or envious, or even interested; but were they trying to impose or trade, except through necessity or native awkwardness, upon them? What did they want? I could not make it out. Not even money, it seemed. A good time? Yes, but no permanent adoption. They would be off again. Why were they standing about like visiting mountains in a delicate landscape, mountains that were even careful where they put their feet? "Horrible people!" The words nearly came out on a sigh. They'd strip the Curtins bare if they could, go off with the pictures and the jade in sacks, mixed with their skulls and their chopped-off arms and feet. Only for reasons and for one reason they could not. If they were not always on their guard, their movements would be beautiful, like animals are beautiful. Then, on a look from Clarissa, I saw Julian come to a decision. "Father wants us all to come down to Ashways before the weather gets too bad. We usually all go down there for a month at *this* time of year. Won't you come too?" A bold move to concentrate the situation in a country house. After their usual, just perceptible swerve at a proposal, they accepted.

* * * * *

Three weeks passed. It was late, and again a bell, this time a telephone bell, rang gently. I heard the accurate italicised voice of Julian asking me if I, too, would come down to Ashways for the week-end. As I said I would (I had never been there before), I added distinctly: "But I'm no good with them," and gathered that it didn't matter, and understood that strange things must have happened before that family made to a rather barbarous person like myself the suggestion of an appeal for help. And I wondered why the powers who arrange things had picked me out to sort that family, and resented it, and was amused and rather afraid.

* * * * *

Harvest at Ashways, radiant, serene. We picked hanging apples and bit on hot peel and sweet ice within. Seven people, parents and their children, secure, intelligent, assured, against two wolves. Before I came there had been situations, a series of them, but no quarrels. They do not quarrel in that set. Not among themselves. Outsiders are pursued in fantastic vendettas. Outsiders stand no chance. I had just begin to decide that the brothers had some claim on the whole family estate and were waiting their chance to spring the news, when Clarissa came into my room, and went, as was her reasonable habit, straight to the point.

"It seems to me," she said, "that like any other primitive persons they might be more understandable if we knew their tabus. So we each decided to keep notes on anything we observed and report."

They would, and they had, and they'd find out a lot. "Well?" I said.

"The obvious ones first. Lavatories. The usual reserve of people who generally don't have them, and are only too thankful to use them when they get the chance. No particular inhibitions. Sex. It seems more what they expected us to have than what they've got themselves. Fabian and

Clinton both say that they're never so drunk with the people they pick up on their nocturnal expeditions that they can't tell whether the police are likely to arrive or not. Which does not seem to indicate a repression. On the other hand, they don't seem able to put up with people of colour."

"That's the half-brother," I said.

"Do you really think so? Then that does seem to be definite."

We did not get any further because there was to be a lunch-party. The Chief Constable was coming, and in the library I heard John Curtin telling them what a Chief Constable was.

"But don't you ever read crime books? You really should. When anyone is murdered in a *country* house, it is always the *Chief* Constable who arrives and makes up his mind *who* has done it. Either that, or else the Inspector from *Scotland* Yard finds out he has done it *him*self."

"Be accurate," said Clarissa. "Don't mislead them. It's almost always a guest in the house."

I watched them say nothing, noticed that there was something, a fatigue perhaps, in their silence. Later I had an idea, and was able to say to all five cousins before dinner: "I've spotted a tabu. It's police."

"*Most,*" said Julian, and before he could add "peculiar" was silent. We all were. Until I caught myself babbling:

"Of course, they've always lived up-country, in places where there aren't any, and it may be just the idea. Or perhaps they got across the military police in the War." As an idea it lacked vitality. Suggestions like that mean nothing to the Curtins, but it passed without comment. I felt that something more was expected of me.

"It seems to me," I said, "that it's time someone forced their hands. Curiosity like ours has no business to be wasted." The Curtins did not like this. Perfectly courageous within their sphere of courage, they did not admit people whose hands have to be forced. Then we all turned round. They came in, and I saw the two men, rather splendid in their black and white, formalised as they could not be in their easy clothes. I said:

"If they were several centuries back in time, poetry would be written about them."

Clarissa nodded: "Edom o' Gordon and his men." She had a pretty step and a delicate perception of her own. Her training had made what was natural, choice. She looked up coolly at her cousins, one stared at her for a moment, then both looked away. Oh the fine brutes among the small, dark, lean creatures! While she had nothing to fear, who should have had everything to fear—in Edom o' Gordon's time. Was she woman enough to lead them a dance? The youngest would be led. Was she up to it? It seemed as if we were the hunters now. Was that the truth of it? Had we been all along their hunters who were their natural prey? Were the Curtins up to it? I was, if I had to make them.

As the Chief Constable's lunch had passed without incident, the evening went soberly enough.

In the library after dinner, Clarissa played Corelli on the harpsichord. Her mother embroidered, her father listened. Of the rest of us, one played a crossword puzzle, two chess. One talked to me. The cousins sat together, pulling at their pipes. I noticed that they reduced people to domestic life or tribal occupations. In that house conversation was the exercise and the sport, and the brothers were bad for one's conversation—so non-committal that one never could be certain if they were stupid. Non-committal and pent-up, and by that time we were become the last. It was then that Mrs. Curtin said: "Did anyone ring up?"

"Only the Constable," said Mr. Curtin. "He says he wants to see me again to-night. I can't think why. It's most unusual."

John looked up from his puzzle: "Could EGPA, by any exercise of imaginative phonetics, be the name of a central african tribe?" He asked this of his cousins.

MARY BUTTS

"Can't think of one," they answered, hastily for them.

"What a pity," said Clinton, "that your brother isn't here. He might have known. And we really do regret him. Where is he buried? We were wondering if you'd like a really *good* fetish to put on his grave."

"I guess he's all right." Then, after another silence, "What does your Chief Constable fellow want?"

"He wouldn't say. I gathered that it was to ask me something. Has anyone heard lately of any petty crime?"

"What a bore," said Fabian, "the police are."

Clarissa played on, delicately, deliberately, accompanying her brother.

John said: "You know you never really told us much about him, and he was, after all, as much our cousin as you. And the *natural* result has been that we want to know *all* about him. *How* he died and what you thought of his mother. I suppose she is *dead* too. And *what* you thought about him, and what the neighbours said, and how you got on with your *nice* bantu relations; and whether he was like them *or* your father— And whether"—the requests were becoming a chorus—"he wanted to be *like* a white man or a black man. You needn't think it will make *any* difference to us."

"And I must go and see about the Chief Constable's room," said Mrs. Curtin, "in case he wants to stay the night." Perhaps she was a little sorry for them, but equally intended to give her family a free hand.

It went on: "Was he married?" "And which kind?" "Or *half* and half?" Having made our modest inquiries, we turned round in a half-circle, ten eyes interrogating four.

Again they backed and blinked, and I saw what I had always suspected, and knew that I had been blind not to have known, their ferocity of hate and fear.

"He was a pretty poor lot," the elder said.

"What particular kind?" came the chorus, getting into full cry—"reversion to the bush or to victorian England?"

"Not the sort," said the younger this time, "that a white

man wants for a brother. It's as well he's dead. We couldn't have brought him to you people over here."

"But why not? Why didn't you bring him?"

"I tell you he's dead." (Unconsciously they had insisted that he was alive.) "You can't bring over dead men—"

Then Julian said soberly and gaily: "Then you must do your best and give him a kind of vicarious *after*-life. These fascinating hints are *not* enough."

"Are you sure," I said, "that he is dead?"

Clarissa stopped playing and turned round on the harpsichord seat.

"Are you *quite* sure," said Julian, "that you didn't *murder* him yourselves when he was tiresome? It might happen *so* easily. One is so *apt* to be prejudiced—"

There was the noise of a car outside, steps and voices. Mr. Curtin went out. "I'll see him in my study," he said.

Seized by my idea that they had lied about their brother's death, my impression had been blurred for a moment. I looked again. Julian, pitiless, was pleased. So were they all.

"I thought from the beginning," said Clarissa, "that it was that. You've murdered him. Now didn't you?"

Above the slight rustle of excitement and lightly moved chairs, I heard a sound like a low howl escaping and immediately lost on the air.

The elder was snarling: "What d'you mean by saying such things?" They had half risen. It was too tense to be true.

Julian went on: "But that is what we have been thinking. *All* the time. Do tell us *how* you did it—"

Mr. Curtin and the Chief Constable came back. "Another of these extraordinary cases of cattle-maiming. Colonel Thornleigh wants to borrow some people to watch the farm to-night. I wonder if you have had any experience."

Two falling bodies under whom an angel's hand has been slipped. I heard the proposal—heard, understood, accepted, complied with all in one movement, and the two brothers were out with the Constable's men in the night.

Five Curtins beamed on one another until I said: "If that's that, it explains why they're shy of the police."

"Were they?" I was asked, and again saw the suggestion miss fire.

"They'd be *sure* to understand about cattle-maiming, that's why they went off," the Curtins explained.

I persisted: "Yes, and weren't they thankful that he'd come about that?"

"I'm quite positive," said Clarissa, "that he's not dead at all. The only thing to do is to go on till we get them to admit it, and send for him to come over here."

* * * * *

It was just before dawn, dim, spiritless, not yet lit, as though night's pure dark had given out, never to be replaced, and I was aware of Clarissa and Fabian at the foot of my bed. I was to come downstairs. In the library a fire had been kept up for the cattle-watchers, and there were thermos flasks and food. The brothers had gone up to bed. All the Curtins were down. The police left.

"*Where* are they?" I said, falling into the family italics. "Did *they* maim the cattle?"

But Julian broke out shrilly, a cry in his voice: "It appears it was true—that there is something in—in the *preposterous* pleasantry that they killed him. We were told to move quietly and separately along the edge of the wood, past the farm. I came up and they were *behind* a tree, and I heard one of them say, 'We needn't have done it.' And *complain* of the fright Thornleigh had given them. And ask if we *really* believed it; and if we were safe; and if they thought we should try to blackmail them. Then they laughed. I nearly came round the tree and said I should speak to the Chief Constable *at* once. Then I realised what they were and what they might do, and I had to go on *watching* the cows till we *came* back and they went to bed—"

"Essential daylight, colourless and clean" filled the

room. The fire sulked. The hour was unpropitious for the turn of the event. Besides, what were we to do? Julian went on: "I made an *under*-statement. They spoke of their victims in the plural; referred to 'them.' The woman, I suppose, their stepmother." Situations which sink in. All their little peculiarities which had hitherto delighted us, reseen in this light. Revision at dawn. Of murder; of blood on black ivory skins. Polished boxwood and scarlet; two bodies who would stay dead. Two men upstairs, sleeping, who had made corpses of their own flesh, a brown stain out of bright blood. *After such knowledge, what forgiveness?*

"Futile beasts," I said.

"That won't punish them," said Clarissa, "—they're not clever enough."

At the same time, everything now was in its place, everything they had said and not said, everything they had done and not done. The worst in coming to the worst had made order, proportion, light. We knew now how ignorance and cruelty had bred fear, and fear murder, and murder more fear, so that the desire to further which they had killed twice had never since run free. Prisoners? What need to make them prisoners who had walked into their own trap?

Curiously enough, this was not the line the Curtins were taking. The debate, getting actually shrill, was whether or not to wake the Chief Constable up at once, or wait till he had had breakfast. Their reactions were as much on time as those of the wretched brutes upstairs. Who were, after all, upstairs? Who were asleep—or talking? What would they be saying to one another? After all, were we quite sure? I asked that; held up Julian Curtin's disgust and alarm with what seemed to me to be a reasonable question. Repeated it, while five sets of mixed statements reiterated their point of view.

A blank, absurd hour for such an awakening. Reluctantly they went back to bed. I went back to bed and had only just fallen again into the exquisite sleep that follows shock, when I was called to face the real day. Breakfast came and went; the Curtins came and went; and it felt as though in every room in the house there was a pair of them, each proposing to do the same thing in a different way. Colonel Thornleigh left unenlightened. Mrs. Curtin had not come down. Only Mr. Curtin and I sat at our meal, asking each other no questions.

It was then that the two cousins came down, and in their walk and voice there was a new unrestraint, in the way they ate and used their hands. Something assured, raw and lewd, a relief and a new assurance that would bawl at us, now they thought they had found out that what they had done would serve their turn. Not as they had meant it to do, but enough. In fact they had been sharp enough to see how their supposed crime had enhanced them. "Meet our cousins, the murderers," as they thought the Curtins would say, and to profit by it, not adroitly, but with a sufficiently ugly swagger. That it was all an utter miscalculation did not spoil it as a spectacle, as they snapped down a sausage at a bite; and when they stood up, stared insolently, feet apart, pitching their huge bodies from their hips. It was their hour of satisfaction. Like all hardy and adaptable men, they cared little for the nature of the event, so long as it could be made serviceable. In this case, a crime had been proved to have been unnecessary, and now it seemed that instead of losing by its discovery they had profited by it. They were in no danger from these cousins: they feared them, these cousins. The poor little fish. It had worked out all right, the murder they needn't have done. It had *worked*.

Behind shut doors the Curtins were fluttering. A thousand delicacies of intellectual perception and interesting angles of approach to life coming together like puzzle-pieces—to make a quite different picture. Not a picture anything like the Curtins' picture, the gallery of significant forms they hung in their front windows. Called into their council, I thought they looked smaller, and more alert; the blood-rhythm of one generation of a family almost audible.

Julian was repeating: "I heard it *last* night, *standing* behind *a* tree. They actually murdered him—and his mother."

"Hardy sons of the great open spaces," said I. "What are you going to do about it? Their half-brother and their stepmother and probably several others —"

"Do?" Five voices intoned the word— "Do? Go to the police *at* once."

"Absurd as it may seem," said Julian, "we are accessories *after* the fact."

"This isn't a detective book," I said unkindly—"the Chief Constable's gone."

"I am going over," said Julian, "*on* my bicycle—*at* once."

Leaving two women, a father and a mother, who, presumably, did not know what had happened, to the care of three young men who had two murderers to deal with, who might try it again.

"It's absolutely necessary," said Clinton. "Not a moment's delay."

Fabian squealed: "Thornleigh will cable to the Cape police at once. They must be quite upset looking for them, and that's why they left."

"To come over here and hide with us," said John venomously.

I am not sure whether Clarissa intended to catch my eye. I asked: "Who's going to break it to them? They're bucking about in the dining-room, entirely convinced that they're masters of the situation."

Fabian said quite simply, "Why?"

I explained.

"It's quite impossible," they all said. Then Clarissa:

"The best thing to do would be to ask them in here and tell them what we know, and tell them to go away. In which case, I think, they should have a start of the police. You know, they may only have been bragging—"

"In the *middle* of the night; *behind* a tree," said Julian. I remembered that it was not my family.

"You always had a way with them," said Clarissa unkindly. "Will you go and fetch them? This must be settled."

I have not forgotten how difficult it was to make my mouth smile, nor what it feels like to walk off somewhere on an errand of that sort. I put my head round the dining-room door and said: "Come into the library, you two, for a moment."

"What about?" said the eldest lazily, yawning in my face, a beast's stretch to his jaw.

"Plans for to-night about the cattle."

Damn them! They were murderers, and they might murder me. They shouldn't find the whiphand so easy. It *was* fair.

I went back and heard them following me, strides that could overtake me down the dark corridor, quiet to the feet. One stride would catch me up; one spring bear me down. I put away imagination as I opened the library door and faced the Curtins. Turned into a comedy that was rather over-strident, a little over-seasoned with false excuses, the true truth of the situation was on us.

How would the Curtins handle it? It had not occurred to one of them to run away. Excess of imagination or defect?

All irritable alarm, Julian was on his feet, saying: "Now I know. I heard you last night, behind a tree, actually admitting that our preposterous supposition *was* true. That you are *both* murderers. *More* than once. And we asked you *in* here to *tell* you to *go* away—immediately. After twenty-four hours we shall go to the *police*. If you refuse to go, we shall do it *at* once. The twenty-four hours are to give you time to leave the country. It's most astonishing that the police in *South* Africa have not been here *al*ready."

I felt embarrassed for them. Painfully and unnecessarily. I did not want to see what they looked like.

"What in hell d'you mean?" the eldest said.

"What I have *just* been telling you. I am speaking for us all. It is *not* possible for Clarissa to see *any* more of you. While, until the police know, we are in the *position* of accomplices *after* the fact. Most unusual. *Quite* impossible—"

I do not know why the youngest of the wolves looked at me. Then I said: "You'd better get out. They mean it."

"You are murderers," said Clarissa severely. "The only thing for you to do is to go away at once."

"Parasites on us, and a disgusting prey on society; d'you want to leave here in handcuffs or your car?" Fabian fluted at them—"and don't try to kill any of us. You won't get away with that."

"That means you go when the going's good," I interpreted.

Now I was able to watch their faces. Insolence at first augmenting their surprise; then immediate watchfulness; and then, as the seconds passed, a veil over the watch, a fade-out of all contact between us and them. They got up, narrowed eyes half closed, their shoulders loose, feet that backed nearer and nearer towards the door. Mouths that said: "Fine way to treat your own kith and kin," and "lousy bastards," and more curious endearments, but on the whole a brutal collapse, a poor savage show, and a complete ability to disappear. Something to laugh at, nothing to cry about, and only to be feared in a lonely place.

"You've got twenty-four hours," Clarissa cried after them. We waited. By general agreement the library door was locked. A quarter of an hour passed. The front door was invisible from the windows, but it was then we heard the particular shriek and bang of their fast, dilapidated car.

"Contact with the criminal classes," said Julian. "Disgusting. *Most* peculiar."

Green

"Don't you think, Madonna Loring, that it would be better if I went down to see?"

"I'll think of it," she said quickly, and he noticed a slight hauteur in her voice.

"We are sure, alas! that she takes too much to drink, and we know that my son does not. And you have heard what people say about her friends. Nick would never allow me to know the Taverners, so is it likely that he will have them to his house unless she insists? And if she does and he refuses, as he certainly should, she will fall out of her own set, and most of his friends will have nothing to do with her. The Derings have hinted to me that they might have to drop Nick. I hardly like to tell you, Ambrose, but they said—" A paraphrase followed for several sexual and social irregularities.

"Don't you think I might go?" Ambrose Alexander said this with loving earnestness, with whimsical adoration, leaning over a narrow space towards an old woman, upright by the fire in a dull-gold London room. Inside her tight silver wig and her mask of paint, she was yielding to treatment. In one hollow centimetre of her mind she knew she was, and that she would send Ambrose, because he would bring back an exciting story, a story that would justify malice and moral indignation: that could also be repudiated without strain. He owed her a good deal, she thought. He was a Jew. His function was to please. He did please. A slim, supple young man to run about was essential: to confide in: to reassure her.

For his part he was willing to oblige her. There were good pickings in that family, and benefits apart, she was giving him what he wanted—a chance to get his own back on her son and his wife. For the six months before, for the six months since, their marriage, she had been ravenous for its discredit. The discredit it was for him to supply. But a full meal, this time, and more than a meal, a provision, on which she would never satiate, of the wife's blood and sap. What she wanted would serve his turn; but when he thought about her, and he preferred not to think about her too much, he misunderstood her degrees of consciousness, the balance of her scruples, her ignorance, her appetite, and her fears.

"If you are to go down and see her, how can it be arranged? It mustn't look —"

"They had better not expect me. If I could have a car and it should break down, then I could simply be there, and they would put me up for the night."

"That's a good idea. I'll pay for it. But, mind you, Ambrose, it must be a real break-down. I won't have any lies."

"Madonna Loring, it shall go up in flames to make my word, since it is really your word, good."

She looked away from him, a little sentimental smile disturbing the corners of the old thin mouth. If only in her life she had heard more men say things like that. He meant it. Ambrose was a good and noble man. Of course he would not have to burn the car. That would be too extravagant. Even for the most disgusting news of her daughter-in-law.

Splendid that Ambrose was going. Her son might be in agonies about his wife: her son might be wanting his home again. She would give Ambrose messages to make it easy for him to come home for help. She foresaw decent divorce, and when Ambrose was gone, walked up and down the long room between the azaleas and the inlaid chairs, rehearsing a long, hideous, and wholly satisfactory scene with his wife.

Until the nature of the interview, from being a source of pleasure, became a kind of pain, and she noticed that she was not sure how far she wanted to be able to trust Ambrose there. Later she rang him up.

"Of course I'll pay all your expenses, but don't be too extravagant. I've just thought we may need all our money later."

She had said "our money" out of romantic delicacy. Ambrose relished it differently. It had been share and share alike with Nicholas, who usually forgot about his own share. Then, a year ago, Nicholas had found out that intermittent rebellion is exhausting, and had conducted an entire revolution instead. Six months later he was married. Now his landmarks were off both their maps. Only their débris remained—nothing but skeletons and broken boards where his places had been. A devastating escape, but Nick's mother had herself to thank. And hatred of his wife, which had been her refuge, was to become her revenge. Against Nancy Loring, Ambrose knew nothing— had not heard much—*Le dossier accusateur de toute jolie femme.* But to be kept by Mrs. Loring; he must keep Mrs. Loring; give Mrs. Loring what she wanted, a daughter-in-law unkind, unchaste, and, so far as possible, unkissed. It seemed that he might have to rely on his imagination. After six months they were still living out of London, in that small, remote house, where no one that he knew ever went. Without a car, a telephone or a horse. With cats and an old boat and books. That did not promise disillusion yet unless the girl was bored. What was there to find out? Could he return and report bliss? A spring wind filled the curtains of his room; coal-dust from the unlit fire charged its delicate touch. With his eyes on the tree-tops breaking leaf he could only smell London. He did not particularly mind, but at night with the fire burning he could feel Mrs. Loring behind his chair. Boards cracked before and after her tread, step of a bully with small feet and ankles swollen a little with age, and there was a sound of gobbling already, and appetite unglutted, and punishment for Nick shaping once she had got him back. Once they had got him back.

Need he go at all? Could he go in theory, or, if he went, in theory provoke Nancy to behaviour whose character could be decided on later, and Nick actually into appropriate disgust? There is nothing more difficult to deny than a casual event whose importance rests on its implications. It is said that you have been to Biarritz with friends of doubtful character.

You do not know the people.

You have not been to Biarritz at all.

Prove it, if you have not been conspicuously with other people anywhere else. The force of your denial will fly loose, attach itself, and strengthen the accusation. You will have been at St. Jean de Luz, where you met, and were notorious with them there. It is this fact that lies at the base of all non-resistance to evil, that the resistance becomes a neutral agent, equally able to strengthen what it attacks.

Ambrose felt that he need not be too anxious. There is always something wrong. If it were not yet conscious he had only to give the unconscious a name. While it was equally possible that the girl was bored, loose or a slut. If not, she was going to be. The elegantly set problem absorbed him, in whose solution he ignored himself, his emotion for Nick, his curiosity about Nancy, his fear of the mother—about whom he assumed himself to be particularly cynical and gay.

Two days later he ran out of petrol on a remote road a mile from their house.

*　*　*　*　*

Nancy Loring asked her husband: "Who was it called the sea the 'very green'?"

"The Egyptians, I think. The Red Sea and the Mediterranean. What about green wine?"

They were looking out at a green plain which lay as far as the horizon on their left, and their house stood on the shelf of a grass hill beside the plain, tilted in the sunlight to another green. High trees stood about the hill, and a short way outside, across a lawn, a copse crested its last bank. The plain had once been the sea, an estuary savage with tides, now narrowed to a river, tearing at its flow and ebb; where all winter, for every hundred yards, a heron watched its pitch. There was no dust: no sound but birds and air; no colour but green. There was every green.

In late April the top greens were of gold. Across the plain there was a march of elms, open hands with blood inside them, tipped with saffron fire. The copse was a stuff woven out of the same green.

They went out. On the small lawn were cats, black and white enamel in fur. One watched its lover; the lover watched a bird; the third, bow-stretched and upright, ripped the bark off a tree. Two kittens tumbled over like black and white flowers.

They followed one another through the copse. Each willow trunk was a separate man and woman. They came down the farther side to where, when it had been sea, the plain had worn a little bay under the hill. There was long wet grass where the tide-mark had been. They came to a dyke and an old house. There were willows along the glass water, very tall; along it and over it, one flung across and an elm tree drowned in it, its root out of the ground in a flat earth-cake. The house was a deserted farm. An orchard reached it, down a small valley between the rising of another hill. There was no path. They went up through the apple-trees, through a place wholly sheltered, where no wind came but only sun; where, when there was no sun, there was always light; so that in mid-winter, in the stripped world, the seasons did not exist there. They called it the Apple Land, remembering there something which they could not recall, that seemed to have the importance of a just-escaped dream. The orchard ended sharply in an overhanging quickset, and a sharp climb to the top of the hill. To follow the valley to its head there was a glen on the left, sickly with flies and thin shoots and a scummed choked stream up to a short fall, almost in the dark, which was not quite wholesome, whose pool was without stir or light. The way out of that was also sharp and steep but quite different—to a shut cottage on top and a garden with tansy in it, and herbs used in magic.

Through lambs running in the up-fields they came to their village, and bought a morning paper, cheese, apples, and cigarettes. They came back another way, by a high-road, by a lane, over the open grass along a ribbon their feet had printed, green upon green.

* * * * *

Ambrose Alexander reached the house as they had entered the copse. A shy country servant left him alone. He was pleased that they were out; he stood back by the door from where he could see the whole length of the room.

Across the table an open ordnance map hung like a cloth askew. There was a chessboard beside it, and men half tumbled out of a box, and a wide bowl of small mixed flowers. There was a stone bottle of ink and a dish with sticks of sealing-wax and stamps, pencils, and a seal. There was a dog's lead and a pair of leather gloves. A red hand-kerchief was knotted up full of needles and wool. When he handled it one ran into his palm. There was an oil painting of Mount Soracte and steel prints of forgotten gentlemen; and on the black chimney-shelf a fishing-rod crossed with a gun. There were books of poems, and on murder, the roman occupation of Britain, chinese art.

Mr. Hunca Munca, the mouse, climbed to the top of the kitchen chimney and looked out. There was no soot. Up to the age of five every child laughs at this version of that joke; but to Ambrose it was as if the room was calling him, very plainly and in another language, an outsider. It was not what he had come to hear. He stared out of the window and up the hill. There was no one. Then he went upstairs. Under his feet the old boards had no friendly squeak. Like old servants who might talk.

Their bedroom had a rose-brick fire-place and a line of persian prints. Under the mirror, piled in a shell, were strings of glass flowers and fruit. Everything was in order, polished and very still, and the bathroom full of things to wash with. He went back to the bedroom, supposed that in one of the shut drawers there was a shameful secret among soiled linen, persuaded himself, opened it, and in it there were folded silks, bedroom books: two more murders, a County History, *Per Amica Silentia Lunae*, Sterne. A cat looked in at the door and yawned before it went away. Under a scent-flask was a receipted bill. He looked out of the window at the very green.

There they had been all winter long. They did not seem to want to go away. Told nothing, saw no one who would tell anything, asked for nothing. He was discouraged. Propriety, simplicity, the routine of country-house life. The house went on talking out loud; not without passion but with directness that annihilated. Down any passage there might be met a wall of fire. He looked at the bed over whose foot-rail hung a bright shawl and a fur.

The persian pictures were perfectly proper. In the dining-room cupboard there had been two bottles of beer. He went downstairs, heard no approach on the soundless turf, so that they were on him in an instant, as instantly recoiled, and a moment later were overwhelmed in his cordiality and excuse.

Disentangling themselves from him, they exchanged a word together, out of the house. "What has he come for? Car broken down? Whose car? Who's given him a car?"

Nicholas Loring was annoyed; his wife uneasy. There was nothing to do but feed him, and not to go after the swan's nest that day. Swans stay put, but are more interesting than a townsman ill at ease, vocal and supple and full of admiration that did not try to be more than a display.

Voluble and mobile, Ambrose had a trick of statement, one to each sentence, followed by a denial, a reversal of it in the next. So that which seemed, sentence by sentence, to be a vivid reaction to life, cancelled out to nothing. To no belief at all. Nicholas, folded-up in country quiet, was now without illusion and irritated by what had once stimulated him. Ambrose had no belief at all. And Nancy saw that everything Ambrose said would mean nothing, and felt giddy in her mind until she felt sick. They were his hosts and they must stomach him, feed him, and endure him to an hour they had not fixed. They were saved from spiritless irritation, and she from fear, by curiosity and the involuntary hosts' calculation of the time when they would be able to lose him. Ambrose understood this, and that he must stay the night, and that at present no mere breakdown of his car would get him the invitation. He saw himself after lunch led by Nick, grim, courteous and embarrassed, to restart it at the top of the hill.

* * * * *

They came to the end of lunch. Nicholas was listening to Ambrose, to what he had once heard, year in and year out, and now had not heard for a year. And after a year there was no more pleasure in it or surprise at the changes. It was as if he knew it by heart, for the first time at last.

Ambrose was trying hard with a parade of emotion, trying to praise marriage, their withdrawal, the serene country; displaying himself as the neurotic townsman, the alien, whose pride it was to humble himself, to look into paradise through bars. A peep he owed to them: "Is that safe, Nancy?" turning to her from Nicholas.

"I think so," she answered civilly, not at all sure. He is trying not to cancel out, she thought. Why? He can't do it for long. Why is he here? He does not like me. Would like me to be vile so as to hurt Nick. Nick he loves and hates. Then that he had once loved Nick and then hated him, probably for his marriage and now did neither, or in different proportions. What was he there for?

He said: "Suppose me at my rôle again—the old serpent. You used, Nick, to call me that, and any variation that struck you from 'you dirty devil' to 'Lucifer.'"

"Lord of lies," she murmured.

He heard her. She was ashamed. He looked steadily at her and smiled. "You're right, my dear. I'm just as much that variation of the fiend. Only neither you nor Nick need the serpent in me any more. Serpents"—he added—"are not sentimental. That was useful once to Nick. While who has ever heard of a mother-snake?" They took that in.

"There was a time when Nick needed an old, contradictory bloke like me to leave all doors open and let a spot of reality in. His mother" (the pause which left her unqualified perfected suggestion) "she would have shut the lot, and everything open is the only answer to everything shut. But now—" He went on to explain that Nicholas, now he had welcomed the reality Ambrose had provided, had made his own freedom and been given love. It was true. But Nicholas must be repersuaded that he owed it to him. Doors that have been opened can be shut. One implies the other. They could begin on him again, he and Mrs. Loring, and Nick would be well retrapped. The doors would be shut and the wife outside. Only it would take longer than he thought, and Mrs. Loring would not see the delicacy of it. He must find out how to persuade her that the cup of deferred blood is richer.

Rapt in these thoughts he started smiling at them. Nick was moved, but remembered that once he would only have been moved. Ambrose had opened doors once, or he had thought so. Until he had noticed that he had only slammed them to and fro, chasing him between draughts. Until he had stuck open a certain number that he needed for himself. (Who wants to live with every door open?) His exits and entrances were now his own, and by one of them Nancy had come in: helped to fix open a few more, and,

by one of these, first Ambrose, then his mother, had gone
out. That was what had happened in terms of doors. He
softened, feeling that he could afford to. Old Ambrose
had come down for some sort of thanks. Or perhaps for a
share. Share of the rich strength which made things easy
with Nancy: easy to give and take: easy to go in and out:
to live: like music, all the musics. Ambrose was by himself
as he'd always been. Nancy was thinking the same thing,
that here was a man alone all his life and always would be
alone; and thought of him on a toadstool and with people
round him on toadstools, and that he spent his time picking their stalks from underneath them and his own stalk.

Then, the strength mounting in her also, she wondered if Ambrose had been necessary to Nicholas, to that
woman's only son. Was it possible that they had shaken
Ambrose off his fence? Was this visit, after all, a no mean
congratulation and praise; one of the mysterious triumphs
of love? She forgot his subtle opposition to their marriage.
Was this old Mrs. Loring's last defeat? She judged it most
improbable and forgot her judgment. Only remembered
that it would be good if it were true. If it were true, they
might some day be able to forgive. She looked at Ambrose,
very simply. It seemed a far cry to "mother's gigolo." He
observed her, went to the piano and played the letter-song
from *Figaro*. Whistling softly. *And the sounds of beauty flowed
and trembled until they seemed to triumph . . . over the hard hearts
of men.*

She brought him over his coffee. There was not a cruel
animal behind Nick, only a vexed old woman, who had
been lovely, who would never feed on her son again, or
with septic finger-nails scratch at the bloom of her own
youth. She had been ungenerous about Ambrose. How
hateful is the wife who does injustice to her husband's
people, to her husband's friends.

She lit his cigarette, and stood by Nicholas' shoulder,
wholly herself and part of him and part of the very green.
Part of Ambrose? Yes, for this moment, if this were true.

* * * * *

They took him out, a tramp across green, from green
to green, entertained him with birds' nests set deep in
thorned twigs and split light. There had been tea and toast
and chess, an evening to get through and a night. He stood
between them at evening at the door of the house. Now
in the sky there was a bar of the green that has no name.
He was standing on grass darkening beside dark green.
She had said, "*It is all Hermes, all Aphrodite.*"

He had been bored and concealed it, with the night
before him, becoming unsure of himself. Dinner, chess,
music, country-talk. A drink? They had filled up his car
and put her away in the village and refused to let him go.

They gave him a drink and a rabbit cooked in onions.
He had gained nothing but the fooling of them, and, if
they did not know it, they were slightly bored. The worst
thing that can happen to a liar is to be believed. If he did
not notice that, he suffered, as Nick indicated in intimate
outline, his serene and final detachment from his mother.
Confident, they told him their plans, about excavations
and gardening, and Nick's new book, which was not about
himself or even about people. He had to listen, and by
that time it was night, grey, windless, with a squeak in it.
The great chimney flared. Standing inside it one could
follow the sparks up its square tower to a square patch of
sky. Innocent as wine, as dew. He sneered. Outside was it
innocent? Innocent for them and strong. His room was
away from theirs. On that side of the house the night could
do what it liked with him. The night would have him to
itself. Nick and Nancy would have themselves to themselves. He would have nothing to himself but himself and
night. Oh! there was someone who might come in and sit
beside his bed. Madame Nick might come in and talk,
smile, and suck in her thin, red lips. Keep him awake
because she was hungry. She would not mind dark green
night.

He would have nothing but lies to feed her on: have to invent her a meal because her sort of food wasn't in the house. He was getting childish. With their stupid innocence they were doing him down. What did Nancy want? To give him another drink: be sure that he was comfortable: a game of chess before bed. "Glorious game" he must say, but it took longer to play than he reckoned. A shy woman, what she did was better than her promise. Later she said: "It is good for your complexes, Ambrose, to win things and be praised." For that he should have let her win. God! But he could not bear to evade the game. And it put off bed, and whatever it was that tapped outside on the windows its peculiar code.

But when he went up, the soft air surging in put him instantly to sleep.

* * * * *

They woke next morning with a distaste for him in the house. He was to go after lunch, and the morning seemed an hour-series that could not be lived through. There was no reason for it, only that they did not care now if his visit marked a triumph. They wanted him out of the way. There were interesting things to do and he would not do them. Nancy decided that she would disappear, on the excuse of leaving Nicholas alone with his friend, and came downstairs first to see that Ambrose had his breakfast in bed. There was a letter for her from Nick's mother. That hardly ever happened. She went outside to read it, barefoot on the cat-printed dew: split it open and read:

"*My Dear Child,*
"*I wish this to be entirely between ourselves, but I have an idea that Nicholas' old friend Ambrose intends to come down and see you. Please be very nice to him. You know how it is—he was so fond of my son and has suffered the break since his marriage. Of course it couldn't be helped,*

*and I am so afraid of emotional friendships between young
men, but I am sure you have nothing to fear now. Don't
tell Nicholas anything about this—and also what I meant
to say is—don't be upset or offended if he should try and
flirt with you. It means absolutely nothing. He has a very
fine nature really, and is not at all interested in women. I
just want there to be no misunderstanding, not that Nicholas is likely to think anything as long as you are careful,
only I do not wish you for your part to be led away. I explain
this badly, but I am sure you will understand. I hope you
are both as well as possible.*

"*Your loving Mother*
"*Angela Loring*"

The crisp dew melted between her toes, and their colour
changed from pink to red. One hand held on to her curled,
cropped hair. There was a moment when nothing happened at all, neither image nor concept nor sense impression. She came-to, first to the small bustling wind, then to
a bird. Then to a draught of other life-like voices, shrieking
from London, recorded on a square of thick white paper.
It was mad; it was comic; it was dangerous. She ate a light
breakfast in silence. Anyhow it was tiresome.

She said: "You will want the morning with Ambrose.
I'm off." But Nicholas had his plans also.

"Look here," he said. "I forgot that I said that I'd see
that man about—"

"Take him with you."

"It's a trudge. I got mud to my knees last—"

"Am I to keep Ambrose?"

"I mean, if you could be that sort of spirit—I'll be back
before lunch."

"Very well. Do you mind what happens to him?"

"I'm leaving him with you—" He grinned, and there
began to be less of him, a hand or an ear or a foot left, and
the rest out of sight, and then the whole of him out of
reach.

After she had been alone for ten minutes she began to feel holy, and inside herself an immense preoccupation with power. She went upstairs, put on a gayer sweater, and delicately painted her face. So Ambrose had come down to see if there was anything to be done about Nick. Through her. If she had been easy, to have her; easy or discontented or jealous of Nick. Very likely Mrs. Loring, *mère Angélique*, had sent him herself and repented, and so written. She had thought such a thing possible? Wanted such a thing? Wanted her son's wife a slut and had not wanted it. Wanted Ambrose back? In her mind there was the old woman's name written-up and scored through. Then she went out and called lightly up at his window from the cool lawn.

"Come down, Ambrose, it's a perfect day."

With sweet animation and pretty phrases she made Nick's excuses, and took him the plain way up the hill to the village for a drink.

He had better go, he thought, there was nothing doing here. He was separated after the night's deep sleep, cut off already from what had been yesterday's preoccupations, and those of weeks and years and even of a life past. Indifferent for the moment to their reassertion, like a man drugged, but not as though it was well with him there. So that the only thing was to get away. Go before lunch and cut its pointless coda. God! was Nancy, the woman beside him, talking, running a primrose through his coat, trying to flirt with him at last? The gentle admiration of last night turned pert with a grin behind it. She went on like that all the way to the village inn. He had a drink. He needed it. He was imagining things. She was a gay baggage after all, and he'd interested her. She wanted to know about himself, did she? She'd got rid of Nick. What was she saying?

"It's good of you to tolerate me, Ambrose. After you and Nick. What a marvellous friendship we might have. But oh, my dear—!"

"What do you do me the honour of thinking about

me, wife of Nicholas?" There was another drink before him. Put it down. It was quick work following this up.

"This visit has cleared up so much, made almost anything possible. And now we are friends, I feel I must say anything to you that I think."

"Go on."

"Anything? You mean it? Then, Ambrose, I shall begin about yourself; and first of all I'm going to tell you something you're to do and that you are not to do."

"I'll obey you." Her voice had light music in it.

Now she leaned across the inn table, *dulce ridentem,* a shadow in her smile, making him aware of her awareness of him.

"You are a great man, Ambrose, but oh, *mon ami,* love Nicholas, love me, but don't, don't—"

"What am I not to do, lady of the place?"

"You should not, you must not. Ambrose, you are not to let people call you—you are not to be so mixed up—with old women who exploit you. I'm a woman, and I'm not an old woman, but do you know what some old women are like? They adore your looks and your sweet manners, and," she added rudely, "how? They want you physically, of course, but not simply physically; and they've their own way of getting that. And when they've got what they want, or not got what they want, then they make comparisons."

What was this? She was serious, she was smiling. There was a smile set against him and eyes lit with cold fun.

"Whatever dowager takes such an interest in me?"

"Oh, my dear, with so many about, and you so liked and hard-up. Why, this morning I had a letter from Nick's mother, for you to be returned intact. A perfectly wolfish howl. How did she know you were here?" The smiles were working easily on her lips, but her eyes were steady. Steady as two carved stones on rock.

"I think you should be kind to her; kind as you are to Nick; kind as you are to me."

She was making a sing-song of it, her head drawn up,

her throat strained a little under the high collar of bright wool. Then relaxing: "Forgive this candour," she said; "I know how they can be useful, these women. Only if you can't do without them, you must learn how to keep them in order. Nick was a little annoyed that his mother should write such a letter. Keep her in hand. You remember about Peter Carmin and how his friends got him out of the country—"

If she had been alone down there with him at the house she would not have been safe, in spite of the green.

"May I see the letter?" (He must say that.)

"Nick has it." That was what she must say. She could say what she liked. She was in her own land. It was then that she heard his surrender.

"Tell Nick I will write to him. I think I had better go up now since the car is here."

Its noise drowned her light farewells and excuses.

* * * * *

She dropped back softly between the hills, by the first way, through the Apple Land. Round the green bay, through the copse, until outside the house she was looking at the plain and the trees' open hands. Her husband came suddenly round a corner of the house and saw that she was alone.

"Gone," she said; "and before I come in take this letter into the house and read it."

In Bayswater

"Some passages in the life of an only son."

I

HE FOUND THE ROAD behind Westbourne Grove where there was the cream and laurel-green cottage where he wanted to live. He had heard that it was to let and was persuaded that it would be cheap, because of the neighbourhood, because there was no tube, because of the Portobello Road. A woman made of dirt-stiffened rag was its caretaker. She told him a fantastic rent. He had begun to live in the cottage years before. In the last resort, he liked to wound himself observing his own piteousness.

He crossed the ivory boards in his muddy shoes. There was clear yellow paint inside and a round window over the porch, set in deep wood. He put his elbows in it and listened to the wind in the poplars and thought that he was in an old, resting ship. If four shared it, it might be possible. He had not four on whom he could rely. A clean laurel grew in the back yard. He picked a yellow leaf and wrote on it and put it inside his shirt. The great window at the back was made in small panes. He wished he had a diamond in a ring to cut his longing on it. The kitchen was flagged. The larder had a marble shelf for cooling and in summer the butter would not run or the milk sour. There was a glass and white wood cupboard, and shelves for books.

"It is nice," he said to the woman, "but there is no geyser in the bathroom." He knew that she knew that he could not pay the rent. He thought, how, if he took it and could not pay, a life of beastly evasion would begin and corrupt the still beauty. He had no nerve to dodge bills, the technique of frightening him had been too developed. He went out, the leaf pricking him, and forgot to give the woman her tip, so that the wretchedness might be completed by a bad exit, and the shilling still be there for tea.

The round window followed him that was the house's eye, a ship's window, the shape for the eye of the wind. Small, square windows are good, and wide plate sheets; well, he could not have them and must go back to the sort that rattle and stick, that look out on mean arrangements and illuminate them.

These are the fancies of a man looking for a house. His next was the Portobello Road because of its crime. It was a fair walk, as Londoners count it, into a hollow full of bright shops, a market and a crowd, a moving, merry place. There were squat glass pillars full of sweets, called cushions, of the texture of silk. There were little pieces of meat classified and no carcasses. The poor like thick gold watch-chains, and little earrings stuck on cards. He pretended to be envious, while he had no sense of it at all. He imagined a freedom, but the rich vitality, the bestiality, the arrangement of wit, innocence and corruption had no relation to his nature.

He wanted his tea.

The leaf had made a small sore. He pulled it out. On the yellow underleaf was a red line he had scrawled: *From the house with the round window we are kept out of,* and his name, *Alec.* The letter was broken by the veins of the leaf. He put it away. He did not notice the people who had noticed him unbuttoning his shirt. He walked away to the right into a district of tall houses whose doors stood high above the streets at the top of high steps. Some had pillars. The dogs ran along lifting their legs against the high, frayed area rods. The road also ran up.

Into a city of charwomen. They climbed out of deep areas. Soon he saw they were everywhere, descending, rising, in their rhythm; young in glazed cotton furs, mature and very pregnant, old with scum in their eyes. Rooms would be cheap and include the services of one of them, and that would make a gesture.

Rain began. Wetted at dusk, the streets' patina of filth gleamed like stale fish, and out of the crests of the houses came noises of weeping that never was, that never could be comforted. A stiff old gentleman with white whiskers and a red face let himself into a boarding-house with a long bright key. Alec saw him and remembered that the family of a man he knew lived in one of these streets, and that his friend used to live with them. If he called, there might be tea, and he liked the idea of contact with the man again. He filled a coloured disc in Alec's mind, violet and blue with little gold flecks. He looked up and saw the street. At the first number there was a brown visiting card with the man's name under a bell that did not ring. With his lips against his fingers Alec called up the tube. His breath beaded its mouth and moved a clot of grit. A woman let him in. He went up the high stairs that smelt of dust. At the top of the stairs he found their flat, the door flush with the step. He was half-enchanted, saying *these are not natural*, forgetting he had come for human contacts and tea. A little old woman opened the door, dressed in dull silk, and a small coat of black wool over it. Her wedding ring was of bright gold and very thin like her hands. For an instant she peered at him and then began to smile.

"Come in; you're a friend of Charles, I expect. I'm afraid he's not in, but he may be back." He was drawn inside, and separated from his hat and stick. A tall, sullen, pretty girl left the room at once to make him tea.

* * * * *

"You see," she was saying, "I am Charles's mother, and that makes it so difficult. How can I say anything against my own son? But sometimes I must . . . before my daughter comes back. A girl's innocence should be respected. Once it's gone, it's gone for ever, as Landor says.... But he drinks, my dear boy,—you'll forgive a short acquaintance and an old woman, I know. He drinks, and stays out half the night—all night, and I don't know what his journalism brings in, but he gives me nothing...."

It had been going on some time, and the impact of the idea, substituted for his idea of Charles, was like the pricking of the leaf. He took it out of his pocket and split it down the back. So a generous man like Charles was a cad to his mother. —What was she saying?

"He says he is fond of his sister, but he does nothing for her that a brother should do. He brings men to the house who ignore her. He says she is not smart enough. He sneers at her. There is something in him all the time that makes me afraid."

Rubbish. What did she mean by that? This was not interesting. It was mean. As Rutherford he stood for charm, as Charles he was becoming wicked, just simply wicked like a man who starves his dogs, and also obliquely, medically wicked, responsible and irresponsible, a double treasure for the connoisseur.

"I'm so glad you came. I like to meet his friends. Charles tells them I am a spiteful old woman. But I am all alone, and I have to keep it from the girl."

Why? Poor old thing. I don't suppose she has to.

"We all thought him a good fellow. He is our authority on periods and décor." That ought to please her—mothers like to swank.

He wanted to hear more, and was beginning to be ashamed. He did not attend to the shame, and was arranging a fresh cast when the girl came back into the room, staring contemptuously over the tray. He took it from her. She blushed and scowled. There was bread and margarine and with them a superb cake.

The delicate voice spoke like a gramophone, round and round, to no one.

"My daughter is a good sister, she loves her brother Charles."

"Don't, Mother."

"Why not, my dear? Wasn't it only last week that you replaced the eyeglass he is always breaking? I know it cost ten shillings, and on your salary.... I tell you about this, Alec, I knew that you were the one Charles calls Alec as soon as I saw you, because of what you said about his being an authority on dress. Oh, my dear boy, if you saw his room, the filthy state in which he keeps his things, his rubbishy novels, his ukulele that makes such a wicked noise, I think; the cigarette holes in his sheets. I know I am a nervous old woman, but some day there will be a fire, and he will burn to death and we're very fond of him, all the same, aren't we, dear?"

"Mother!"

"But, Mrs. Rutherford, what does he do that you don't like?" He wanted his appetite quickly glutted.

"Charles ... I can't bear to go into it ..." She paused and winked: "I must leave you and see about dinner. Char-women can't cook, and I'm determined that my children shall have one good meal a day. Charles ..."

He was left alone with the girl. A more abstract part of him had already sketched a mask from her pale bold face, and hot ignorant eyes.

"Your brother Charles ..."

"You must not take my mother too seriously. She does not quite understand about young people. Charles ..."

He thought: You are ten years younger than he, you silly maid. You want smacking. And he said:

"Yes, I agree, but what does Charles really do?" He rearranged himself, raking back his beautiful gilt hair.

"Charles drinks—he leads a bad life, whatever that is."

"We would admit nothing, but that he is sometimes drunk."

"There was a night here once—anyhow he thinks dreadfully. He told me to read a poem once about a bad woman. Mother was frightened—I know too that he is friends with a woman who is not married and who has a child. He would not tell us that it was not his child." Alec thought: But this is ordinary rubbish. I'm wasting my time. Good advice, and I'll go. He said:

"You should try and be matey with him then. You should go out with him, make him show you people. He might not drink so much if you were sympathetic. Nothing is so beastly as when brother and sister aren't friends?"

"Mother would not hear of it. You don't understand."

"What don't I understand—" —I'm off, but I did say the only thing that's always true when I told her to be matey.

The girl went on: "Charles does not think that one can do anything wrong. I don't understand these things. I never go out except to work. It is lonely."

He forgot the stiff lines of the mask he had made of her, lost himself in psychology, and psychology in pity.

"Well, now I know that Charles has a sister, perhaps your mother will trust me." This is going it—I am off home. "Make my apologies to your mother, I have an appointment."

"What did you come here for?"

"I've been looking for a flat."

"There is one to let on the floor below. We have the keys. Mother, let us show him over the flat below."

The mother came out of the kitchen. "Do you like apple dumplings. I hope you'll stay to supper and only hope Charles will come in. I've kept my hand for pastry." She led him affectionately downstairs.

The flat was frightful, a low room with jumping panes and sprawling flowers and yellowing paint. A hot blue bedroom. From the streets he had fallen into domestic anguish, and into rooms that were the interior version of the streets' unrest; and though the retreat was open, he was not sure of it, because the old woman was a witch and would diddle him, the girl her apprentice, and Charles their conjuration. He saw Charles as a stone idol that walked. He was damned if he would take the place.

"Charles. Charles. Charles."

Someone was coming upstairs. To his active ear the slow step sounded deliberate. Here was Charles coming, who did not think anything wrong, who was cruel to his sister. Who would not take his sister out. Who had an old woman cooking for him upstairs. Whom Alec knew as another person. He was out of the door and after him.

Charles marched past him, did not look at him. He followed him, feeling kicked, up the black stairs. He saw the girl beside him suck in her mouth, and then a frail call: "Charles, my dear boy, here's a friend you'll be glad to see. Alec whom you've told me about so often. He is staying to supper." And lower, "You will be nice to him, won't you?"

They crowded on each other into the little room.

"What in hell does he want?" asked Charles. "I'm going up to my room to be sick."

"Have you no respect, Charles, for my drawing-room?"

"None."

His sister screamed. "I can't bear it. I can't bear it."

"What can't you bear?"

"We were having tea with your friend and showing him the flat, and it was nice and amusing, and you can come in and shame us."

"And what would you do if I didn't? Exploit me till there was no telling which was your son and which was your husband, eh, Ma?"

Drunk—dangerous. Might be sick.

"Rutherford, hadn't you better come up to bed at once?"

"In the absence of that woman's spouse, I am head of this house—

"My fathers drew the righteous sword

For Scotland and her claims,
Among the loyal gentlemen
And chief of ancient names, ...
Like a leal, old Scottish cavalier.

"In Bayswater we have other occupations."

He had taken the hearth-rug position, his arms open, grasping each end, working his olive neck. They waited. "Charles, why do you mind us knowing your friend?"

"Alec, I must apologise for these people. This is why I don't bring people home. I am as drunk as drunk, and where's some food?"

"In the kitchen. I'll bring it up to your room if you're going to be sick."

"I'm not going to be sick. Is there anything to drink?"

"You know—"

"I know there is going to be some. Go out and get it, girl, and we'll play *pass the keystone.*"

"Give her some money, Charles."

"Damn her, why should I?" The girl went out. Alec rushed after her.

"Go back, my dear. I'll see to it. You must let me. I insist. It is abominable." This is not possible. He sings: *His golden locks time has to silver turned.*

In the street Alec shouldered people left and right, ran into the wine shop and out again with the sour drink.

When he got upstairs, the women were talking low in the kitchen, and up and down the tiny sitting-room Charles was pacing, talking, striking at the air. An ugly boil showed above his collar, a patch of skin on the heel above his shoe. Alec noticed that a great ring was gone from his elegant yellow hand.

He stood in the doorway, licking his mouth. Then he said: "Here's the keystone," and then: "I say, Rutherford, wouldn't you be better in bed?"

"How long have you been here?"

"About an hour."

"What's she been telling you?"

"I never knew you drank like this."

"Turn it into a nice mime, man. That's your job, isn't it? What did she say? Tell me, or I'll wring your neck."

"She minds your drinking. What mother would not?"

"Go on."

"Oh, and the way you keep your room; you've got such a flair for beauty, you know."

"Good man, you've told me, now I'll kill her." He spun Alec out, lifted him, dropped him, hitting the ground with him, and went into the kitchen. There were screams. Alec rushed in. Mrs. Rutherford was sucking her hand. Charles was leaning against the dresser, tears falling down his face. He spoke first:

"It is finished. I am going up to bed." He went out on a light swing, and as lightly up the bare attic stairs.

"This is too awful. Mrs. Rutherford, I am going to take the flat below. I may be able to help you. I could come up at a sound. You are all alone here."

"Bless you, dear boy, bless you."

He was just conscious that this was the sort of good deed to be done quickly. He ate her dinner, he went out to telephone, he slept on the sofa. The women whispering in their bedroom were quiet. He sat over the fire. There had been no sound from Rutherford's room since his door had shut. Suddenly his mother in a red dressing-gown came into the room and sat down by Alec.

"Dear boy. What an entertainment for you. Must I tell you that it might have been worse? Poor, poor, poor son of mine. To think of his singing like that. You know we really are people of that sort. The last poor ghosts of a great family. May I have a cigarette?"

She sat slim and straight, head back, hand up, like a boy. Alec saw the boy. He saw the room and its implications. He thought he saw the possibility of romantic adventures. He saw his retreat closing. He acquiesced.

II

One of the charwomen was creeping about his bedroom. Alec stood about the living-room afraid to touch anything lest the dirt-scum should rub off before the woman had given it a semblance. He could feel her revolving slowly, on an unfresh, quiet morning, when his mouth was sore and his body dazed, with only the sleep interval between him and the dreadful stories upstairs. What a family— compact of malicious and sexual crime, tragic lives and comic deaths. He remembered a great-aunt who had had twins, who had crawled to her husband's bed and left the bodies there, and had hung herself from the chandelier, and her toes tapping the foot of the bed had waked her husband in the morning.

... The girl would leave the room with her irrelevant hauteur and the mother's voice would drop to a hiss and out would drop a toad and Charles would improve on it. *Putting the jewel in the toad's head.* Phew. There could be a series: Bayswater nights.

The flat was horrible. He slept at one and two and three, and woke at nine and ten and eleven, and often went out without washing, rehearsed, idled, ate too little, ate too much, till late night, like a black madness, drove him back. Not to study, talk and imagination, but to a dogged run up the black, smelling stairs. There he found them, not often Charles, not always the girl, but always the old woman, and a series of obscene, absorbing stories. The flowers he brought them withered in the vases, the classics they borrowed were not read, and it seemed to him that if he took them away it would make a position clear of which he was afraid. He was on a tide and felt it, with reprobation, with amazement, with anguish, curiosity and fear.

The mother fed him, and he sometimes cooked for her, but she would not learn his dishes though she praised them. There was always praise. Instead of a small clean green house and some pretty bits of furniture, praise.

Charles, since that night, had been charming. He had not come there often. He kept his disc in Alec's imagination, night-blue, spangled with gold; and another arrangement where he might murder his mother, and terrify his sister, and refuse to explain why.... He was in a circle by himself. Alec heard his soft bitter voice, whose sound was lost in the mother's reiteration of praise.

"Charm, my dear boy, of course he has charm. All my husband's people have charm. He reminds me of poor Lord Byron."

"Where has he gone, Mrs. Rutherford?"

"Oh, to his room to work, I hope."

Alec thought it must be cold up there with the stars shaking over it.

"He drove Mrs. Sumner out of it this morning. What a state it must be in. You are so particular, Alec. I like to see that in a young man. There is an uncle on his father's side—"

Alec felt for the cigarette he had long ceased to enjoy. It was the first time she had got down later than a grandparent. It had been saga as much as scandal. She had said "uncle." That might mean that they were coming to the history of living beings, not death-gilt heroes and heroines he had dressed in their costumes as she had moved them naked in their sins.

She had a husband "away at his work and shortly to return." She was preparing him.

"His uncle Ramsay won't speak to us."

"Because of Charles?"

"Because of something that happened before Charles was born." Among the various properties of Uncle Stewart's career had been a collection of obscene books. "He was like Charles about his bedroom, and when he died they were found. I sometimes think that Charles may have something up there."

Charles knew any number of amusing things that had happened about cod-pieces and beds and medicines and make-up and songs.

"Of course you must not think that I mind the classics—I don't think it's a book, but he locks the door, and if only he'd trust me a little— Do you know what he said to me when I asked him?"

"I heard him tell his sister she had a mind one could make toast at—"

"He said *to the filthy all things are filthy,* staring at me with that ridiculous eyeglass. An eyeglass with the clothes he wears." She fretted on.

In the afternoon of the next day he was alone with the flesh-raw flowers, and when he had thought of blood and flaying and Assyria, and the uncommunicative shapes of cuneiform, he had backed to the door, and stood rattling the handle and let himself out and then went upstairs. There was no one in. He pretended that Rutherford might be in, and for the first time went up his stair. His door was not locked. Alec's conscience went on squeaking like a ghost.

The room was stirring in the thin wind.

There was a pale stone Buddha, an iron bed with a red blanket, and a night table with a marble top, and a blue quicksilver ball. A nice set. He saw these and began to look for something to see.

It takes time to look at books. There was a basket-handled sword. No fire-place. The servant's room. Pink tooth brush. Did his mouth bleed? A chest of drawers the colour of mustard to write at and dress. A piece of silk on the wall in Charles's colours. The wine-dark. If he finds me here, I came up to borrow a book. The devil take him. He never told me he had these....

He squatted down on the boards.

There were all the Italian writers and portfolios of fallen columns and standing columns and well-heads whose contemplation should occupy a gentleman's leisure.

There was a Boccaccio, on parchment, the page spaced with small witty cuts. Alec turned over on his face, and an hour later, put them away with guilty accuracy, and went downstairs.

If there was a secret, it was hidden. He had not believed in it, only hoped for it as he might hope for a drink. He left the women alone that night, and the night after, Charles came down to his rooms, and a friend came and another, and they sang, but Charles would not sing, and Alec fancied he might be going to cry, and put off telling him that he had gone up to his room, because one confidence might force another. He knew now that everything would happen in its time, and this was the root of his perception, the excuse for his weakness, and made him a happy man.

The next night they were not cordial and he hardly noticed it. The night after, he was making a stage-model and there was a sharp knock and he had let in the girl, sulky and liquid-voiced and fresh from tears.

He noticed that he would like to force her into a corner of the room, twisting her arms, and supposed that one or both must be in a high state of erotic excitement.

"I'm not supposed to come," she said, and scowled, then, with a prepared vulgarity that scandalised him: "You won't let on to Ma, now, will you?"

He wanted to say: "My dear, it is quite proper for you to spend an evening with me, and I shall not make a mystery about it," and felt again that mixture of disgust and vital interest, when she fell down into his arm-chair and began to shiver without crying, so that he could only say: "What is it?" and at his gesture, she exclaimed: "What must you think of me?"

He looked down into the hot eyes, not at acting become obscene through excess of lying, but at raw hunger. It was personal and impersonal. It was the impersonal that interested him. Her race was boiling there. She ought to be singing, not squirming there like a typist, singing another bit of that infernal saga that was coming up-to-date, that was coming up-to-date.

Poor ravenous kid. She should be given flowers and kisses and taken to bed. *Cover her with flowers.*

"I'm glad you've come—listen to this." He went to the piano and sang the pretty song, and played some Mozart to sensitise and detach himself. When he joined her she was bolt upright and sneering:

"What a good chaperone a piano makes."

"What is this fuss about propriety? It is awfully silly."

"I was only thinking that we need more than a piano upstairs. That's why I came. That's why I came." She said it the first time with sober tragedy, the second time like a caress.

"Has Charles been unkind to you again?"

"Oh, là, là. Don't let's go into that. Please, Alec. Yes. Yes. He sneers at me. Oh, God, why aren't I dead?" He thought: I'll get the truth out of that girl if I wring her beastly neck: "Now, look here, tell me the truth."

"Yes, Alec, I will. He sang a dreadful song about—I can't tell you, but you can guess, and when Mother told him to stop and he wouldn't, I ran into the kitchen, and he followed me in there still singing."

"Now, mind you tell me the real truth."

"He frightened me. I ran downstairs."

"You must explain it more. You haven't told me anything to believe."

"I can't, I can't. Oh, comfort me, comfort me."

They're all mad. I must start from that. They're all mad. His brutal temper is making the girl neurotic. Poor little beast. Is it a trick to get hold of me? No. No. Charles is off his dot—I needn't be careful—it's awful. "My dear—"

"Alec, it's silly to mind, but when I minded he snatched my little seed-pearl bird out of my frock and threw it out of the window. It was very old, and I haven't any ornaments."

Alec found he was beginning to cry, and when he checked himself, the sense of danger rose behind the pity and interrogation and balanced him. He was leaning over her staring when Charles came into the room.

"What have you been doing to the child? How dare you throw her bird out of the window?"

Charles took no notice and said to her, "I want to talk to Alec, wouldn't you be better upstairs?"

Alec, expecting heroics, saw her face swell into a puffed, white, whimpering mask.

"Rutherford, you leave that girl alone. She came down here with a horrible story I don't believe."

"Believe it, man. It will have truth enough to suit you."

"Until I know it's a lie, I must protect her. Nothing upstairs makes me believe anything but that you are all mad, but she is too young to tell nothing but lies."

Charles frowned: "Will you listen if I tell you the truth?"

"You said that her truth should satisfy me. Suppose it does?"

"So?"

The girl turned in her chair. He thought of a daschund lying on its side.

"Sit up." She sat up immediately, a young gentle-woman.

"It is good of you to take care of me."

"Look out," said Charles laughing.

"Man, how dare you laugh when you have driven the child so crazed, she doesn't know what she's doing or saying?"

"Alec," said Charles, "are your intentions honour-able?"

"God, man! Are yours?"

"What are my intentions? They are to leave this place to-morrow morning, and my mother can try my father for a change."

Alec was just going to ask Charles humbly for the truth,

when the girl began to wriggle and chatter, bolt upright in her chair, turning her body from one to the other.

"Charles, please, please go away. This is the only refuge I have. It hasn't been all fun being shut up with mother. Alec, you know I came down ... I was afraid it was wrong, but I came because it was quiet, and you would let me cry. Oh, Charles, you might give me a chance. I will tell Alec all the truth."

The men felt that they were acting in a story from a magazine, the present race-fable. They saw each other. "You go to bed," they said.

It was not easy to get rid of her.

"I hate Mother as much as you. Let me stay with you. Show me, and I'll be the kind of girl you like. Give me a chance. I ought to have a chance. You are my brother."

"I agree there," said Alec, and immediately the image of another kind of living was clear to him and he said:

"I wanted to live in a small green and white house that was quiet with a tree, and a round window and stones on its floor. I came here instead without wanting to. That was mad. Without being mad I have lived in an asylum I am going to rationalise for myself. I give in to it. I do not understand what you are all about. But I'm going to."

Mrs. Rutherford slipped into the room.

"My dear, what are you doing here? I am very surprised. Alec, what is my daughter doing here? She's not a bohemian, to be in a young man's room."

Alec and Charles each noticed the other was feeling sick.

"I followed Charles down to get my brooch."

"What brooch?" said Charles.

"My brooch he threw out into the yard."

"It will never be found," said the old woman, "you had better go upstairs."

"It does not exist," said Charles.

"Something exists," said Alec, and then: "Charles, what have they done to you?"

"It is time," said Charles.

The old woman said: "Haven't you done enough for one night. If you will excuse me, I will take my daughter to bed."

Charles said without violence or pleasure: "Will it surprise you to hear, Alec, that I have just come in?"

"There is rain on your shoulder," said Alec. "You have just come in."

"Then I could hardly have been bullying my sister. At present I have no hat."

"Stay here with your friend, Charles. I did not know about this. I will get as nice a supper as I can, and call you both."

Charles fell into his sister's place in the chair by the fire. Alec said: "I smell burning." He did not move. They both said: "It is nothing," but Alec ran out of the room, mad with the feeling that he must be there first, and up the chocolate stair he would see history-making, saga-history, the drama and the psychology caught for a moment in the event, the historiê.

Upstairs in an iron tray on the kitchen floor Charles's *Decameron* was burning to death. There was the white core, curled edges that glowed and went out, brittle metallic pieces lifted in the draught to the four corners of the room. The cover his mother and sister had torn off lay on the table like a sham. Their mutilation had left a block of sheets, too well sewn to come apart, whose lit edges had gone out. Many loose sheets were burned away. The book was dead.

He did not hear them following. He stood about. Poor Charles. His treasure. This was what they did when there was no one looking. He was convinced at once and became Charles's man. He wanted to put it all away, just to hide it, then to bury it. He burnt his fingers on the tray.

"Charles," he cried over the bannisters: "Charles. Come and see what they've done." Charles came.

"There they are," he said, "now do you see?"

"Yes," said Alec. "I mean I don't quite, but I want you to forgive me. Let me do something. Oh, your book, your book!"

"It is the way they relieve themselves," said Charles. "She is malignant against the pleasant things, and the kid is mad with thwarted instinct. That's what they do."

"What can I do for you?"

"Nothing."

"For God's sake don't say that."

"I didn't like the way you came in here. You told them, I don't doubt, that I was the devil of a fellow."

"You know them. It was like going on falling."

"All right."

"I'd better tell you. I sneaked up one day to your room and read there because they said—"

"That there was something obscene there."

"No. I did not tell them."

"Are you keen on my sister? Why did you stay?"

"No. I was interested. At first I was really taken in. Then—"

"When my mother overdid it—"

"I felt that I was in a current—I wanted to find out the truth. I was inside the houses of these streets. It is the opposite of my values. I wanted to get through this way into what *is*. Living with demons made me a cad. I am begging your pardon. I will pack and go."

"And leave my mother responsible for the flat and rent."

"What am I to do? I'd beat the girl and wring the old woman's neck."

"It is time to shuffle the cards. You might stay and see what we can do."

Alec felt beaten, forgiven, blessed.

"They're still here," he said.

"Coming in too," said Charles. "It is more than a stanza, it's a canto. I'm glad you see that." He guided them in and pointed to the floor.

"That is what you have done to my book."

"If I were you, I would be ashamed to have such a book for a girl to read."

"How did she come to read it? She sped up to my room at your orders."

"You must have left it about. I found her hysterical."

"So did Alec. Stop it, Mother. You have overdone yourself this time. It was also a valuable book. I had meant to sell it and have given her the money. However, she amused herself with it another way.

"Why couldn't you have laughed at it? It is a jolly book. You've got its sheets for domestic uses."

"Alec, would you allow your sister to read it?"

"I should be ashamed of her if she couldn't."

"Come," said Charles. "I am going to bed. I am going away to-morrow. Perhaps, Alec, you can give me a bed for the night."

"They have all left me but you."

"You have my sister?"

"A girl. You are the head of the house."

"While my father lives?"

The girl wailed: "Alec, persuade him sometime to forgive me." He went across to comfort her, and when he put her through the door he heard Charles saying:

"Prospero burned his book: they burned mine: my book is burned: they could not bite, they hid the tooth: they could not see, they stole the eyes. I am starving. I am blind."

Alec's heart climbed up his throat; he took Rutherford away. He remembered the streets, three weeks back, where there was weeping going on that never was, that never could be comforted. He would like to have had the girl, too, and run all night from one to the other, and patronise one while he worshipped the other. He felt sickly and refreshed himself, remembering that he was finding out a truth.

He saw Charles undress, feebly, dropping his clothes for him to pick up and fold, gaily, silently.

He said: "It's a pity we've no drink."

"Have you any tea—China tea?"

"Yes. My mother sends it to me. She is kind—"

"Tar and jasmine. Make some."

He fell into his bed and lay flat, smoking. Alec came back.

"It's been going on for two years. Since I came back sick. I thought they might give me a roof. I meant to shape the girl. I heard a bolt snick. I was curious too. There is a great smooth tide we call a rost. I was drawn on it.

"I don't know why it happens. Why the old sow eats her farrow. Why the farrows are eaten. I couldn't make the girl see, though there's not much difference between a paralysed rabbit and a paralysed fox.

"She's not omnipotent either."

"Why didn't you quit?"

"Fatigue. They are wretchedly poor."

"But, tell me. I heard you speak brutally to them."

"Oh, man, when there is nothing but untruth, one must *make* a reality, or become one of the lies. Any reality will do. It is a quality that one famishes for.

"I made myself part of what she said, to give her truth, which stops madness, which is release for her and for the girl. I am a man of my race, I want truth. Universal truth if I can get it, anyhow particular truth. Even my décor I hitch on. More tea. But she won on me. I am brutalised, gelded, spoilt."

"Listen to me," said Alec. "I have got some cash. We are going to take that house."

"What house?"

"My house with the round window, the dear place."

"I should improve it. I tell you I'm next door to mad. I even need food."

"You'll have it. You must let me do it for my own sake."

"All right. I used to have a will. I suppose one can recover even from a mother. You know, I have a terror that one can't. I am very sick to-night. My God, what harm had the book done them that they must destroy it—the clean page. When I was a boy she gave us things to break, she was a scolding housewife that soiled things in secret with grease.

"She told me the great poems were filthy. 'I am guarding you against yourselves.' *An exile I have washed me clean.*"

"Peace," said Alec. "We'll do better by our own children."

"I've lost faith in truth. I'll leave no children. I'll do my bit to end the world."

Alec devoted his life to him.

"This persecution is over for you now. Don't you know that? Do you hear?"

Rutherford tore away the clothes and began to toss.

"They murder, they are murderers—"

"We're at an end," said Alec, "that is sure. At the end of a set of evils. Slowly, one after another, they're going to be eaten. There won't be any left."

"You mean," said Charles, settling down in the easy bed, "there is going to be destroyed *all things but beauty alone?*"

And Alec to whom beauty must be mixed with love slept beside him.

III

It had been Alec's intention to take Charles away, but next morning he found him occupied and disagreeable, inert in every part but his body. Alec was shy and took his cue, accustomed by life to these disappointments. He had an idea of paradise that was a state uninterrupted by breaks in fortunate continuity. Upstairs it would be quiet for a time. He did not know what the mother and the sister would do, but they would find a way out for themselves. Man must do that, and those people always do. The worst of men do the most impossible things, have to do the most

terrible things. *God is not mocked.* He winced that he could
still think like that.

He loathed his occupations till they relieved him. By
the evening he was tranquil enough to say: "There will be
an empty week. Perhaps a week and a week. *A time and a
time and half a time.* We shall begin again. These Scots families carry Scripture with them. There is the father to come
back."

He passed the girl on the stairs with her head up,
slowly stepping. He wished her an illegitimate baby and
went off.

Two nights later a little old man hopped upstairs in a
dreadful hurry. Alec was afraid that it was not time for life
to become again a condition of music, but went about his
room remembering what that condition is.

And Charles was not interested.

"Pa's back," he said. He called him that always, with a
spit, and "Ma" with a contempt that masked hunger.

Alec could not bear it and took him out to dinner, and
with friendly cunning gave him all the drink he wanted,
letting him choose and suggested "tell me about your
father." Charles, glowing at a red velvet bench, refused.

In the street Alec said: "I think I shall walk home," and
Charles said: "Do you mind if I come with you?" and in
Holland Walk Charles sang.

First he sang:

> "*My father is a clergyman, a good and honest man,
> My mother is a Methodist, so I do the best I ca-a-an.*"

"You said he was a schoolmaster."

"No, he was a priest."

"Oh," said Alec, excited at the Roman mystery, "how
did he get out of it?"

"He left a note on the vestry pin-cushion, after he had
celebrated mass, that he had lost his faith. But it was because he loved my mother. He has never lost his faith."

"How has he combined the two?"

"Not at all."

"But what has he done?"

"Perhaps he maternalises her. He has been the great cuckoo squalling in our nest."

"And the cuckold?"

"I expect so. She hates him now."

Then he would talk of nothing but of some discoveries made in Etruria, but he talked so well that Alec's mind sprang wide and he gave him his attention, keeping the rich morsel of story to enjoy alone. Charles had brought a camp-bed and placed it along the opposite wall at the foot of Alec's, and slept there, neat and formal, chilling his host.

Alec saw the father next day running up the stairs with a bunch of flowers. He was like a greying dog, and by no means, in himself, a formidable man. Alec gave up the effort *de se taire* and began again observations that would end in spying on matters that spying would not illuminate. In his life he had known too much ill luck to believe in good luck, but still felt that it might be induced. When his sitting-room door did not shut easily, he left it open. When a friend came, he held him in talk on the stairs. Charles was out all day, came in late and sober, asked politely for his bed, slept in it folded like his figure on its tomb; did his share of the breakfast, ate it and left the house. But on the fourth day he asked for his father. He was restless for a little, and said, "I must see my father." He went into the bedroom and drew a comb that smelt of sweet oil through his black hair, and went over his face with a little wad filled with brown powder.

Alec, who made up well, in the theatre, never did more than wash and whip a wet comb through his magnificent hair. He feared that he would not be able to go upstairs again. A saga is not heard by inference. He was sad, and was careful not to examine the point of anguish behind the disappointment—the sense that he and Charles had nothing in common . . .

Before he had expected him, Charles came down.

"How did you find him?"

"Not so bad. There are times when I quite like him. My mother improves when he first comes home."

Alec was disappointed till he had tasted this.

"My mother gives him such a time. He still thinks her incomparable, like an infatuate with a mistress he condemns and can't live without. Not that he condemns her. He only wishes they were both angels before God. Oh, how he wishes this business of living over, and so do I, and so do all our house."

"I don't see that," said Alec. "I still like things, green leaves and frisking and the good hearts of friends."

"No," said Charles. "I want venetian palaces, which, once and for all, are not to be had, and cannot be won."

"While your mother is the worst housekeeper I ever met. She can't make a pattern of plates on a dresser-shelf." This annoyed Charles and Alec was not sorry. His irresponsiveness had bruised him. My little son, do not take sides in a family quarrel. My mother's advice. Damn the old ladies. They knew things.

When he got home that evening, he found a little blue note that Charles's mother would be so pleased if he would come up and meet her husband, he was very solitary and so liked young people. Alec's going upstairs was like the passage of a nightmare, slow, and swift in extreme opposites, and he was not himself when he pushed in the door, but a stuttering greed for sensation of which he was no longer connoisseur but glutton. He grinned at the bowed backs about the fire.

The girl would not turn round, or look up. He thought he would tell Charles that when she was old she would be a nasty woman, and remembered that no one knew that better than Charles, and that Charles must not think that he talked clichés. . . .

Charles was shewing off a point of erudition.

The old man listened with respect. Alec listened, fidgeted, had no comment. He was crying to himself that this was a Volsung house, and they should be singing. Charles's ivory stick in the corner by the fire was the sacred tree.

But they didn't grow round Charles. Yes, in a way they did. Alec did not see exactly how. But he would have liked to hear them sing.

The old man said: "Don't you think, Charles, it would be very interesting to have an article on Byzantine monasticism in the new quarterly. I'd rely on you a good deal."

The girl said: "Do you remember the wonderful dance you took me to when you wore the gold dress and the curled purple beard?" and Charles said: "Yes, and you wouldn't stay out of pure, sullen refusal to play—"

"I had warned her, Charles, that it was not a proper place for her, but I don't doubt you'd find her more broad-minded, or shall I say more corrupted, now? But here is Alec. I'm so glad to see him again. Didn't I tell you, Father, all he has done to cheer an old woman up?"

"Do you know, Alec, she has broken the most horrible silence about that dance? What truth is there in them?" Alec felt readmitted. . . .

The old man began to fidget. He did not look directly at his wife and daughter, but obliquely at the men. Alec said: *he was once a priest.* An operation of magic was done to him: if he had eyes, he has seen something outside the course of Nature. I say that it depended on his eyes. They say that it did not depend upon his eyes. He has heard confessions. He has elevated the host and censed it and given extreme unction and called Mary an ivory tower and exorcised ghosts. Here he is with wife and children. He has done too much.

The old man belonged to the majority who do not approve—say of cats or earrings or 'bus tickets. He tried to get a denigration out of Alec, who could not think of one. He was wondering at him and trying to remember a piece of theology, when Charles began to give his father a piece of his mind.

"I tell you, people ruin their lives trying to mean both

sides of a question as both sides. You can mean a question one way or another, or as many as you damn well care to invent; but you are not to mean two opposites at once. Of course you can mean them if you do not think of them as opposites. You can mean *everything*. But then you have to know what everything is, don't you know . . ."

So Rutherford was drunk. A good beginning for the night. Alec began to ask him to come to bed.

"I want Father to see what I mean."

"I see that you are drunk, sir, and in your mother's drawing-room. I have known since you were born that you would come to no good end. You say that you can make no money, that I never gave you a profession. Your mother needs a winter coat. Look at your collection of books—"

Charles spat into the fire and sat rigid, while Alec's heart beat.

—"I do all that my circumstances warrant. My son should supply my deficiencies. I am a much ill-used man, and Mother, Mother,—she is not kind to me."

His voice ran up. Alec stared and shrugged to himself. Rutherford flung his arms round his mother's neck. "We understand one another, the old lady and I. Don't we, Ma?"

Alec knew that the gears had been changed, and the engine that had balked would now climb. He blew his nose and looked over the crest of his handkerchief. Charles and his father might be going to cry, no common tears. The old lady had unwound a small roll of braids, tacked on blue paper, and began to knot some dirty threads. Alec cocked his head. That was a web. She was making lace. She makes lace when her men are beginning to cry. The girl looked as though froth would bubble out of her heavy mouth. He lost his sweet feeling for Charles. Charles was part of a play. Not even protagonist. He had no time to feel ashamed. Sometimes love is restored to the quiet soul that Alec wished to have and that his simplicity encouraged and prevented.

Would the song never begin? It did not begin. They bickered. Then Mrs. Rutherford said: "Why should he sell his things when you could give me a coat if you cared to. If you had kept your post in that secular school, we should have been well-off. There's a man for you, worrying about his soul and not his wife—not even about his pretty daughter."

"Don't, Mother."

"There are times when I must speak out. Do you know, Alec, that whilst she was being born, four old priests sat outside our house, in a cab, cursing her as she made her first cry, and me for bearing her to a man who had been one of their priests. Isn't it like them, the shaved men!"

This was reward. There are rewards and fairies. Was this fairy land? Certainly not. "You must not make those curses real," he cried and was not noticed.

"It is she makes them real," the old man cried.

Alec wanted to hide his face....

Mrs. Rutherford and her daughter went to bed. Alec recognised that brightness in the air which marks the appearance of a form of life to which man is not unusually sensitive. His mother would have said: *There is magic about.* The father and son discussed projects and literature. Gradually they began to move. One looked for cigarettes behind a photograph, the other for matches, for a handkerchief, for a suitable piece of coal. In the cramped rooms they swelled, and round Alec grew shadows that met on the small ceiling, drove into one another, mixed and moved out. The son said:

"I shall go and see if Mother is all right," and the father: "I want to ask the girl something." The women slept together. The men did not go. Alec saw the women laid out like saints in neat iron beds, the old woman thinking, the young woman feeling. Nasty, ill-educated girl. No. Charles's sister was capable of thought....

Charles was not drunk enough? How much would it cost to make Charles drunk enough—drunk to ecstasy, not drunk to witless braggings, drunk to possession by the dark daimon?

Outside, the miseries were streaming up through the roofs, the constant incense that did not even smell nice. It was not much of an exchange for the old man for the sweet scents of his altar. He remembered a barrow of cherries fresh with rain outside a Paris church. His innocent cocky youth made a face at him and dropped its mask. Misery—*Miserere.* —There was no lord. We are not allowed to believe in a lord any more. There is a great prince in our hearts. Rutherford knows that and I, he and only I, that we are lié'd for ever: But that prince is in prison. I take him out when I can, and Rutherford shuts him in. I want the salvation of Rutherford's soul. Do I mean anything when I say it like that?

The salvation of his soul means that the prince has come out for ever. A thing that has never happened in the world.

Alec left them moving about and went downstairs to bed.

Charles came in to breakfast and said that he had spent the night wrangling, and then gone for a walk in the pale morning rain. He added: "Are you sure that you do not mind if I stay here, because the old man is getting ready to turn me out of what he calls the house?"

Alec said that he could stay for ever, but that it seemed strange because his father had asked for his opinion on several important matters and had listened with attention. "You will see," said Charles. Alec went out to work. Observation had become a creation like a piece of needlework to be picked up, added to, and perhaps be finished.

A few days later Charles said: "I have made a great mistake—I wanted a recommendation from an old friend of Pa's, and I asked him to get it for me. He promised, but he warned the man not to give it."

"And what will that cost you?"

"A great deal, I am afraid. It was for an excavator's job in South Italy. I shall not go now."

"Oh, Charles, it is insupportable."

"It is," said Charles. "I sink and it lies on top of me. How dirty one feels when one says: 'I am doing my suffering.'"

Alec saw that it was a small, beastly tragedy. Charles could do that work, it fed his imagination and would feed his body. It would lead him back to consideration, honour, luxury. He thought that Charles must have these in order to be himself. The old man had lain in ambush for this. Alec hated him and tried to be rude to him, but he went on looking peaceful and wretched, fussing about the rooms, never leaving his wife, still asking his son questions. His son answered patiently until, two evenings later, he went up to his father and said:

"You are trying to ruin my life and you still pick my brains, you wicked old man. The sooner you die the better."

Alec had expected something more from Charles than this commonplace. It was a little better when he added: "In spite of you I will live and do the work I like. My mother and my sister can starve. They are your job"—and the old man skipped with rage and said nothing. Alec laughed, too, when Charles added: "I will not accept your responsibility," because he articulated like a good Scot.

The girl opened a rosy mouth and sang:

> *"Charlie is my darling, darling, darling,*
> *Charlie is my darling*
> *The young—"*

"Blackguard," shouted the old man.

"Hit someone your own size," said Charles, lifting his noble height, and above his laughter, Alec watched and could make nothing of his eyes.

"You will never come into this house again."

"Do you challenge me? I am going out now and my last state will be worse than my first."

Alec followed him out. "You've done it, this time,

Charles." He made him no answer—Alec wanted to catch at his sleeve and was afraid. Only a woman could do that. He had to stop a sob of excitement, pain and humiliation. Then he thought that Charles was going out to drink and had he enough money to get as drunk as he wanted to get? He crumpled a ten-shilling note into his hand. It was taken without recognition. Alec went into his sitting-room and left the door ajar. Not for an hour. Before midnight, Charles, who had fallen in the road before a 'bus, was carried up, they presumed to die, and laid on his mother's bed. There was a dry hole where Alec's heart should have been. He helped them that night, and, when the doctor said that Charles did not seem intoxicated, went out on to the stairs and cried and thanked God. He wanted to help more and went back, and from the living-room he heard the girl crying in hysteria, and her mother controlling her with great sense. The doctor was in the kitchen. He went to the bedroom door. Charles was on the bed, black and white and young, and by his side his father stood, in exaltation, his hand lifted, absolving his son; and, as Alec saw, absolving himself also, not from past malevolence, but from carnal generation and from women. Alec also saw the father exulting in the son, and afraid that he would see what was being done to him, and that Charles had seen, and was curious, angry and amused.

Just then the mother came back, past Alec, into the room and spoke cheerfully: "My son is not going to die."

IV

After his parents thought that Charles was as good as dead, Alec did not leave the affair alone. Independent of his preferences he had an eye for truth, he was preoccupied with Charles. He knew that Charles wore masks. If Alec could not unmask him, there was trouble about that might strip him. He was not afraid that anything common would be exposed. If he had thought that, he might have been afraid and gone away because he was looking for something that was greater than life. Instead, in sensual fever, he evoked pain on this man, ready to stage him and weep over him at once.

After his accident he took Charles away into the country and talked to him about his complexes, his father's complexes, his mother's complexes. He was invaluably silly to Charles. There was an idol once taken round Scandinavia in a cart. He went about through the villages with Alec. He did not tell him anything.

Alec decided to find Charles a woman, a girl of parts to play baggage. He brought Charles back to his people's flat, his visual mask red-gold that had been yellow-gold. Alec explained that he could not find the money to take another place; probably Charles insisted. They lived again in the pagoda, Charles on top, then Alec, and a creeping woman in the basement. She cleaned for Charles's mother and the old lady sat on the dresser and they would talk. Alec's contact with the district was over. He had described it to his friends. Over the street there was a set of empty rooms. In league with Charles's mother he let them to a white girl called Billy.

The flat was damp. Her furniture came tied up with ribbons. She went about like a blooming, fresh toadstool on its stalk. From the first Alec lost interest in her, but his instinct for treachery made him bring her upstairs to see what the old woman would make of her. They made it a favour to have her, she made it a favour to go. She asked for a footstool. The easy tea-party became formal, a duologue between the old woman and the young. The girl hated her, deep in her sullen pool. Alec was bored. Charles had bruised him. He could take the girl or leave her. He might take her since his people disliked her. Billy rose to go. She engaged the party to return, dropped a little veil half-way down her face, and went down to her flat. She put on a dirty dress. Her eyes set into grey glass beads. She

lay with her hair in a fish skeleton the cat had left by the
fire.

Alec went away for a short tour. He came back into
a windy, violent spell of spring, and found about one
quarter of his flat occupied by a young man. He said that
Charles had put him there and had paid the rent. He was
called Festus.

"He wrote to you for permission, but the address was
lost. I will go at once if I'm in your way." Alec's sentimentality was not vulgar; his weakness, by which he meant to
inherit the earth, was also kind.

"Of course not, my dear boy. You must stay of course."
He was not sorry even when Charles came in looking like
a tree trying not to put out a leaf.

"Festus was homeless between the jobs."

"I gave in and did what Charles told me."

After tea Festus washed up.

"Hard, bright and sweet," said Charles at the slight,
elastic back and drew in the ashes with his stick. "I am very
fond of him."

"How long have you known him?"

"A long time. He rationalises his affection for me."

"I can see he adores you." The small change chinked
in Alec's pocket. He had set the stage and he was not to
play. He was a young saint and an old saint walking in a
paradise that was a cold hillside.

This was something that Charles had found for himself. Charles was warm. There was a deadlier cold about.
He felt himself run upon icy sticks.

"Is he as mad as the rest of us?"

"Yes."

"Only adolescence I suppose?"

"He is formed for his age and very intelligent. But you
must be right. By the way, Alec, why did you bring that
girl, Billy, here? Mother is saying that she won't know your
cast-off mistresses. Festus would like to save me from her
and I can't gratify him—"

MARY BUTTS

"Your mother wanted the place let—" He was pierced
and weary; "I can't please everybody. If you keep a tene-
ment, you try and let it. I see what unites you and Festus.
Some new humbug about sex. I'm sorry you don't like
Billy. I'm off to look her up."

"I hardly know her."

At the door he turned back to see Charles lie back and
smile at Festus as he brought in the dish-cloth to dry it at
the fire.

Billy let him in, yawning inattention. Billy at home was
new. He sniffed about. On a table representing a mush-
room there was her photograph in chiffon and a rose.
Stuck on the frame there was an abominable portrait of
her in orange-peel and buttons. She shewed it to him.
"Festus did that."

"Did he give it to you?"

"No, Charles."

Really. She did not see that it was not kindly meant.
What fun. He readjusted.

"How is life getting along?"

"I'm waiting for my contract to go to Los Angeles.
It is all settled. The director is taking me over with his
wife—"

"Or as his wife?"

"I wouldn't think of such a thing. I'm getting my
clothes—"

Swank of the métier. Why try it on me? We all starve
together. Play up. "How many people are dying of love for
you, Billy?"

"I'm tired of love. A little quiet spinsterhood suits me
at the moment—"

Pale hands I loved. Dear—dear. He thought of a piece
of white, smooth, dead wood.

"Sergius wants me to marry him and go to Russia. I
might."

"But you're married already."

"Only technically, after all. The Soviet would divorce us."

Lord, the vanity of these fancy-girls.

She began to be eager.

"Do you know, Alec, if I had not been brought up a Catholic, I should like to be a Buddhist. What do you think I'd better do?"

"Be a Buddhist."

"I can't get over what I've been taught. A clairvoyant told me that I was once the wife of a Samurai. A man no one can see follows me about. What do you think of reincarnation? I haven't seen him for a long time."

"Seen who?"

"My spirit-husband. Some day he will materialise and give me everything I want."

"Meanwhile you might as well go to Russia with Sergius?"

"Why not? I want to get this life over, you know. It's dull."

"I'm surprised to hear you say that." This ass I tried to foist on Charles. I must tell him this.

"He comes when any danger threatens me. He tells me what I am to read. Once I was staying in a house when a murder was done and I saw him. I don't know why I am telling you this, Alec."

Nor I. "Have you seen him lately—since you came here?"

"Not at all. Your friend Charles would be sufficient to keep away any real psychic manifestation—"

"You don't like Charles?"

"He seems to be simply negligible, that's all."

"And Festus?"

"He seems a nice boy. It's a pity he's so neurotic."

"What's his trouble?"

"Oh, he imagines it is his duty to kill himself. Didn't Charles tell you? I imagine it was Charles put the idea into his head. He is just the sort of man to suggest morbidities and give them a greater value than normal facts. Festus has had a hard life. He has told me all about it. His father was a brute—"

"It sounds a plain doctor's case. But he mustn't die. Charles wants him."

"I can't see that Charles ought to be considered. His life is spoilt already. Can't you see he is rotting where he stands."

Alec wanted to bounce. Wanted to box her ears and smack her behind. Charles had not told him everything and she'd guessed. She had asked him in to say what she had said about Charles. She had poured dirty water on Charles. She had a spirit-husband. That bright, righteous lad was going to die. Charles would be upset. Oh, dear. They could not have it to themselves because Billy was here. Billy at other people's houses. Billy drunk, Billy sober, Billy broke, Billy amorous, Billy-by-the-fire. Two men called to see her. Alec was sent to fetch more cups. Two boys with a car. Festus was not that kind of boy. One of them took his chair. Billy was standing up. Beasts. He went away.

Charles was rotting. He saw Festus out of doors, giving Charles blood out of a spoon.

"She says you're no good, Charles, my Charles."

* * * * *

"Follow up," said Alec. "Let it be quick, let it be quick, my God." It had happened quickly. He had left Charles to his darling and gone off with Billy. She was always ready to talk about them, but he left it to her. He asked her to interfere, to consult Charles about Festus, but this she always refused. For reasons she would not give, for no reason, because Alec did not understand, because Charles was responsible, because no one could approve of Charles.

Alec said to himself, "Charles does not come to me. I am entitled to find out what Charles is like." Then he discovered that Billy saw Festus, and was doing her duty on behalf of him. "He spent yesterday evening with me, and I've found out all about it."

"No one has told me yet," said Alec, "why he should be killing himself at all."

"He thinks that he is fated to kill his father," and this from Billy seemed enough, because Billy did not understand pride, innocence and torment. He could not think of a better answer. Festus had gone to lodge in another house.

One day Alec was coming in quietly, he heard Charles talking to Billy in her room. After the first interest and inhibition of listening, he listened. A high voice and a low noise. The acute interest went out. He was irritated and knocked at the door. They did not say "come in" at once. He went away.

Billy said: "That was Alec. We'd better ask him down."

"He will find out what he wants without our telling."

"He might think that there was something between us. Will you fetch him?" Charles looked at her and then, slowly, did what he was told. Alec would not come. "Tell me yourself."

"Festus is going to commit suicide."

"Can I help you?"

"I don't know."

"Are you trying Billy?"

"Alec, will you take Billy away?"

"No. How can I? She doesn't count. Why do you want that?"

"For the sake of the clean issue."

"I don't think, Charles, you are quite the man to manage a young suicide." Charles sighed. Alec went on: "Why don't you take him away yourself? And you mustn't be jealous of him."

Charles giggled.

—"From the look of you I should say you could do with a change. Can't you leave town?"

"I don't want to at present." Charles went away.

Alec began to shiver. It was then he prayed for it to

come soon and suffered because he had deliberately offered Charles sense.

Charles had earned sense.

He went downstairs after him.

"I'm sorry you're troubled. Please let me be of use."
Billy said: "Festus has gone out by himself. I think we
ought to follow him."

They went out. Billy in a purple coat, Alec in grey,
Charles in black. Through the dull spring streets and the
grit-laced air they hurried to Festus' lodgings. He was not
there. "I know where he sits." Charles walked them to
Holland Avenue. It was getting dark. They walked on the
right side under the trees. "There he is." Alec saw a dark
boy upright, alone on a bench. He looked at Charles. Billy
said: "I suppose I had better go. He ought not to be left."
He wanted to push Charles on and hold him back. She left
them instantly. "Not her," he said to Charles, but she was
sitting on the bench, a black cap at the back of a white
neck, and purple shoulders sloping.

"It is your place and all you'll do is to save it up against
her that she took it."

"The pubs are open," said Charles.

* * * * *

When they got home, they called on Billy. "It's all
right," she said. "I've got him to promise that if I'll help
him to do it later, he'll put it off for three months. It's a
bargain. But he must have company."

"We'll all keep him company. Good for you, Billy. Now
I must be told why he wants to do it at all."

Charles said: "He is going to do it because he believes
he can never express in himself his idea of excellence."

"But we none of us can. Why can't he see that. Why
should he want to? The vanity!"

Billy said: "I said I would go round at eleven to his
rooms. I'll tell you everything in the morning—"

Alec was dazed. His mind would not focus.

There was a tightness and a white blur. He felt he must strangle or be strangled.

"Is she doing her best d'you think, Charles?" he asked as they went upstairs.

"The pubs aren't shut," said Charles.

* * * * *

They sat in the saloon.

"Aren't you letting Billy have all the responsibility? Can you trust her? I wouldn't. You won't like it if anything goes wrong."

"I am enjoying myself so much up to the present."

"Why do you let Billy act for you?"

"My hands are tied," said Charles.

"They're not, they're not," Alec shrieked. "Use your great wisdom."

"I have none. Let the female do her part."

"You're afraid of the responsibility."

"I am *not* afraid of you or Billy or myself. Believe me, Alec, in the past I did everything that suggested itself to me. Now we are on an ideal plane, and I have no ideal solution."

"Ideal plane! Can't you see it's an adolescent neurosis?"

"Believe me, it is like that now, and nothing less. Let the flesh do its bit."

Alec did not think of Billy as flesh. Charles frightened him. Charles was playing up. He squirmed.

"You'll be in an awful state." And what state am I in throwing silly fits before my friend in his necessity? When it's over, I'll help.

They did not go to Festus' lodgings because Billy would be there.

Next morning Alec woke up feeling sick. Billy was about, very brilliant.

"I've sent up a note to his mother to let Charles sleep,

whether the charwoman wants to do his room or not. Go round and call on Festus."

"Won't you come?" She was uncertain.

"No, I must get my place straight. I've left everything because of that boy. I should like to—"

He could not bear to stand about. He went.

He found Festus dead in his bed. He sat down beside him, feeling very cold.

Get the news to Charles. I have to do that. Thank God the girl didn't get here first. She mustn't see him. So that's what he took. I must find the landlady. *In any case you leave a body behind you. Such a want of method.* Can we persuade them it's accidental? We must try. Charles would wish that. I must see about . . .

But he walked out into the street, and, at the impact of the air, he swam and drank it.

Festus is dead. Charles knows it, but he has to be told. How unfair.

I'll tell Billy and she can tell Charles. That's a frightful idea.

I've got to tell everybody. I found the body. Who killed cock-robin? It's quite all right. I hardly knew him.

Take Billy down a peg. Petty cat. Suppose Charles says nothing. If Charles doesn't come off it—

Come off it, you bitch. Leave us men alone. The pretty dead. People go mad and die to illustrate Charles. The illustrated life of Charles. He tore along: with a thick throat shouted up to Billy on the doorstep: "Festus is dead."

She flung out her arms, and strained her palms on the door frame and opened her mouth. She stretched back her head and then led him in.

"Had I better tell Charles?"

"No," shouted Alec, "you go and tell the landlady, tell the police, tell the postman. I am going to Charles."

On the stairs he met the charwoman.

"There's a glove, sir, from one of the gentlemen who was here last night." A huge motor-gauntlet like a dead animal.

"None of us. What gentleman?" Suppose Charles should come downstairs.

"Last night, sir, a gentleman called. Before eleven it was. I heard him with his car. One of Miss Seton's young gentlemen. He took her for a ride in his car and they didn't get home till it was nearly two, I heard them."

"Give it to her."

"Oh, oh, oh." He sat on a stair. We left him to her. He asked her to go. She said she would go. She did not go. He killed himself.

And well the car Love guideth.

Follow up.

He walked firmly upstairs, straight in and up to Charles's room. Charles was awake, propped up, his elbows tucked in to his sides.

"Charles. Festus is dead. He took poison last night. I found him. Billy did not go to him as she said she would. She went out in a car."

"Dead is he," said Charles, and threw himself out of bed, into an overcoat and went out past Alec. "You can tell my people."

Alec told them and went out after him. There was no Billy. Beside Festus' body, Charles was giving directions to the landlady and the police. He gave Alec telegrams written out to send. They worked all day without speaking to each other.

They had the inquest and buried him, received his family and sent them away. They ran it between them. After two days' absence Billy went about among them again. When they could not repeat the story, she told it. Eventually she did all the telling. She invented a mysterious silence when the men began to talk about their affairs again. The she left the flat and went away.

Alec followed Charles about. It seemed to him that Charles carried a quiver of shafts when a shot meant salvation.

Brightness falls from the air. It had fallen when Festus died. He wanted an arrow to stick. He followed Charles up to his room. Charles had offered a contact like brushed velvet. Alec wanted a kick or a blow. Charles sat up against the wall. Alec, sitting, reached across the table to him.

"Do for God's sake tell me, Charles. Do you understand about Billy?" he cried at him. "Did she know what she was doing when she left him that night? Did she want it to happen? Yes, want it to happen? I can say it now. It's a good thing she's gone. What does your mother say? You must admit, Charles, I've been reasonable and asked no questions?

"*Approfondir* the business for me, for pity's sake.

"Aren't we friends enough for that?

"Stop playing the velvet cat. You've played it since that morning. Can't you see you're being too proud to shew your broken heart? But I know it's broken. You might occasionally come off it with me. I'm not in training for a hero. I've been helping you bury your friend, and a ghastly week it's been. I'm going off for the week-end. I wish we could go together."

Charles listened to this. Alec became ashamed and stopped. He had exposed himself to Charles. Perhaps all this had happened that he might be lured on. Like a split plum he was lying in Charles's mouth to be spat out. Excess of shame squared him against Charles. Charles said:

"Let us take Billy first. There is a common girl, detached from the pre-occupation of her class-type, and who dares not be bored. Her ennui was like a vacuum, into which everything was sucked.

"You brought her here. You have an uncritical reliance on the female principle. After the example underneath us. You have not got the key of the mothers.

"I suppose you thought that Billy would satisfy your

curiosity, but not as a rival. She cancelled out with my mother, but that was no gain for she was unready for fresh action.

"I was asleep with Festus. You got tired of Billy. I'm not her size. There was Festus like a thin rod incapable of evasion or compromise or the least adaptation, stripping a male reality, and you two around clapping your female disks.

"We laughed.

"Then Festus' little obsession came to a crisis—"

"What was it?" Alec muttered.

"A simplicity. He had stripped certain aspects of virtue and when he found that he could not exactly reproduce them in his daily life, he decided that he was not fit to live, and must immediately die.

"There was also a boy who was better than he was at his job.

"I made the mother's circle till you came along and charged the air with that blonde bitch. A young man does not do it easily. She got going. He died as easily as falling off a log.

"They were getting on quite nicely, you remember. She was busy saving and pushing us gently away. He was full of gratitude and simplicity. He felt he would not die, and wondered how I could have been so right without knowing her. She withdrew and he instantly died. And there rushed into her vacuum intoxication, orgasm, flesh for dreams. She will feed on that for a time. She will be something for a time. And that's that.

"These were your arrangements, Alec, to enlarge your theory of me; to illustrate, explain me, punish me. The developments took their own line. When I could not act, I stood out. Now you are shocked, but you will find that you have gratified your nature. You will not describe its instinct to betray, you will only feed it.

"I betrayed you when I practised my feminine element on you. Superficially you sentimentalised yourself into

pique, into indifference, but your instinct found Billy. She
has done the job for you. My boy is dead. My mother will
be stimulated."

"I can't stand any more," said Alec. "Kick me, kill me—"

"Or cry to you. That's your sensuality, but I'm not
under the obligation. I am on exhibition here before you,
but I give my own show—"

Alec took out his pocket-knife and sawed the blade into
the hard bend of his wrist.

The blood and the good pain saved his reason.

"You are right, you have given your own show. I see
myself. I am your slave. I will go away for ever and become
not your slave. Some time I shall be at peace and not your
slave. I mean I understand and thank you for this explanation, for your show. I'm going off because you'd be
justified in treading me in like a slug—you'll feel better if
you know you'll never see me again—"

"By no means," said Charles.

The Warning

THIS HAPPENED in the kind of house people live in who used not to live in that kind of house, who were taught to have very distinct opinions about the kind of people who lived in them. Yet, now that they have gone to live in them, they are rather different than when the other sort of person lived there.

Difference between the architecture of one generation and another? Or a kind of spiritual modification? Both, without doubt.

So it was not on ancient stones that the sun shone, nor chimneys warmed by generations of fires that the sea salted with spray. Only in situation the house might have been built by a king, a Ludwig of Bavaria, with the sea for play-boy, whose imagination had led him to make his palace of art, instead of perched up on mountains, under the sea:

> ... *bowers*
> *Where the ocean powers*
> *Sit on their pearlèd thrones*
> *Through the coral woods.*

It is strange that none of the world's play-boys have ever thought to do that; yet this house was set in such a place where the most enterprising of them might have meditated it. There, three hundred feet below, the full Atlantic poured its waters in and out of a cup. There you enjoyed night and day the entire conversation of the sea. There it sang, swore, snored, shouted, whispered, yelled. "Dancing floor of the sun" there, on a reef where contending waters met, it leaped in seven waves, whose hair shook out the prisms of seven rainbows. There, round that reef, the pattern the tide draws in a white line takes on the shape of the Bull, the one beast off a cattle-boat that staggered up on to its black back and bellowing, faced the raving of the green water beasts; and there in the still seething his outline rises before a storm.

There, at the pull of the moon, the tides draw out half a mile. Draw back across lion-bright sand, a delicate flat-race, sea babies at the water's lip, coral and crimson weed and a starring of shells, pearl beads and glass and yellow stone. In every colour but the sea colours. Each one smaller than the last. A perfectness.

There, in a world jutting with empty stones and airy as though you stood everywhere at a great height, the cliffs have clothed themselves; and you look down or you look up into a cross-work of gorse and bracken, blackberry and bryony, threaded with the drip of streams. There, all summer the rose-campion waves a scarf in its face exactly the opposite in colour to the sea. There in the middle of the bay the sand has blown itself together into one place, a dune thrust out from the land, a child carried upright in the belly of the earth; dunes the couch-grass has covered, the grass that never stands close enough together, so that between each blade you can see the skin-pale sand.

And there, round about the house at night the hedgehogs squeak; and night and day, in every tone of voice, the sea says out loud its stupendous secret which is the meaning of everything, the tuning-in for the music of the spheres; and men often listen attentively, understand, and instantly forget all about it; while a foot above their heads the gulls mew like cats.

There, it was only natural that with the summer the friends of the two friends, the husband and wife who lived in the house, should come down to see them. Inevitable, too, that they should arrive all at once and spread themselves about the village, in the tar-and-whitewash cottages of the fishermen; or at the ancient Inn, now pretending to be a hotel; or plant themselves under canvas in the

corners of a field, under a stone hedge beside a planting
of willows, whose green wands, cut in autumn to weave
crab-pots, quivered "upon the wild sea-banks" in summer
cat's-paws off the sea.

Equally the husband and wife were glad that they
should come. But with the pleasure went the knowledge
that there was friendship and friendship, friends and
friends. Their intimacy with each had been a separate act,
a special creation, extended over time. Would they all instantly harmonize with each other? They would not. It was
a question for delicate arrangement, for judicious pairing.
The naval officer and one of the painters. Not the other.
The stage-and-hunting woman with the sailor and the tow-
haired politician whose job it was to restore ruins, rebuild
for a very different habitation the ruins of past West
Country life. She would think his opinions a boy's barbari-
ties; know his strength and his kindness for a man's. The
journalist was for all the pretty women. There were not
quite enough to go round.

"Except," said Marcia, the wife, nibbling at her pen,
"Caroline, with two babies in tow, and the divorce she
doesn't want in the least."

Julian, her husband, said: "Why doesn't she bring a
nurse?"

"It's the new idea of mother-love. Besides the expense.
You can't get one here ..." There rose before their eyes
the picture of Caroline, slender and very young, her wide
tormented eyes, her tangle of curls, the delicate coltishness
of movement young maternity was turning into grace, desertion and sorrow had made a little wild. A creature made
to adore and be adored—now torn defenceless from such
petty shelter as the graceful scamp had afforded her when
he made her his wife. The graceful scamp would end the
graceless scoundrel, as the wise Frenchman had prophe-
sied. The lovely lass—what distressed both husband and
wife was the stamp he had left already on the girl's delicate
wax. Along with the innocence that made them weep was

an ignorance that appalled. Corrupted innocence can turn ignorance, a damnable state of the soul.

While the immediate question was how to blend a grown child and two babies with a number of people who were strangers to her; and the men strange to children of any form. Men are rarely conscious of exquisiteness in the young, shapes of delight that seem to them to combine the dangers of a live bomb with the disadvantage that it cannot be thrown over the cliff and has no pin to take out. No, Caroline must have her special hours, a separate play-time.

This arrangement broke down. Not wholly, not disastrously; but since the same plan had to be followed with most of the rest of their friends, the summer became more and more a service of time-spans, conditioned by a constant and vigilant effort to bring people together and to keep people apart; and inevitably the last became the more important, and separation the chief term of their hospitality. The wide porch up the steps with the green benches and deck chairs, the summer's outdoor room, where the earth turned over on its side and fell away down to the sea through flowers—half cocktail bar, half restaurant—now seemed the place where everyone else was happy and they were not.

In their bedroom, in candle-light and mid-summer dusk, Julian said: "I don't see where our fun comes in. They are all right, with the view and the tea or the drinks or whatever it is, while we keep wondering whether someone who doesn't get on with somebody else'll take it into their heads to call; and if they do I have to take them along to admire the stream. And now that eldest of Caroline's found its way here by itself and its mother will come and look for it, just when Toby and Violaine have settled down side by side, telling each other about their operations."

Toby was the sailor. And Violaine. It was not quiet easy for either of them to speak temperately about Violaine— the tall woman, who had been brought there a month before by another friend, who had gone away and left her there. Much as a pretty launch, dressed for a regatta, might give tow to a racing yacht, its mast stripped, rising to the heavens, in that building for speed inside the winds that makes such a ship the tallest thing in nature.

Together they were sure of one thing—that here was a gift, a peculiar finding of treasure. Jar out of some rare earth, and inside it something at once familiar and rare. While friendship was in its second state of crystallisation. The first recognition over—would it harden out into its pure shape? Was it a late frost crystal? Or a superb flower in a cut glass, to be hurried on to the fire, so as not to shame it with the miserable change in its beauty? Too early to tell, but not if they could help it. For with her went, more than an ambience or a memory, a statement that was the opposite, among other things, of the outside of the house. Forms that had once "composed the beauties" of all three, forms like lost moulds, dies for their stamp, and to have Violaine near them like a new mint; who were all three exiles and from a life that it seems is more and more passing away. To build a Civitas Dei in such minds as theirs, lay up its pattern for itself. Until such time as it will return, and stamp itself again upon its outward images.

Another thing that was perfectly plain was the gulf fixed between Caroline and Violaine, a gulf they had made no attempt to bridge. Why not? For reasons that made them blush. And then blush for blushing. So hard it is for one kind of person to enter with the inward being into the life of another order of society. Yet that was what Violaine herself had done when she left her Border castles and the dark ruins of her house, her salmon rods and her horses to plunge into the world of the stage-world, not as actor but as spectator; and her friends half great persons of the world, half women players with their lovers and their sorrows. A world of which the wife knew little and the husband much. As he knew less of what his wife knew well, the world of what is called the Young Intellectuals, the Intelligentsia. A name that has given itself away. Yet she had lived it once, lived through it very thoroughly. Was in a position to judge young entry—the kind of lad Caroline had married—as Violaine the puppy she was walking, her husband the quality of his own art.

So, with so much enlightenment about, it should not have been hard to adjust, and tactless of La Bruyère to wake up his little platitude, asleep in the attics of memory, and send it sauntering through their heads: *Rien n'est aussi difficile que le commerce des hommes*— What was to be done about Caroline? When surely the only question should be: What was to be done for Caroline? Caroline, ardent and sweet, quick-witted and true, a lass with a delicate air? What also had been done to Caroline—taken, a child from some awful home in the middle of God knew where, from a place not marked on any of their maps. There Arthur had found her, enchanted her, married her; led her a dreadful life. It was pure Prunella. Made her the mother of two lovely children; spent too much. Was unfaithful to her; encouraged her to be unfaithful to him. Left her penniless. Taught her the fashionable immoralities and the slang of cheap intellect, the formula of bolshevized behaviour. Substitution for such simple faiths she had not believed in much. Deserted her, forcing her through the prospect of starvation to the divorce she loathed.

Quick-witted, such education had not made of her an utter mess, held by such simple loyalties as duty to her children and love of him. Grief also at the harm he was doing to himself. Not bad, but not enough for a *credo* in the world in which she found herself. Was she in herself sufficient to develop and enlarge?

The husband and the wife listening to all this believed that she was.

Yet, like a term from another series suddenly intruded, star-dust from the tail of a very different comet, they still observed that there could be no introduction of Caroline to Violaine.

Reasons presented themselves. Violaine's health, her

trigger-set nerves. Her unawareness of the existence of small children, too young to sit a pony or throw a fly. Still less of children whose parents had lived in the fear of that new disease, the Repressions, more dreaded than ever the smallpox, for which the prophylactic was behaviour which would have sent their parents off to learn the habits of civilisation in disgrace. Nurse's business, only there were now no nurses to do the rough work of licking into shape. (How far has economic pressure given point to the theory which banished Nurse, to replace her by over-strung young parents, whose fatigue their young, with the demon perception of infancy, know instantly how to play up?)

This took them some of the way. But what about the starry evenings, when the babies were in bed, and the terrace room hummed with voices and the clink of glasses, and three hundred feet below to the purring sea? Waiting for the moon to rise, watching the stars come out, when "the sounds of beauty flowed and trembled" as from inside the house Julian played Mozart. Hour of the moth, when they brushed by, each with a lion's head, black eyes and white fur. A mystery. Or a baby snail, his still transparent house in black and coral rings. A young hedgehog, tender-quilled. The toad. These were their night-callers, the faint coloured stocks giving out their perfume in little floods born on the night breeze off the sea.

No, she had better not come if Violaine was there. Was it because they were all so much older, the War-generation with its unspoken secrets, that complete assumption of a common experience? In part. Because they were all such old friends? Not all of them were.

"You can't go on feeling sorry for a person all the time," said Julian.

"She loves us too much," said his wife suddenly.

"She kisses me too often," he answered simply, "outside the Post Office with all the garage men grinning. Hangs round my neck . . ."

"That's true," she said, "she twines." Reflecting on the

counsel handed down from mother to daughter through the ages, how only to pretend to be a vine.

"It's not *natural* . . ."

His wife said: "It's Arthur. You don't realise—husbands train their young wives. And when I first met him his chief asset was the way he sank on to the floor at your feet, and looked up through his eyelashes. The way every woman from a matron's size down was encouraged to lean against him like Leighton's 'Wedded.' I did. He never forgave me when I told him to stop when he put on weight and the bump of his *derrière* could be heard on the floor."

"What I mean is," said Julian, "someone ought to tell her *when* to do these things. Not with a village watching. Or," he added candidly, "anyone."

This did not take them much further, though agreeable in itself. Then, little by little, there became perceptible a certain restlessness in Caroline at the mention of Violaine. A touch of curiosity; eyes that once or twice implored. With that the other pan of the balance moved a little when one day Violaine asked:

"Who's that pretty little woman with the children I saw coming out of your gate?"

It is easy to answer a question one has waited to hear, easy to draw a picture for her of Caroline; try to elicit interest, sympathy. Violaine without doubt could be useful to the child. Violaine was saying:

"Of course it's pretty hopeless looking after these young things who've got their lives into a mess. Besides, they always turn in the end and blame you." Easy to protest that, for once, this was impossible. Easy, too, to bore Violaine. It was dropped. Easiest of all, when the wistful look came again into Caroline's eyes, to explain how useful Violaine might be, with introductions to designers—and, privately, to a world more seemly than Arthur had ever chosen to show his wife. Part of their broader plan came in there—to lift the child out of the intellectual slum, the mental house of ill fame this young pioneer of our future society had offered her for home.

"And when her life is settled again, I shall tell her about her bearing . . ." Which done—and accepted—they saw the pretty ship set sail again, dressed for a blue day and a following breeze. *Départ pour Cythère,* as they both prayed.

It was two days later that the wife was led to the indiscretion which brought the delicate structure of their lives crashing down, with a harsher sound than a card-house toppling. Or compare it to a lid lifted off a simmering pot, showing under the bubbles a stew not designed for human food. Caterpillars out of the garden or inedible snails. Slugs even, and for herbs a few rank weeds. (Lately a fleet of henbanes had sprung up on the waste land outside the garden gate. A sending from Pan knew where, set on empty soil, as though even the weeds feared them, henbane from whose grey leaves the hyoscine is distilled that Doctor Crippen gave to Mrs. Crippen. Henbanes, on which and on no other plants, a swarm of black caterpillars were riddling to rags. A cycle in nature which struck them as sinister, no matter to what scientific terms it could be reduced.)

It was late afternoon when she turned to Caroline and said:

"My angel, you are passing Violaine Standish's house. Would you leave this note?" And saw her up the garden path, a lovely child in each hand.

"It's only to say I'll be down to-morrow for a cocktail at six."

This to her husband. Twenty-four hours later she heard the latch of Violaine's gate click behind her. She walked lightly, whistling, the hostess dropped and the housewife, the mother, the wife, and the apprentice British matron. A guest mounted the path, a guest come home to a meeting sweet with tradition. To a friend in the making. Over the edge of the ring of Violaine's high bearing, into air it gave power to breathe. The door of Mrs. Penrose's house stood open, the best rooms in St. Enys. In Violaine's sitting-room in the low window, two arm-chairs were drawn up. Twenty yards off the sea broke in a light thunder. Flood tide after a Biscay storm, its backwash sweeping the Atlantic coast, line upon line of breakers marching in under the lightest breeze, a limpid sky.

She sat down and opened a book. Upstairs Violaine would be changing shorts for trousers, dinner-dress at St. Enys if you are slight as a larch and as tall. Casing her tanned legs in grey flannel, cut and creased like a man's. Running a heavy comb through her hair, brushed back in short waves, the tiny sea of brass she carried on her head. The arms in her checked shirt would be bare, arms that matched her legs, the wrists so turned to make the senses ache. Only the tips of the fingers cut perhaps too short, a thought too square.

She heard her enter the room. Half-turned to the sight of something that instantly cut her smile, held it half-shaped. For what after seemed for a very long time. For Violaine at first did not come and sit down beside her. It was she who turned, slewed half-way round, while Violaine stood beside the table piled with glasses and books and records, her eyes on the high seas, her brown nostrils wide.

She was saying:

"Who in hell was that little woman you sent to see me last night?" Marcia knew instantly catastrophe when it arrives, crashes out of the invisible into the visible world like the clown out of the cupboard or the pantomime cat down the chimney; or at the play, the hidden witness to all impossible secrets when he knocks over the screen.

"I sent no one. I asked the little Caroline Adams to leave a note on you about this evening. That was all."

"That doesn't interest me. Perhaps you would like to hear what she did. She chose to come late last night as I was going to bed. Yes, then, with a howling child on each hand. Asked to see me. Got past Mrs. Penrose, who knows my orders. Gave me your note and sat down unasked. Yes, stayed. A friend of yours I had in decency to receive.

"Sat where you are sitting now. What could I do? Took hold of my hand and stroked it. Said she'd been longing to know me; had watched me from the beach. Told me she admired my hair, the way I moved. Told me she thought me beautiful. Asked me about my health—intimate questions; and was I doing this for myself, and did I know how to do that?

"And all this time the children were whining and yelling: 'Mother, we want to go home. Mother, who is this lady? Mother, can't we go home to tea?' and running round the room and spilling my cigarettes and messing about the records, and falling down and shrieking, and starting to play and starting to shriek. First one and then the other. Then one got hold of the back of my chair and the other little brute hurled itself on me, and they both grabbed and pushed and fell about and kept asking questions. And one got hold of my jade figurines and the crystal and threw them down; and all their mother did was to tell me that *you* said children should be allowed to handle precious things to get the feel of them young. I can see you allowing anyone's brats to paw your things.

"And all this time she was cooing and stroking, and I had to sit still, knowing the next second I should insult her. How should I know how to control such people? A friend of yours, I could hardly kick her out of the house. But, my God, I shall if she tries it again. The slut! I'm not surprised that her husband left her. How did he ever come to marry her? Got her in the family way, I suppose, and she whined him into it. And, Marcia, I warn you if she tries it again, there will be trouble. I'll not answer for myself if I have any more of that insolence. And I can't help wanting to know what you mean by knowing such people and letting them loose on people who are defenceless because they are your friends—"

Defenceless? The storm went on, not shrill, high and clear, deadly with its steel edge. An edge to which Marcia's own brow was exposed, bare. Or was it her eyes?

And "Steady, Violaine," was all she found to say. "I was a fool to send her with that note. For that I apologise." (I am paying too much for this—for that child's folly. We guessed Violaine capable of this. Yes, be a little formal—) "If I had dreamed she was so foolish I would never have let—" (All perfectly useless. That's not Violaine's point. What is? That she must whip herself into a fury, ultimately to punish herself. Long-tortured body, long-thwarted pride. Called nerves. A contact she loathed. We know all that. Oh damn and blast the little fool! —What is she saying?)

"I can't see why you waste your time on such people. A mother! Fine sort of a mother, keeping those wretched kids up to all hours, howling in other people's rooms. Poor little devils—fine chance they'll have.

"And she's not the innocent little sweetness you both think. She had her reasons for coming. Those morons have. I only want to warn you she'll get nothing out of me; that if she tries it again, I'll not answer for my temper."

"Is she answering for it?"

(It's no good my repeating and repeating. What am I listening to now?) Violaine was sitting beside her, visible only in profile, her hard brown hands making gestures of tearing and destruction. Exhibiting something destroyed to scorn. Now she was asking how well Caroline knew the other men of the party; men she had referred to by their nicknames; and who had asked her to call Commander Norton "Nibs" and give details about his inside? Marcia writhed. These "imposings" which are more deadly than vice, the want of training that hustled youth and sorrow behind a screen.

Violaine was perfectly right. Perfectly wrong also; only

her wrongness did not matter in comparison; her rightness was essential. The subtle contract broken on which human association depends. What is implied when you say: "People do not do these things." And where was Friendship's Garland, the wreath she and Julian had made with such splendid flowers and nailed up over Violaine's door? Or the posy of gentle blossoms with which they would have comforted Caroline? Not the roses and bays for Violaine's proud head, but such plants as columbine and love-in-a-mist. Love-lies-bleeding—oh damn love. —Stop protesting, however coolly, to her. Walk out over the scattered wreath as lightly as you can. Don't stop to pick it up.

Marcia was on her feet now, making—not excuses— but sincere and aloof apologies to a stranger. A tall bony woman, dressed as a man, flung now in a deep chair, her face lined with long endured atrocities of the body and spirit. Cause or effect? Eternal nagging problem. Her body was like a sword used for stabbing—ultimately herself.

"I can let myself out." Only half an hour before she had heard the garden gate click behind her, advancing towards that house with joy. Now she was walking up the cliff road in strong sunshine, in light become a burden as it does when the interior light has been turned off; quenched in another's darkness.

*　*　*　*　*

She sat beside her husband, in the terrace-room. Aghast they looked down on to the roof of the house below, where Mrs. Penrose kept the best lodgings in St. Enys; the house with its strip of lawn the road divided from the sea. Up through the gulf of air the sea-thunder rose. He said:

"When you got back so soon, I could see that something was wrong. From the way you walked up the road—"

"Two perfectly good garlands gone west. We shall doubtless make fresh ones, but—." He finished for her:

"C'est toujours moins involontaire."

Later, in his evening bath, she heard him singing, the theme-song of their household, of marriage, in times of stress:

"Never mind if things look glum
You're sure to find there's worse to come—
Every silver lining has a dark cloud inside—"

Smelling agreeably of violet salts, he sat up in bed, again the candle-light crossing the last mid-summer light, reflection of the sun on the Atlantic disk, as the planet rolled over, along with Mercury and Arcturus and the rest.

"Find me the bright side of this," she asked.

"What's the bright side of a hollow tooth?" he said, finishing the quotation. Suddenly she sat up also, clasping her knees: "You are angriest with Violaine and I with Caroline."

"Well, haven't we agreed it was stupidity made her do it, and curiosity and Arthur; that Violaine's forgotten more about manners than she ever knew; and hasn't Violaine got bats in her belfry and haven't we always known that?"

"Agreed, but don't you see—you can have Caroline for yours—but Violaine was one of my Muses, and in this life you want the Muses to be their very selves, not turning on a little hedge-sparrow for singing out of tune?

"And what are we going to do about it?" A question one partner does not always like to be asked. Julian said nothing. There was silence. She sat still straighter up:

"I know. One thing is true—this that has happened is the greatest of all cautionary tales. I shall make it into part of our saga and our children's children shall tell it, and the awfulness of its warning shall go with them from the very first time they go out into the world."

"So, like a good housekeeper, you'll not let any of it be wasted."

He drew her down beside him.

The House-party

To Jean Cocteau

H E WANTED TO GO and stay with them, in the sea-washed, fly-blown, scorched hotel along the coast, whose walls were washed primrose above the blue lapping water, where one mounted to bed by a plaster stair outside above the shifting sea, under the stars shaken out in handfuls.

There might be peace there. Under Vincent's wing a man could stand up a bit. Vincent was English, tender, serious, older than he. Vincent wanted him to come. Was no doubt cajoling, hypnotising away certain objections. Objections that were always made about him, especially by his own countrymen, the Americans who made a cult of Europe, a cult and a career, not quite perfect in their transplanting, and conscious of it. As he was conscious of the virgin energy and high intelligence which made them a reproach to him. Also, that in certain directions, his adventures outnumbered theirs as the stars the dim electric light-bulbs of the hotel. No they would not want him, and Vincent, poor fish, would sweat blood to fix it so as not to annoy them. And at the same time risk his old friendships on his behalf. A fool, but a sort of glorious one. Glorious fools pay. Meanwhile he would go—and not be a nuisance to Vincent. Take a back seat all right. Give Vincent what he had to give. An audience, someone to *play* with. Worship carefully disguised. If Vincent bored him—. An essential meanness in the boy reminded him how he could take it out of Vincent, Vincent who was standing by him; not out of Vincent's friends. A cracked little specimen of a gigolo, after a year in prison for something he had not done, his comfort was to be revenged on the good. Vincent should pay.

Great André also was staying there; the silver hill, the lance-point of the boy's world. Vincent would present him. He would have something to worship as well as Vincent. Make Vincent jealous? No, no, no. Perhaps he'd find out how to behave as they behaved. No, no, no. God help him, he'd play no joy-boy tricks.

He had met Vincent at the Casino of the great town, and had heard about the fun they were having, the harmonious, mischievous house-party ten miles along the coast.

"International relations going strong. I'm still on speaking terms with Dudley and Stretton, Winkelman and Marjorie, Edouard and Clarice; with America, Mittel-Europa, England and France. And since André came I've never had such a time or known such a chap. Like lightning and Mozart."

Not a word about the social lift André's presence implied. Only response to his longing to be there, and a little diffidence.

"Dudley and Stretton are difficult, Paul. Tastes very definite and standards unaccountably high. It works out that they don't like anyone who isn't in the arts, or pickled in New York, or else extremely important socially—"

Paul said: "I'm a pickled New Englander. That's to say that I'm much better family. But you can tell them I won't interfere. They won't even see me except across a room at meals. I suppose they can stand that. If I come, it's to see you—I know what's due to people who have been kind to me."

Vincent smiled. "I see a good deal of André. I expect you'll meet him too. I'll take you a room for to-morrow, and when the high cultural atmosphere of Dudley and Stretton gets a bit too much we'll amuse each other—"

Paul saw him leave the Casino and shoot across the bright gardens to find his car—a young man whose large bones the flesh covered delicately, who, even indoors, set the air stirring. Not noisy at all, but easy, as if his life was nourished by a fountain, whose very deep waters rose and sunned and spread themselves evenly, and mounting kept everything they touched astir. Paul, shooting craps at a bar, remembered a sentence Vincent had quoted, "The generosity of strength," supposed Vincent had it, and his heart felt the little nick of pain which was his form of worship; he knew that he did not mind saying, even to Vincent's face, that Vincent was his superior.

A moment later he began to reflect on his simplicity. These scrupulous Englishmen were easy to make. Because of their innocence, because of the insolence implied in "the generosity of strength." He counted the knuckles of his small, rosy, gold-wired hands, tried the pointed nails, jerked up the arm to feel the bicep, who had once been an athlete, looked in the mirror at his pretty clothes and handsome childish head, spoke to the barman in faultless French. To reassure himself. It was all he had to take over there to people disorderly with treasure of mind and spirit. Of bodies also, but he knew how to exploit his—

Vincent, rushing his car along the hill coastline, was saying that the ill-used brat should have his treat.

He had acquired Paul in a moment of occupation with human wrongs. The boy had been handed over to him by another man as a hopeless case. It had seemed to him that Paul's life of dissipation, malice and despair, occasionally touched by a kind of nipped sweetness which flowered only into unwilling loyalty, was one form of a universal condition, a rot nibbling at a generation. This gave him the power to illustrate the particular by the general, translate the boy into boys, and take valuable notes. His feebleness lay in an observation he had shirked: that all Paul's qualities, his vices, his sincerity, his aspirations, and his affection had been steeped, as though his body in filth, in some essence of the sordid which made him repellent. Apart from the blindness of generosity, a connoisseur in bad smells might have accepted the handsome lad, courteous when he liked, ravenously grateful for scraps, and rather chic.

Vincent looked out to sea, over jade dancing, called it a drawing-room ocean after the Atlantic, and kicked himself mildly for ingratitude. If only Paul could be dipped in it and brought out clean. He knew that what he needed was purification, from what corruption he did not quite understand. He concentrated too closely on the horror spot of the story. The boy's imprisonment for folly; his desertion by his friend. The savage sentence; the appalling illness that had released him; the details of his third degree. Little Paul naked and terrified, and beaten up. Questioned to insanity; flung for weeks into a filthy cell; chained to a black murderer running with sores. He had infinite pleasure when Paul responded, told him how peace of heart and self-respect ran in like small tides "into the mess it has made of me. Don't suppose that when I'm with a person like yourself, it doesn't do good to my character—"

Vincent knew that behind the small admission there was a continent of waste land and reserve. Also that it was sincere. Paul brought him presents, a cigarette holder in almost good bad taste; popular fiction that had impressed him; once, God knew how acquired, a lapis snuff-bottle stoppered with coral, the most gentlemanly chinoiserie, full of oily permanent eastern scent. Paul loved to give, loved himself for giving. Vincent was touched. He enjoyed presents too. They played with them together. Vincent was persuaded that Paul did him good, not by exercising him in charity, but by taking him out of his group intensities. Paul had lively adventures, good because they were ordinary debaucheries. Yet in each there was something distasteful, as though the prison and the hospital had left a taint and a sepsis. The sea racing below on Vincent's right was the sign of purification. For purification was necessary. A saturation—in what? Vincent did not exactly know. He only knew an essence that washed his spirit daily as the sea his body, the wine in his throat, music in his ears. What was it? He resisted the easy race-temptation to call it by old names, religion, God's grace, because they had once been counters for it, possibly were so still. But observing great André with his crowd of lads, who came for an hour, for a day, flashing in and out of the Frenchman's darkened room, a word had crystallised out for such activities. Kourotrophos, a bringer-up of boys. Not much more than one himself, Vincent brooded its meaning, half ashamed of its emotional charge, the humility and elation it brought him. If he could not show Paul the Good, he would bring him samples, rub his nose in them if necessary, pitch him, kick him into it, scrub him. Hold him up a glass to see his restored cleanliness. For the spiritual-sensual reward: to hear Paul say that it was good, clean and on his knees. And see the little thing run off translated, his small gifts liberated, reasonably at peace.

Beside the classic sea, the classic title took form: Kourotrophos. He saw Cheiron, Pallas. In the same land, built of gold and violet rock, barren, but *a good nurse for boys*, André; the dead scots officer who had licked him into shape. He meant to try a practice hand on Paul; for someone in the future, the friend of friends, who at the start would need that. Paul was just a try-out, with a dash of affection in his sentiment towards him, and a slight kick.

Vincent was an english type, mutely convinced that he was there for a purpose, accepting the discipline of the virtues as preparation for an unknown. A particularly unknown unknown at this time, with religion and love and pride of land and race off the map, and the unconscious the cheerless substitute. Meanwhile he had to be observant, study the iron puritanism in which Paul had been raised. Was that the soil which had grown his corruption? He decided finally that it had only set the stubborn will that resisted catharsis. They had read together the story of the Butcher of Hanover, and he had noticed that the horrible fairy-tale had struck Paul with terror. Also that it had excited him. Which suggested a Hoffman in Paul? Really, really. But Vincent had spent an hour or so of his imaginative life in the old quarter of Hanover, in and out the over-hung, cobbled passages and crazed buildings, greased and glazed with old blood; still alive, this time with painted, emotional boys, followers of men's oldest profession. Current hysteria, gossip, intrigue, on a mediaeval stage. Mystery of stairs that lead nowhere and doors that do not shut, and round the corner to Augustus' Live Wire Bar.

Throw fire, crystal, salt between little Paul and that place, where Vincent could have strolled and picked up wisdom; where the absence implied the presence of his lord. He left his car at the hill garage and ran down the terrace stairs of the small town, past gay, plaster houses roofed with round tiles, along slots of cooled, highly seasoned air; a ribbon of liquid sky on top; and at the end of each stair a patch of still water, divided by masts, the basin of the little, prehistoric port, till he reached the hotel on the quay. He had Dudley and Stretton to appease, where, from his point of view, appeasement should not have been necessary; and it is hard to entreat those we love. He could foresee the iron stare at Paul's name, the lip-twitch of contempt, and, incidentally, the glance of apprehension.

He ran up the white, sea-cracked stair and knocked at André's door. In bed, God bless him, in a room where the sea-light sifted through wooden slats; the red silk of his pyjama coat falling back up dark ivory arms. Ready for any emergency. Ready always to talk. As by magic, he spoke immediately of Dudley and Stretton. "Any news from the Upper House, *mon cher*?"

"I've news for them," said Vincent. "Listen, André, I've a *déclassé* little friend—"

"You always have—so have I. Well?"

"—I put it to you, André, the boy ought to come. You'd think that, after his past, his countrymen would be hunting him round with bouquets—" He tried to find the French for scapegoat.

"*Bouc émissaire,*" said André. "I don't suppose they chose a valuable beast."

Then it was like a ride on a wave, repose on the sea's back, when the Frenchman said: "I will arrange it—he has a right to stay where he pleases—Dudley and Stretton can't have everything their own way. Leave it to me."

They embraced, and Vincent felt as if the sea had lifted him gently on to a firm beach.

* * * * *

In another room of the hotel Dudley and Stretton's sails emptied a moment and flapped in a pocket of the rising gale they were running before to well-earned fame. Vincent had said "check" when he had gone straight to André to sponsor this deplorable specimen of their native land. In their sun-steeped rooms, filled with objects of comfort, utility and impeccable taste, they yielded to distress. Dudley picked at the typewriter, Stretton sat on the edge of the bed. The sea danced at them. They were saying that no European ever could or ever would understand the way rumour reached New York, and booked its passage by return of liner under new and horrible disguises. That people would talk; that people might say they were friends with the boy if they were seen in the same place. It was all very well for André, a prince of the arts, and for Vincent with his shameless english indifference to public opinion; they had extra cats to whip. Stretton was tall, fragile, ageless, beautiful. Dudley was handsome, quick, serviceable. The pair two formidable hunters, out for the lion's share. In the civilisation of Europe, kind, ruthless, observant pioneers. Neither aware of the power of their arms, the prestige of their fresh strength. Both aware that Vincent had put their queen in danger, intentionally or not.

Dudley clattered off a letter on the typewriter. Stretton put on a record. *I Ain't Nobody's Darling* pointed the situation. He took it off and substituted Mozart. Perhaps not perfectly appreciated, the lovely air flowed out above "the hard hearts of men."

The day after, while André took a cat-nap after two hours' unbroken lunch conversation, Vincent hurried along the sea-bordered rock-path to the station. In the train Paul soiled his hands, clinging to the black-dusted rod in the corridor on his way. The train ran into a tunnel, into the mountain that rushed down to the edge of the dancing beach. In an instant he had passed out of flashing air into brownness, into hell's neck, after a paradise of blue stone-pines. The boy suffered in it, and from more than fear that its filth would soil his smartness. To his literal, primitive fancy it was like what hell would be, hell where he'd been before, hell where he belonged. Only this tunnel had an end, which ran full into a station, where Vincent was waiting for him beside more sea.

Together they left hell's mouth, Paul trotting a little behind Vincent's stride, and glad to run to earth in his sunny room and arrange his pretty properties. It occurred to Vincent, as he watched him displaying trifles, that there were people without house or land, with a dressing-case and a photograph frame for anchor. Paul said: "I suppose you couldn't get me a window table downstairs? I can promise you not to look at Dudley and Stretton. Or rather I shall leave it to them. They can cut me or not as they please."

"I've fixed that for to-morrow—André asked you to dine with us to-night." He saw Paul start, harden, and then sitting on his bed drop backwards, his forearm over his eyes.

"What is it, lad?"

"I don't know; but you take me out of hell into heaven. It's all you. I know that. I'll kiss Dudley and Stretton if you like."

Vincent jumped. That wouldn't do. Keep 'em apart. Quite simply, because he was ashamed of Paul. Also he remembered their iced politeness when they had seen him once before, the night he had taken Paul to one of their parties, when he had been at fault, and Paul had acted in character. "Let them be," he said; "you can make friends with them later."

"You mean," said Paul, "that I may be fit to know them later?"

"I mean that if you clean up and cheer up you can meet them later on your own ground."

* * * * *

At dinner Paul sat by André, at the head of the table, opposite Vincent. Beside him an Englishwoman, neither ugly nor old, who had Dudley beside her; and by Vincent, Stretton; and by him a pretty, watchful French girl. The long table, with a Frenchman at the head of it, which was the hotel's show-piece and alarm. An annoyance and bewilderment for the old soldiers and older maids who filled the *salle à manger,* when the conversation rose above the clash of plates and the shifting of the sea.

> "*J'ai du commerce sexuelle*
> *Avec mon colonel*
> *J'ai connu, charnellement, mon commandant—*"

seven gay voices sang when the courses were late. The Englishwoman was teasing André, who was whittling green olives into improprieties. As Paul passed a carafe he was nodded to by Stretton, and asked where he had been, as though his address had been a public lavatory, and he given a chance to conceal it. It was like being let out on parole. No, it was not parole, it was freedom. He told them all a story, suggested by André's anatomical reconstructions of the olives, and they were silent.

He felt walls closing on him again. Like the walls of his prison that his body had somehow got out of and left the rest behind. He was listening now to their talk. About the same thing as his story, but excused because the words were different, and mixed up with implications he didn't understand. That was cleverness: that was hypocrisy. They were like bright flies hatched out of dung, and he the beetle content to roll its ball. He thought about that until he caught André's voice again, half-way through a tirade on the theatre. He'd seen the play. Coolly Stretton asked for his opinion. Again, what he said was not *like* what they said. He flushed. André sheltered him. Stretton illustrated André's criticism with a New York production. He was analytic, weighty. By chance, wrong on detail. Paul corrected him eagerly. Silence. With a pinch of assurance gained, he invited André and Vincent to the café on the quay. André refused gently. Vincent carried him off.

The little town was built on terraces chipped out of the mountain flank, between two precipices, round whose base even the Mediterranean flung itself in spray. It was very still in the little port, white docks ran in sideways along stale emerald water, an utter security for little boats. The quay stones, salt-bleached and fretted smooth, where the cables rubbed, were laid with rust-coloured nets. Eternally torn, eternally repaired, untidy girls in black gowns, with black-brown necks and dusty, dark curls, mended them. But at this season, at night, the open bay looked as if it were divided by a wall, pierced with round holes, blazing with circular light, behind which could be heard voices and music; the space between the wall and the quay shot across by launches turning and tearing, ripping the water's green back; and little ceremonies of recommitment to land or sea took place on the quay, as the commander of the battleship welcomed or was welcomed. And every room along the front or up the terraces roared with sailors, their pockets full of money; and the town girls out with them to supply the honey; and nine months later, after the christening of too many grey-eyed, flax-haired babies, the Curé would get out his annual sermon on the sin of fornication, until the next season brought more ships from newer and richer lands.

But from the day the ships arrived one could observe the girls' black overalls and dingy espadrilles shed, to be replaced by wall-paper cretonnes and shoes whose high heels turned over unaccustomed ankles; and shiny, pink wood-fibre stockings over olive legs. While the gramophones worked to death, and the tin pianos beat out jazz, and the cars of arriving and departing officers swept light paths on the bent road up the hill.

Much later the noise became more concentrated by the water's edge, more expressive of the emotions of drunk men struggling with a foreign tongue. Finally the ship police would load them into boats, groaning; the last cargo would shoot out, to be replaced at dawn by men with fresh leave and stragglers returning from the great town where Vincent had refound Paul. It had not occurred to him that it might be more than a spectacle for an american *deraciné* to see the men of his fleet out on a spree. Only he noticed a difference in the quality of their pleasure. He was at a play of which Paul had seen the rehearsals. Might at any moment run off behind the scenes. For Vincent the play was just sufficiently amusing; but Paul had imported something with him from the great town, where half the earth swarmed up and down an esplanade, where each vice had its location, and even the lamp-posts and bicycles were over-sexed. Sailors talked of the swell joints and the swell girls they had found there. Paul stood the drinks. He was sparkling with excitement. The sombre child, alternating at dinner between timidity and impertinence, changed into a sharp-eyed lad in the know.

For some days before, as well as for some nights, Vincent had observed a shadow about the quays. First because it had tried to sell him an obscene book, then because it tried to sell André an obscene book, then because it tried to sell everybody an obscene book. Then because it was obscene. Of no race or of any; grey, green, greasy, with a few horned teeth and black nails; its clothes a patch-work of hotel leavings, its speech a kind of American, pronounced with a lisp, the chi-chi of the East. Referred to as the Pimp. No name, no associates, it would appear and be gone. It knew a whore-house, a cinema. Lived by finding the people who wanted those places. Found them. Of no age. Probably an immortal. Vincent composed of west wind and tree sap, the wine, beef, apples and classic literature of an english country house, was affected by him as by a bad smell. In the café he went over to speak to Stretton, escorting the little French girl. Danced with her once, introduced her to a sober, charming sailor, turned and saw Paul, leaning along the bar with the Pimp. Stretton must have seen him. Anyhow, he pulled the boy's shoulder round, surprised at the shock inside himself.

"What d'you mean—speaking to that filth here with us?"

Surprise from Paul might have cut his fury; defiance justified it—but the boy said: "No, no. Please take me away. It was not my fault. He spoke to me. I'm afraid of him."

The man glanced, cringing at them, and began to melt away, merging into the crowd at the door.

"Don't play into Stretton's hand then." Thoroughly cross he replaced him at the table.

Timidly Paul looked up at him. "I couldn't help it, Vincent. I saw him once or twice about before. I don't quite know what he is—" Then as "All right. Tell me why you're afraid of him" framed in Vincent's throat, the child's notes went out of Paul's voice, and the self-conscious, self-righteous debauché spoke: "Why should I mind what Stretton sees? If you're ashamed of me, you've only got to say so and I'll go—"

"Say go," said a guardian angel tartly to Vincent. As generally happens, he told it to shut up. In fact, "Shut up" was all he said aloud to Paul.

* * * * *

"Pan," said Vincent, on a terrace on the top of the world, overlooking the sea in which some day Solomon is supposed to drown it, "what's Pan to you?"

"I guess," said Paul, "he's my god."

He seemed to want to hear something about him. Vincent sketched the varieties of his cult. He did not neglect him as a god of sex, but down the gulf below them a yacht race was standing in, on blue-roughened water, the true wine-dark, a handful of silver slips. And as he watched them, all that was natural in his training and imagination made him breathless with love. Inattentive and unprepared later to meet reserved sarcasm from Paul—"That's all I know about Pan—what's your idea?"

Paul's answer was the smile of contemptuous pity a novice might get from a nasty old priest.

"I could show you a bit more about him if you came with me up the back streets at night."

"Only drunks and drunks and more drunks. Like the Prince Regent's waistcoats."

"There's more than that—you'd see how people get away with it—what can I do—" The dark blue stone eyes were shining again; his smile to himself, an acute sensuality outside the romantic attitude to sex. Vincent whisked the car back down the hair-pin bends and wished it would grow wings, fly away with Paul and punish him, and show him a life so different that back streets or high hills would be Tom Tiddler's ground to him. And it felt as though he had exchanged a cake of soap stuck with nails for a crystal ball when he joined André after dinner, alone.

Then Stretton came in. He said, "Where's your interesting experiment, Paul Martyn?"

"Out somewhere, I suppose. I'm not his nurse."

Then they listened to André, brought their lives to illustrate his. They loved him.

Dudley knocked. "I've seen your Paul below. He asked me why I was ashamed to be an American. I didn't know that I was."

Vincent did not understand their problem. The hag of unspecified bad conscience hobbled in. André was tactless.

"He will not make a scandal for us here, will he?"

"Of course not. And he asks rude questions out of defence. Let the boy enjoy himself his own way. What reason is there to turn him into a bad copy of us?"

"By all means," said Stretton. "A glimpse into the mentality of the Pimp at second-hand might be useful."

Vincent felt an impulse to go down, fetch Paul and beat him. Both ways Dudley and Stretton cramped his impulses. And for nothing would he miss an evening of André's magic mind.

Very much later he looked out his bedroom window, high up over the slip of cobbled square. Dancing was over and carouse and rows. On the other side of the hotel the sea lifted quietly up. Here and there a window of the old town showed a square, rose or orange. Somewhere a concertina gasped a dying breath. A line of plane trees rustled, and drew a delicate shadow on moon-whitened stones. Out of the house shadows an occasional cat slipped. He washed himself in the moon-quiet. Then saw that there were two people about, presently visible in the open square—Paul and the Pimp. At the foot of a stair they turned and mounted quietly together up the town. Vincent stayed still. So that was what Paul did when he went out to play. Follow him out and ask to be taken to see Pan? The shadows seemed to be coarsening and thickening. He remembered the smell of thyme—sweet, rank, classic grossness. He cleaned his teeth a long time. The stuff was called euthymol. A whiff of magic about; great indifference to Paul. He slept.

Paul woke late next morning, and with the nervous anxiety common to his race began to feel for symptoms of disease. Throat sore, mouth "like the bottom of a parrot's cage," nerves no worse than usual, but outside scrutiny. Normal awakening under abnormal circumstances. He should have been rather pleased with himself, but part of his conscience was raw and in raving protest. He hadn't come to Vincent to behave like that. Hated Vincent for the stab of remorse which made it necessary to suppress tears. The spasm passed and he smacked his lips. Stretton wouldn't have dared to go where he'd been, and Vincent wouldn't have cared. And André. He bet André knew more about it than he'd let on. All the same, he hadn't meant to keep the rendezvous he had made with the Pimp at the bar before Vincent had turned him away. Why in hell had he? Why in hell shouldn't he?

He got up, groomed himself with concentrated attention, and went out. At the tip of the breakwater, under the pepper-box pharos, André and Stretton were sunning themselves. Paul had on the coat he had worn the night before. A pocket crackled. He pulled out a sheaf of dirty drawings and sat down to reperuse them. The breeze blew one along. Stretton retrieved it, glanced at it and rose politely to return it. Impudence seized Paul. He walked back with him and showed the whole lot to André then and there. André laughed; but both were embarrassed by Stretton. High intelligence and boundless information uncorrected by wide experience takes all comfort out of criticism. But because André laughed and chattered, Paul though he had triumphed. Would not let his sexual curiosities drop. Again he bored them. André finally let him see it, and was told in French too rapid for Stretton that there was no need for him to play the prude. He lay sprawling by André, his tight, smart looks displayed beside the worn seraph, laid out, light as blown steel, along the stones. Blind with need for response he became reckless, using *tu* and calling the Frenchman by his first name. Knew himself further and further separated from him, until he yelped from his starved little heart:

"D'you know, André, you seem a hypocrite to me. When you were younger you raised enough hell. You're getting affected."

André, infinitely wise and unwise, whose memories were of Paris, poetry, the adventure and passions of a unique personality, did not want to be reminded of his incomparable adolescence. How it could be visualised by this little animal. He raised himself on his elbows and began an apostrophe on aeroplanes, men, birds, bird-priestesses and the hawk of Horus. On wings. Stretton tossed back the thread as it wove over Paul's fair head laid comfortless on his small, clasped hands. He held hard to the belief that all they said was only his own life dressed up. It was because they weren't honest and had read things. Suddenly he got up and almost shrieked at André: "If you'll excuse me, I'm going. I can't stand any more. *Ta voix m'agace.*" Stretton made a gesture. André carried on, his voice the minutest division of a tone higher.

He lunched with Vincent. It had been agreed that Vincent should leave the long table, to which he had not been reinvited, and join him for one meal each day. His outburst at André, his failure with André, had let loose a storm of sensibility and a need to confess. Vincent was cold. Paul began to explain again how good Vincent was for his character. It was a dreary shock when the Englishman said: "Then what were you doing out last night with the Pimp?"

He saw the boy retreat into himself, trapped. Then plaintively: "I can't speak to you now, Vincent. Leave me alone, please." He saw Vincent shrug his shoulders, unaware of the pity which could have won him forgiveness.

Vincent went to fetch André, Dudley and Stretton for a run in the car. Found André on his bed talking, supported on his elbows, and morally by Stretton. After Paul's small, musical drawl, French tired his ears. He was oddly unstrung. Paul's presence, which could not separate him from André, divided him from Stretton. All three whom he loved, and differently.

Stretton said: "Paul has told André that his voice gets on his nerves."

The pit of Vincent's stomach made itself noticeable. "What's it been about?" A few careful sentences, terrible in their scrupulous avoidance of condemnation, gave the meeting on the quay. Stretton holding his mirror up to nature. A superb mirror, reflector also for his petulant, stern beauty. He might as well have struck Vincent when he left the room to tell Dudley the car was ready. Vincent looked at André, to watch his mouth set in its divine smile. It did not. He turned over nervously.

"Vincent, let me speak frankly. Before your *protégé* came, and Dudley and Stretton were so perturbed, I had though them unjust. I meant, in fact, to take the boy up. To give him the run of this room. See if one could help him. Teach them a lesson in kindness. I see now that it is impossible. To begin with, he is a bore. Bores are unhelpable. Then he is corrupt. Not on account of his life or his taste in art. And I rather liked him when he said that my voice got on his nerves. It gets on mine. I am speaking of the quality of qualities."

Bitter-crystal waters of lucidity. Vincent nodded. "But, André," he said, "I had him here on trial. I know now it is no good. I'll send him away."

"Not at all on my account. It is you I am considering. You let your heart run away with you. The boy adores you, but some day he will play you a dirty trick. You don't know these little boys as I do. And you English play the *grands seigneurs* in a world that does not admit their existence. And—" (the clause was flashed in) "I do not want any scandal here."

Very well punished, Vincent said: "All right, André, I'll clip his poor little claws. I shan't cut him myself because of what happened to him in prison when he was a child. I hold that because of that a lot should be forgiven him. We'll run up into the mountains. I'm going for the car."

"Nasty pill," said Vincent, stopping in the corridor to feel his wounds. So much for the Kourotrophos. He had risked André and Stretton on that piece of swank, and had been very properly put in his place. Was it for that he was nearly weeping? Not at all, he observed, sufficiently a pupil of the french mind; but because his little kouros could not be brought up. Would never "put off the old man like a garment." The filth had gone too deep, he was dyed in it. Vincent knocked at Stretton's door.

"Coming?" There was discussion in the further room.

"Dudley wants to know if there will be room."

"Yes, for the four of us." Dudley appeared, perfect, neat, complete, hands in pockets, his look pitched straight at Vincent. He did not mean to come if Paul were asked. And he was perfectly right.

Worse luck. They were perfectly right.

"Only us four. Are you coming?"

"Yep."

They dined on another terrace-rock, hung over space; a cloud hiding the gardens and vineyards of men. All that was visible was other stones, staring like animals at the shifting, glittering sea. They sat until the sun turned its dancing-floor into a lacquered parquet, a gold path for his dip into the ocean baths.

Vincent told them the memories of Atlantis, Hy-Brasil, the Apple Land. André told them about Basques. A Basque and what had happened to him swimming in the basque country. A story which would have pleased Paul.

The boy spent an afternoon chewing the cud of stale excess. Inclined for company, he went down to the hotel front, on the quay; and there, as though newly risen from the dead, was the Pimp, pestering a tourist. And when he had pestered him, he made straight for Paul, sat down beside him, and carried on, as though it had never been interrupted, their conversation of the night before, held in a dim-lit maroon-hung brothel of the old town. There followed suggestions how they might be useful one to the other.

"You gotta pull on plentee smart guys. You bringa them to me."

In bright gold daylight. The only creature who wanted to speak to him. Misery rose in Paul. The man became a spectre of his imprisonment: of all that cut him off from other men. He was a louse out of his filthy cell, who had crossed the water on his body: fattened on his secretions. The rich pleasure he had taken in the man became a fearful punishment to him, who believed in punishment: who had been punished. As he stared away from him, the green harbour water plaqued with gold, the old stones tufted with wild flowers, the fringed mountains against the low sun, all the shapely, brilliant beauties of Europe's cradle became alive with obscenity; neutral forms for the foul to make plastic. His very precious ring, the gold snake with the diamond sunk in its head, was a small fiend in command. A late fisherman landed a net of flapping, dying, sea-people; snatched a small squid from the salt-running pile and held it up. Once Vincent had caught one—Vincent so easy and happy out in boats—and had told him how they were motifs for decoration on cretan jars. An awful people they must have been. Between the squid, the Pimp and his little ring he was being damned alive. He could not tell him to go. He must go where he was bid, as before he had gone to prison. A calvinist ancestor appeared.

"My great-great-grandson, it pleased the Lord to damn you before you entered your mother's womb. It is so, even though you should learn humility and bless Him for it." The squid's arms writhed. The fisherman, young, gay, beautiful, held it up; flashed his white teeth at the small crowd round him, lowered his head and bit till the eight arms fell limp. Lifted his slimed face and laughed. Paul, now nearly mad, shrieked.

The Englishwoman walked along the quay, looking for friends. She saw Paul and smiled at him. He staggered up, agonisedly produced the pretty manners of his upbringing.

"Come and have a drink with me," she said; "are Vincent and André back yet? You didn't go with them?" The Pimp faded.

"No," he said; "I'm afraid I've offended them."

"English people ain't easy to offend. It's your american nerves." He looked to her also like a child. "What have you been up to?" she said.

"Vincent is angry because I spoke to that man. I didn't mean to. I'd give anything to get away—"

"You've only to cut him and he'll run."

"But you didn't know. I can't." She saw that it was serious.

"Vincent told me something. If you want to live differently, you have only to tell Vincent. He's patient—"

"God knows I am sorry, but what's the good?" All the same, when he looked round, the harbour was again a place for ships. "Thank you," he said, "most people are decent to me now. And when they aren't, I dare say it's my fault."

They dined together, waiting for Vincent. But by the time he returned, Paul disintegrated again. The English-woman spoke to Vincent: "Go and look after that kid." Vincent, only half-willing, found him in his room; heard only a petulant, self-righteous harangue on Vincent's mis-conceptions about him—which he answered grimly enough with André's sentence: "You could have been adopted, given the freedom Stretton and I have: to teach them charity, and you something more about life. And André, who is infinitely merciful, saw it was no good."

Paul said, "Yes, for a Frenchman, he is merciful. But he would never understand. I think that man below is the devil and that he is following me."

The agony in his eyes, blue stones, glazed and burning, convinced Vincent. "Let's look at it clearly," he said. "Why did you go off with that man?"

"I don't quite know. You see, I'm more accustomed than you to that sort."

"Sort of swank then?"

"Perhaps. You've had such luck, you people. I was just as well raised. And if I'd had your education—"

"Cut that out. If you want education, you'll get it. I'll

tell you this, Paul—" The countryman of Blake took a long breath, lifted the apricot-tanned head, darker than his hair. His eyes counted paint-flaws on the wall, his imagination aware but sightless. He said: "That man is an ambulatory, mediterranean sore, living on the viciousness of our vices. But I think he's a shadow, d'you see—the image, the signature of a very living thing that is your torment. He is nothing, a corpse, a nuisance; but he may be under orders. Orders he knows even."

Paul amazed him, breaking into sobs, the unfathomable hysteria of the damned. He took him by the shoulders, almost to his heart, and said: "You have only to summon your courage. It'll come: and he'll melt."

But Paul sobbed on, racked noises leaving his body, as a man might spew up formless evil spirits. Vincent hitched him into the crook of his arm, each jerk of the slight shoulders registered against his heart. Was this the beginning of purification? He caressed, careful not to talk. Paul at last lay still; then sat up suddenly, slung his fine ankles to the floor, went to the *lavabo* and washed his face with hot water, with cold, with cologne. Drew a wet comb through his hair, worked on his cheeks with a powder-wad.

"Thank you for letting me cry. It did me a lot of good."

"Where are you going now?"

"Down to the lounge. I don't think he'll come there. I've got a book."

"What sort of a book?"

"I like it. It is about the sort of gentlemen my people were; like yours. The sort I might have been." Vincent was conscious of the whine, the sniff, mixed with the utter truth. He sat on the side of the bed, pensive and fatigued.

He went down to the garage and saw to his car; and there, among its intricacies, anchored himself against flights on to planes of suffering which produced the phenomena of one fair boy weeping on his bed, and one green, gap-toothed figure dodging on the quays. Also distaste, division and disgust among a band of friends. He ate up his car's insides like cake; here was something precise to *do*, for people who where dependents on his car's flights for pleasure. He had worked himself into a serenity, a little too ardent to be sane, when, rising from his knees he saw the Pimp, looking in at the garage door, pulling something out of his loose pocket, a book or a box.

"Get out!" he cried. The man's mouth moved; it sounded like whistling. Something flapped. He went off. Up the moonlight-stair Vincent had watched on the last night.

He left the garage and crossed the square to the hotel. It was getting late. In a corner of the empty salon he found Paul with his book. A child sent to Coventry, in the arid, frivolous, depressing room, his face was still scorched with crying.

"Vincent, for pity's sake, don't give me up. It is true what you said; there are evil spirits around me. I've been too kicked to fight them alone. You invited me out of hell into heaven, and it seems I brought my own hell with me. For pity's sake—"

And pity like a naked, new-born babe striding the blast. Vincent flung himself off down the corridor to André's room, and found him alone. "André, I've sent that child sky-high, and it seems to have kicked him permanently off his legs. I'm out of power; I can't handle him."

The passionate sentences, thrust into literal French, intrigued André: "Oh these little boys with more sensibility than wits! I know them. Send him up to me."

He went back. "André says you're to go to him."

"I'm ashamed."

"Do as he tells you."

"I'll try."

Vincent sat on the foot of André's bed. All lights were out but the reading-lamp that lit the Frenchman's hands, the gay, dark, imagination-worn head in rose-gold shadows. Paul drew up a stool to the bed and sat between them, leaning against it, his hands on the sheets.

"*Mon gosse,* what is this trouble about? Vincent tells me that you are afraid of the Pimp. But Stretton says that he saw you talking to him last night."

"I did worse than that. I went with him up to the old town, with the sailors. To-day I saw him again. He would speak to me. To-day I saw that there were evil things all round me. And I see the man everywhere. In places where I know he can't be. He is a devil. I am being punished again. I am always being punished—"

André scribbled a note and gave it to Vincent. "Take that down to the *patron.* It is to say that if that man is seen round the hotel again I and my friends leave. That should settle it. Will that do, boy?"

When Vincent returned to his place Paul had drawn closer to the bed, and André's hands were invisible, the boy's face laid on them.

"My little one, you are young and handsome. Clever at some things, Vincent says, and neither poor nor sick. What is it that spoils your life?"

Paul answered in a low voice: "It has always been the same, André. When I was at school. People were unjust to me. I hadn't laughed much in years till I knew Vincent. He can make me giggle. And in spite of his friends, who hate me, he brought me here and introduced me to you. And my filth's followed me just the same. I'm in prison like I was before. Then something that separates me from you. Dudley and Stretton are quite justified. I shall never hold it against them that they won't know me. But I'm sorry I was rude to you to-day."

"It isn't that," said André, looking out as Vincent had done, summoning his angel. "It is your attitude to life, to people, that is wrong. Don't you know that the kind of general insolence in which you take pleasure makes people your enemies—separates you, as you say? When your charm is all you have, you ruin it, and wonder that you are ruined. If you used it, you would have friends, and your devils would vanish, and your life fill with pleasantness."

"But I am better, much better, much more moral since Vincent—"

"When did Vincent preach morals to you? Morals are an excuse for a boy of your sort, to justify your tempers. Or hags to ride you to hell. Leave your little virtues alone, and attend to the virtue which gave you Vincent. Don't you know that God does not like us for the things we think good. For the rest, courage—" He pulled a silver ring down his arm and slipped it on the boy's wrist. "Wear that to-night if you're afraid." The lovely, tired voice ran on, with passion fatigue seemed to strengthen, and all the vicissitudes of man. Paul kept his face laid on the hand he clung to, the bracelet that had changed wrists lighting the sheets. "Remember the old woman who had been pious, at heaven's gate, who was secretly afraid because when she was a child she had stolen cherries from a tree. She told Peter all the good she had done, and while he called up God the Father, prayed that the cherry-tree had been forgotten. Until God answered, 'Let her in. After all, it's the woman who robbed the cherry-tree.' It is a sin to wear thorns when God meant you to wear roses."

Vincent, silent, curled-up, heard Paul's rare, short, flute laugh. Knew he was listening to the Kourotrophos, the bringer-up of boys, André, the peacock of the world, who had borne the cross. Paul was smiling at him, and now he had lifted his head, Vincent saw André's hand wet with tears.

It was late. It seemed as if there was a huge balance in this room, a scale filling up and up against the other which had been filled. Paul's face was hidden again, this time on his knees. André spoke on; but Vincent dreamed that the scales held the life and death of Paul. If the high one sank, a cup would sail in down a light ray (he imagined it through a hole in the shutter slats). There would be a lance with it and an aureole for the boy. If it did not, well, he could only see a seedy man with green teeth following them about.

There was a knock at the door. Without waiting Stretton came in and stood for a moment against André's bathrobes. André said: "A moment, Stretton."

Paul sat up, but both he and Vincent had time to see Stretton's face, set like the Lucifer of the english imagination, in blasting pride and contempt. A son of the morning, visiting a son of the morning, his eyes were on Paul, the scorn in them a thing to cross dreams.

André said: "Come back in a quarter of an hour." He went out. The high scale stayed in air.

Paul got up. "Thank you very much, André. You've done me a lot of good. I'll say good night now. I'm very tired. Good night."

Vincent followed him. "Well," he said, "now can you have a little faith?" and saw Paul look at him with lost sweetness that hardened again through misery past comprehension to a coarse denial that would never leave him again.

"Almost," he said, "I had. It was like music that you could see. Till Stretton knocked. Then it turned not real, flat, a bit of pretence. Stretton did it. He meant it too. He's in with the man on the quays." And at Vincent's agonised laugh: "I'm not so frightened now. I reckon I can get along. But not as André meant. Or you. Not after the way Stretton looked at me. He's put me back in my place. I know now that the filthy can never mix with the clean. He won't forgive you in a hurry either. Or André, when he's thought it over. D'you think I need give him back his bracelet? The boys in Paris will make a fine story out of it. Sorry, Vincent. I hope, I hope— Oh, only that Stretton will never be able to bitch you as he's bitched me."

Vincent felt very cold—utterly tired. He took Paul's wrist and slipped off André's silver ring. "If you ever want it back, you will only have to ask for it."

"Thanks, but I shan't. I'm off to-morrow. Run in to you sometime if you care to remember me. I should like that— Vincent, you're a poor fish to take it so hard. It's my business. I shall be gone before the rest of you are up. Good night."

Lettres Imaginaires

I

M<small>Y</small> D<small>EAR</small>,
      I have learned that I cannot speak to you any
more as to my temporal lover. If I tried you would force
me into sentiment, and special pleading. I might appeal
to your pity. We have not known each other very long, but
I am assured that with you such a demand would be a
piece of ill-breeding.... There is an image of you in my
breast and an image of the world. But truth does not lie
in these presentments.

Let us suppose then that you have a Pattern-laid-up-in-
Heaven waiting to touch my elbow as I write.

"Sir, you and I have loved," but that's not it.

"Sir, you and I must—." I find it difficult to continue.

The business should be commonplace, but a bizarre
streak seems to accompany my lapse into passion. It has
been a freakish crucifixion—from a delicate approach, conventional as a harlequinade; for ten days we loved one
another—as I thought with some quality of passion. You
assumed my nature, I took on yours. The change of spiritual
hats was no loss. No one knew. We were too sure to need
confidants. There was no one to forbid. Our aptitude was
perfect and our opportunity. Then one night we had arranged to meet, and you sent me a strange telegram. Two
nights later you came in late to our little restaurant and
said: "This won't do. I smell burning." Now I like fire. I
looked at you and saw you were Wyndham Lewis's drawing
of the starry sky, a cold Titan, a violent Intelligence. You
were holding away from you a jewelled image which was
myself. Then I knew that friend I might be, or mistress,

but not lover. That dance was ended. Essentially you were "through" with me and resentful. But I do not love like that. I will not have this sensuality and this friendship. I march to a better tune. I will not listen while you play both air and accompaniment with your heavy alternate hands.

Dear, I was tired that night. Couldn't you have been gentle with me? It was not lust that I wanted then, or philosophy, only peace. I sat opposite to you, "tower of ivory, house of gold." Your eyes narrowed. Then, with some ingratitude, you damned me for the vitality which had sustained you. Gallic realism? perhaps—your Latin analysis stripped the beauty you had enjoyed. I matched my wits with yours, answered your questions, parried your threats, folded myself in my sex, offered you a delicate candour.... You were not pleased. Then I saw that it was not a game. Throughout your analytical protests there was a recurrent note. I understood that I was target for some sacred male encounter with its own might. Scorn for me was to reanimate your virtue—assure you of something you had lost. But then I could not make the analysis. Your sneers were too effective as you held my image from you. Your brilliant eyes swept past mine, you spoke with your hands. Then, with some irrelevance, you said there was nothing to make me unhappy. I was a cocotte who had attempted your seduction.

Sadism? Well, yes. Innate need for violence, vulgarly called love of a row? In part. But there is an x in the equation. Not since Valentine....

It is too soon for this to have happened to me again. It is making me cry and quiver. I remember how by your Sussex fire you laid my head on your hands, and crossed the hands I clasped lest my virtue should escape you. My rings had bitten into my hands. Your eyes were dark and profound, heavy with peace. I would not have had you change yet to this pursuit of a truth whose "chic" lies in its perversion.

All this in three weeks. You say: "She will get over it."

II

It was too soon, my dear, to be hurt again. That's my text for to-night. You should never have comforted me if you were going to submit me again to torture. All my life I have been accompanied by a ghostly pain. Lately it has become substantial, and I have recognised it in some absolute sense as cruelty. First there was Valentine, then you. You know how you found me—grey and sullen—wasted through too much knowledge. You knew what I had come to see.

There were your compassionate words, you've unsaid them. Can't you understand, you fool, that you've unsaid them?

* * * * *

Look here. You must not imagine that this is a complaint, a whining because a man has refused to love me. You are under no obligation to find immortality in my "white and gold and red." But I think that you should have made up your mind. Do you remember what you said—"If there is any goodwill that can help you through this business, remember that you have it." Within a month you faced me across Porfirio's table—my evil personified. What does it mean? You see I have the mind's curiosity to understand and incorporate. It sustains me, nearly all the time. You need not have loved me, though it would have been better that you should. But your voice is flaying me like the noise of a scythe on stone. Why should my vitality have moved this impulse in you? Through you it returned to me augmented. Did you hate it? Did you crave to diminish it yourself?

Love, dear love—how dare you speak to me of love?

III

You have said that you do not trust life, so why should you trust me who am, at best, one of the "naughty stars"? And I imagined that I was to be your reconciliation.

From such divergence where could we have found a meeting-place for love? If I, "the brother whom you have seen," could not enter your house, where will God come in? In my vanity I thought that where one went the other followed. Sir—you have undeceived me.

What did you call me? "*dangereuse*," "false," "essentially outside truth." Has that last phrase any meaning? To me, it is plain tripe. I can only tell my part of this adventure. Louis—there have been times, often before some humiliation profound as this, when I have known myself for an artificer in a better way of love than men practise in the world. That does not "prove me base," but may prove me dangerous. Did I offer you too much freedom, too much passion? When I stripped myself of jealousy and possession, did I strip you of some armour you would not be without? You allow me words. I might talk with you on those matters till dawn. But love is not a conversation.

An adventure has been lost. We shall not be together again, and in love how can one have the adventure alone? You hardly admit the possibility. I said, "I could make it damned good." You answered: "Damned it might be."

Am I to go through my life looking for the lover whose pace equals mine? Is it always illusion that turns me here and there, saying that I have found him in my perpetual error?

The pilgrim rescued the lady in the dewy wood. There, without explanation, he left her to face the Blatant Beast.

IV

Last night when you had gone with your friends I sat down on the floor among the nutshells and cigarette-ends, and cried at the fire. I was alone in my house, and you had all gone home, "lover by lover." I was left, out of your thought, out of your dance. Not one of you but Leila had thought to say that it had been a good party. An empty wine-bottle rolled across the floor and chinked against a syphon. It frightens me when inanimate things move about. It can be lonely here, past midnight, under the great shadows of this roof, not easy to leave the fire and mount the gallery stairs and slip into the icy bed. Before I decided to attempt it and take aspirin, I wondered if this fire which you have lit—and will not share—has an "absolute" value, a good-in-itself apart from you—and from me. Eventually one takes the way from one's kind.

This afternoon I went out in the rain and through the streets, not faint with desolation but in tranquillity, with my love.

Pathological?

Later

I am waiting for you now. Will it be the same if you do not come? How can it be, when my eyes are starved, my quivering touch cannot fasten. I want our old ritual. I want to play it—to satiety. Don't you remember you would sit by the fire? We'd be alone. I would sit on the chair-arm behind you. You lay there, silent, relaxed, as life flowed from me to you. Did you know what I said as I kissed your neck—that I laid my peace on you—the peace you've not had? "My peace, not as the world giveth. . . ." Your astonishment made me laugh. I slipped from the arm on to your knee, and crossed my feet, and swung there. I can see you laugh. I can see your quarrel with life remembered to be forgotten.

"Oh, my dear, you happened, but just in time, only just in time."

And I believed it. My eyes went hot because of the miracle. I used to watch the flush on your thin face, the sudden fusion. . . .

You used to laugh. "Was there ever woman said such things before? Witty fool!" I would slip from your knees on to the floor and crouch there, looking up at you, silent.

Then it was your turn.

You are not coming to-night. I was mistaken. There is no adventure alone.

V

Half an hour later—a knock. External shapes, the walls, the coloured glass on the dark shelf, became like scenery, flat, two-dimensioned. Crossing from the fire-place to the door, I knew how my body bent as though the great chair had risen and clung to my back. You were not there, but a boy with onions. It happened again. I said: "It's not Louis—it is not."

It wasn't. I saw a girl with a suitcase and umbrella and several kinds of fur—a girl you have not met. She wanted a bed for the night. The sequence was amusing.

That evening we compared our beauties on the floor, by the fire on the white rug, burnished our nails and our hair. Our scents and orange-sticks lay between our feet— my long pink toes and her short ones.

She threw down her mirror. She must speak.

She had gathered—indeed she knew. I had given my-self—and to more than one man. I was not married at all. I did not seem to mind. Did I know what I was doing? I was giving men what they wanted ... I exacted nothing in return. Did I know the "awful degradation" that was over-taking me? No one could be more passionate than she— but never. Her fiancé would come back from the front and kill her. (There's a chance for Ivan.) She was proud to think that she would come to him. Just all of her— (Price sixpence. Please see that this seal is unbroken.) Incidentally, she considered me a blackleg in a pair of silk stockings. . . .

She has left me to wonder, though—without passion—whether you, Louis, are despising me. (She does not know about you.)

You have called me pure. Do you still think that? Did you ever think it—with your mind? I don't care. If love of truth can make me pure, I'll pass. And so, what woman cares a pin about chastity? She tried to frighten me, damn her.

Then later I saw her puny man, and lunched afterwards with Bill, and drank with him, and comforted him in sexless amity; and then came to me, as there has always come, the answer to her fear.

VI

Well, my dear. We've had it out? I repeat if it had been another woman, lovelier, wittier than I—Dolores, Bill's wife, or some other *amoureuse*—you would be dead now, spitted on a dagger. Or the lady would have hung herself on your door-knocker, leaving you to explain. You are not grateful for my moderation. Yet you behaved rather well. You were skilfull. I watched you manœuvring to reduce our affair to the terms of the harlequinade. When you explained that you were not worthy of my least regard I grasped the setting and gave you your Columbine. What did it amount to? That I, who had brought you peace, had become the devourer of peace. There was no greed of which you might accuse me, but you made your case against a vitality which might destroy.

"It is my deepest opinion that a philosopher must avoid love. I cannot—though I have wished to—recognise your life of intuitions corrected by intelligence. It interferes with pure mentality." And then: "Dear, I have wanted to—I wish I were different. But I mean to draw back before I hurt you any more. It is intolerably disagreeable to see you suffer." Your eyes pleaded for my departure. I stood before your mirror, colouring my mouth. In that glass I saw your magical presentment. In it was mirrored the boy scientist, the 'Varsity philosopher, the emotional adolescent. Heaven's hound called herself off. I left Soho, and you, and the tragic-eyed woman I passed on the stairs. I was almost at peace, on the edge of contemplation. I did not cry when I reached home.

I am become a dawn-cat, pattering back with torn ears and fur. A month ago there seemed no beauty my body could not accomplish. Loved One, there is a great gulf outside formal time between our Sussex days and these.

"When the Lord turned again the Captivity of Sion."

Sion has gone back into her Captivity—"credit me," as Stephen Bird would say.

* * * * *

It's all right, Louis—you are not my lover. You are a boy, and have sharpened your senses on the scent of my skin and the colour of my hair.

As a lover you are nothing. But the truth of your presentment does not lie there. I've found it. This also is true. Herein lies your originality. Most minds in the world are cheap, sterile, insincere. They impart their stale flavour to the whole. But I have tasted your mind's fruitfulness and passion like salt and fine bread. There is your way, your truth, and your life. And I have lived with you.

VII

To-day we met—almost as strangers. We both wished to resolve our affair into formal acquaintance. We finished a bottle of Burgundy. Old Porfirio, who had watched this and other of our affairs, was pleased to see us. He had noticed that M'sieu came no longer with the tall Mademoiselle. There is a gentleman tucked away behind that round stomach. Do you realise that he is not licensed to sell liqueurs?

We walked down Drury Lane greasy with banana-skins, and you held my arm and spoke of Anne, that "wafer made out of the blood of Christ." I could not point out the ritual error while you were telling me of her trust, explaining that her confidence appalled while it elated you.

O sacred *naïveté*! Has it never occurred to you that I have behaved to you in exactly the same way?

That's as may be. I could have sneered, till I looked up and saw your face. You might have been a flame enclosed in ivory. You were thinking?

To you: Endymion, is it all one moon who in the innumerable phases of women turns to kiss you? Adolescent, sensualist—are all women alike to you in the dark?

We walked under the portico of Drury Lane.

Khovanchina—I do not understand the full implication of that music, except that it united us for a moment, to separate us, I think, forever.

When we came out the Great Bear trailed over Covent Garden, and the empty pavement rang, and the stars leapt in the bitter sky. The music had ravished and troubled me, but your cold elation gave me the fear of an animal that knows it is to be beaten. "It's all there," you said, "in the last Act. The negation of your passion—your pleasure and your despair. There is the end of being, voluntarily to become nothing, to evade—courteously—your angel of the adventure. Withdrawal, stillness, immaculate contemplation—there is escape with victory. Isn't that better than your daring and your temperance?"

We came to your door, went upstairs without speaking. You did a strange thing. You came beside me, music in your eyes—and on your lips. Then, your eyes closed, you flung yourself down upon my breast, and clung there.

I held you, sitting upright, dazed. Then I heard Jim on the stairs. He came in and found us very quiet. I went home.

* * * * *

You're a brave man, Louis. I cannot accept final futility, Dostoevsky's bath-house full of spiders, the ultimate rat in the ultimate trap. You are a great man. I "also have known a lot of men," but have not met one before of such intelligence.

You can put them away—things which feed you: Mozart and Tchekov and Plotinus, ballet and *décor,* your physics which only vaguely impress me, your economics with which I do not agree. You can put them away and bank on the ultimate bankruptcy of all cognition and passion. I love you, I adore your quality. I'm too proud to fight.

Varya.

VIII

How am I fallen from myself
For a long time now
I have not seen the Prince of Chang in my dreams.

To-day I went out on the word of a lying map to look for hut circles and kist vaens in the mist. I believed also that there would be ghosts on the moor. I found those I had brought with me, awaiting me there. The mist filtered down and covered the world. I wandered over those soggy uplands, and listened to the silence made audible by running water and the odd settling noises of the bog.

It was not the stone age that pressed round me, but my metropolitan ghosts. I found them translated in that iron land whose focus is a prison and a house of torture. The images that haunt me—the horror in Valentine, the shadow of the war, the starvation of the human spirit, the thwarting of creation, the power whose symbol we call cruelty—rose out of the moor, ghastly familiar. When the sun strikes it after rain it is the colour of raw flesh. Find me the greatest common measure of these things.

IX

You asked me once: "What can I give you that other men cannot? My intelligence—perhaps—but not my person, or my wealth—I am hardly a sexual athlete." And then the demure smile, and the stroke of the moustache. Dear fool. Am I to accuse you of idealising me? Don't you know that there is a sensuality in me no one has ever satisfied? I'm tired of echoing Aspasia and Egeria, but with you I've been romp and *amoureuse*, shared the "ardours demi-virginal" of the Kirchner Girl.

We've had the profundity of infinite lightness. With you I've danced my solo in that equivocal ballet of the world.

X

Prince of Chang—I think of your pale face and high cheek-bones, your narrow brilliant eyes, and you seem to me remote as that Prince. You might be an enamelled lord, and I once an embroidered lady, two pieces of *décor* in an age and city remote as Atlantis.

I have now been a week on these moors.

> *Great London where the sights are*
> *And the lights are*
> *And the nights are.*

The memory of our affair is not dead, but it has become a magical *objet d'art* like some awful tale of India or Japan where the raw blood beats through porcelain and cloisonné and jade. What has Ivan made of this? Nothing. I haven't told him. I'm learning to offer myself in instalments. Besides, it won't make a tale yet, and to cry the raw pain aloud would not be fair. It is not his dance or his crucifixion. It is hardly his business. But I cannot give him what I would. I've been too starved. There are better ways. All the time the moor watches me and the granite hills. The cold streams hiss between the boulders, the mist is soft as thistledown and cold as death.

There are better ways than this acceptance of mutilation. We are creatures in time, Ivan and I. Years have knit us, of love and adventure. He is my temporal stability. But we three together? The moor is destroying me. Here nature and the Beast—Sologub's Beast—are one. The moor is a repetition of the war. The town is a microcosm of the moor, stripped of its grotesque beauty. I am a tiny seed in such a mill. There are better ways. When he and I first sat by the fire, I remembered you, Prince of Chang. There is a *pas de trois* in love, two cannot dance.... Another way of saying that I don't see why I should not have you both. The result of the frustration is that I am bored. I sit here, sucking smoke up a tortoiseshell tube. The taste of you burns my memory—like the vile cigarettes of this abominable place.

XI

DEAR BRUTUS,

I am in town again—with more humour than when I left it. At least I watch the completion of our cycle without further illusion. It is like this. Since Sion has gone back into her Captivity, she will drink freely of the waters of Babylon. My dear—you don't know—women who can stand this can stand anything. I do not know what absolute value it may have, but I remember the night when the thread was cut that tied me to temporal needs. I have lived in a world become translucent. But I cannot gauge the quality of the illumination beyond. My feet have been lighter on the streets than on the day you said that you loved me. Then I strode through them, part of the combers of the wind and the hurrying stars. My bird had left the bush and dropped into my hands. Now there is neither bush nor bird but a stillness like sea-fog. I am relaxed, passive. Then I remember. "For God's sake don't stop loving me. I have everything to learn. Make my world new." And then: "You have come in time, only just in time—" and the tears force themselves out of my eyes, separate as stones, and each a microcosm of my disappointment. But the worst you've done is not these. All that I might have written, all that I might have perceived, the adventure I saw and have not accomplished—these I can present you. You begot them. You aborted them. Now I am barren. That's the worst you've done.

* * * * *

> "*Complaints are many and various,*
> *And my feet are cold," said Aquarius.*

This is your side to this tale, and I, perhaps, be none than a green-sick girl.

Last night in your rooms, I could not but laugh. You were so glad to think that you had steered your canoe safe back to interested acquaintance once more. Dear Brutus, there was nothing to forgive.

VARYA.

XII

> *Faint white world,*
> *I stand at my door.*

There is snow on every plane of the street and over them a mist, an ice-gauze. There is nothing more. I can live without you and without any man. Yes—"Be sorry for your childishness," and dance again and run about the world. Nothing more. Not for you. The air is an unshaken silver net. It hangs in suspense outside of time. So with me.

Remember the last act of *Khovanchina*. I do not know whether I am alive or dead, but that there is another state through the antithesis of life and death. There is a cloister for passion. You by denying, I by acceptance, have come to the same place. But there are no final vows. O Tranquillity. There are no more grey-walled houses set to watch us or conceal, or scarlet 'buses grinding up the Tottenham Court Road. There are only masses and spears of light, coloured, interchangeable. All things are dissolved into their elements, all things dance.

Athis. . . .

A Lover

THE TWO FRIENDS sat together, talking over the last night's party and particularly one man who had been there.

They were very old friends, the young actor and the woman who had given the party, who had come up from the remote country to find out what London was like; and because she knew how to give parties, people came to her house; and she had already seen a great deal of what happens in London.

They talked of the people who had got off at the party or changed partners when it had got to its riotous stage: of the two men from the Ballet who had danced: of the punch it had taken three days to make and three hours to drink. Going through it all carefully, she with an eye for failures as well as for successes; for people to ask again: for people to forget about as soon as possible.

All this cleared away, she came to what she had been waiting to ask and her friend to answer—the amiable, fussy man, something of a match-maker and rather concerned for this woman who lived alone in the white victorian house with tall rooms good for parties and a balcony over a walled garden ending in trees. (This happened some years ago, when parties were still gay, before they took their agonised, bitter, debauched twist.) Perhaps it had something to do with her, though she never interfered, only people who came to the house at their worst sometimes left at their best.

"Now tell me, Alec," she said, "about your new friend." She noticed at once how his voice changed, charged as he spoke with unaffected grief.

"Alan, Alan Courcy—that's his name in case you didn't

A LOVER

get it. French—not Huguenot—Revolution, I believe. I'd
rather like to tell you about him."

"I'm listening. Go ahead."

"I got to know him because he's a great actor gone
wrong. Met him on tour—in another company. He'd understudied Richard III and went on suddenly. I saw it by
accident. He played him like a flame out of hell. White,
too, and piteous, something I shall never forget."

"Reading the character? I don't quite see it. Or just
touching up his own personality?"

"The last, I suppose. But it was thrilling. Finished work
too: no raw edges. Then I got to know him."

So it all came out. The family behind this Alan Courcy,
a mother he adored and quarrelled with and could not
do without; a stepfather he played up against her so
abominably that the hapless man periodically kicked his
stepson out of the house. Some money. No need to work.
Badly knocked about in the War. An equal gift for painting; for quarrelling with managers; for destroying his
work unfinished. For believing in himself: for disbelieving
in himself. All of which meant in Alec's simple mind that
it was a case for his dear Anne, with her trick of harmonis-
ing people. She must take Alan up, persuade him what a
wonderful fellow he really was; what a wonderful world it
is. Get him to become his promises, some of his promises,
all of his promises. Alec was a sentimental optimist about
human beings. Though when he saw the pair of them
together on the stage of his own mind, his actor's eye hesitated. It was not quiet so easy to see them playing opposite.
Anne, tree-tall, calm and light. Alan—a conceit formed in
his mind, surréaliste image of a dachshund and a serpent.
Heavens! how the man did wriggle about. He could see
the small, pale, nervous body flinging itself from side to
side in an agony of self-assertion and self-depreciation and
viperish verbal depreciation of others. It would take all
Anne's earth-power to restore that to its original well-being. It was Alec's article of faith that there had been well-

being once. Besides—besides—there rose in his mind the essential of Alan Courcy's history, the shattering, appalling fact round which his murdered youth was impaled; and as he turned again to Anne, she saw his kind eyes full of tears.

"Besides, Anne, besides—there is the thing that happened to him. That it should have happened to him of all people." It passed quickly through her mind that this Alan did not look the man to be the victim of one annihilating fact, a man too flexible, too diverse. But Alec was an honest creature and not stupid when you discounted the sentiment.

"Go on," she said.

"He told me when we first met—he was all to pieces after playing Richard. He has never told me not to tell. It was this. He was in Vienna before they ruined it. Just-before-the-War Vienna." The sigh passed their lips without which the name of that city is never said. Alec went on: "It was there he got engaged to a girl, a proper engagement, family and all. When the War happened he wrote and wrote. Heard she and her people were in difficulties. Brother after brother killed. Then there was the famine and he sent money. Money, you know, and love and hope. After a time he got no more answers, but he went on. Then, directly it was over, he dashed across. And couldn't find them. Utter strangers in their house. Jews. Went to their country house and found it in ruins. There had been some local fighting, and he says they must have left it in a hurry; that in a fallen-in summer house he found her handkerchief and a book; and the beginning, only the beginning, of a dreadful letter to him. I saw that. He carries it about and he read it to me. She had never had one of his letters. Nor the money. She knew nothing. Except that he did not care for her any more.

"At last he got on her track. They'd been driven, her mother and one sister, away to some other town. Became beggars together. Till she died—of starvation, really. A quick illness and no heart left. The woman who had tried to nurse her told him. 'Alan,' she said, 'I'd have seen it out if you had. But you've gone and I'd better go too.' Then she died. By the time he got there they were all dead. He says he died, too, for a bit. Perhaps he's never come back. Lots of us haven't. Only one feels that we all ought to be damned decent—to see if we can help him pull through. I can't help feeling it's a bit up to us."

By the time he had finished speaking, tears were running down both their cheeks.

Half an hour later Anne saw Alec, on and off the stage the eternal *compère*, out of the house. That he had just filled his role she saw laughing; but she was not laughing when she turned to her desk and wrote to ask Alan Courcy to dinner.

* * * * *

"Anne Clavel, dear, I suppose you'll be saying that I must take the job with a lowly and thankful heart and work up the part, and not tell the producer that a cockney accent goes badly with iambic pentameter; and that Shakespeare talked a nice country accent with a burr— warm, like a woolly caterpillar. How tiresome and moral and athletic, and how very very good for me.

"Yes, I will. You're the only being on earth I would do it for. You are making things different. Taken a fool, trying to have a private life as much like des Esseintes as possible, out of his dark room. Opened *all* the windows, let out the musk and amber and let in garden smells. Only why did you do it? Why? Why? Why? Why in hell or out of it should anyone bother about me, licking perfectly disgusting sores in the dark?"

"I don't know," said Anne peacefully, but gratified, "I don't like septic wounds. And I couldn't stand the tortoise."

"The tortoise?"

"Don't you remember? He had its shell set with car‐
buncles to watch it glow as it crept round, and it killed it;
and he could see the stones still shining in the dark of his
infernal flat until it occurred to him where the stink came
from. Some of your memories were too like that tortoise
for me." Alan had left the deck chair and was lying on the
grass in the garden at her feet. At this he dropped a mo‐
ment, his face hidden resting on his arms. She could see
the slight shoulders quiver.

"*Mon vieux,*" she called after a moment, very gently.
The ravaged, petulant head turned up to her again.

"Witty, searching beast of a woman. I didn't know
whether to laugh or cry. But I won't be like a tortoise gone
bad—even a tortoise with jewels stuck in it."

"I never said you; only some of the things you think
about."

"If you weren't so utterly right, and didn't make it
rather funny, I'd lose my temper and show you what sort
of a nasty, catty, self-pitying, little martyr I am. But oh,
Anne, what put it into your head to see through me so
comfortingly? When I came to your party, I actually found
myself behaving like a human being. I'm usually rather
awful at parties. Drink too much and either cry or else
insult my hostess; and instead I found myself indulging
in an innocent frolic." Anne thought: It had better come
now. She was more and more moved as by something that
seemed rather exquisite, wild and young and wounded,
that had stopped fidgeting and lay on the grass at her feet,
still and appeased, as if waiting for some word which
would come from her to make him stand up and let fall a
great burden and then move—swiftly and harmoniously
and with joy. Like a man delivered from the hell of his
own mind. And from more than his mind. From what had
been done to him. Like many women after the War, she
had been busy patching up; spending herself on it, still
young enough to expect too much, old enough to suffer,
but not wholly break her heart.

"It was Alec," she said slowly, "he told me."

"Dear old Alec! Such a—*comprimé* of all the best traditions of the stage. So good"—his voice was gentle—"that I bore it the other day when he put his hand on my shoulder and called me a priceless old fruit."

"Be thankful it wasn't 'laddie.'"

"You always have an answer—the sort that puts things in a better light. It would be intolerable if it wasn't true. Anne, Anne, Annette—Anna Perenna, the moon-in-and-out. Which shall I call you?" He twisted round suddenly and sat staring up at her. A dreadful change came over his face, the eyes staring, the body taut; the bright restless eyes, brown-irised, the whites shaded with blue, starting out of his head. Anne thought she had never seen eyes so haunted, so crazed with hopeless escape. Flight down the corridors of the mind, each one that ended with a door, and nailed to it the same dreadful bleeding god. We each have one to meet, but this man's was Eros crucified. The girl he loved, dying out there so slowly, one victim out of millions. Out in Central Europe where the folk-wanderings meet and cross and destroy. A long time ago . . . Heavens! what had ancient history to do with it? But man had thought he had made himself a reasonably safe place out there in the heart of those lands, where Dacia once stood with its chain of towers. Till Trajan came and took the Red Tower and the city of Smaragethusa, and there Rome had made for herself Vindobonda, and for us Vienna. One of the Holy Places Cities, last seat of the Roman Empire. In place of so many crucifixions, a place of delight. A fountain of wit and sweet laughter. Anatol's town. . . . He was saying:

"So you know? Of course you know. Why shouldn't you know? She died. She died. Now you know all there is to know, Anna Perenna. I'm glad you know. For now you know all there is to know about me. For her agony hasn't redeemed me—it's made me a maimed cad. A spiteful liar. A man too hurt to use his gifts, who takes his shame out

MARY BUTTS

in miscalling other men. I'm not a man. I couldn't protect her; I was caught in the Army with the rest. I was so sure as I went strutting about, and though I call myself a Christian and a Catholic, all the time I see another god, something very old, with a filthy leer, who likes hurting people. He's had his joke—he's still having his joke with me.

"But you are not laughing, Anne...." He flung himself forward and laid his head down on her knees. Her fingers touched the little drakes' tails of the soft hair along the cleft of his neck.

* * * * *

This time it was Alec who sat at Anne's feet, looking up like an affectionate and enthusiastic dog.

"Wonderful the change you've made in Alan. We're doing a Sunday show and you ought to have seen him at rehearsal. Understudied Biron, and had to go on again at the last minute. His body doesn't fit, but he made it. The sword and ruff did what they should and often don't and helped him, and he forgot what he does when he's nervous and goes all stagey—took a flying leap into the part, and you saw little Alan Courcy turn Renaissance lord. It went as though it had been sung—you get what I mean? The young Shakespeare, working up to a hell of a climax—stuck in the rest of the play as an excuse for that speech—and Alan was his rocket. Going up and bursting out on top with stars. You should have heard him, mounting his part:

> 'But love, first learnèd in a lady's eyes,
> Lives not alone immurèd in the brain—
> In valour is not love a Hercules,
> Still climbing trees in the Hesperides?'

"And when he came to the persuasive solemn bit at the end: 'For woman's sake by whom these men are men' he spoke it like a gay prayer. His English is naturally very pure. A little pernickety—after all he's part French; but

·178·

when it comes to a show like that and the classic stage, he's got it where he wants it."

"I wish," said Anne, "I'd heard."

"I wish," said Alec, "you had. For at the end, my dear, he was praying to you."

"Not to his memories?"

"Well, it's been you who've treated them so as to make them fit to pray to," said Alec sturdily. "Besides, he's told me as much."

* * * * *

Again Anne was very pleased. It was the appeasement of nerves that pleases many women, aware that through them has come consolation, a certain order and proportion, virtue set free. Pleasure that, when Alan came to call and tell her about it himself, came with a sensual stab.

The spring came too with its wave of green fire, and they became lovers. Even, at his suggestion, marriage crossed her mind. His family encouraged her. His mother especially, his half-French mother, the elegant old lady, anxious, ironical, profoundly observant and attached to her son. Exhausted too, as Anne noticed, with a life-time of dealing with him. Did she understand him? Did she not? Was she, *au fond*, wise, or did she suffer from that vanity, that essential blindness of the parent that seems to the lover so shocking and so hopeless? Anne asked herself that, when she noticed old Madame Courcy to be as much amused as impressed. Impressed she certainly was and thankful, with even a touch of hope that in itself sounded like a warning. For every time she heard her say: "Anne, child, what wonders are you doing with my son," Anne could hear, undertone and overtone, fear and something like derision concealed. A little afraid for herself, she summoned the lover's faith. Again, whatever he was, Alan had the trick to make her passionate and to make her laugh, two things sufficient to fly away with judgment and again she knew it.

She was the fountain at which he drank, bathed, adorned himself. With altered step he had begun—she saw it and his mother endorsed it—to *move about the house with joy.* Yet she soon noticed one thing—that he never bought her anything but cheap flowers, and these with excuses she did not expect, about poverty which she knew, within that range of expenditure, did not exist. And, though he was always at her house, he rarely took her out, and then with the same excuses. It was queer. Then one evening he told her that he was on the track of a sister of the Austrian girl who might still be alive, and putting aside every penny to help her. Well and good, but it occurred to Anne that a possible wife could hardly be asked to share for ever such an excess of charity.

And when he spoke of this his voice grew shrill, the small lithe body flinging itself about, and he would wander about the room from chair to chair, find nowhere to rest. This progress she knew and that it ended in quiet, his body laid down again at her feet, his head with its soft blown hair come to rest on her lap.

But that evening, after trying the fourth chair, he got up again and, apropos of nothing, cried out: "Why should I bring you presents? I know I'm supposed to bring you presents. Convention demands it. I sent her presents, money, all I had. I went without the decencies of the other men in my mess and she never got them. They never did her any good. You've got everything you need. What can I give you? My rotten life to pick up. Fine gift that, my Anna—"

She took this quietly. It seemed to her inevitable that it would come to a struggle between the dead girl and herself. A struggle that, for both their sakes, she must win. That it was fair for her to win. The little Elizabeth would not mind. Was not going to be allowed to mind. She waited till he had done and said:

"I wish, Alan, that your french mind would run through what you've been saying. What *are* the parallels? And when did I ask you to give me presents? Only there comes a time—a way—when the dead must bury their dead. It's the only way to keep them properly alive. Otherwise they're apt to stink. You say you're a Christian and a Catholic, and you know our authority for that. Only just look at the sense of what you're saying. You're not to give me presents (for which I've never asked) because once (under tragic circumstances) you gave them to someone else who didn't get them; all bolstered up with camp about convention and lies about me. Alan, dear—"

"Anna Perenna sits there, the Moon-Woman, and talks about logic to the Man in the Moon! But I earned that, I admit. Oh, I'm a nasty bit of work. No one knows how nasty—" He came across, took her by the throat and began to kiss her:

"Doesn't she know I must punish her for being so lovely and so wise and for purging the cad out of me?" As he thrust her back among the cushions, her body began to relax, and he lay beside her, nibbling her lips—"Best French logic"—and heard her laugh from her throat. Then silence close together for the lovely words, murmured but distinct:

"*A la très chère, à la très belle*
Qui remplit nos âmes de clarté—"

And a moment later, as if to himself: "Go away, Elizabeth, my dear, your time's over." "To Paradise," she whispered, drowsed and trembling at his touch. The long couch in the room where the spring wind stirred held them easily, and his presence shut out everything but the wandering airs and high up in the trees the talk of doves.

* * * * *

A few days later he said: "Let's go to the Ballet. We must to-night. I've got the seats." Anne agreed. Before she

started she looked at the programme. There was to be one
called "Le Beau Danube" they had not seen. She remembered what she had heard about it, that it was written
round the Danube waltz, with one heart-breaking *pas de
deux* for Lopokova and Massine. (Critics had called it a
return to sentimentality, but those two knew what they
were about.) Then that Alan must know: that he meant
them to see it together for a kind of adieu, a last salute to
the dead.

She met him and they went to their seats. They were
not very good seats. While a little worm of observation
coiled in her mind suggested to her that, if she offered to
pay for them, he would be pleased. So, preparing for some
sort of crisis, hoping for a finale or some revision of their
relations, she sat still until the curtain rose.

There is still power in that sweet tune to make the
shattered children of the after-War world weep. Not because they love like that, or that they would like to love like
that. One of the recurrent love-moods of humanity that
our society at the moment has no use for and no response.
Only, as presented by the two great dancers, one of tears.
In that ballet there is nothing but their dance, when the
passionate modulation before the end is worked out by
their bodies, in a rapture based on sweetness based on
grief. A voiceless song accompanied their movements
across the empty stage. They were dancing the death of
their love, but the song said: "This is Vienna's death." As
he lifted her and she mounted in his arms to the passionate
air, the heart of the youngest of all ancient cities was broken with their hearts. A dance that lasted ten minutes. It
took several years to kill Vienna; several centuries to make
Vienna. And all these three times were the same time. Nor
are we used, like the ancient world, to the death of cities
who have married civilisation each with a ring of their
own, which cannot be made to fit another hand.

It did not seem necessary to compare their thoughts.
They sat straight side by side, each in a precinct of pain

and delight. Watching a dance of love, love when it is nearest to death. Death of Vienna. Death of Anatol. Death of Saki's Clovis and Comus Bassington. They were dead. They were dead. Had those dead boys found any Paradise in which to go on playing? (Was it a spoiled Anatol she had sitting beside her?) As the curtain came down, "No," said something distinctly.

The next was the "Boutique Fantasque." Alan did not want to stay. "Not after that, Anne, please." Anne wanted to stay, because she loved the "Boutique," because it was something like bad discipline to run away, instead of tuning in to another kind of joy. A better kind perhaps of a very different best. "Stay and laugh," she said. She often gave in, but this time she did not want to give in. Or, when Alan began to sulk, damn well mean to give in. "Alan, stay and play." "Play!" he cried out, turning his ravaged head: "My play died with that. Why should I stay? Tell me that."

She said coolly: "Because of courage." For a few moments he stared down. "All right," he said at last. The curtain rose again. She leaned forward, ready to lose herself. Not quite. Aware from time to time of a fleeting look he gave her. Of the kind a lover would rather not see.

When they had left the theatre he said: "I wonder how long it will continue to amuse you, going about with a corpse. Can't you see, you blind woman-thing, that I died when that died?"

"The answer is that I should dislike it very much. Only I'm not and you haven't."

"You're like all women—you only see what you want to see. And what you want with me, God knows. I can't even ask you out to tea. I'm sorry to be so poor, but the tickets cleared me out."

She knew these pettish fits. At first she had thought to tease him out of them by a cheerful generosity, and for a time it had seemed that she *had* teased him. The afternoon suddenly palled.

"I am going home to tea. And I'm not going to ask you

because it's my housekeeper's day out, and I have to get it myself, and it's such an awful bother putting an extra teaspoon into the pot. Besides, think of the expense." The tube station was mercifully near. She knew him hesitating behind her. Would he dash after her as he had sometimes done and, penitent, eager, exceedingly forgivable, laugh at himself? Explain all over again: "I come all over beastly about money because of *her*." This time he did not follow. She reached home unhappy, vexed at the stab of—worse than pain—of contempt that nagged at the being of love. The love she thought they were making, and of which she could never be utterly sure if it was makeable or not.

The tiny crisis passed. It seemed more and more as though she had accepted to marry him. Not that there was any hurry. Then one day they were together at her house when the news came that Alec was very ill. He was going on tour, a first-class tour, to play lead. He could not go; and when he recovered he would be out of work. It was possible that if an expensive treatment were given instantly, he might recover enough. Anne got out her passbook and looked at it thoughtfully. Did sums. Asked Alan if he could help to make up the right amount.

"We owe him a bit, *mon ami*. No two people had a better friend. Besides he is one of the very few who will pay back and pay back quickly." She had not time to be horribly afraid before she heard Alan saying:

"Twenty pounds? My dear girl, I'm afraid I can't do that."

"But Alan, it's only a loan and a short one. You've told me your income. You've no real expenses. You're living at home—"

"I'm out of work if it comes to that."

"My dear, you could have gone touring with Alec. They wanted you; he wanted you—"

"And leave here—you—this?"

"As you like. But don't call yourself out of a job."

The usual fatuity followed: "I thought you wanted me
to stay." And she must make the obvious reply:

"For myself, yes, of course. But for you, and also for
myself—don't you understand—I want to see you act."

He said with a sneer:

"And play second lead to Alec." There was a nasty
silence. Then he began to tell her witty stories of life on
tour, and left her, promising to go home and see what he
could do. Left her reflecting. He had said no more. He *had*
changed his tone. Perhaps he had seen for himself what it
would mean if he did not help his friend. Anne wrote a
cheque for her part, and went round to the far harder
business of persuading Alec to take it.

* * * * *

The next day she went to Kensington, to Alan's house,
to the tea she shared once in a week, alone with his
mother; a visit now become a custom between the old
woman and the young. The ritual was that Alan should
appear later to take her away, dine with her or take her
out to dine. Still Anne could not determine what the old
woman thought. Was it her french training, ignoring what
she could not prevent? How far was she in her son's
confidence? Were they together—uncomfortable suspicion—using her—as a medicine, a cure, a prophylactic
against something worse? (Stupid. Of course they were.
Exactly how much?)

How much *did* he tell her? Anne smiled and blushed.
Well, old Madame Courcy was the right kind of mother
to appreciate that.

They had tea in the garden. The old lady began cheerfully:

"Alan will tell you when he comes. He won't have had
time before. It's sad that your poor friend Alec is so ill, but
they've offered Alan his part on tour; and, thanks, my

dear, to the way you've encouraged him about his work, he's accepted it. He says, too, that he's sending Alec something to help pay off his illness."

Anne stared at the grass. A caterpillar on a blade stood up on its green tail and waved a black head at her. Two worlds, caterpillar world and man world for an instant in contact. Anne thinking man thoughts, the caterpillar, caterpillar thoughts. So Alan had sneaked off and stolen Alec's job. (Innocently she was responsible. She had told him about Alec's illness and his need and the tour he had accepted.) On such conditions the loan she had asked for had been granted. Alan would have the work and the pay and the fame, if any. And be paid back the money he had invested which had obtained him these things. He, the spoiled gentleman actor, too good for this and too gifted for that. The bitterness that is the reverse and the measure and the proportion of love welled up dreadfully in her. The amateur had robbed Alec, Alec who gloried in his profession. The profession Alan gloried in being too good for—the fine art of the actor—picking and choosing and turning his back on the mill to which Alec offered his body as a grindstone.

(And how had he got the job? Was that the way the money went? Was it possible? Anne only knew that anything is possible.)

Madame Courcy was looking at her:

"Have I distressed you, child? I mean, do you not want him to go? Of course you don't, but you've always been so sensible and intelligent in wanting him to work; in seeing what his work might do for him. Only it has been a shock, the separation—I see. I have been careless. But if you only knew, my dear, how I have come to rely on your courage. It has not always been easy to be Alan's mother—"

(Tell her? Tell his mother? Why not? She would not understand by herself and she'd better. And if she's a cheat also, I shall know. Those last words of hers sounded sweet. If they were, then she's worth truth; and if she'll stand the truth, Alan won't quite get away with it. . . . Besides, I'm so angry, it's bound to come out. . . . Lovers can't be cads. . . . How dare he do that to love?) Hoping piteously that Madame Courcy would understand, grimly prepared for an explosion of mother-love, she said:

"It is not that, *Maman*. It is because Alan had no right to do that." She explained with her head averted, her eyes on the caterpillar, now gathering itself up, head to tail, in a loop, and shooting forward its own length, to wave a moment and repeat. Very neatly done. As if, too, it was showing off. Alan like to show off. *I am a worm and no man*. She began to look hard across the garden to a tree, the tree the French called Golden Rain, most beautifully in bloom.

"You see, it takes away one's respect that he should do a thing like that. And how can one keep love without the honour that goes with it? I mean I can't. And forgive me the priggishness." To her great comfort, Madame Courcy's voice reassured:

"I see, my child. Of course I see. Yes, I am glad you have told me. It is as well to face these things." Blessed french mind, accepting things as they are; keeping values pure and intact.

"I quite see that he has done wrong. And what it means to you—for you have tried. We have all tried. . . ." (Anne thought: Even if she would be glad to be rid of me, this woman is honest. Not a touch, thank God, of "my son, right or wrong.") She heard her add rather grimly:

"I think we will speak to him when he comes in—and yet—" Their eyes met and both women nodded.

"You mean, *Maman,* that it might put him off acting for ever if he is told not to be a cad and to leave this?"

"Yes, I fear that. You see, I know—oh how well I know—his perverse mind. Presently he will be saying: 'You made it a point of honour, when I had the best chance in my life, that I should not take it. . . .' You can imagine what he would make of that."

"You are absolutely right. Dear God, how difficult it is." And from the mother's face she understood what a life-time had been.

"*Réfléchissons-nous.* And what perversity it is again that you should have so stimulated him—for this.

"It has always been like that. From his childhood—how often I have been unhappy. Feared too for the woman who—how do you say it—should tackle him. But except for the *amourettes* with the lower classes and with, shall I say, *grues,* he avoids our sex. Always it must be one who is paid to please."

Anne sat up sharply. Of course he was that sort. All the horrible things, as is their way, were coming out at once. If she had not been drugged by the Vienna story, she would have known that. Now it was intolerable with what distinctness she could see him making love to a girl of easy virtue from the corner tobacconist. And did he get his cigarettes free? Reaction was making her beastly. He had called her Anna Perenna. Moments of exquisiteness flashed back, flashed past. Flying things, coloured and winged, to lie preserved only in the amber of memory. She heard herself saying in a sensible voice:

"While we must always remember the Vienna business. To have lost one's first young love like that. When a thing like that happens there is always something final about it. Something for which one must have extraordinary patience, extraordinary understanding. After which, heaven help us all, perhaps we can never expect too much." Madame Courcy interrupted:

"Vienna, my dear, what was that?"

"Why, about the little Elizabeth, about Babette." (Perhaps he didn't tell her. That's nonsense. He tells her everything, let alone *that.*)

"Babette Cosmas he was engaged to and who died so awfully." (She is staring at me. This is like finding a person you supposed a Christian hadn't heard of the Crucifixion.)

Clear and distinct she was being answered, plain words within the range of cat and dog and no and yes.

"Babette—bless our hearts, why should he say that she is dead? Or that he was engaged to her? Yes, they were a family we knew very well, in Vienna, just before the War. Charming people—she was a good deal older than he was. He made a few calf's eyes at her as a boy will. Engaged? She was engaged already. Married when we left and managed to spend the War with her baby in Switzerland. They had property there. They all managed to get through all right. I still hear from them occasionally.

"Child, you were angry before. Now you are white. What is it? Speak out. We have not kept secrets from one another."

As Madame Courcy spoke it seemed as though, instead of trees flowering and new grass and borders opening with flowers, they were sitting in a place that was a desert pocket, full of clean dry stones. In the middle one large stone, like an idol, called The Truth. And why all the time had she been calling the place a garden, when actually it was made of dry stones? Bones among stones. *Can these stones live?* Instead of the heart's desire, a stone. All this time she had been serving the image of a love which had not been there. The moon had come to Endymion; Endymion had got the moon down under false pretences. After all the moon is a stone. Who was it called the moon a "luminous stone"? In the centre of everything there was this large stone. A stone instead of the heart's desire. It occurred to her that perhaps she now saw the stone because she had wished for truth. Truth in love. No love without truth. There was singularly little consolation in it.

"I will tell you the story Alan told us," she said. "The story that was his passport, through Alec, to our society. To me most of all. The story we believed utterly."

She told it, the passion and death of Elizabeth Cosmas. Which had not taken place, whose shadowy and metaphysical existence had so affected her own. With its details: the money Alan had sent, the things he had gone without, the money he hoped to send. His mother listened silent. At the end she said:

"There was no one like that: no one of whom that story could be true. Nor was he in the Army for more than a few months at the end. Clerk's work at some base: his health alone made a commission out of the question. On that account I never suffered the least anxiety." Then, "I remember, Alan said to me once, quoting one of your modern poets: 'I must find a gesture of my own.'"

"He seems to have done so." The old woman waited a few moments. Then she said:

"My dear, I have one question to ask you. From you I know I shall hear nothing but the truth. Can you forgive him? If you do not yet know, say so; but I believe it to be one of the occasions when if you look in your heart, you will know the answer." Anne did not hesitate at all: all anger apart, the mother was quite right. She knew the answer, as it were prepared for her.

"No," she said.

"I understand. With you it is inevitable." Anne nodded. The old woman stared down the garden, in which she saw no more flowers.

"It is not necessary for me to say that I am sorry that my son has done this to you."

"Done it to love. If I stayed till he came and we taxed him." She went on staring; both women thinking the words he would say: "I'm glad you've found me out. I'm glad I've been exposed to you. Now you know exactly and for keeps how vile I am." Roll himself in his poisoned shirt, till she, too, was fiery with the prick of his disease. Now there was just time to escape. No gifts at home to remind her. Half an hour would purify her house of the memory of him.

She picked up her long gloves. No need to hurry. The gods had this in hand, and she had already escaped him.

"Good-bye, Madame Courcy. Thank you for all your *gentillesse* to me." She walked across the green grass which had turned to stones.

What am I leaving her alone with in this garden? Something she did not know before. Thrown him back on her? I had to. Leave him to her. What have I to face— some pain and more shame? But if she were not his mother, she would no more forgive him than I would.

Widdershins

EVERY DAY HE WOKE to the desire to take the world by the throat, and choke it. He had no illusion that the world wanted to be saved; still less that it was ready to be saved by him. Ready!—it was punching at him with agonising blows, to be rid of him, once and for all. He woke up. Even that was not true now. It had been true once, but now the world was getting over any slight alarm he might have caused it. It was leaving him alone, to realise the wounds it had given him. Sometimes it was even tolerant and trying to patch him up.

Oh, God!

He was in the middle of London, in a dull hotel bedroom, stale with travelling from the Shap moors, where two years before he had gone away to think. He had called it thinking, but he had gone there to lick his wounds and dream. He was just intelligent enough to notice that he had not thought, and that what he remembered was certain moments of action. Certainly he did not understand that what he wanted was magic.

He lay, and remembered something about himself: that he was called Dick Tressider, that he was a mystic; and that among the people he met the word meant a snub, a cliché, an insult, or very occasionally, a distinction: that he knew a great many people who almost realised his plan, and yet did not: that he was a gentleman. He had not thought of that for a long time. London had reminded him. He damned the place and ordered his bath. He shaved, and put on his good, worn, country clothes, his heavy boots, his raincoat and leather gloves, all without pride in his strength, or tonic from his unconventionality. He ate a country breakfast, and looked up his appointments. He felt that he was held from behind by the short hair on his skull, and cursed the city. But what he needed was magic.

It is doubtful if he understood the idea of progress, but whether he did or not, he disliked it. It may be certain, but it is obviously slow. He had his immediate reasons too. He had tried every association which tries to speed man's progress; labour and revolution, agriculture and religion. In each, it was the soundest point in his perception, he had seen one thing and the same thing, which was the essential thing and, at the same time, did not come off. Meanwhile, labour and revolution, agriculture and religion were entirely sick of him. He knew, if any man living knew he knew, that sometimes things were improved, or rather that they were changed; and that in individual action there were moments of a peculiar quality that expressed the state in which he knew the whole earth could live all the time, and settle the hash of time, progress and morality once and for ever. What he wanted to happen was for some man to say a word of power which should evoke this state, everywhere, not by any process, but in the twinkling of an eye. This is magic. Lovers did it, especially his lovers; and saints, when he and one or two men he knew were being saints, with a woman or so about to encourage them, at night, in a smoky room. There were moments, too, under the hills, breaking-in horses, when it came, the moment of pure being, the co-ordination of power.

But the universal word did not come off. He was over forty now, and he was losing his nerve. He was beginning to spit and sneer; and, since he could not find his word, he was beginning to grin, and hope for the world to ruin itself; and rub his hands, and tell his friends in their moments of pleasure that they were damned, not exactly because they had not listened to him, but for something rather like it. And, as very often they had listened to him, in reason, they were hurt.

Because he had not mastered the earth, he was beginning to hate it. Hate takes the grace out of a spiritual man, even his grace of body. As he left the hotel and walked west through the park, and saw the trees coming, he drew in one of his animal breaths that showed the canines under his moustache, bright like a dog. "Grin like a dog, and run about the city"; but then he understood that this was one of his empty days, which might be filled with anything or nothing.

"I must fill it," he said, and he meant that on this day he must have a revelation and a blessing; which is a difficult thing to get to order. He went on to the grass, in among the trees, which are a proper setting for almost every kind of beauty. Their green displayed his tan and harmonised his dress. Their trunks drew attention to his height, the grass gave distinction to his walk. It was early, and there were no pretty women about to make his eyes turn this way and that, greedily, with vanity, with appeal for pity, but too scornfully for success. The trees went on growing. He looked at them and remembered Daphne, and that she had said once: "Stop fussing, Dick. Why can't you let things alone for a bit? Think of trees." Silly fool of a girl. Wanted me to make love to her, I suppose. He had said that at the time, and still said it, but he added Daphne to the list of people he was to see that day. Like men of his kind, at cross-purposes with their purpose, there could be nothing fortuitous that happened to him. Everything was a leading, a signature of the reality whose martyr he was; for he could never allow that he had made a fool of himself, and only occasionally that reality had make a fool of him. So he pinned the universe down to a revelation from Daphne, and took a bus to Holborn to get on with the business of the day.

It is much easier for a man to lose his self-consciousness in Holborn than in the female world of South Kensington. He went first to see a friend who was teaching a kind of Christian anarchism made dramatic by the use of Catholic ritual. He was a good man, patient with Dick, who trusted him. It was one of the things that made Dick uneasy that the works of sanctity and illumination are now distributed through offices, and he saw himself a terror to such places. His friend Eden was out. The typist was a very childish one, with short hair and a chintz overall, and she did not suggest the Sophia, the Redeemed Virgin, Dick was looking for. He shifted his expectation and saw her as the unredeemed and improbable virgin, which is the same thing as the soul of the world, and prepared to treat her for the part. He was hungry by now.

"I'm Dick Tressider," he said, "and I'll wait for Mr. Eden." He dropped his stick, picked it up, lit a cigarette, and walked once or twice up and down the room. "D'you know about me?"

"I can't say that I do," she said. "So many gentlemen come here for Mr. Eden."

"D'you know Mr. Eden well? Are you conscious of what he is doing here? I mean that it's an expression of what is happening everywhere, of what is bound to happen everywhere, man's consciousness becoming part of the cosmic consciousness?"

"Mr. Eden never says anything about it."

"D'you know this whole damned earth is going to smash any moment?"

"Mr. Eden says that if there are any more wars we shall starve. He's trying to stop it."

He grinned, and showed his wolf's teeth.

"I tell you. It'll make precious little difference what he does. You look as if you might understand. Come out and have some lunch."

She got up obediently. She remembered that she had heard of Dick, that he had been a soldier of some family and some service. Also he was a tall figure of a man, not like the pale, ecstatic townsmen who came there.

He took her to a restaurant and ordered red wine and steak. He crammed his food down and asked her what she thought about love. Immediately she was frightened. She was not frightened of seduction or of a scene. It was pure fear. He saw that it would not do, and sulked at her, pouring down his wine.

"I don't want to waste time. I've got to get down to reality. Tell Eden I'll call in later."

He took her out, and left her at the door of the restaurant, without a word.

He walked about London, through the streets round the British Museum, on a cool still afternoon without rain, past the interesting shops and the students, and the great building of stone. He wanted to persuade men that they were only there to illustrate the worth of the land. He did not want to see Eden, who would be busy trying to stop the next war, and getting people to dress up. He knew what war was and how it would stop these games, more power to it. It was all up with the world, and the world didn't know it. He would go to tea with Daphne now. It would be too early, but that didn't matter.

At the Museum gates he saw a man he had known who said: "Is that you, Tressider? I didn't know you were in town."

"I came up last night."

"Wishing you were back?"

"Wishing I could smash these lumps of stone or get men to see their cosmic significance."

The civilised man winced. The idea might be tolerable, but one should not say it like that.

"I am going into the Museum. Come along."

"What are you going to do?"

"Look at things."

"Some earth-shaking new cooking-pot?"

"It's not a question of size, is it? Come along."

He had to run beside Dick, who flung himself over the courtyard and up the steps.

"I read a jolly fairy-story about this place," he said. "Some children got a magic amulet and wished the things home, and they all flew out. Those stone bull things, and all the crocks and necklaces."

"I remember. They found a queen from Babylon, and she said they belonged to her, and wished them all home, and home they went."

Dick looked at him with a sideways, ugly stare.

"I know. You like me, don't you, when you think I'm a fairy-boy. A kind of grown-up Puck? You like me to like rot."

"But I do," said his friend. "I like that story myself, and was glad when you recalled it."

"Do you know that the only thing we've said that meant anything was a bit of your talk—'She said they all belonged to her.' That's the cursed property-sense that keeps this world a hell."

"Oh damn the property-sense! I was going to look at the casts from Yucatan, and I always forget the way."

Dick was staring at a case of bronze weapons. He put his hand easily on the man's shoulder. "Don't you understand that that fairy-story is true? They could all fly away out of here. It's as easy as changing your collar."

"Do it for us then, Tressider. I'll come along and applaud."

"My God! You people will find a man who can do it for you, and worse things, and soon. Someone you've treated as you treat all people. Take it from me, Brooks."

Madder than ever, thought Brooks. Won't think, and can't play. "All right. The room's at the end. Come along."

It is not easy to get on terms with a cast the size of a house, whose close decorations mean nothing to anyone except to an archaeologist or an artist. Dick lounged and stared, and leant up against the central plaster lump.

"What are all these things for? I suppose you think you've done something when you've dug 'em up out of the earth."

It is exceedingly difficult to explain why a thing is useful when you like it.

Dick smote it with his hand.

"A lot of good those'll do you when the world busts up."

But Brooks was thinking what a type was there, leaning on a sacred maian monster, a fair, ruling, fighting, riding man, and what twist of breeding had turned him prophet *à la* Semite, "sad when he held the harp." And that the harp that once—etc.—was now completely cracked.

"All right," he said, "we'll leave antiquities for the moment. But it's a speculation worth following: Where did that civilisation come from, and did it have any contact with Egypt?"

"Egypt? They knew about the soul there, and I don't care where their jim-jam decorations came from. Civilisation's going. The world wants a man whose contact is primeval."

"Oh does it?" said Brooks. "I suppose you mean yourself. You're about as primeval as a card-index. Come and have some tea."

And at tea Dick asked him sweetly about his children, and sent messages to his wife, and told the story of his uncle's funeral with point and wit, and left Brooks, to go up to Daphne, with his affection intact, and his doubts.

Now it was evening. The 'bus climbed up the side of London, and above the screaming children and the crowd going home from work, it rolled like an animal ship; and from every contact Dick sighed and withdrew himself, until at the five roads at Camden Town he felt something coming to him which had come before. "This place is not here," he said. "I can lift myself out of it, in my body. So!" He sank down a little as he said it, and answered himself. "The things you hate are only your body being knocked about by phenomena." Then the place disappeared, especially a public-house with a plaster tower; but there had crept up through it tall, perpendicular folds, which looked like dark grey rubber, which rose and passed in from all sides. But he was free, both of the houses and what replaced them. He lifted himself like a clean man out of the sea, and rested in his mind, which was now full of order and peace. He wondered that he had ever minded anything, and at the end of the ride stood several men drinks in a public-house and roared with laughter with them.

Before dinner he came to Daphne's house and rang the bell. There was some time before anyone answered it. Then her old nurse came, and looked at him without knowing who he was. He came in, and took off his raincoat before he said: "Is Miss Daphne in?"

"I'll see, sir," she said, and led him into the living-room, which had tall windows and a balcony on to a garden full of trees. The wind, a new thing, was moving in them. It was almost night. Next door was Daphne's room. He heard the door open and shut several times, and brief voices. The room was very empty. He stumbled over a rug, and saw the shining boards and a gramophone gaping with the lid up, and records on the divan among the cushions. He did not make himself at ease by the fire. He understood that they had been dancing. He walked up and down the room, wondering what they would give him to eat.

It was all right. The peace was there. He would tell Daphne about it. Daphne would give it back to him with assent and vivid words. Perhaps he would take Daphne out to dinner. Her youngest sister came in.

"Please forgive us. We're in such a hurry. We've been dressing Daphne. Would you mind coming to see her in her room?"

He remembered Daphne's room, rows of books and glass balls and chinese pictures of birds and windows that stepped out into the air. He followed her sister, and as he came in, heard Daphne's cry, "Hullo, Dick!" that was like a battle yell. In a minute he was treading into a sea of tissue paper that rustled like snakes. The shutters were closed. All the lights were on. Here was night, suddenly and

strongly lit. As Daphne came to meet him, her sister fell
on her knees, and followed her over the carpet, pinning
something at her hips.

A woman he did not know was sitting on the couch
looking at Daphne. The old nurse was somewhere behind
him, by the door.

"Shall I ring for a taxi, dearie?"

"In a minute, Nurse, I've a few moments to spare."
Then he trod on the paper like a man and saw her. She
had on a green and white dress, and crystal earrings that
touched her shoulders, and a crystal at her waist, slung
round her neck with a green cord. Dick remembered
enough to know that it was a dress that is not seen in shops,
but is shown, "like an ear of corn reaped in silence" to
certain women on certain occasions. He saw her feet in
silver sandals, her hair like a black, painted doll's, a curve
drawn out over each cheek. On the dressing-table, white
with powder, there was a bouquet in a frill.

"Dick, I'm going out to have a glorious time." She did
not look at him twice to see what his heavy eyes said.

"Val, my dear, is my back even?" Valentine got up and
took a powder-puff and dusted her sister's white back. She
sat down again at her mirror, and called at him into the
glass where she could see him. "Dick, sit down. You know
my cousin, Mrs. Lee?" He would not know her, but sat
down and stared, and saw that Daphne was like a tree in
glory. And that the colour of her mouth was due to art. It
was not trying to be anything else. If it was kissed, it would
come off so much sticky paint. The room was warm, full
of scent and whirling with powder-dust. He tried to hear
the wind rising. He wanted to swear at Daphne and hit
her. In the mirror, he saw her little head sink an instant.
He knew her. She was thinking, "Oh, Dick, don't spoil my
pleasure." Well, he would. Then she whipped round and
smiled at him, deliberately, brutally, and he knew that he
could not.

She was pulling on gloves like curd, picked up her flowers, and moved across the room.

"Nurse, ring for a taxi. Angry, Dick? I'm going to dance all night. Oh, it's good to get into decent clothes—"

He said vulgarly: "It seems to me that you've got out of them," and she looked at him exactly as she would look at a man of his kind who said a thing like that.

He felt his power drain out of him, his poise, assurance, pride. He had come to tell Daphne about heavenly things.

As he waited and hated her, she forgot even who he was.

"Say you like my dress. I must hear everyone say it."

"I suppose it's fashionable, but I remember you in the shrubberies at Pharrs in a cotton dress. You came for a walk with me."

"Oh yes. I remember Pharrs—that reminds me—"

It had not reminded her of him. She turned and went quickly to the glass again, and spoke to her cousin beside him.

"Terry. I'm not certain, but I think it wants a head-dress." She pulled out a wreath of bright green leaves and set it on her head.

They were like the leaves of no earthly laurel. He shuddered and called, "Daphne!" Her cousin agreed with her.

Her taxi came. She said: "Dick, I'm sorry I've had no time to-night. Can I give you a lift down town?"

She flung on a sliver cloak, and he followed her down the steps into the cab. The wind was rising, and drummed on the window-glass. They ran in silence down London. It was very cold. He saw where she was going; into a high square house, and down to dinner with a black and white man, down golden stairs.

She looked at him again.

"Cheer up, Dick. Don't you like to get back to it all when you come to town?"

She had won. He had not known how to express his disgust; now he did not know if he felt it.

"I suppose I miss it sometimes."

"Look here. We've a party at the Savoy on Saturday, and we want another man. Will you come?"

He would not come. Anything might happen in the world, but he would not come.

"I'm afraid I should be out of place. You would find my change of values too complete."

"Should we indeed! There are several Paradises, Dick. Me for this Paradise."

She had known all the time. He must say something destructive, inimical, quickly. Only she had forgotten him again.

"Oh," she said, "it's cold," and drew her silver stuff round her. Without concern he put his oily rough raincoat over the silver, the white and green, the milky back that came off a little. She made a little face, said, "Thank you," and forgot.

The wind roared through the square. She opened the door, two half-crowns in her hand.

"Here's my share. Good night, Dick. Come and see me some time. Good night, Dick."

He did not want the taxi any more. He only wanted to meet the wind, and let Nature knock the nonsense out of him and the memories. He took the half-crowns from her, and she was out into the street before he could find his stick. He did not help her. She was gone. The wind roared past. He paid the man, and at the last instant before night, saw her run up the steps, and the wind take her cloak and open it. He saw her bend like a full sail, and balance to the wind. He saw her head go down, and her silver shoes run up. The door opened; he saw her run into a tall yellow arch, and the black door immediately close on her again.

Brightness Falls

THERE IS NO HEAD or tail to this story, except that it happened. On the other hand, how does one know that anything happened? How does one know? How do I know that Max did not invent it? Only, if I invented it that he invented it, it doesn't mean that what he thought he saw happen, happened as he thought he saw it. And I am profoundly suspicious of those two women. They are after something they want, and won't be happy till they get it; too careless to reason or even condescend to describe. Light-hearted minxes or spae-wives or immortals, and on top of that Parmys, I suspect, is a little sorry for herself. What has she got to be sorry about, if the story Max told me is true? And I could not sincerely be sorry for him either; though there I can't precisely say why. Except that we all have to take our chance, and to be married to Parmys must be an adventure.

He came into my rooms "hot and bothered," as our nurses said, obviously with something on his mind he was determined to be truthful about, and indignant that he should have such a truth to tell. I saw at once that it was the kind of truth that slips through the fingers, that is to say, a fishy truth; and that I should have to exercise the virtues of friendship without their reward. Max is not a stupid man, but I knew that night he was going to be stupid, and from the highest motives. And he was in trouble and alone. It was about Parmys, of course. When all's said and done, we do hang together against our women, and not wholly from rational reasons. All one finally discovers is that, when they urge us, the loveliest and wisest become all one with the slut.

He was saying, "I feel I've got to tell someone, and it

might as well be you. I won't ask you not to repeat it, because you won't be able to. And no one could injure her reputation over it. Only mine. Either for sanity, or for not being God." It was plain that he was annoyed and surprised that he had not been God.

"I don't believe in a word of it," he said. "The explanation lies in some kind of hypnosis; and it is going rather far if she has come to trying that on me. You see, if I allowed myself to believe what she wanted me to believe, I might credit the whole caboodle."

He threw out the rather naïve argot at me. Slang makes us feel safe. Yes, and by a contact with some sort of reality.

"What sort of caboodle?" said I.

"Witchcraft," he said, "spells, magic; all women's occupations, by the way. Or the whole slush of theosophy: auras and reincarnations. You know I am not the man to stand for that sort of thing. Candidly, my mind is not sufficiently trained to examine and explain."

I told him, with perfect truth, that I could think of no woman than Parmys less likely to practise witchcraft or theosophy.

He said: "I agree. It's one of the things that makes it so impossible."

I reflected on the number of times the impossible turns up in a man's life.

He went on: "I told Parmys to keep out of it. Like I do myself. Whenever the infernal things crop up, I irritate as much as I can. Talk rationalist press stuff, and when that won't do, I try Freud. That's good enough at the moment with the kind of woman you meet out. The truth is, I'm as sensitive as a cat, and as ignorant as we all are. While Parmys—you may know that over our marriage there was some occult link?"

Knowing him, I had supposed that he would think so.

"—I mean—I minded nothing then—but there was some blend of passion, friendship and wonder which was different from all these. Like a separate quality—detached. It gave us some strange moments, which were perhaps our best. It was like a place, slightly to the right or left of where you are going, that marches with you; that is occasionally lit up from inside. Not quite an ingredient, normally, of the greatest love. But we had it when I married Parmys. Only, gradually, it annoyed me when she said it was the key. Besides, she was wrong. You can't *turn* that key. It is never any good doing that."

"Did she ever tell you to turn it?" He did not answer. I said again:

"Tell me more about this place that moved on your right or left. What did Parmys call it?" Hoping that he would go on talking to himself. He hesitated.

"I don't remember. She loved chinese balls. I can see the living rose of her hands against their dead ivory. And there were witch-balls. She did say that when you looked into them you saw yourself there, and the one who was with you. Yes, and she said once that there were places about like it."

"Like what?"

"I can't explain that till I come to it."

He began to talk to me again.

"I was right to take no notice of it after the first."

It is no use denying that women resent us when we say about our relations with them, "after the first." I mentioned that. He said:

"If they'd only consider what Nature is instead of their own desires. Anyhow, Parmys shut up." I ran through the marriage of Parmys and Max. How we had all blessed it; and if there had been a touch of thankfulness that we hadn't fallen for her, that had probably been sour grapes. We'd said of him: "Max is the only one of us for her. Max is absolutely all right." Because there was a daft touch in him which might carry him through. He was not being daft now. He was going on.

"This story fits nowhere. If our divergence on this one

thing had limited our contact, there was so much besides. And I thought that side of her nature would take a proper feminine course; that she'd become an Eastern Star or a Purple Mother and content herself that way."

"Good God," said I, "Parmys a Purple Mother. It's unthinkable, whatever it is."

"It's american," he said. I thought of Parmys with her bright wits and her elaborate "side." Her husband went on:

"She just said no more about it. When I noticed that, I hoped it was because she was beginning to think as I do, not a mask for devilry. I think I found it best not to think at all."

"She did not seem unhappy."

"Not at all. And what is a bruise or so to a woman as supple as Parmys? You know how cynical she is, and how little secretive?" I did, but also how childish. He went on:

"She took more than ever to the world; tore about in it in a flurry of clothes and people. Especially with that tall woman who races, Cynthia Montgomery. They were everywhere together. There was no unhappiness between us, just a small parting over a thing which does not exist. We lived as we have always lived, and were no end pleased to see each other at night. And all the time it must have been like an army with banners—"

"Or like water from the reservoir emerging from the bathroom tap," said I—but he was talking to himself again—"or from a fountain in a place that is right and left. I mean in a garden," he said. Now I didn't want him to start to dream again.

"For goodness' sake tell me what has happened—" He licked his lower lip endlessly, trying to rehearse facts, disputing with contempt and fear.

"I tell you those two women, Parmys and Cynthia, went about together. Parmys with Cynthia; and they danced and went to parties and were in the eye of the world. Cynthia had never done anything else, but Parmys took to it again. They'd go out like lacquered idols. Their extravagance was a scandal, only they looked glorious. But they brought their troubles to me. I used to tell Cynthia to trust Auntie, and she did. They'd a nice fatiguing taste in mischief."

"You did not feel you had lost Parmys then?"

"No. Her pleasures were mine, in my way."

I did not see how that could be quite true, but it could pass.

He said:

"Now I think I can tell you. It has been difficult to tell you, so as to tell it straight. And keep the quality in it. I took Parmys to a show, some decorative art stunt, because Cynthia wanted to redecorate her bathroom. We saw a man there, and I asked her who he was. Parmys said: 'Oh, that man. Gothic fonts.' It must have been Cynthia's bath we were after, because I remember saying: 'You can't wash Cynthia in a gothic font.' She didn't remember his name, and kept trying to. Then she heard some people talking and said: 'That's his name, of course, Corandel, Dr. Corandel.' She was rude about his exhibits, loudly and inopportunely. Then she forgot his name again, though she was introduced to him later on. No, she was reintroduced. I remember she said that she met him once, years before.

"I never heard anything to his discredit. He's a high connoisseur, and makes enamel plaques. Parmys said they were exceedingly bad."

"Sounds innocent," I said.

"It *is* innocent. There was nothing to be said against him. I doubt if there is anything to be said against him now. Then, it was about a week later—I remember, we were dining somewhere, and Parmys ordered a cream caramel, and called it 'Corandel,'—'Caramel, Caramel,' she corrected, staring the way she does. Also, that same evening, we went somewhere, and someone asked what was meant by a Coromandel screen. She started, and went over to the man who had asked, and said that she didn't know and had always wanted to and could anyone tell; and nobody could."

"This story, then, is all in terms of food and the applied arts?" said I.

"It has nothing whatever to do with them. Nothing happened after that. Cynthia was away in Wiltshire. If Parmys missed her, she did not show it. Perhaps about the house there was a sort of winter hush—I mean when one hears things too distinctly, or does not hear them at all. Parmys was in the house a lot, and several times I think I was expecting her to say something important, not about our tabu at all, but about her friendship with Cynthia; or whether she would condescend to have a baby. She did not say anything, but she was loving and gay as ever—oh yes, she once asked: 'Do Corandel and parallel rhyme?' As if anybody couldn't hear, as I told her. She said: 'Oh, it's like that, is it. Assonance, not rhyme. That doesn't make much difference. I must go on with it.' Then I did say, 'Go on with what?' 'Go on listening,' she said. Do you know what she meant? I don't know what she meant."

I didn't know. He went on:

"But the little cat had made me begin to listen. I didn't want to listen, but I found myself attending to noises. In November the third week was still, you remember. A few leaves left to fall, and each one I thought was like a little word that you just couldn't catch. Light and brown and so few of them—whispers in the air. I used to stand at the windows and watch, until I thought of coral and pearl and how red and white they are."

I said: "I'm sure Parmys didn't listen like that."

"No," he said. "I did, who didn't want to. With her it was like waiting, though she was distracted and busy, like a flower full out and full of bees. But with me it was the idea of listening, for what I shouldn't hear because it wasn't there. It got on my nerves; and then, one night, I could see she had gone daft on some interest that had nothing to do with anything. Like a fairy child, for all that she's thirty. Staring and inclined to sing. I said something, and then she said: 'There is magic about,' and I said, 'Drop it, can't you,' and she sang, 'Oh no, we never mention it,' turning away. After that we had the formidable, chic Parmys again."

"After that?" I said, doing my best.

"Nothing for ten days. Yes, there was another word-play I tried to ignore. Only a boy from Dartmouth, who asked me what was meant by the Coromandel Coast. I told him that the name had passed out of use for that part of the Indian sea-board; and heard Parmys laugh and say that it didn't seem to be a lucky noise.

"Next morning I came into her room and sat on her bed. I remember thinking that her quilt was like a neat green and gold sea. She was picking feathers out of it, and drowning them in a teacup. I remembered the boy the day before, Peter's nephew, and mad about old voyages; and I told her, I don't know why, what I'd read in an article, that in Lincoln's Inn there was an old map of the Coro-mandel Coast.

"'Oh, is there,' she said. 'Oh hell,' and when I asked her what hell had to do with it, she said something about a long, long trail winding. I asked her later if she missed Cynthia down at Pharrs, and she answered, 'Oh no, not at lovely Pharrs. Excepting that November is the worst month down there.' Meaning, I knew, that all the ghosts are supposed to be out there then. I ignored that; but then I asked a question, because I felt it was dragged out of me—'What has Corandel to do with Cynthia?' I said. 'Don't know,' she said, 'don't know. He had a house round the corner from hers once. No good came of it. Now he's staying down there, not at Pharrs, but in the old house at the edge of the wood.' I thought of palladian Pharrs, and the little piece of the earlier house sticking out across the lawn. There was nothing to be made of that, and I said so. Tell me—up to now, do you make anything of all this?"

If there had been one mercy in this infliction, it was

that it could hardly be turned into a story of Parmys' infidelity. Once that is out of court, one is free to be interested or bored. I had made nothing of it, but supposed that there was more to come. Some secret between Cynthia and Parmys. It is getting more and more inopportune to suppose that women have no secrets unconnected with sex. I supposed that Parmys was shielding something Cynthia had done; and I remembered that once I had heard her say that we must take care of her, because Cynthia, for all her high manners, was innocent of heart. So I told him to get on with it.

He said: "That was all until the thing happened. How shall I tell it?"

I saw him pause with that look of admiration and fear one can see when a man is greatly moved by something his intellect does not recognise, and he appears half as animal, half as God.

"I was waiting for lunch when Parmys rang up from the Savoy. 'Come down here at once,' she said; 'come down at once. I must have you to trust. Come at once. Come at once.' Even over the 'phone I thought her voice sounded no longer distinct and cool, but like the sea beginning to rise before the wind. I went down at once, very irritated. After all, Parmys had lived freely. Why should I be dragged into a business that was not in common between us, and would necessitate explanations I was not willing to hear?"

"You assumed it was the business, then?"

"Yes, I did; and that it might be a trick to drag me into it. And when I got down, I found a double cocktail of the kind I like waiting for me, and that annoyed me too. It was too simple. 'Listen,' she said, 'drink it, and eat those sandwiches. We'll need them.' I asked her why—and women are maddening—she said: 'Not two, only one now. We must be there before them. I've been hearing those noises again, like a storm rising. Not in my head—people and advertisements. A hawker would sell me caramels, a man at the bookshop was arguing about parallels. There was: "Go to Arundel for architecture" in the tube; and that infernal Coromandel again—'

"'You'd never hear such a word in the street,' I said to her.

"'Oh yes, I did. Name of a horse. I backed it—out of perversity, I suppose. Such a lot of noises, Max.'

"I wouldn't let her move me, suggested that we should go in to lunch. 'Oh no,' she said. 'I got here half an hour ago. I was coming in anyhow to see the man who sent me the coral links, and I was waiting. Then I saw Cynthia come in with Dr. Corandel. And Cynthia doesn't look like a queen and huntress any more.'

"I thought I saw it then; that Cynthia was having an affair with the man, and that Parmys did not approve. Not out of morality, she'd never condescend to that, but for some reason that was probably a mask for jealousy, and dressed up as psychic. I was going to say this, when she went on: 'They didn't see me. We've got to go to Lincoln's Inn and stay there till they come. He is feeding her now on the wrong things, especially to drink, inside. When they get there, I'll do what I can. But you must be there too, to mind the lot of us.'

"Then I said things: not what I had meant to say, but about the size of Lincoln's Inn and its partial privacy, and why Parmys knew that they were going there, and how we were to find them, and why she drank cocktails; and almost that I'd see her damned first. And her answers were: that it would be in Lincoln's Inn, because in Lincoln's Inn there was a map of the Coromandel Coast. Then, and here she began to entreat me, that Cynthia had a lawyer there, and would certainly have to see him about money directly she got back to town; and that it would be on the green lawn at the back of the hall, 'because that was one of the places, and one had to go through one to get

to the other. We have been there together, Cynthia and I.'
I cannot tell you with what irritated reluctance I followed
her."

After this, I admit I was pleased that I had not married
Parmys. Cynthia I hardly knew, but I suspected the high-
strung female friendship and the cruel jealousy of Corandel, the amiable connoisseur. Cruel also to play Max up.
No, she had not done that consciously. In some way he had
failed her—what an over-spiritualised woman calls failing;
and it may have been an inevitable reaction to drag him
into a mystery he was not to share. But I was all on his side,
if ironically.

"What was the anti-climax to this?" I said, confident
that he would admit one, once it had been suggested to
him.

"None," he said gravely; "but, impossible as it sounds,
a real business. Brass tacks of a kind, and I wish I knew the
nails. I had better go on telling you straight through.

"We got on to the Benchers' lawn at the back, through
a little door Parmys said would be open and it was. The air
was wild and mist-softened, moisture everywhere, but
without shine. Like a picture that might easily become another picture, and has to be very good to stay put at all. It
was all so dull, a London pool, and not deep enough. Deep
enough, God knows, I have found it. Parmys was looking
at me with friendship, and that hardened me, until I saw
her harden herself. Against me, I suppose, and she had
need to, for I was beginning to be afraid. She smoked and
we walked about, inside on the grass, always with her
eyes—and mine—on the little door. The wind began to
pitch about, shifting up from the west. I remember the
grit of the gravel, the softness of the turf. I stamped and
shivered. 'Patience, oh patience,' she said, 'patience with
Cynthia, patience with me.' There seemed nothing to do
but be patient, and then with a surprise that was like a
sudden note or a sudden light, Cynthia came in with Corandel through the door by which we had come in. They

were walking fast, straight along the path by the hall. They were going somewhere. Then, from being sick at Cynthia's name, I was suddenly aware of her extreme distinction and beauty. A kind of wonder, pity and admiration. Also I saw that beside her, Parmys looked coarse; and again that that was because Parmys was like an archaic goddess stored with raw power. Not my wife, not Cynthia's friend and *belle-femme,* but something that is in the foundation of wise woman and child. Half-moons of black hair crossed Cynthia's cheeks; she moved like a lost star. I heard Parmys say: 'Mind Corandel for us,' and I followed her as she walked back to meet them as they came along the path. 'Minding' seemed to mean that I was to get Corandel out of the way. I was rather knocked sideways. You see, they had come. Parmys' calculation, I know it was calculation, had been right. Also I wanted, for the first time, to know why they had come.

"Parmys walked up to them, and said to him, as though she knew the answer, 'What are you up to?' There were no greetings between them. I saw Cynthia shy like a sensitive horse. 'I'm going on,' she said, 'to the old house.' 'No, you're not,' said Parmys, 'you'll never go there with him; and he can't take you round the other way.' Then to Corandel: 'You go.' Now Corandel hardly paused, but came straight over to me, and we walked away together. I was past embarrassment. I *knew* the thing had not been pre-arranged. Apart from what I trust in Parmys, it would not have happened like that. Now I wanted to find out what had happened; and, so are we trained, to spare Corandel if possible. And I allowed the second instinct, which did not matter, to spoil the first, which did. 'I think,' I said, 'that my wife and her friend have not met for some weeks. Let's leave them while they talk.' Then I added, 'Perhaps you will show me the map of the Coromandel Coast.' Just that, a kind of equivocal burning of the boats. But it was a right thing to say, because without embarrassment, annoyance or surprise he said—sleek under his silk hat and umbrella—'How strange women are. Who would have thought she would have noticed that. Or the set of the houses.' 'Notice—you mean?' I said, trying a tone of easy confederacy. 'The map,' he said, 'and, of course, the houses too. But then, she's been down to Pharrs. I suppose she's one of them. Which is your house?' Then he understood that I knew nothing. We were mounting some steps, and it was as though he were suddenly possessed—made automatic and afraid. For he turned round and walked away fast in the direction he would have gone with Cynthia, at an oblique angle towards Chancery Lane and, I think, the Strand, without a word, the wind blowing up behind him. There were people about, but I could still pick him out. There was someone following him that I just did not see.

"Then I went back to find them. There was no one about, and they were on the edge of the lawn, a little apart from each other. There was a tear running down Cynthia's face, but as if it did not belong to her. Parmys was staring ahead into the empty, rising level of turf. Being full of curiosity, and now of love, I went up beside them. Parmys nodded to me, and went up to Cynthia. I saw her take her left wrist, putting her arm round her, holding in her right hand Cynthia's right hand. 'Look now,' she said, 'look again. It is here.' Her voice was like strings of gold and silver, love and something detached, or even matter of fact. A sort of jade dark cloud blew up, and it began to rain. They took a step forward; indeed, through all of this we were walking very slowly across the grass, into the wind, I beside them. But this is true also, that I couldn't stay beside them, because they were half in, half out of another world. Also, they changed. Before there had been Parmys resolute, and Cynthia distressed; now there were two shapes, abstractions of women. The cloud was right over us and the wind lulled. I saw Parmys press down on Cynthia's wrist, and Cynthia steady herself on Parmys' hands.

"After all this detail I'm trying to come to it. They were

walking up to and along with a place that I could see in flashes. Up to and along with. They never seemed to me to be quite inside. What I got was the changed quality of the old London scene. How shall I describe it? Say that everything was enhanced to fantasy and to breaking-point. I was peering at it, when a large drop of rain fell, and I did see. They were beneath a fountain like a tower, on long terraces divided by strips of water clear as glass or driven like plumes into the air. Beyond that there was some kind of wooded country, coloured like spring. I heard Parmys say to Cynthia: 'Here it is again. But what happened to you, my dear, when he followed you to Pharrs?' Then the answer: 'I knew that I was hunted, there and back here again. I couldn't get into the cedar-house, let alone out here. There was always the white house and its copy at Pharrs. I was to go there with him, to where it is, away to the right behind us.' I remembered that was the way Corandel had gone, and heard Cynthia saying: 'But if he has gone there, he's inside it now; I told him too much, and what'll I do.' Then the tune of *What'll I Do* came into my head and annoyed me. I was seeing the place they were almost inside all the time, but not always clearly. Parmys must have caught the air too, because she went about afterwards humming it, but cheerfully. She answered Cynthia by showing love for her, not by speaking, but tightening her hold on her wrists.

"'After all,' I heard Cynthia say, 'we have to go there some time.' 'Not yet,' Parmys said. 'It's the place, but it's bad and small. We're not ready yet to be able to get in, and take away what has been lost there, and watch the house fall. Corandel went there on his own business, and much good may it do him. Look into our own place again.'

"I stared with them, and saw again the fountains and terraces, the unobtainable blue air. Not perfectly. At one time they were in a hall of dark red wood, and there may have been music. I knew too that we were wandering along over the common grass at the back of Lincoln's Inn, away from the hall. There was a bell noise, and then whatever was there was not to be seen any more. We three were standing alone, out there in the wet and the wind."

I wondered what on earth they had done then. The first question after a thing is over is often revealing. I asked Max. He said:

"They turned to me, discreet and sweetly smiling. Triumphant, I thought, and a little sad. I said nothing. In a minute we had got a taxi, and went home."

I asked him what happened then.

"Nothing. You see, I didn't ask, and if they wanted to tell me, they didn't. They were charming to me, but they were like children, enchanted, drenched with some abnormal radiance, and inclined to giggle at the same time."

I could not believe that he had not tried to find out more, but he explained:

"I was annoyed again. You see, I had helped them, and I thought I had earned their confidence, and to be given credit for what I had done. After all, I did not fail them, and I saw part of what they saw."

I asked him if he had behaved as if he had.

"No," he said. "No. That would have been going too far. I'd been scared, which was more than they had been. And it may have been hypnotism, and hypnotism may be anything. I was speechless too with trying to make up my mind. And they were simply enjoying themselves. Yes, and I was proud of Parmys too."

"And jealous?"

"Yes, that too. But not of Cynthia. But of the way their folly had been rewarded. Ignorance, credulity, dangerous practices turned into imagination and love."

I could never see why they shouldn't. The world seems annoyed that any sort of hand can win. And I was sorry for him, who seemed as if he could not be judicial, indifferent or all in. I asked him again what the end had been.

"At first they were delightful. I think they were a little shy. But they began to cheer up by the time they wanted their tea. When they'd had it one could feel something new coming along."

"What sort of thing?"

"An enormous lark. Physically they were so refreshed and lovely, they would have been bound to do something. Anyhow, they got livelier and livelier; out of their clothes and into them again, telephones, taxis, dancing somewhere; more mischief—"

"Did you go out with them?"

"No, I would not do that."

Mappa Mundi

I

PARIS IS NOT a safe city. It is never supposed to be, but so often for the wrong reasons. Perhaps the only place in the world that is really and truly both a sink of iniquity and a fountain of life at one and the same time; in the same quarter, in the same place, at the same hour, with the same properties—to even the same person.

It is no use, or not much use, to know it only as a spree, or as an aesthetic jolt, returning very sophisticated about it. Like all the great feminine places, behind its first dazzling free display, you come quickly upon profound reserves. After the spree a veil is drawn, a sober, *noli me tangere* veil. Isis, whose face on a first swift initiation you think you have seen, even to the colour of her eyes, Isis you believe you have kissed, withdraws, well wrapped-up, grown instantly to her own height—as is the property of a goddess. Colossal, as Apuleius saw Hecate, and made of stone which is a goddess's material; and for lover and mistress you are left with an image, remote as St. Geneviève where she stands looking upstream, an inviolable city behind her.

Properly snubbed, or enchanted, if you remain, above all if you live there, you learn that the delights of that first spree are repeated and confirmed as pleasure does not often repeat itself. Not only these, you find that there are others, possibilities of thrilling ways of life that do not depend on wealth or sex or the excitements between midnight and dawn; vistas of well-being that touch the commonest acts with the service of the Goddess and her law, the quality of sheer living, sufficient in itself, as Tamar Karsavina tells in her book.

That is as far as most people get. Wise men stay there; more than the ghosts of good Americans settle down to the bliss of it. Only remember we are dealing with the Goddess Isis. Her forbidding veil is off and not for a long time replaced. She moves now in transparencies. Only do not pretend to yourself that you have seen her eyes. Still less her smile. Least of all perhaps, do not ask what she is smiling about.

If you do you must be prepared for other things to happen.

There are people who do. That is how I account for what became of Currer Mileson, the American boy I met outside the Café des Deux Magots. Who was seen, who was seen less, who was not seen. Until he was never seen again. It was a business people explained in various ways— so far as it was explained at all. Until they gave it up. For he had come to Europe, so I gathered, all by himself out of the Middle West; and there one supposes were a few people who said: "that wicked Paris got him." Which about sums up, perhaps omitting the adjective, all that was ever said.

Yet American boys usually take some killing—if Currer Mileson is dead. As nuts they are tough, and as eggs hard-boiled. Their imaginations having less historic exercise than ones over here, they are inclined to be superficial—that is, romantic. Or, their national culture not yet achieved, when they do not despise they gobble. Or, anxious to assert their capacity, become culture-fans.

Enough about American boys. As rare and no rarer than rarity the world over, there are some of them who do not fit into any convention of their land.

I knew he was a rare one when I saw him, sitting alone on the round-the-corner part of the *terrase*. The beautiful lean body, immense strength the generations had fined, even to over-fineness. All length that old age would make

gaunt, and wild bright hunter's eyes. Eyes that were looking east, towards the shabby end of the Boulevard St. Germain where behind the Boul' Miche rises the Sorbonne,
and behind the Sorbonne, the Rue du Cardinal Lemoine,
where Strindberg ran away from two crossed sticks when
he was finding the philosopher's stone.

We had met before. I sat down beside him and we each
looked. The spring sun made one's senses ache as they
ache nowhere but in Paris.

"Have you ever thought?" we both began at once. Both
meaning the same question, but it was he who explained.

"Have you ever thought what lies behind this city—
above all behind the ancient part we're sitting looking at?
What, if you go at it long enough, comes through, comes
out, what you walk into when you're awake and when
you're asleep?" I stared at him. He went on:

"It's easiest on the Quai Notre-Dame, by the little old
shop where they sell books on how to raise the devil. There
it's pretty well done for you."

"What about when you're asleep?" said I.

He turned half round to have a good look at me, as
though to be sure of my face for the first time:

"So you go there too?" he said. I nodded.

"Here? In Paris? But I might have seen you."

"Here and other places—places I have really known,
got inside of, worked into myself."

Like him I sat, my face lifted towards the quarter
which is the womb of Paris, where her young still go and
her secret poor. Down the street where the broken bits of
Julian's baths lie about, which he built when the legions
occupied the little city of the Parisii called Lutetia. Stones
cluttering the grass railed off from the pavement, round
the house full of symbols of the real story, the Cluny Museum. All the Parises were about us, behind us, on our
right and our left. Only before me, invisible behind the
high roofs, stood the matrix of Isis' temple, the darkened
shrine. He went on suddenly:—

"What do you think is the meaning of it? What do you see there when you go? What is it, that kind of sleep?"

"Well," I said, "I think, I'm nearly sure, that then, in *that* way, we are seeing, or even being shown, as much as we can see of what is really there."

"Why do you say 'sometimes'?" I hesitated.

"You know what dreams are—even these sometimes begin and sometimes fade away into quite ordinary dream-stuff."

"Mine don't. They're as sharp and separate as two kinds of being alive. But this other thing that happens when we're awake, that we're watching here right now, sitting on the edge of the Boulevard St. Germain—that's different, that's another thing, isn't it?"

"Yes," I answered slowly, "I'm pretty well sure by now that it's not the same thing at all; that these two experiences are different. If your sleep and mine are a pair, then we are moving about in places we know, and we can recognise this place or that. Only more real. Only in splendour. Great houses and courts and terraces climbing the sky from squares and steps and streets. A perfectness.

"When we're awake, as we are now, sitting together, it is much more like ordinary living, extended in time." He interrupted: "That's it. Trailers for half the films that have made Paris, or a hundred and one ways of Queer Street."

I agreed. I have a weakness for Queer Street, and people who have that are soon past being astonished at anything. So I did not ask him the questions I might have asked, but took it as I found it that a boy from the other side of the world should have walked straight up one of my own particular streets. A long way further up than I had ever gone.

I followed his eyes again, pitched high on the roofs on the other side of the street beyond the trams.

"It's there it all begins," he said. "Every corner you turn will be the next and the last. How'd you describe that?"

I tried again: "An extraordinary, a unique sense of all sorts of mixed pasts, a sense of the ancient city and all the fury of life that went to make it. Especially for me, in Villon's time and in the seventeenth century. That and"— he gave me a quick look—"that and something else. Like something out of which they *all* came. A matrix, which is Paris and the secret of Paris."

"The pot-boiling," he said, "and the bubbles coming off the stew."

"You can go home," I said, "when you've prowled enough, and pick it over and make plans and patterns. Even maps. But I think we're right to be careful, to keep this wholly separate from what we see in sleep. For there is nothing glorified about it." The look in his eyes troubled me, the look of a hunter of his race at a terrible quarry approaching from a long way off, a quarry that made him the hunted as much as the hunter.

"'Glorified' is the word," he said. "Alone there in a light of a finer quality than day. Funny I didn't meet you. D'you know the white cliffs with the poplars and the fountains, east of the city near the old fortifications?" (I did, it was one of my "places," and I knew the Orphic alphabet too.)

"No one to speak to—just a few lovely quiet people about on their own blessed business. All Edens man's been working on. But what are the great birds?"

"Of course you're right. It *is* two different things. But what luck on my first trip to have walked back straight into the lot. History by day and Plato's patterns by night— *Garçon!*" He ordered two long, golden, starry drinks.

Like two travellers we compared notes. Yes, any time of day did, but a misty dusk was propitious in the broken hill-country at the back of the Sorbonne. Yes, and we both knew the ancient church at the foot of the wicked slum, called after Port Royal; and I had broken new country in the three great parallels along the river, of which the lowest was the Rue de l'Université and the highest the Rue de Grenelle. To us both had come the moment when walls slid in and out, to reveal others; both understood *crains dans le mur aveugle un regard qui t'épie.*

Pure past or pasts, with their mystery and their passion; and as it were *through* them, the over-powering sense of one energy roaring through each, the crucible, the power-house in which each was formed.

After such wandering you could go home, turn over in your mind what you had walked through. That was why I had spoken of maps. For by now I had in my mind a chart of the place, of a Paris upon which the city of our time was no more than superimposed. One aspect of a central fire, or the womb of Isis, eternally fertile, eternally bringing forth. An activity of which we were the latest *eidola.* Admitted perhaps to this knowledge because we had not been content with her carnal gifts, had never boasted that we had seen her face.

Not even in our dreams, though there was no intellectual work, remembering or researching. There we strayed. Into the courts of her perfected work, the threshold of the completion of her labours; within and beyond the *simulacra* which were all we, in our bodies, could share.

It is one of the curious things about such experiences, whatever their reality, their ultimate significance or insignificance, that no one can discuss them for long. (It has been years before I could bring myself to write this.) After that morning we saw a good deal of one another, Currer and I; and though we knew perfectly what each was doing, what each was thinking about, we never spoke of it again.

Yet I thought of him as well, this young man, strayed round the side of a planet, carried across an ocean to stray again, awake or asleep, in two wholly new forms of experience.

The dreams, so I concluded after some meditation, were safe. So long as you woke up in time. Nor could you prevent them, nor had I ever come to harm in that country. Rather I loved them, as a promise and an exquisite reassurance; knowing too that like the "sensible fervours" of prayer, they were not to be sought or asked for or even longed after, but, like the grace of God, only to be enjoyed.

So much for the Goddess's more legitimate work. No, it was the other business, this waking awareness of what one could only describe as the "goings-on," the furies of dark energy, for which our Paris, with its brilliance, its exquisite sobrieties, was the mere shell—it was there that I felt less happy about him.

He did not know (for one instance) that along the line of my three glorious streets was once the waste place where the witches met—*quartier des Sorciers;* that when it was known what had happened in the little church by the river, the judge ordered a cloth to be hung over the crucifix, in sign that man if he could would spare God the knowledge of what had been done there.

He did not know, and I shied at my own guess, why the Tour St. Jacques stands alone as it does, or who the Child is who visited there.

He did not know the things Strindberg did not tell— even less than the things Joris Karl Huysmans told—in part.

He did not know that it is a curious fact that Madame de Montespan could not even get buried properly.

He did not know that the work of Isis implies the opposite of its own activity, that the Courts of the Morning stand on ground won from the Waste Land. He did not know that there was a were-wolf in Paris as late as the Franco-Prussian War.

He did not know what Hugo meant when he wrote about the Wicked Poor.

Any more than he knew what the Surréalistes were up to.

He did not even know the Song of Paris, how every century she had taken civilisation and made it dance to her tune. Built it and sung it and dressed it, prepared it for the table, for the assembly, for the bed. For prayer, for wit, for treachery, for rhetoric, for devotion; for its life and for its death.

Nor understand what goes with this and what must go; until the ανακαταστασιζ, the renewal of all things, which Paris will be the last place to notice.

Puis ça, puis là comme le vent varie—that most dreadful line of a terrible poet, the most dreadful line in french literature of the dead men rotting on Montfaucon, might have been written about a girl's scarf, fluttering in the Tuileries in a spring gale. Might be said of the Goddess, flirting with her admirers.

I went across the river, to the Paris of the Empire and the Third Republic, but only depressed myself by the sight of women buying lovely things I should never be able to afford.

Across the Seine, still high, still racing with last winter's rains, ancient Paris sat watching the light splendours that had risen across her stream. So that it seemed that a giant, straddling the river, would have one foot in time and one foot out of it; and little doubt, for all the contrast and the easy splendours, on which side the Bird-Priestess who under Isis is the city's daimon has her nest and lays her eggs.

Anyhow all mine were in that basket, and I walked home across one of the bridges that have a spring to them like a bent bow.

II

The next time we met was in the Rue de l'Happe—this was in the days before the playground of the Wicked Poor had become one of those spots for vice without tears in which Isis specialises the first time you meet.

I had not thought to find him there, "on the zinc," and the centime-in-the-slot jazz, among the youth in their coloured linen and skimpy suits.

It appeared that he was expecting someone. A friend

just over and calling loudly for adventure? He did not want to tell me about it and he did. It was an exquisite night. I suggested a cooling walk along the quays, away from, not towards, the Tour St. Jacques.

We strolled west under the moon. The Paris moon, of all moons the most nostalgic. For what? For everything. Love-in-a-mist at eighteen; for a night spent with a vampire in a vault; for a court ball; for an adventure at sea. For staying in Paris for ever; for running away from it at once. For delicate vice, for sanctity, for a great laugh—the moon who creates out of all these longings the final mood of divine high spirits, for which again only Paris has the receipt. The laughter no other city can evoke—except Vienna before we murdered her—the joy and daring she distils out of one like a dance, a running up and down between the alcove and the stars.

Shadows on the moon-candied stones, cat-black and sharp. It was late. Spring night or no spring night, the city was indoors at its play. My companion in his tuxedo was black and white too, the stones not paler than his young cheeks nor the night brighter than his eyes. Nor any hunter moved on a lighter step—I thought of great woods, and of his forbears' watchings in the woods for the feathered, silent warriors of the Five Nations, stepping, score by score, on the war-trail in the night. Then noticed him (we were silent) glancing right and left, checking his step as if to listen. For this friend?

With my mind on secular things, "Who *are* you looking for?" I said.

As though already I was not there, and his question to the wide world (as our questions often are), to *anyone* who would answer:

"Have they never spoken to you in sleep?"

As I have said, you cannot dwell for long on these things. My active mind was on the Boeuf sur le Toit and the friends I had left. "No," I said, was suddenly glad, now

I came to think of it, that they had not. Even if they were the souls of just men made perfect (as one hoped).

"No, they never speak— Why?"

"Well," he said, with again that flash across his shoulder—"believe it or not, when it happens in the other way, there are some about who do."

"They're *not* the same thing—" I began, pedantically. Then suddenly felt as if I were pulled up short. By an intense cold. As though the little perfumed breeze that rose across the river were iced. Blown off some glacier—a breath, but a more than polar chill. And if you are to believe Dante, there is ice in hell. Then from behind, a shadow I could not account for all but caught me up. Came up and dropped back into an angle in the walls. A little dark that had been following us, catching up and falling back, all the way, a thing that I had noticed and I had not noticed. A shadow thrown from one tree to another, travelling with them as they bent in the night airs on the embankment over our heads? I did not think so. Somehow I was wanted away. Instantly I wanted myself away also.

An interesting adventure, a perception to play with from time to time, wet one's toes in that sea. This man by my side had plunged straight in, with more intuition and even less knowledge, was already past hailing distance from the shore.

Argument and near-panic raced up me together.

"Don't," I managed to cry, "come away. It's not safe. Come to-morrow, and I will tell you everything I know about it"—I caught his arm and it felt as if it was something a long way—an infinite distance—off, and cold, and made of something else; and between us something that was not space, and cold from where cold comes from, was separating us. I heard myself saying:

"Ariadne it's like. You can't go without your thread."

Hearing his answer:

"He's got it. He's past the Minotaur he said. Round the next corner he'll wait."

We had been standing facing one another. Now we began to walk again, and into my mind flashed images of men who had been too far. The young publisher who vanished on Olympus; the man in Buchan's story who discovered the corridors and that space, like murder, is "full of holes." We hurried as though driven. Already our feet were on the incline that leads up to street level again; as with the tail of my eye I saw the shadow dart out of its hiding-place.

Just at that moment a taxi drew up to the curb at the top.

He did not follow even so far as to put me in; nor the taxi wait so long as for me to see what happened to the American left alone on the white moon road below the street, beside the stream.

It was an hour later, at the Boeuf, that I remembered to wonder who had paid that taxi, and how he had known that he was to bring me there.

I was with friends. But not to one of them could I say: "I've been out with a man who was followed by a ghost, and I left them making friends; and because I was upsetting its vibrations, it drove me away."

Next day this dumbness Montagu James describes as "common form" still held me; and it was three days before a mixture of conscience, curiosity and Paris high spirits sent me out to try if I could find him again.

I learned nothing at all; or rather that he had been seen, and that he had not been seen; alone and not alone (or possibly with a friend beside him, or with a bad character at his heels) by the concierge of his hotel, the *dame du bureau,* a waiter at the Deux Magots and one or two of his acquaintances.

Pensive, I left them, and walked east towards Notre-Dame along the Quai Voltaire.

Oh but the place was sweet! On the Quai des Fleurs I

bought some. Country flowers, larkspurs and *giroflées*, and the orange marigolds the French call *soucis*. Looking up at the towers of Our Lady of Paris, thinking of Our Lady at Chartres, who could believe—in the demon who from her roofs looks down upon the city of Paris? That ubiquitous demon they can make into a door-knocker and the simple tourist's souvenir; who may even be a fake, a restorer's idea for a devil. Who, set in the crown of Our Lady in Paris, is yet the best known portrait of the Evil One that exists.

On my way back I passed again by the very dirty deserted house, beside which an alley runs back into the web of old streets at the wrong end of the Boulevard St. Germain. A house that saw the Musketeers in and the Revolution out, high-pitched, crazy, the kind of house etchers love, rat-worn, with something abominable about it. On my secret map a black spot and a question-mark—*crains dans le mur aveugle*—and the alley beside it is filthy. If you could not see the far end nothing would make you walk up it. You never meet anyone in it, and from the river end I was half-way up when I saw him cross the mouth of it; and I could not be sure if the figure at his heels was accompanying him or not.

I hurried up, to find myself in a street market, in a crowd walking round in circles, and on the Boulevard a knot of trams, all starting at once.

It was clearly, perfectly Currer Mileson, seen with something of the small perfection of a figure seen down the wrong end of a glass.

Reassured, I walked back to the Café des Deux Magots.

It began to get about that he was gone, to get about and be contradicted. I said nothing, and as I have told, he was new to Paris and he had no close friends. No one to start the inquiries which set the machinery of society in action. It was some time after that a man from the *Sûreté* came to see me; and I suggested, which did not please him, that Paris was a city in which one might easily be lost.

"Have a look round here," I said at last, "and see if I'm hiding him." It was the quietest of still days. The torquoise and gold dust of early summer—*maquillage d'Isis*—lay upon the city. Yet a picture, a map of old Paris, suddenly clattered on the wall, the *agent* turned his head, and a curious silence fell between us, like a shutter between his incredulity and my reserve.

You can only really give to people the kind of truth that is serviceable to them. I dined early, and when dusk came shut myself in to consider very carefully what I knew that I could be sure I knew, in the policeman's sense, in any sense, and possibly in another.

I ought to be able to believe that Currer Mileson was doing no more than wandering about, neglectful of his meals or the people he knew or his bed. That overwhelmed by his discoveries, by the release of certain imaginative and intuitive faculties, he was working off a crisis in himself. That in time he would either snap out of it or be picked up by the police. "Partial loss of memory" was the phrase that rose—until I considered the sense of it and began to laugh rather shakily.

Yet it was the obvious way to approach it. It was what I should ordinarily have believed, even in the face of far stranger-seeming evidence. Only this time I did not believe it, I could not believe it, a single image recurring to my mind continually—of a young man to whom an order had been given: "step out of your body." An order he would obey (the means given, the means would certainly be given) as lightly as he would change his shoes.

Swept up, hurried off into an extension of that knowledge we both shared. Only an extension I had the sense to keep out of or the inability to pursue. *Something far more deeply interfused.* That was it. So far that he would never return.

It was after this that people came to see me. Americans mostly. People I had met and people I had not met. Few, or very few, with the idea that I had harmed him or even had some private knowledge, but (as I did not at first understand) as if some of them, at least, had a question to ask me they could not ask themselves. They came for help, and I had no help to give that would have helped them. Yet they seemed to feel that I felt something, and would one day produce it on a plate. One of them got so far as to hint about "vibrations"—but they none of them knew Paris.

Now and then I would try them out. In the Rue Férou—did they remember who had lodged there? Or did they know Jean Goujon's fountain, in a panel of which the inner genius of water is shown in stone? Or who had died on the Pont Henri-Quatre, calling upon a Pope and a King to meet him within a year before the Court of God? (A point which taken only provoked a reaction about the Templars and homosexuality.)

Or at Versailles even—had they noticed the silver birch that stands alone in the rough field beside the choked tank between Petit Trianon and Hameau?

Or that in the Bibliothèque de l'Arsenal there is the manuscript with the squares, and the receipts for letting out what, as Montagu James says, most certainly ought to be kept in? Or the emptiness of the Boulevard Arago where, for all its broad leafiness the horses shy because of the work that the guillotine does there? Or? Or?

It was during this time, too, more than once, as I had seen it that night on the quays, a shadow would follow me home. A slip of dark I could not account for; and like Punch hiding behind the curtains, so it used my windows. Hanging half in, half out when my back was turned, as though keeping an eye on me to see if I knew enough either to be drawn in or to interfere. One evening it leaned out, shamelessly stretched up over my shoulder, as though to follow the page on which I had been writing down my helplessness. An eye it had on me, but I did not know and I could do nothing; and that was what it wanted, what it had come to find out. And all the time I was aware of this also; that there was a step I could take, simple and obvious, that I was a person with a key in one hand, a box in the other, without the wits to make them fit. Like Punch it sniggered at me, like Punch it was somehow annoyed.

Until one night it gave it up; and this time I was so certain of it that I hurried to the window, to see what appeared like a thin blackness swarming down the face of the house, dart across the moon bar in the narrow street, to be swallowed up in the dark of the opposite wall.

"Goddess," said I, "keep an eye on your servants."

But it seemed, too, that she was laughing at my ignorance; and as the summer drew to its height began to be bored with me, having given me, and in more ways than this, of her best and of her worst.

The *agent* came once more. This time he was more amiable. It seemed that Authority was still asking questions. Strange as it seemed, even the most insignificant of Americans were not allowed to vanish utterly. As one European to another, he implied that I would see the point. As if one of them, supposing they came from the place they said, supposing there was such a place for them to come from, mattered more or less.

Especially, as I pointed out, the object of his inquiries did not seem to have made a good job of it. There always seemed—just to be a little ghost of evidence that he was still occasionally seen. Then, for the sake of trying to say something, I added.

"Last time, Monsieur, you would not admit that your city was a bad place to be lost in. Yet would you admit that it is a place where you might make a bad friend?"

His answer surprised me:

"I entreat you, Madame, to tell me what you mean."

"I have told you all I can tell you, and you know that."
Again there was silence, again our eyes met, and this time it was his eyes led mine to the map on the wall.

Then he surprised me even more. He crossed himself:

"I am not of Paris—I am from Corsica, I; and I do not mean its brothels or its criminals, but I say there are parts of this city that were better burned to the ground."

I nodded: "That is why I do not think you will ever see him again. Can you not get a corpse, any corpse, and satisfy them as to its identity?"

"That," he said simply, "will no doubt be done." Then surprisingly: "It is not you, Madame, who could bring him back?"

"No," said I, "then there would only be two of us. Besides, I assure you that if I could I would have done so long ago."

He stood there, no longer the Paris policeman but a tall man from the pure mountains in the South. And he believed me.

"He met then?"

"A shadow. Who has drawn him into the shadows. But remember, he was good. He may come to no harm there."

"How is that possible?"

"I mean that on the other side of the shadows there is another country, the Courts of Morning that lie only just outside the gates of Paradise. When you are off duty, pray for him."

The map on the wall was still.

From Altar to Chimney-piece

HE WAS EXQUISITELY in love with Paris, his *sweet pro-found Paris*. Great Paris—

> *where the sights are—*
> *where the nights are*
> *and the lights are.*

In love as young Englishmen used to fall in love with her, who had come to her just after the War, after doctors and hospitals and sanatoria had done their best and worst for them. After the country-life prescribed had done its best; and after a year or more had sent them out with the minute drop of sap, without which health of body is no more than the carrying-round of an active corpse and health of spirit does not exist, running once more in their blood. A supreme tonic was all that was needed, and here Paris played its lovely part; and, though it seems incredible now, just that part of Paris the newspapers have learned to leer at, which has now become an american side-show and an alcoholics' parade, Montparnasse. Montparnasse— at that time still old and shabby and merry and wearing a crown of little stars at night. Twelve years ago, when Vincent first went there, it was still like that, still french, still serenely uncomfortable, still adorable and full of great and famous people and those who would become great. Famous Americans too, but come to enjoy France, not a bad copy of New York. Their imitators, their failures, their complex-ridden repression-loosers had not yet arrived to violate and corrupt it. It was not until five years ago or six, that a demon of vile intelligence stepped off the boat-train, crossed the Seine at the Pont Royal, followed up the Boulevard Raspail to where it meets the Boulevard Montparnasse, and at that wide, untidy, sun-struck, tram-clanging cross-roads halted to see what he could do to change all that. He found a quarter in a princess of cities where people were being good because they were being happy, because, after the lost years, a small tide of earthly joy was rising gently in that place. Or winding in and out of it like a little stream no evil thing could cross. A place where, even if people suffered, the sorrow had in it something that was exquisite, a touch of rapture, as though the pain was about something real, a necessary part of something like immortal life. A place where men and women were beginning to live again, beginning to make up for the years that the War had taken. A place where work was being done, by people of all kinds and races; and France at her work again, modulating, civilising, evoking, praising, setting free.

In those days you could see, springing, timid but sturdy, like plants an east wind has shrivelled to the earth but whose roots have lived, men and women in bud again, hardly able to believe the blue air's caress, on the warm soil firm and nourishing, but lulled by them and fed—looking out at life again from the shoulders of Paris, from the arms of France.

This story, suppose one could bear to write it, is not about how the demon changed all this, how those who should have guarded the stream let him across. Or how, like a good strategist, he attacked the French where they are weakest, telling the proprietors of hotel or restaurant or café how much money they could make by giving the nastier or more ignorant kind of American the drains and baths and bars he thinks are civilisation, because they are all he has to distinguish him from the least finished kind of man. Hell found no difficulty in transporting them, the men and women who think art synonymous with vice, and delirium tremens an ornament if acquired in an artists' quarter. These and the hangers-on of all the arts, their failures, the silly-rich, the neurotic, the intolerably-re-pressed. They came—and the place is hardly recognisable now. They came—demoralising their hosts, who grew fat and brutal and time-serving under the rush of dollar bills. They came—and the old delights went, the love of work and the love of play. The love of a party, work, solitude, study, indolence or an exhilarating row. Love of loving Paris, of good wine, good food; love of one's friends, one's enemies, one's beloved. The lovers went, as the old cafés were pulled down or came back after an interval of hammers and scaffolding in new and horrible clothes, with doubled prices and waiters ravenous for tips, and with no eye for the old clients who made or would make their Quarter and their service illustrious. The great arts withdrew with the men and women who practised them, and with them went the lovers and the men and women who were beginning to live again. They went—to be replaced by the parasites on all the arts and all the passions, the men and women harlots and the fashionable purveyors of sexual excitements disguised as art. And with these, *their* panders, not of social or sexual tastes, but the neurotic vices which follow fashion and have nothing to do with desire. Also the men and women whose hell had not been occasioned by any dislocation of our society, but by the putrid state of their subconscious selves, occasioned by fear, by over-indulgence and sometimes by the intolerable repression of american life.

Anyhow, their arrival closed Montparnasse as a temple of Æsculapius; and Vincent, the young man who began this story, went to live in another quarter; and for a time, again, it was well with him.

* * * * *

Years passed, and Paris remained in part his home; and as happens to people who become imaginatively conscious of a great city, he came to have a private map of it in his head. A map in which streets and groups of build-

ings and even the houses of friends were not finally rele-
vant, or only for pointers towards another thing, the atmosphere or *quality* of certain spots or spaces or groups.
These maps are individual to each lover of a city, charts
of his translation of its final significance, of the secret
workings of men's spirits, which, through the centuries,
have saturated certain quarters, giving them not only character and physical exterior, but quality, like a thing
breathed. Paris is propitious for this making of magic
maps. While one thing that Vincent, the Cornish gentleman, found out was that the hillside, across the river from
the Tour St. Jacques to the top of the Rue du Cardinal
Lemoine is still given over to witchcraft, a winding stream
of passionate and infernal air, in and out of the old Latin
Quarter. Also that, in Passy, there is a river-strip and a
small low terrace (now in the hands of housebreakers),
looking across to the river over green tree-tops where the
tears cried in the Revolution are still audible. A blind rain
among the almost visible gleam of ancient silks, the tapping of heels, the stir of powder, a terrace where the soul
of elegance still breathes, and, like the heart beating, one
hears the passionate continuity of french life.

In the Rue St. Dominique it is difficult to tell the living
from the dead, and he could never be sure if he were not
buying cherries off a talking ghost. The west wind sweeps
them out like leaves, in handfuls, especially at dusk, when
the Eiffel Tower is putting on its crown and the necklace
which hangs to its feet; while the wind roars in the mouths
of old courtyards, springs like a cat in and out of their
corners, and with its broom sends out spinning leaves, torn
papers, ghosts and the street-swarm, to scatter them on the
starry, roaring space before the Invalides; where, looking
down towards the river, you can see Imperial Paris with its
crowns and tower. For Paris is a city divided—not like
London, with all that she has of splendour and govern-
ment, of learning or pleasure or art on one bank of its
stream; and the other a place not one half of the city has

ever set foot in, being given over to workmen at their meanest. But of Paris it can be said that the right bank of the Seine belongs to the world, and the left bank to France. This could have been said once, and is still partly true—but this story is not about a city, a few bars only out of the Song of Paris, and perhaps, of something more than Paris. So that for its introduction, a few notes on the present state of that capital will serve.

Two years after the War imagine Vincent at least half-healed, and as the years pass, see him half-established there, but going less and less often to his first love, the quarter of Montparnasse. He has struck roots here and there, in a small Passy flat and in several french homes, in a few cafés and restaurants and among certain groups, english and american. He would arrive now at any time or leave—for his small, ancient home and estate, which was in Cornwall, and of which he was a careful steward. Less consciously now and more by habit he would leave England—for that exhilaration which is also rest, for that delight which is peace and Paris' loveliest secret. For, like many men of profound patriotism, he liked less and less the way England was going, what she was doing, and still less what was being done to her.

While this also was true and he knew it, that, since the War, he had never achieved full life again, not quite. He did his duty as a small country gentleman, kept up his classics, his science, his contemporary letters, his friends. Had neither—and he noticed the omission—either love-affairs or any work that implied creation. Not up to the limit of his powers. For he was a man to whom quiet power would have come in life, in his case perhaps in moderate public life, with a fair chance, too, of private and enduring passion. "They castrated me, after all," he used to tell himself. "I'm just wholly alive, but only just. I can't use all of myself. Like a man who plays clock-golf perfectly, but not on the links. There must be a million or so like me." Not quite forty, he had not given up the hope that the check

was inside himself, that the minute barring of his energies
and impulses would disappear of itself, if the right, exactly
the right, stimulus came. Scrupulously honest, he was hard
with himself: gave life every chance to have its way with
him. And it seemed that life delicately evaded him. "It is
like being thirsty, a thirst only one drink would satisfy, and
I don't know its name. Still less if it'll ever be offered.
Neither I nor anyone who is in the same boat." This is not
a state which can be talked about, but Vincent was a much-
liked man. A man, lacking at any time the power to seize
life by the throat and strangle it into submission, he was
one of those who work joyfully for whatever in their age
is best. The stuff out of which the "perfect, gentle knight"
was made; and at any time, in war or medicine, in govern-
ment or agriculture, in works of organisation or mercy—a
man who needed, for his full development, a law, a worship,
if possible a congregation and a church. At best, a hero.
These he was equally without, in the west of England from
where he came by long descent, or in France. Or among
his friends, who were all in the same state; who also, that
being one of the reasons why they were his friends, knew
it. The adventures of such men are important because,
whether they are fatal or not, they are honourable adventures, and because they are significant of our time. For it
seems that none of their traditional occupations are able
to take them over and use them as they once did, neither
religion nor politics nor any traditional occupation, no cause
or leader or conception of human relations with the divine.
However they have survived as individual souls, the same
minute sap-gland, in them just saved, seems to have dried
up in the clan and the group—almost in the nation; and
its loss has left the most vital of human affairs somehow
inadequate. Insufficient to take a man by the shoulders
and swing him off into full allegiance, able at once to take
the rough with the smooth, to judge as well as to save; to
pour a life into a chosen mould, and feel it in the end
sufficient, a mirror for all that there is. What is wrong?

Was it his own fault? It was too easy to say "yes" to that. While he knew that he was not without ambition, and that it has never been easier than it is to-day for a man to boil his own egg. And not only the worst men. There is still a modest place for the Vincents. Only Vincent who had never wanted more than a modest place, whose instinct was to give his life up to something greater than himself, found that he did not want *that* modest place. ... He had a dream of himself as a little fish, standing on its tail and bowing to one of the present Great—say a newspaper lord—on an Albert Memorial throne and being asked why he did not do anything. His answer was like the Bible: "because no man has hired me." On which the man on the throne would begin to tell him all the things which a "straight, intelligent Englishman of goodwill" ought to be doing. He heard himself say, "I'd sooner be a dago-moron than serve you: but I'm a fish: that lets me out." And then he tried to run away on the point of his tail, until he noticed he had changed into the little Sea Maid who walked on knives. But that was for love's sake. For what love was he bearing a life-time's loss of honourable employment? For a love which had left the earth? Gone off somewhere behind a space-time curtain into the inconceivable?

It was this that drew him and his friends to artists. They had something. Mysteriously tiresomely, or noisily or crossly, or savagely or piteously, the arts went on, weathering the chill dark storm, blowing across the earth as if from outer space. Yes, art was still going on, most certainly in literature and particularly in Paris. The men and women who did it had something they held to and which held them. Theirs was essential health, and it was among their hangers-on, or—and here he smiled—among their admirers, that the death-rate was so high. But all men cannot be working artists, not in the strict sense. If the artists' secret was one form of a universal secret, there must be a re-statement of it, in terms equally life-giving, for his sort of man, for every sort of man. Nor was it, he suspected, quite enough even to meet the artists' full needs. For two things are needed to-day, an art in the terms of Dante or Æschylus, which is also first-class in terms of our age and of itself.

When he came to think of it, he did not know any writer or any painter whose work fulfilled such terms; but only for such would their art be enough. While they were all suffering from a singular new set of prohibitions: forbidden in the past to refer to the Deity as a wish-fulfilment, they now seemed unable to refer to It as anything else: unable to mention the lavatory, they forced the reader to spend more time there than he would in fact. While the bed, once tabu because too stimulating, now appeared discouragingly as a trap, baited with all the ills that flesh is heir to, source of disease and abortion; or, if not in the body, of the cruellest terrors of the mind. As for painting! Why was Titian able to paint a picture of Sacred and Profane Love, while, to-day, no one but a bad painter would try? Vincent noticed all this, noticed also that, traps or not, beds did not come into his life, who filled them with no more than his own lean body that he kept in scrupulous condition—for what?

Time after time, a moment would come and a desire— to fling himself out, abandon himself to the flashing hurry of contemporary affairs as they tore past him, a ravelled web of cross-colours, a stream whose rapids so many bodies he knew were shooting, their heads bobbing under and out, their hair splashed with spray. Or piled like mounting salmon before some obstacle. Which usually turned out not to be there. Or, more frequently, turned out not to be the barrier they thought, but something different, neither to be changed nor circumvented. Part of the structure of reality, in fact.

Still, he envied these swimmers, those delicate or vigorous, fastidious or powerful specialists in pleasure or dissipation, in the pursuit or power or wealth or notoriety, or of social or sexual success—rioting in their Paris-playground, incomparable *terrain* where, for once "work was play and play was life." But what play? And what life? He sneered, as near as ever he came to a sneer, at it and at his inability to yield to it. While the image of the Poor Fish pursued him and distressed him.

Par délicatesse
j'ai perdu ma vie.

Here his humility protested. Who was he to compare himself with Rimbaud? If he had chosen to forget "the ardours of an incomparable adolescence," it was because he had preferred to go about his own mysterious and delectable business. Vincent's youth had passed on Vimy Ridge, in hospital and on the Somme.

Meanwhile, there were artists of contemporary Paris, and the modest collection, part prudent investment, he was making to set on the shelves and along the panels of a Cornish manor-house. There an Atlantic sun and airs from half-way across a planet would look in on the café scenes, the abstract plates, plants, pots and musical instruments, the austere landscape, the magic horses of contemporary painting.

"I have brought back tangible treasure," he would console himself—"for the more I look at some of these, the more I like them. I have brought back, too, a piece of France." Noticing that whoever brings home french work does that; and finally, that what he had acquired owed as much to the spirit of the land as to any particular painter. Or, in another way, that in France, the most individual artists are more the transmitters of a supreme tradition than of themselves. Matchless discipline! Was he dying slowly for want of the version of it proper to himself?

If he had been driven away from the famous crossroads where his life in Paris had begun, there was still a half-way house; still in the Latin Quarter, still itself, still brimming with young life; a place where there remained a taste of the old delights—the Café des Deux Magots on the Boulevard St. Germain. At the end of the still noble part of a noble street, on the edge of the space in his map coloured "witchcraft," it stands close to the river at its most adorable strip—the Quai Voltaire. He would sit there, with the pleasure at the back of his mind that comes from the right geographic situation, from being perfectly placed with regard to the whole environment. At any moment he could get up and go for an enchanting walk, with, a few yards off as he crossed his sorcerer's line, a hint of danger about it. A delicious sense of walking into the part of a town which was literally supernatural, charged with it, a charge put in during a part of the Middle Ages, too strong to wear off. Also that he, and a good proportion of its inhabitants, were in tacit agreement about it—and the less said the better. Meanwhile, one could always retreat, back to "the Maggots," as a swimmer out of the haunted caves of the ocean to the warm beaches of a pleasant shore.

It was there that he met his American girl.

She was the freest of free things—a young woman sent with her people's blessing and a sufficient allowance to stay in Europe as long as she liked. (He could never quite make out what her people were, her credentials were not those of some of the New Englanders he knew; but he judged the situation to be that.) Of course she was to return—to an address which geographically baffled him—filled with the last culture; her pretty gift for painting improved, with ravishing clothes and interesting friends. Something like that seemed to be the old people's kindly wish, not nervous about her—that, heaven bless it! not in their tradition—for she had friends who would keep an eye on her, and her own good sense would keep off undesirable foreigners. Thee would be plenty of the right American boys there, for sure.

This, at any rate, was Vincent's kindly translation. He saw her saffron scarf fluttering along the Boulevard one spring morning, heard her little heels tapping on the pavement and "registered"—the word had just come in—nothing but delight. She *was* enjoying herself, bless her! He saw her eating cream-topped ices and wave her spoon; and when some friends of his spoke to her, he spoke to them; and finally took her to a place where the ices were larger and better, and fed her several more. So they became friends.

After that he saw her every day, with that utter Paris-freedom which allows people to do exactly what they want to do. Not all people. In practice, the people who achieve it are the people who are "most right." Others, unless they are strong in character or long-practised in evil-doing, find that liberty a snare at least; at most, a terrible thing. These fall continually into traps they have set for themselves, create imaginary barriers and fall down before them, feel emptiness where others find open air and conjure up demons to people it. She was not like that, he said, his lass with the delicate bones, her coaxing, slightly hoarse voice, her sharp young appetite for everything. Vincent immediately forgot to think of himself as a piece of middle-aged war breakage, and tore round with her all night and half the day.

If he had thought of himself as a little older or a little younger, it would have been better. Older, he would have assumed authority; younger, he would not have thought to let her be. As it was, he used often to withdraw himself respectfully, in a sort of homage to her youth. While all the time he noticed that he was asking himself questions about her. For one thing, he could not find out how much she really knew. Was she really so keen on everything, and so intelligently? Or was she—it was an uncomfortable suspicion—a kind of wonderfully trained automaton, for response to whatever was presented to her, but without criticism and without real choice? Without effective memory, and the working-over the creation it implies? *Was* it sheer youth, trying everything at once? (Or was it looking for and would it find something that was outside the range of his understanding at all?) Was she a puppet, who might even now be dancing to lures he had never heard? Or a bit of both? The last presented appalling difficulties. Suppose the part of her that was not an exquisite doll had no connection or the slightest real interest in what was important to Vincent, to Vincent's race, to high European life? Suppose she represented another, an in-the-bone-and-nerve raw thing, a tricky race-mixing? A wild animal with an instinct for adaptability, inquiringness and protective mimicry that masked—well, something that since the Stone Ages man has been muzzling, keeping on a lead, destroying, lest it should destroy him—even though it were one of his eyes, a part of his right hand? He could not place her in any of the Americas he knew something of, in New England or the South or the East or well-accounted for New York. While "from somewhere near Kansas City"—and where *is* Kansas City?—was the nearest he ever understood of her address.

These tiresome questions represent the further side of the moon of his love for her, the questions, as he afterwards remembered, he had put about her from the first; that had grown until they made shrill noises at him, in proportion to his love, the other, the visible side of the moon. Was she real, or was she not? For if she were real, his real, she was too good to be true. If the child were true, there was no imagining how far she would go nor the miracle it would be to have the care of her, "to watch, to encourage, to restrain, the royal young creature by his side." Was she infinitely sophisticated? Or nobly innocent? Or of such intelligence and native virtue that she *did* know, dealing with good and evil like a young warrior from heaven? Her "Come on, Vincent," "Look, Vincent"—her eyes, the curve of her parted lips—was their strength that of a spirit or a wild beast?

It was one of Vincent's simplicities that he did not see what value he might have had for her; or that, whatever she was, she was a young girl, and so, to some extent, what the man who took her in hand expected her to be. That

what he had to do was to assert himself, muffle any protests with "that's what matters over here, sweetheart" and
a kiss. He had not learned from life how much time and
trouble kisses save, still less the romantic figure he might
have seemed to her, had he been a little more explicit, had
not assumed that she could place him as an English girl
would have placed him; not realising that where the tradition is different, a common language may be a trap. In
fact he made most of the mistakes we make in dealing with
young America.

What happened, when it happened, happened quickly.
The quickening appalled him, who forgot that however
long it may take to prepare, a fall is a matter of seconds.
Later he reminded himself, that if it had not happened,
he would have given himself up to his love. Taken back
with him to the West Country a strange woman; and that
it was not without some mercy—even her mercy—that he
had been prevented. That if he had seen an infernal curtain lifted, he had been left with a closer apprehension of
the world. For a curtain was lifted for him, but not before
the last minute of the last act. The rest of the story had
been played on the stage of Paris, as if before one of those
drop-scenes which came down close to the footlights, leaving the stage a strip, for the actors to enter in twos and
threes and the chorus to dance across. A drop only lowered for scenes whose significance is momentary, while the
full stage is being set behind.

They went about with artists as before, but Vincent's
friends were usually English or some French; it was
Cherry, the girl, who had discovered and furiously cultivated some of the Americans; who, so far as he could see,
had taken over all that was left of Montparnasse. He found
himself telling her: "Of course you have to make an art of
your own now. Your great men of letters were so much
pure Europe gone across the Atlantic. Now you've half a
continent wanting to express itself, instead of just New
England. Though how the place managed to breed Mel-

ville and Poe . . ." But these, as he expected, she had hardly
read, while the others were no more than school-books to
her. What excited her was a number of quite young men
and women, whose master was James Joyce; and what *they*
were about, he could never quite determine. Unless it was
to turn themselves inside out. Very natural to youth, but
he did not much like their interiors, not quite wholesomely
raw they seemed, and furtive and afraid, wanting in candour and simplicity of perception, in faith and essential
courage or the rudiments of fine taste. He even called
them to himself a set of unprincipled little bastards, black-
guards or milksops in the making. Which was not at all
fair; but, in his heart, he was blaming them for having
hurt his Paris, who of all their countrymen were least responsible; whom poverty kept reasonably sober, who were
not to be blamed for not knowing what they really wanted,
or for the growing-pains of a nation, or for homes where
the wrong things were held in esteem. For in America it
would seem that a cheap and strident idealism often takes
the place of true discipline, the love of country or of mankind. All this he made himself allow for, reduced himself
to wishing and wondering why, with all their chances,
these boys made no effort to make over their lives with
some sobriety, pray for peace and quiet and practise them.
They spoke as though nothing had ever happened before
they happened. What was worse, they wrote—some of
them—as though man had never put pen to paper before.
Incidentally he noticed that they were not without friends
among certain young Frenchmen, busy on the same experiments. But, then, on this last point, the Frenchmen
would not be able to judge.

Perhaps the abyss that Vincent saw opened, that for
an instant he leaned over, gave him a glimpse of something final, as the colour of the infernal spectrum might
be held, for a split second, in a drop of dew. While if, at
the same time, his glimpse was his salvation, the danger
and the escape came together oddly mixed, treading on

each other's heels. And it was with difficulty that his mind held, clearly and continuously, what he had seen. As he told it to himself and as I learned it from him, he called it "the translation of a translation of a translation."

"We're at least two languages out," he said. "But at least we both make the same thing of it."

What happened was this.

Between Montparnasse and the Boulevard St. Germain, the tide-line between the rest of the city and his magical strip, there lived an old woman of some consequence, in herself like a received and accepted and perfectly reputable witch. A local sorceress, and therefore, to some extent, international, long become part of the landscape—who *might* accept an invitation to a fashionable christening, but had never been known to resent it if she were not asked. Her spells were composed with the help of the English language used as if it had never been used before; and were not calculated to inspire fear. She had a house in impeccable taste. Her entertainments were formal and much sought after. But the people who were always to be found there were Cherry's young Americans. And their French friends. The art of the latter was based, partly on a mystical reliance on the subconscious, partly on extreme Communist theory. In essence a belief in magic—"*Le Moi est le Verbe, et le Verbe c'est Dieu.*" In practice, a measured brutality, a logic of destruction, all somehow made elegant, flashed with "chic" by the qualities of the french mind, its instinct for proportion—even in the realm of chaos and old night. While for reasons Vincent could not make out, the French who knew everything and the Americans who knew nothing, met, at the house of the old woman in a kind of uneasy dance.

One day it was Cherry who insisted that he should visit her. He asked: "Why do you young things go there? Why do you want to go? You can't have much fun. Your best behaviour and no drinks. Yet I believe you spend half your time there, when you aren't with me. While what I'd like to know is—which is the agreeable change from which?"

She gave him a little smile with closed lips, what he thought of after as a far-too-wise smile.

"She's an old dame of course. I reckon she likes it that way."

"Why should a flipperty-gibbet like you mind what she likes?" The girl hadn't an answer—she evaded all such answers. Yet go she would, and now she would have him go with her; and amused Vincent by telling him how very carefully he must behave. Though he did not believe it was snobbery; always he had felt her to be far more interested in her boy-friends than in any of his celebrities. He did not know what to make of it. He flung it away from him, determined to make nothing of it at all.

From the beginning he had loved her. For the last few days he had fallen in love with her. No one knows what that is—only the infinite variations of what it looks like. But this one property it always has, that the beloved becomes harmonised in the lover's sight. As though seen in some magical glass, which mankind has always insisted, and probably rightly, that the image it gives is nearer to reality than any other. Closer for the instant, but liable to vanish, liable also to burden the original with its loveliness—(for it is rare, for women, at least, to wish to live up to the image the lover has seen). So Vincent saw Cherry now, marvellously the same, but now all true, all one. Girl of the Golden West, young maid *"prochaine Aphrodite,"* ready for adventure, yet a wife in the making. He would take her back to the West Country for her journey's end —the end that is a beginning; incorporate her into the saga of England by way of the saga of his house. He had put it to her lightly, a few nights before, during a wild evening in Montmartre. She had danced away, said "no," implied "yes." It was the look in her darkening eyes he had not understood.

He was now asking her again:

"Cherry, my heart, will you make up your mind to it and marry me?" She became very serious:

"Sure, I ought to tell you. You come up to tea with me at Miss Van Norden's, and after that you'll know—I mean, I'll know—I mean—." So he had seen many small beasts pursued and casting around, but he was not thinking of things like that. He drew her hands to him and kissed her small brown wrist-bones. For the last week a clean and quiet content had been entering his life, as a man sees—not the other side of wood, but a path that will lead him there; and already, ahead, a thinning of dark branches, a promise of open country not too far off, at last. As, with a turn of passion, he drew her to him, she did not draw her wrists away; it felt almost as though she were pressing them against his mouth. He expected her to dance off, but instead he saw her, now standing upright, straight before him, a young gold tree between him and Paris-winter fire. A moment later, she was fallen between his knees and her shell-curled head was burrowing blind towards him. She was saying: "You're strange too. It's another kind of strange, but I tell myself it's the kind of sort that's quiet because it's strong, and so strong it can afford to be kind. Like one kind of strength, whatever people say. Sort of thing I thought I wanted—till I found something else. Or what I'm like myself. I thought *that'd* cure me of being afraid, but maybe it hasn't. I'm not sure I'm not afraid still of what they call life—." He supposed that she meant that life hadn't turned out what she had expected, not like *him*. That she expected him to give her courage again; and he was filled with the infinite—there is no other word—delight of the lover on whom the beloved calls for help.

"Life," he said, cheerfully, "it's our friend from now on." He gathered her up. It was all right. The beginning of the way: first with this precious thing—

"I didn't know that you'd found life too much already."

"Like hell I have!" She answered harshly, with a wriggle

out of his arms, where for a minute or more she had lain exquisitely, and a spring on to the arm of his chair. He saw her face in the mirror. It had not the Artemis-look of the girl he had met a year ago—but the look of another hunter, who had become the hunted. A song tolled in his head:—

> *Thy lovers were all untrue,*
> *Thy chase had a beast in view,*
> *Thy lovers were all untrue.*

Then:

> *Time the old year was out—*

What sort of passing-bell was it? A rare accompaniment for a man about to take his young love out to tea.

They left his warm flat and went down the wide, shallow french stairs, side by side. In the grey street he thought that the small gilt curls growing under her scarlet hat were like some delicious fruit, gilding winter with promise; and that her face and her slight body and flying legs made her like a boy-angel. He strode beside her, tall with pride and possession, and approval that she should choose to walk, like a country girl and not like a town miss; and that her walk was fit for the wild land, hills and dark valleys and hollows and sea-terraces, where her home would be.

They reached the house of the old woman, across a courtyard in which there were true city trees, whose branches stirred in the small bleak wind as though they wept. The long room was full, and he, except his hostess, the oldest person there. Why was it full of young men? Why should they go there? Cherry seemed to know them all. English or French. While it had about it the indefinable air of a group, meeting in a familiar place. But what a place to choose, an entertainment as conventional, indeed it reminded him of it, as the hospitality of a cathedral close. If indeed the Frenchmen found the formality agreeable, would the American boys, come to Europe, as he knew, to throw off all restraint?

There was tea on an ancient table, before a magnificent fire. Their hostess sat and spoke to them, one by one; giving the newcomer a little more of her attention. Then he noticed that, after a time, people found themselves in circulation. One after another, in twos and threes, and one or two accompanied by her, they would make the circle of the long room, down whose centre ran more heavy tables. Exceedingly slowly they went, a flowing stream, turning their heads up from left to right to look up at the celebrated collection of pictures, or down on to the tables, at books and manuscripts and *objets d'art*. With pauses and repetitions, jerks and restarts, but always round and round the same way, counter-clockwise; so that, unless you caught someone up—and that you somehow felt was a thing you should not do—you hardly met anyone who was there.

The first time round, the old woman herself had taken him. He saw Cherry with a pale Frenchman, what he thought of as five bars ahead. The pictures were superb and he enjoyed them. But when he spoke to her across the tables, he felt that he had not been discreet. Much later, when he had been round again, once with a stranger, once by himself, he anchored himself with a bun and more tea in a dim corner, and it came to him how strange it was; and that this was a place where this party was going on all the time, a ritual of some particular significance, a kind of enchantment. (In situation the house was off his magic-map, too far west, between Raspail and the Boul' Miche. He remembered this almost with relief.)

It grew dark. Candles, many of them and nothing else, were lit. He still sat in his corner, his teacup balanced on his knee, opposite a famous picture which was his excuse.

For many years after that winter evening's entertainment, he ground and burrowed into his memory to recover how Cherry had appeared. They had hardly spoken to one another, he purposely insisting on nothing, believing that she was trying to see what he looked like among her friends. All that he could, with infinite effort, recall, was that she had been very quiet, possibly uneasy, respectful even to the old woman, who, and he disliked her for it, patronised the girl as though she had been some little silky dog. Again, that on their round-the-table dance, she had been partnered by a pale young Frenchman, in a light suit. The dying light had shown up his bright hair, the dull white skin of his nose and forehead. This was the sharpest image Vincent's memory threw upon the screen; and that he had called the Frenchman's hair "green-gold" and smiled at it and had not liked him. His eyes were probably grey to match, and Vincent's mind insisted that they were red-flecked on the whites and red-rimmed. He had seen that, inside his slack clothes, his body was slack and would be slacker. Cherry and he had talked, when they had spoken at all, without looking at one another. Her French had remarkably improved, low and vibrating. That was all. All. All. All. Night-out, day-in, he could recall no more. The talk of the room—in rapid French or most pronounced American, ran past him. All gossip or the latest experiments in the Arts. That was the old woman's *forte,* as all Paris knew. The stratum of public-school boy which underlay so many of Vincent's judgments, kept insisting that if they were really doing so much to the Arts, they would talk about it less: until his sense of justice corrected him, reminding him that they were in France, where it is not incorrect to speak of the things of the mind.

Yet everything in the room that had to do with the Arts was ancient, and the picture that had anchored him, a Fragonard. While, among so much lively and controversial youth, the decorum was peculiar. There was animation, no doubt, but spiritually, if not actually, in whispers. His own lass had appeared actually prim. It had been, too, something more than repression; there was something automatic about it, as of a coterie, a set, repeating what they had often done before; and, behind the hypnotic winding round and round the room, as though there was something known—to everyone in the room but him; something—these were the words that rose—large and raw, yet exceedingly subjective; a common knowledge, a secret, even a mysticism, funny, beastly, witty, mad, untrue—but neither mad enough nor false enough to be inoperative and inactive. Yes, there was a secret in that room. He had quickly become aware of it, but not at the time with any reference to Cherry; Cherry who was walking in his mind in a cup of wind and a lance of sunlight off the Atlantic, where England begins to thrust its bones up out of the sea.

Nor did he wonder, at the time, why she had so completely deserted him, his sensibility suggesting to him that girls at such moments are apt to hide. Nor did he give a thought to the young Frenchman, except to wonder if he had seen him, as he had certainly seen some of the American boys, enjoying themselves in a very different manner elsewhere. Certain of them, highly intoxicated: up to larks, in fact.

It was time to go. He looked round the room at the figures passing. The girl did not look up at him, he had to fetch her. They went out together silent; and when they got into the taxi they were silent. They parted to change and he took her out to dinner; and after dinner she told him that she would not marry him. As she said it, he knew she would not: he would never take her home to the West, nor would they, two lovers, play hide-and-seek there, in and out the curtains of the wind. A sea-noise rose in his head.

"You made up your mind then this afternoon, my dear?"

"Yes, I suppose so. I told you I'd tell you."

"But you haven't told me enough: I mean what it would be fair for me to know. What was it that decided you?" (It means so much to know that: then you know who your enemy is, and believe, at the instant, that you have only to know who he is to destroy him.) Cherry was looking at him wretchedly.

"I'm not going to explain. I know all right. You take it from me—you'll be glad enough."

"You mean, don't you, that I shall find something out? I don't care if I do. You mean that you've been having an affair with someone else, and perhaps can't make up your mind? I'd understand that. While you're only a child, and I can be of use to you." She began to laugh, a miserable laugh, but with a note in it that made him recoil—a movement in the mind which often alters, and for good, the previous angle of vision. It was bad, that laugh, a note in it at once curt and unpleasant, as though there was a dirty impulse behind it. Not the laughter of a slip of the moon. She was saying:

"Had an affair! Can't make up my mind! Be of use to me! Who in hell cares for you and your uses? Child am I! Bet your grandmother— Who cares about being fair to you, you poor fish?"

"I for one," said Vincent, a touch of anger helping him. (All the time she was on the edge of crying, which made her actual words less significant.) He went on: "You had not made up your mind until this afternoon. I think you had better tell me, for, one way or another, I mean to find out." It hurt him to see her slightness, trying to bury itself in the folds and the fur of her cloak.

"Go on and find out then."

"So I shall. As a matter of fact, you're going to tell me now."

"Why in hell should I?"

"Because I'm going to leave you with the memory that you'd that much courage." She said hurriedly in a low voice:

"It sounds somehow different in English, but you can take it I was in with that set before ever I knew you: belonged there: wouldn't leave them if I could. You were

Blaise's joke. That's why I told you you'd be glad to be out of it."

"In with what bunch?"

"The lot there—there this afternoon. You can make what you like of it." Then he remembered the young Frenchman. She sprang up. He saw her out of the restaurant, into a taxi; and came back to his table, the room swimming across his eyes.

* * * * *

Several days passed before he pulled himself together enough to do a little serious thinking. *What* was behind it all? He was not so stupid as not to know once he came to think of it that he had a great deal to offer the girl. Why had he been only a joke? Had he been *only* a joke? He asked himself the rejected lover's questions: "Where did I go wrong? Who did she prefer to me? What should I have done 'to lure this tassel-gentle to my wrist'?" That she had perched there an instant, several instants, he knew. What had scared her off? He suffered, not, as he knew after a short time, so much for her, as for what she had meant to him. By means of her he had sensed a way by which his full life would have been restored to him. She was not that life, or only a part of it, but married to her, he would have been able, at last, to use all of himself. Nor had his love been selfish, he would have done his best to insure the same fullness, of thought and experience, for her also.

How had they missed it? What was the meaning of that laugh? He remembered her warm confidence at first, in the summer and in the spring. That had not been *all* acting. In the early autumn he had lost sight of her, but not for long. What had happened during that time? And, above all, what part had the shadowy room in the house whose doors gave on to the courtyard full of weeping trees—what part had it played, and its mistress? Conscious inquiry came hardly to him, outside his code and training,

near spying; until he remembered a Frenchwoman of distinction who knew everything that happened in Paris, and
went to call on her.

Alone, in her salon, she spoke very readily indeed. As
a matter of fact, his simplicity took her in, and she imagined nothing personal in his curiosity; while it amused her
to display the strangenesses of her city to a well-bred man
from another land.

From her he learned what he instantly felt that he had
known all the time—that the young Frenchmen—she
could not answer for *ces Américains*—who went to the old
woman's house were a very bad lot indeed. Of course their
idea, as they explained it to the Paris public, was to make
as close a copy as they could of the principles and practices
of Revolutionary Russia. *Ces sales Bolsheviks* were their masters, which meant in practice chiefly in their sexual conduct. It was the same in their art; but there, as many of
them had talent, the results were sometimes stimulating,
exciting, and anyhow very much *à la mode*. But in themselves they were horrible young people. They played obscene practical jokes; they had a cult of cruelty—psycho-
logical cruelty; and those whose nerves would stand it
made a study and a practice of physical torture. They stole
things, very cleverly too, for an excellent joke and a high
feather in their caps; there were people in prison on their
account. They had a system of blackmail which helped
them to live—they were quite open about it—called it a
protest against bourgeois morality. But what made it quite
intolerable, what, as Vincent agreed, implied a particularly
nasty mixture of ignorance and hypocrisy, was their spirit
of which they boasted of cold scientific inquiry. Dragging
science into that *galère*. Of course, she added—she was a
really intelligent woman—Russia was just an excuse, or
possibly, and in parts, a useful model. It had happened
before, was happening perhaps in a lesser degree everywhere, the cult of *le Moi* in excelsis, and of the private
dream. In Art, a cult of the arbitrary use of words to

express the private dream. Of course, if your dreamer were a Rimbaud or a Mallarmé, you got an art to match. "Art," said Vincent, "is not life. At least ..." "*Exactement,*" said the Frenchwoman, and that whatever the art of the private dream might be, the life of it was another thing: usually a much nastier thing. "Subjectively run mad," said Vincent, "but it would all depend upon the dream." "And what sort of stuff are the run of our dreams made of?" said the Frenchwoman. "Who out of a million has an inspired dream? While for the rest ..." "Where will it take them?" said Vincent. "To suicide, often," was the answer, "or back into the Church." She then asked if we had such phenomena in England. He considered. He supposed that we had, though he had never met it; that it must happen, but less publicly, less in groups, perhaps less staged. Tentatively, that would do. "I believe," he said, "that we're a less intelligent, certainly about aesthetics, but a more sensible, people. We do not laugh at life or at each other so brilliantly as you do, but we do laugh at ourselves. I can't see one of us setting out to be a conscientious blackmailer or a thief on principle. Though I've known seduction carried out that way. An English boy of gifts, however bad his character, would find it too much to believe that there was nothing in the Universe except what he and a few of his friends felt. Even if he knew the arguments. For there is a logic of it.

"But tell me some more about it. Have they any women among them?"

"What young men will always have. A number of young women who like them, and so pretend to understand and adore what they are about. It would be the kind of young woman," she added, "who likes to be hurt."

"Do they?" said Vincent, simply.

"Of course. I have remarked it too among American girls, even—I suppose by reaction—those who have been spoilt by their men into petty tyrants. If they do, they will get what they want: they will be horribly treated there.

The stories that one hears! Last year it was the great joke to make the tour of all the houses of their families' friends—good people, you know, of the higher bourgeoisie. Then, when they had established themselves, to see how many of the young daughters of the house they could seduce; the one who had accomplished the most being elected a kind of Commissar of the Alcove. But seduction was not considered enough: the girl must become *enceinte*, and then there must be an abortion—and—if possible, her suicide or death. Oh, there was more than one, I assure you; and a charming child I knew is in a madhouse, and another is a cripple for life. Another—again I knew her slightly—was like one hypnotised. She ran away with him, with one of the worst of them, I mean, Blaise Boissevain. He's the cleverest, too. It is said that he sent her out on to the streets to solicit for him. She went, and afterwards killed herself, but very carefully, so as not to compromise him. She left a letter, too, in which she called him the Liberator, and said they were all pioneers of a new civilisation. They all, and he especially, have some power over women's minds. They are virile, too, you know. It is not a question of that *Apostolat pédérastique* so fashionable a few seasons ago. They leave that to the older men, whom they persecute in a quite particularly detestable way. You know how Frenchmen adore their mothers ..." But Vincent was not at the moment interested in the sufferings of homosexual Frenchman of his own age. "Blaise" was the sound in his head. "Blaise. Blaise." That whisper of a name had passed Cherry's lips. *"You were Blaise's joke."* That pale slug of a lad had been with her at Miss Van Norden's tea-party, turning, turning round the tables.

"Blaise, Blaise Boissevain. I think I've heard the name. Did you say he was the worst?" "I think so," she answered cheerfully. "His young women usually die one way another. And, as happens, his gifts are remarkable. He quite openly practises spells, some based on a desecration of the Host. And they work. But I have horrified you, Mr. Penrose. You know Paris too well to think that one set of corrupt children can affect, let alone typify our civilisation. Only, as you say, wickedness is staged here. It is perhaps safer so." His answer made her, for the first time, glance at him sharply:

"A girl would stand no chance with them whatever?"

"I'm afraid not. Not if she ever got among them at all. You see, if she did, she would not stay unless she liked that sort of thing; unless it corresponded with some hidden need in her or some taste. You see, they are not particularly attractive physically or well-off. And, *mon Dieu!* they are not kind."

"Tell me one more thing," he said slowly. "Why do they meet at the house of that old Miss Van Norden? I went there and I could not make it out at all." All the contempt which it is possible for woman to feel for woman was in her answer. She raised her silver shingled head, twisted her pearls, flung out one full, still lovely arm, its nacre skin shining under black lace. He thought of old Miss Van Norden's boots, square like a footballer's, her lank, cropped, iron hair, her shrivelled body in an overall tied round the middle with a twist of cord, her nutmeg-engraved skin.

"The poor old creature! But is not France large enough for all? It is the hunger they have for it, the Americans. She knows nothing of her circle, nothing. She sees herself—into whose eyes no man has ever looked—as the *salonnière*—her house full of young men of genius. And how it amuses them! To be so decorous: to mingle there, as happens, with the innocent, the respectable, the lovers of ancient painting, the eccentric-art snobs! To go there before some secret party, some dreadful escapade. To leave it—to vanish on strange errands into those ancient palpitating dark streets. They are connoisseurs in their way: to them a bad nut is *délicieux à croquer*. If she knew! But she knows nothing. But if I know anything of them, they are preparing for her a charming entertainment. She is a woman of letters, she takes herself seriously. One day she will find herself embroiled in one of their scandals. . . ." Vincent gathered that, when that happened at least one woman of Paris would laugh. Soon after, he took his leave, with the sincerest thanks, and went for a long walk.

So that was where the girl had been, secretly, all the time. There had been the centre of her life and he had thought her without one; would have given her one. In such a set as that she had found her feet, his young Artemis. There had been her hunting-ground, with such huntsmen—and such a prey. "Thy chase had a beast in view." For an instant he saw himself, as a quarry that had been spared. The thought humiliated, but why had it happened? Some wisp of compassion—of love? Or had Blaise got bored and early called it off? He was not yet in his senses about Cherry, but a reserve of clarity in his nature told him that he would be. Again, he had not wanted a captive, but she a master. And had found it in Blaise. He imagined her intonations when she said *Blaise*. Imagined other things. It hurt.

A moment later he reproached himself, thinking: "I did not love her enough, or I would have saved her. I would have found a way." Until he could not help hearing the angel of his *clarté* saying: "You are old enough to know that you cannot: that is impossible. She cannot now eat natural food. She never relished it: she is feeding now on what she likes. No, she was not wholly an evil child, or she would not have spared you at all; would have married you to make sport for Blaise and his crew." He had the dislike of his kind for the abnormal, though he criticised his distaste, and began to realise again how she had been carried into a world where he could never penetrate. Only the utmost height of passion would have given him the power and the insight, and that he had not felt. "Love one of your own kind," was the answer of his angel, "if ever this comes your way again." He walked fast, striding over a delicate Paris bridge into the darkening afternoon, into the tall shadows of the Left Bank.

Then his mood changed for a moment into a great pity. Pity for the girl, pity also for the boys, caught with their victims in the traps they had set, whose artificial hell was only too likely to turn into a real one. Passionately he wished, as he had often wished that his own wounds had won a better world for them, a world wherein they would not have found it possible to invent the form of life they had. Then cursed himself for a sentimentalist. Part of this Actæon they had spared would have liked to turn their own dogs on them. Then thought that France might have done better by her most brilliant children. Then that their sickness was part of the world's sickness.

He was not unhappy now, walking in the understanding of the meaning of events, which of all experiences puts suffering and disappointment most in their right places; conquers them, if it can keep them there. "Rapture of the intellect at the approach of the fact" this state was called once; and he went on moving in it, until the beginning of fatigue from city-pavement walking pulled him up.

He found that he was not far off from the old woman's house, and an impulse seized him to return there. Cherry might be inside. The thought of a sight of her was still exquisite pain. He would take one last look at her with the knowledge he had gained: one more look at that infernal dance, going on, counter-clockwise round the tables. A first real look and a last, at the people who had taken Cherry away—(was it possible that it might not be the last, that he still had something for Cherry? Could do something for Cherry? Would find a way to take her from Blaise and what Blaise meant?). One more look at the Fragonard, laughing on the wall, work of a saner age. One more look at old Miss Van Norden, who did not know what happened in her house.

He went into the courtyard. The trees were still crying

in low voices. He rang the bell. She was at home. Cherry
was not there. But it was all going on as it had gone on
before, a replica of that day he had brought the girl and
of all other days. "Weave, weave your infernal dance," his
mind murmured. But to-day they did not seem to be, any
of them, the same people; nor could he hear any French
spoken, only American. "They" were not there. Anyhow,
it mattered nothing, since Cherry and Blaise were not
there.

As before, the room was not lit until it was almost too
dark to see; and for some time the noble fire burned by
itself, like a giant rose. He had finished his second cup of
tea, sitting where he had sat before, with the Fragonard
for company. The ancient furniture gleamed, the huge
cabinets along the wall repeating the fire in their panels.
An ancient servant came in and put a taper to the candles,
and the whole room was picked out with gleam and reflection, the repetition of their pointed flames.

As it had been before. One part of his brain had observed for the first time a particular series of brightnesses,
which in daylight had been invisible, as if candle, not daylight, was needed to pick them out. Again they sprang into
being, all round the room, on top or along the higher
shelves of the wall-furniture; something in metal, a series,
a sequence. He could not determine what they were. His
hostess, who had been circling with her guests, came and
sat beside him. She poked forward her cropped stringy
head at him: "Seen everything you want to, Mr. . . . ?" She
spoke shortly. She would not, he saw, welcome stray Englishmen of no particular "chic," who might be using her
house as hunting-ground for a pretty girl. He remembered what the Frenchwoman had said, shared her opinion of the woman. He gave a conventional answer, while
she must have seen his eyes straying along the high shelves
and the cabinet tops.

"Have you seen those?" she asked. He rose with her
and they crossed the room to one of the shining objects,

now level with his head. On the next cabinet stood another: and another. They were all the same. About a foot high, of some common metal, gilt, rough, traditional. But the design was pure, the whole representing a flame or a star on fire, inset with a circular disk, rubbed silver-bright and painted on it in blue, the letter Chi. It was clear now what they were: they were frames, supports, stands for the ciborium, the box—in this case a round of hollow glass, fixed on to the disk—to hold the wafers of the Host. The box taken away, they now made delightful chimney-piece ornaments. He saw it for himself and Miss Van Norden explained, and told how they had been sent her from Spain, and had once been part of the traditional altar-furniture in country churches.

"Those Greek letters are the only relic of piety about them," she added, "and cleaning will soon wear them off. Interesting parochial baroque—and from the country of its origin too. For they are not old." She picked up one and began to rub it on a filthy handkerchief of khaki cotton, on which she spat. The old paint was dry and cracked and the signature of Christ rubbed off at a touch.

"I must be going," he said. "I only wanted to thank you for showing me your collection. It is superb. I shall never forget it."

She was looking hard at him. Her head was like one of those carved out of a dark nut. She grinned. In matter of practice it was not the face of one who does not know what is happening in her house. Her contempt for her body, but not for her surroundings, and for all that otherwise makes life worth living, had something enormous about it, as if a rock could fling its shadow evenly around itself in an ever-widening circle. They were standing near the fire. He looked down the whole length of the room. Point after point, the empty flames burned up the boxes which had held the bread of life broken off them. He looked at her again. The old eyes twinkled up at him:

"Two of my little friends, Cherry and her Blaise, aren't

here to-day. They've gone off somewhere. No hope, I fear, of wedding bells. I'm afraid that some of my country-women have less morals than your English girls. While Blaise's affairs never last long. Just the conventional change of sweethearts, with a new excuse. It's only his endings that can be called original . . ."

She had hardly done speaking when his courtesies followed. Walking slowly down the room, touching with his left shoulder or his right the dancers as he passed, his eyes stayed fixed on the stripped stars of the Host. The Frenchwoman had been wrong, but now he understood.

The Saint

"WE ARE TOLD that they shall burn for ever and ever."
She had listened to his preaching for twenty years.
That evening his voice was unusually hard, but it did not
convince her. Her mind ran on to the conclusion which
would make anything else he said insignificant. "And now
to God the Father, God the Son and God the Holy Ghost."

She felt the sweet evening outside the lights and smells
of the church. The altar lights were lit, and a double row
in the nave, yet the hard light poured in and put out the
candles and the brassy gleams.

A sparrow flew in. She heard the wings drum against
the dark roof. She felt as though her own breast were
dashed there. She turned round. The verger was pulling
the cords of the top windows. The bird flew out. Half the
congregation had turned. She remembered the sermon
and was sorry, and began to attend.

For a quarter of an hour the preacher described the
rebellion of the angels, and the foundation of the kingdom
antithetic to God's. The old lady listened.

For sixty years she had basked in Christ's sun, and
balanced her prayers with works. She had not married,
but had seen how people behave, and out of her experience her innocent mind had polished its mirror to reflect
the heavenly world. She had an image of life as particles
sucked into the charity of God's breath, all but certain
black specks her church and the preacher called the evil
spirits, the enemies of souls. He was describing the choice
they had made, to be outside God, Who was sorry for
them, but could not, because of His justice, exercise His
power. Then he hesitated.

The old lady wiped her glasses, and made a short prayer that God would help him out. He continued:

"Who among them could say what had happened to the devils now, but that they were active in the world? In the dissensions of nations, men might observe their impure actions. Might they not suppose that a child pilfering in the shop was an instance not indeed of the influence of the great angels, but of the smaller powers it might not be inaccurate to call imps of darkness."

She liked that. That was true. All her life she had felt that. Of course there would be small devils, children of the children of grace and light. Cast out from it.

"... Need man despair when he considered this? There was no need at all, did he realise that there lay within a power that lies in all that is of God, a power to make them suffer. Now, by his good actions, had he the power daily to put back the devils sevenfold deeper into hell. Let him realise that. His triumph was their despair...."

But that was terrible. She remembered a cousin of her youth whose body had been found shrivelled on an island off Cape Horn. The ships had passed him, and their fortunate passage had marked off his torments till he died.

"... Until eternity begins with their annihilation they must remain outside the kingdom of eternal love....

"And now to God the Father, God the Son and God the Holy Ghost...."

The people stood as though sucked on to their feet.

On her way home, on a grass strip of garden, three children were playing cockshies at a battered wooden face.

"Who gave you that Aunt Sally, children?"

"That's not Aunt Sally."

"Who is it then?"

"That's the devil."

It hurt her. She walked away through the delicate light, under squeaking flocks of sparrows to her house, and sent her maid out for a walk. Images rose out of the fire. She

watched the angels falling out of heaven in a glittering rain.
One by one she saw them go out like a rocket's flare, and
stand on the earth weeping, leaning on swords still fiery
at the point. And after them their children, smaller and
darker, who had not the comfort of remembering heaven.
She saw her cousin so withered and enfeebled, but death
had come to him with the passing ships.

Lastly she saw Lucifer fall out of the sky, a most beautiful young man with wings. She wept, and went into the
garden to line the bird-box with wool.

It did not end there; the sermon had only strung together the thoughts in the old saint's breast. For weeks she
was comforted with a picture of the devils' return into the
kingdom and charity of God, but she found that there was
no authority for this, and it tormented her.

Then the summer came, with a heat no one could remember. The dust choked the leaves, and when no rain
came to quench it, moved continually, filling up lungs and
pores. In the evening the water in the bedroom jugs was
warm, at six the pipes were cut off and the tap that was
left all day to trickle in the sink.

Outside the town the woods were worn and littered
with bodies looking for rest. The trains could be heard
crawling, bringing more bodies from the great towns, and
carrying out people she knew to coolness far away.

She did not go, but sent a girl and her baby instead,
and went out at evening into the wide Georgian streets
where the grass grew, and the paper whirled in white dust
spirals.

Then, in the night, she would see her cousin, with his
body nearly as thin and light, among the stones.

There was a moment in each day when the heat rose
like a flood tide of water and broke. For an hour the ears
would throb, and there bubbled in her mind what seemed
like black tadpoles, some legged, some winged, red with
interior heat that blew most dreadfully white in contact
with her.

At evensong when she was restless in church, she would look up to the steps and then the altar, and see behind its glitter there were spaces, dark walls upheld by stones.

There was the lamp that never went out, and the Cross tilted forward, and under these the quiet confusion of lights.

She had read once that the candles had been used in the service of an Egyptian goddess. She was sorry for the goddess whose lights had been taken away.

These fancies, which might have spoilt another's faith, brought her in the end to a crisis of pity and love.

The love of Christ she knew, and since Christ is God, and God is Love, that one might love God's enemies, as well as God. She went into the state of rapture, until the idea of the soul in pure union passed out and became a need for action.

Some would have been contented with transcendental benevolence, some would have written a book, she could only add new works to a life of works. She prayed: "O, God, if Thy angels suffer in exile from Thee, remember also my cousin who was a sinful man and suffered in loneliness, for a time, what they must suffer through eternity. Grant that in praying for him, I may pray for them also; in pitying him, pity them also. For the sake ..."

With the autumn the heat passed, but no rain came. The leaves fell in a night, clashed and whirled; the old dust flew among the streets. People had ulcerated throats. It was cold. There were fires on the moor, but no rain. Everywhere in nature there was pain, the cold of hell when its heat went. Her prayers were no more than thunder drops. She understood that her love must make her one with the beings for whom she suffered; that, to do that, she must sin.

One large sin would be enough. The universal God would understand her mortal weakness and let it be enough, and the devils would be comforted.

MARY BUTTS

She wrote out the seven deadly sins to find that for
those of the flesh she was too old, and for those of cruelty
incapable. She thought that she might send her nephew
back to the light women he followed, but he had gone
already and it seemed at least a kind of offence by proxy.

But the next time she knelt to receive the communion,
she saw what she must do, hanging like a picture in the
air. She had the care of the altar vessels. Among them
there was a pre-reformation communion cup of silver-gilt,
used only when a Bishop celebrated.

When she touched it, it had been a cold treasure of the
Saints. Now she saw it red as if there were a coal inside.
She would steal and sell it.

Two days later, but not at a time when she was accustomed to arrange the altar flowers, she took the cup out
of its case, and put a piece of cement there instead. The
use of a weight made her unhappy, but so it seemed to her
that a devil would have acted, or one of their agents here.
Next day she went to London to see her sister, and in her
bedroom in Camden Town took out the cup.

She wondered if she should shew it contempt, use it,
perhaps, to clean her teeth. Then she saw its beauty, not
as a sacred vessel, but as a piece of jewellery, and the
memory of holy cups in stories made her raise it to her
mouth. A bitter wash seemed to rise out of its dry pale
gold. She understood that it had become, for the time, the
devil's cup. She was afraid, until she saw a picture of a
woman with the body of a suffering man laid across her
knees.

Next day she put it inside her muff and went out. At
Mornington Crescent she asked a policeman where she
could sell a valuable piece of family jewellery. He told her
to go to Attenborough's in Shaftesbury Avenue. She got
into the 'bus, but at Tottenham Court Road she got off
and walked through some streets on the right till she saw
a small dealer in jewellery and antiques. There she sold
the cup for fifty pounds, or about one-fifth of its value.

THE SAINT

She came home in a storm. The west wind emptied out sheets of rain; the gutters brimmed on the house edges, and her cat was mewing, drenched against the garden door. Her life began again exactly as it had always been. Only, by what she had done, she knew she had related herself to everything that there is in the world. She said, "I feel myself less lonely now," and once, "I have seen the Son of Man!"

She knew too that when the time came for the loss of the cup to be discovered, she might be afraid and forget for whom she had done it, and against this she prepared herself.

A week later, sooner than she had expected, the Vicar found out. He told her about it, beating with his stick on the flat stone of a grave, and anger and anxiety made him look unshaved. It occurred to her to say the cup, though lost, was not destroyed, and was still carrying its holiness about the world, and also that a man might have taken it to sell and give the money to the poor. She did not say it out of delicacy, and then, later, forgot, and said it to try and comfort him. But he was shaken out of his priest's attitude, and as an angry man turned on her with his version of the wisdom of the world. She listened and, although it made her unhappy, it calmed and strengthened her.

She had known him a long time; now it seemed that she saw truth. She was exceedingly sorry and tender for his distress.

A week later it was Hallowe'en. She was used to keep it as a feast of holy souls, but that night she kept it as a feast of dismissal for those by whom they had become holy. When her maid was in bed she laid the plates on the table, one of bread, one of marzipan cake, one of apples, and with them a decanter of wine. She said grace over them in the name of her now universal God. Then she said, "Come and eat. Come and enjoy yourselves. Forget the brimstone and the ashes."

She saw that if they came they would eat too much, and that she must do that as well. It did not make her laugh as she listened at midnight to the rocking, roaring wind. The casement strained. "Let them in." She shut it again, and poured herself out a glass of wine, and ate a cake quickly. The disciplined stomach stopped her half-way through.

For a moment she thought that there was more that she might do, a deeper summons she might make, but the idea only began and went away. She took the food off the dishes and put them away, and threw the food on to the fire, and stood at the empty table.

"And now to God the Father, God the Son and God the Holy Ghost."

Next day she had forgiven the Vicar his cynicism, that had, without her knowing it, made her angry. She stopped him, in the churchyard, without speaking. He was wretched. There was no news of the cup. It would be, without doubt, sold in America, and the people there would hardly know for what it had been used. It was wrong to despond. The loss had brought him much sympathy. They must turn their thoughts to the active duties of life. He walked along beside her.

"You do not think that they will melt it down?"

He did not.

"Its value, if one does not consider its sacred use, is not so much in its material."

The tide of her tranquillity rose. Then she remembered that she had done nothing with the money she had received for the cup, and she laughed.

"What has been done about the School for Mothers we are all anxious to have?"

"There is nothing to prevent it, but the want of money."

"I have been thinking of that. You know I have a small sum put by, and it seems that so much of the happiness of our town might depend on it."

Friendship's Garland

THERE ARE DAYS when the worst happens so completely that the whole consciousness is dyed to the particular colour of the abomination, when escape is impossible, and one plays rabbit to the world's weasel with just a little bravado, no courage, and no sense of style.

We were caught that day in Zoe's bedroom full of flowers, arranging our hair. We had forgotten that we were the hunted and innocent. They had been after us for a long time. We knew that they were after us; but we were younger, quicker, and more impudent; only too young. We could not believe that, in the end, they would not come and eat out of our hand. Perhaps they will, but only by exhaustion, not by persuasion, and that will not be good enough.

Among other things, they wanted to take away our lovers, not because they wanted them themselves, but because they could not love themselves, and naturally disliked it that we could; and there was money in it, and fear of us. At least, we liked to think there was fear. But chiefly it was virtuosity in the creation of pain, and that we did not understand. "What do they do it for?" said Zoe. "Never mind. I know they've got their knife into us. The great thing to do is to keep them in a good temper, and never trust them at all." You see, we could not get rid of them; they had seen to that.

Then we began to laugh, and make little traps to annoy the blind animals who were following us. Keen noses and no eyes. Intelligences without imagination. Zoe arranged a little bribe of flowers. I could see them smell it—and soon it would be out on the dustbin. They were not people who burn their dead flowers. "It will look pretty and civil. It will keep them quiet a little," she said; "but they don't know how strong I am when I mean to get my own way."

Indeed, I hoped they would find her strong. She was a better fighter than I, but she could not make herself invisible. That is my long suit.

In Zoe's room we could see trees waving over a wall. The summer wind was moving them, and below us there would be tea, and great, silent cars moving so pleasantly in the street. The white staircase of the house was like the easy stairs you fall down in dreams.

The telephone rang by Zoe's bed. I heard a man's voice speaking from any distance, from no distance, from a place outside the world. He spoke a great deal. I heard Zoe say: "Yes, Carlo, of course we'll come," but his voice went on, and I was reading a book when she said to me:

"They want us to meet them, and I said we would. Who says we're afraid?"

"Where?" said I.

"At the Craven. Where Carlo can pretend that he's a man of the world." That made us laugh. We ran about Zoe's room, taking alternate turns at the mirror, and calling "Carlo" and "Craven" to one another till the door opened and his sister ran in. We could not think how she had got there. It was like an annunciation or a burglary. I felt she would be followed by the servants she had run past. She wanted to do her hair and show us her hat. It was a tight, evil hat of scarlet leather. I re-set my sombrero, and Zoe hung a little veil across her eyes and took her downstairs, and we got into the car. Carlo was repeating, "The Craven. We'd better go to the Craven. I've got some news for you, Zoe." I lay back and watched the streets slip past.

We stood about the steps while Carlo fidgeted with the car and tried to make the commissionaire recognise him. He tipped him a wink, he was haughty, he confided in him, he gave him half a crown. He was attended to with the others, but still Carlo hung on, and would not be done with it. His sister was impatient: "Oh, Carlo," she said, "let's go in and leave him to it." Willing enough we were to leave him to it and wasted no embarrassment on her.

Through the noise and the iron streets, even through the racing wind the sun poured, roaring its heat through the wind at the huge buildings and the crowd. Those are the hours when the city pays for being a city, and is delivered over to the wind and the sun and their jackal the dust. All the earth pays, but principally the city. On the other hand, inside the Craven there is no nature at all. These things are not natural, marble like cheese, red velvet, and plaster gilt.

We sat down. Carlo was a long time seeing about his car, and when he came he was petulant because we had not waited for him, and had ordered tea. Only for a moment. He never thought of anything for more than a moment. He was quite safe to forget. Only he always remembered again, and a little differently, so that he could always escape on a misunderstanding, and pick up the line again and again and again. He bounded across to us, and flung himself into a cane chair, petulant, pretty, and artful, and his sister deprecated him while they were both hunting. I knew. It was Zoe they were after to-day, and they had not expected to find me at her house. I could lean back and watch and eat éclairs. They were too sweet, and I got sticky. Then I could smoke in the rich, stale quiet whose murmur was like the tuning-up of birds that never would begin to sing.

Zoe wore a pearl, hung from a piece of jade, on a chain spaced with small pearls. Cosmo had given it to her. Carlo saw it: "I say, Zoe, d'you know you're wearing Celia's pearl?" Celia had been Cosmo's first wife, and we had hoped she was now reincarnating as something reasonably intelligent and plain.

Zoe answered in her small, distinct voice:

"Yes, his father brought it back when they looted the Summer Palace."

The brother glanced at the sister, who looked as though she could eat it, and Carlo said: "I only mean—you don't mind my saying this, Zoe?—that I don't think Cosmo thinks it's worth much. I was going through some papers from him the other day, and he hasn't insured it. Of course, it suits you." His sister laughed, and lifted it off Zoe's breast with her pink paws whose dimples felt like rubber. She said:

"I expect he's left it to his daughter. Anyhow, I'm afraid she'll think it ought to be hers. I don't envy you, Zoe, once you're married, with that young lady."

"She shall have it so soon as she's old enough to wear it," said Zoe.

"You are quite right. But you know in seven years— she'll be eighteen then—will you want to give it to her? We always mean to behave well. But jewels are jewels, and flappers are flappers. It becomes you perfectly."

Zoe lifted her small, apricot-brown head. "In seven years we shall be so rich that I shall have all the jewels I want."

I sorted this. First of all, the thing wasn't real, and later there was going to be a row about an artificial gem. Of course those two, I added to comfort myself, hadn't the wit to choose or the money to buy an ornament like that. It had been left to Cosmo's daughter, who was preparing—who was being prepared—to hate Zoe, who was to be her stepmother. Wasn't it real? It looked real. I wanted to lick the pearl to try it—I did not like to do it then and there.

Carlo's sister said: "I don't know if you've thought of it yet, my dear, but I should send that child off to school. A good convent would be about the best. If you keep her there most of the year, she won't see so much of the Traverses. She spends all her time with them now, and they don't like you—"

I protested—"Oh, not convents. They save you the trouble of teaching it manners, and that's all."

"Manners maketh man," said Carlo, who had not been to Winchester. I looked away spitefully, and saw his sister register both slips.

"What did Mrs. Travers say about me?" said Zoe steadily.

"You know what she is," Carlo hurried up, all anxious friendliness. (His attack was to dance up and down and give tongue, while his sister hunted soundless, ready to spring.) "They want to keep Cosmo for themselves. They make a lot of money out of him. Travers thinks his wife had an affair with him once. Anyhow, you know how people are jealous. She's awfully attractive, Zoe, and she'd like to do you in."

In the mirror in her bag Zoe looked at her face, brown, painted, celestial, a mask to set dark crystal eyes and hyacinth-curled hair.

"Yes," she said stubbornly, "but what did she say?"

A remark like that is pure science, the investigation of a fact. I was pleased.

Carlo answered: "Only that Cosmo's a bit older than you."

"Oh, be quiet, Carlo," said his sister; "it's not as serious as that. At any rate you can be sure of one thing, the Traverses would sooner die than fall out with Cosmo. It would lose them half their business. People in their position can't afford to say what they think. That's a very effective check."

And admiration and honour and affection? One has heard of these as reasons. Only to-day we have to find out what is the reality for which these words are the correspondents. It was tolerable when we used to say the words and go ahead on the emotion they evoked, but now one has not the courage to say them any more.

"Come off it, Carlo," said I; "you're inventing the whole thing." If Cosmo quarrelled with them, would Carlo get the business? To be put away for further observation.

His sister said: "Don't you think that the test of success

is to be in a position not to know people? After all, like all
the arts, the art of life ought to consist in a series of elimi-
nations—the Farrells, for instance. I am always telling
Carlo not to know the Farrells. People like that do one
harm. You never know what harm people will do." Carlo
fidgeted.

"I tell you I've dropped them." And then—"Don't you
see, Zoe, that one has to be careful? The world's a rum
place, and people do such impossible things."

Zoe, who should certainly have learned something
about science, said: "Which of my friends do you mean,
Carlo?"

"Who d'you want to be rid of now?" said I.

Carlo tapped my knee. "You know, Cesca, some of our
set are impossible. Dennis, for instance, and his brother.
It does one no good to be seen with them. They are *mal
vus*, you know."

"One can't afford it," said his sister. "Things get about,
you know."

"What things?" said Zoe.

"It is very difficult. Of course that is not their real
name. My cousins are furious about it. It is not quite right
to trade upon other people's position."

Dear me, those boys were my cousins too. They'd always been called that. Acquitted, after a gasp—the dears!
"Really," I said, but still feeling shame, and too proud to
defend them. They were my dear friends, but I suspected
them of needing defence. And did not know how to defend them. Then I remembered that Carlo and his sister
hardly knew them at all.

"Cosmo adores them," said Zoe, "and helping Cosmo
is my job."

"You'll have your work cut out," cried Carlo, pulling
one of her curls with his rapid familiarity. "And, talking
of Dennis, Cesca, guess who I saw him with last night?"

"My husband, I suppose," I said.

"That's it. They were at the Pomme d'Or, and I can

tell you they were getting on with the brandy. Pippa was with them." Carlo's sister laughed.

"Young wives like us have to put up with that, I suppose."

And why shouldn't they go to the Pomme d'Or and stand each other drinks? I saw my life through a dingy glass. These people had made me ashamed and afraid. They were also my kin. I must lose them and could not. The effect of shame and fear was to rearrange every physical object that I could see. The Craven turned into a temple built of cane and plaster, oily marble and velvet, and I observed the cult there. To be rich—to be *rangé*—to be cute; to cut your friends—to suffer for nothing—to be a cad. Carlo and his sister suffer. They were priests there, and I hoped a sacrifice.

All the same, I was afraid of their temple. Zoe was chattering about where she and Cosmo would live when they were married.

"There's a lovely house in Lower Seymour Street—we could just afford it. It has such a room to dance in. Anyhow, I'm to have it."

Carlo shouted: "I advise Cosmo not to touch it! Doesn't he know that Van Buren has bought all the houses along there to pull them down in two years? That's why they're going cheap."

"Don't bring down the walls," said his sister with her good humour.

But I became suddenly afraid of a pillar with a gilt mask on it that might be coming at us, while Zoe and I were being fattened on éclairs and listening to this and burning our mouths out with cigarettes.

Zoe rubbed out the stump of hers and refused another. So did I, thinking I must find a gesture of my own. Well, I was out of gestures. I wanted to hide. I wondered what religion would do for Carlo and his sister. Then I reflected on what it had done, and saw religion like an anæmic girl, like Peace in a foreign post-War cartoon, not attempting to keep this cretinous juggernaut on a lead. I thought of the Polis, which appeared clean but feeble. I wanted a sanctity to turn on like a tap. I felt myself growing old, my face greasy and stretching under its make-up. Then we left.

Outside, the wind knocked us about. It blew me into a tube, and up north on the back of a shrieking noise. At the end of the tube the trees were rocking in a wind that wrapped itself round me and flung me down a steep road.

"So that is what happened down there," I said, "and I am running home to hide." That is life. That is the world. The wind is doing its best for me. Home is good enough, but a little austere, because one is always at work there.

I noticed that it was evening. Then I heard the old trees. I crossed the wide road and saw it was empty, and came alongside the house, and went into its dull, dark porch and let myself in.

In an instant I knew the house was empty. "They" were all out. "They" never troubled me, but they had gone away. I went into my room and saw the trees. The afternoon had gone over its crest, and was falling downhill into evening. In my room the walls were white, and went up to the ceiling like a pure sky. I saw my own things, coloured wood and polished wood, a persian duck painted gold and scarlet, a green quicksilver ball.

I saw my face in a mirror, grown old. I had not chosen that. I stripped my face of its make-up, and combed my hair into a straight short piece. The wind marched in from the balcony, and dying in the room, it died outside, until there was no sound but that of the oldest of the trees turning. Then it was renewed. Not a cat came in. I lay on a bright shawl and listened to the tunes of the house. Every room had a tune we had taught them, and under our tunes was their tune, which I had sometimes heard, but could not learn; though I think I moved to it when I did not think at all. I did not think of us, nor of the mummy upstairs, nor of the wireless set or the flute, nor that in the room next mine lived the most beautiful child in the world, nor of the seven glass balls for the seven planets that hung in the room downstairs. Or of the cat that threaded the rooms, or the green bath-salt in a jar upstairs.

I listened a long time to a song like the noise made by the footfall of cats, and when I came out of listening to it, I saw the room take fire. Point and point and point that could reflect took light. The low sun covered my face with fire. Outside the leaves were fiery green tongues. The white walls soaked it in and waved it back, so that, when there were not steady points, there were cloths of fire. It was cool. I pulled a fur over me. The fire took the colour of each object, and presently they began to move, and I swung with them. Out we sailed, and I knew that I was conscious of the movement of the earth through space.

I got up and crossed the room and went out on to the balcony that ran round the wall of the house, above the garden where the dandelions were in seed and in flower. There came a roar of wind that flattened me against the walls, and I knew the house was a ship plunging through the sea. The trees were racing us, and a small moon beat up against us up in the sky.

When I came back, and looked in the glass again, my face was half old, like a child's recovering from a sickness. I lay down again, and turned on the light beside my bed, and read a book about the greek Polis which now sounded like a fine folk-tale.

But almost at once I went to sleep. When I woke, the wind had gone again. It was night. Houses at the end of two gardens were pure gold inside. I saw them through black leaves. My light was out. But the great tree had come in and stood on the threshold of my balcony. It did not menace me. It was absolutely silent. But it said: "I guard your door. This place is tabu. Keep tabu." When I saw the branches pass in and point at me, I did reverence to the tree and its precinct; and when I could have knelt on the floor in awe of the tree's sanctity, I saw that it was also myself; and when I got up and looked into the glass again, I looked like a child that has been dipped in dew.

Madonna of the Magnificat

IN THE THIRTEENTH year of her virginity Mary, the daughter of Anne, sat in the dark store-house, listening to feet running in the alley, flicking her tongue in and out. The dark was cool and smelt of grain. She sat on a sealed oil-jar, cooling her soles on its side. A handful of rotten dates shot in through the window slit. Then a dead puppy. She sat still, with shut hands. Then nothing happened in the gold-patched dark. "Pig," she whispered, rocking, her tongue stuck out. Later an arm passed a bunch of red lilies through the slit. She looked at them for a time, then snatched them and tried to look out of the windows without being seen. When that was over, she heard a small shout: "Hail, Mary," and turned and saw an angel that was like her idea of an angel.

Angels are usually homosexual figures, more or less draped and winged. That will do. She remembered that she had never considered the evidence for her being, or for her not being, a descendant of David, and with another part of her mind she was listening until she said without reflection: "Am I to have a husband so soon?" And then: "Need I marry Joseph?"

Meanwhile the angel took a lily from his bunch, turned it white, replaced it and vanished. She stood for a few moments glancing round the shot gloom, not reassured. She ran into a corner. The lily was visible in the dark. She tightened her little skirt round her knees.

In the next room was her mother, who was told everything, from whom nothing was to be expected, who by tradition had something to give. She was preparing something:

"This from you, Miss, who were too impudent to believe your cousin Elizabeth?" But her eyes were going up and down the delicate angular girl, lifting her gown of dust-coloured cotton, till Mary turned with a small smile and shrug, looked into her lily and out again and noticed that her mother was growing old.

"What's wrong with the lily? I saw white lilies before you were born. Shew it me in the dark? ..."

Her mother dragged her out again:

"My girl, tell me about this."

"The angel said I was to become the mother of God now ..."

The pattern changed. She heard her mother hurrying out, gone to tell Joseph her fiancé, her cousin Elizabeth, and the others, Nehemiah, Hezekiah, Jeremiah, Ezekiel, Nathaniel, Peter-Paul, Uncle Simon-bar-Jonah and Saul. They would be turning round and setting off, exchanging texts. She hugged her lily in fear of the old men, and flung it into a corner and laughed at the old men.

It stood propped in a corner, unbroken, burning, illuminating nothing but itself.

She squeezed out of the window. The "lion coloured" hills were driven through by a road. Her people used the paths, and the Romans the road. She lay among the olives till it was evening.

They had lit the festival lamps, and were sitting around, close together, Uncle Simon-bar-Jonah with the lily, on a mat. She stepped up behind her mother. Her betrothed squatted, sallow, silent. She had made him once a beard and hair of curled cedar-shavings. He smelt sweet.

"Let her tell her story."

"There was an angel."

"What was he like?"

"Bright and very tall."

"Had he a beard?"

"He was like—he was young—"

"A female demon, I don't doubt. The angels of the Lord are male."

"His face was hairless, not like you. I know no other man."

"He spake unto you the tidings that you were to bear the redemption of Israel. What answer did you make, daughter of David's house?"

"It's my opinion, Nat, and I'll stick to it as long as I live, that it's not certain what she is. Enquiries don't always follow one's fancy—"

"We had better hear what was said."

"Come along, girl."

"It is my angel, and my lily—"

"They are our evidence."

"Not unless I tell you. You'll know in time, anyhow."

"There is no reason to suppose that the Messiah at birth will be anything but a plain child, such as any man might get with you."

"Abnormally plain," squeaked little Nehemiah, "visage more marred than any man's."

Joseph spoke—"Fathers, I am betrothed to this girl. Personally, I should prefer the Messiah to have a father."

"I have not gathered who is to be its father."

Mary said: "The angel said I need not marry you."

"You know what has happened to Elizabeth," said the Levite. "It makes one not know what to believe."

Mary said: "He had wings," and watched Joseph while they rent the crumb of information.

"In the days of the captivity of Israel—from which forever the Messiah is to deliver us—the heathen had for image an eagle-headed demon, doubtless capable of procreation."

Said Joseph: "The cherubim on the Lord's ark will give us an idea of what Nathaniel means. O, these birds!"

Mary giggled. He was just tolerably mean and amusing, and he did not like her people.

"It's all right, Joseph. Look at the lily."

"How am I to know?"

"The Lord of old spoke plainly by the mouth of His servants the prophets."

"Not plainly," said Joseph. "God is subtle."

He led Mary into a corner and thrust her back into it, speaking very close, his small hard body against hers.

"Little girl, I do not mind. We will call it by a right name and be married at once."

"Then I need do no more work."

"Then the child, whose ever it is, will not be strong."

"How do you know I want to have it?"

Anne shrieked: "Nothing has gone right in this house since Zacchariah had his tipsy dream and the old woman got dropsy."

Mary said: "I'm not old. I've not had dropsy. I've had an angel."

"Angels are incapable of procreation."

Joseph made a face.

"Joseph, why do you still want to marry me?"

"I don't know. It would be better than this noise. These old men don't smell nice."

"Is it because you love me?"

"Yes, perhaps. I don't know—I prefer not to wrangle."

"Joseph, it is all true."

"Quite so."

"Oh, why did it ever happen?"

"Peace, sirs. I am willing to marry her, and let her tale pass and then confirm it."

The air rushed out of seven old lungs.

"Then, son, it is your affair."

The lily fell into dust.

"A question for you, fathers—supposing the lily miraculous, does its change constitute another miracle, and what miraculous element is there in its dust? On this question hangs that of the homogeneity of divine substance. Again—it would be suitable for the mother of Israel's king to make a thanksgiving. I leave it to Nathaniel to prepare. I will teach it her myself. Mary, go into the store-room and sleep."

He left the house. The dark road was full of lights. His

people were about and soldiers. He passed in and out in his clay-coloured gown. His light, cleft beard stuck out. He plaited in his intelligence with his desires. True or untrue the story might be good as true, and so serviceable. To him the divine was an ambiguous element, appearing in life, and occasionally plastic to man. There were two kinds of men necessary, or a man and some men. A man to conceive, and men to execute and adopt in the great *ludus sacer* which is the whole of man's activity, a sport of lions, only subsequently rationalised, whose rule is that every man must win, and every man but one be annihilated.

He tested his positions, while his sensuality grumbled, waiting its turn.

He did not like the moon. He could not follow the stars. In his workshop he lay down and poured the cedar-curls on his head and did not reconstruct a glory for Israel, but a future in which God seemed to have let them down again under an ornate construction that resembled the Roman architecture he had observed.

* * * * *

The next day she cleaned the house. Cleanness attracts light, breaks up a room into point and shine and glitter. Water loosed the colour in the tiles, the mud brushed into dun bubbles, and left moist stone for the sun to suck and polish. At the well the water split and broke like loose glass.

A quick day ran through into night, when the other side of being breathes and wakes. In the morning she had not known how to evade her mother. At night she walked out.

* * * * *

The boy who had thrown the puppy and the date stones and offered the lilies ran after her upon the hillocks.

They argued:

"You can't have the Messiah, you've been about with me."

"They don't suppose you're a man."

"They're marrying you off to Joseph because they do."

"But I saw an angel."

"I guess what it was you saw."

"Anyhow, there is going to be a Messiah."

"I don't believe in the Messiah."

"What is going to happen if there isn't going to be a Messiah?"

"There's a man over there who knows everything. They're Romans. They've been after robbers in the hills. They camp down here at night. I am going to Alexandria where there are lots of them. They're soldiers. The officer is called Panthera. You can come, too."

She followed him.

* * * * *

"Brought your sister?"

"No. She's the one I told you about."

"From the family that does miracles?" He cut on his tablets by a clean fire, the brush of his helmet curled beside him.

"She saw one of the angels, and now she says she is going to have the Messiah, and Joseph's marrying her—"

"Shut up. I'll ask her to tell me."

There were the squares of his armour, his small chin, his nut-shaped nails that were like his teeth. She edged in.

"Do you think it happened to me?"

"If you saw an angel, you saw one. Think carefully if you did. And if you did not see an angel, but something else, think what you saw. And if you decide that you saw nothing, think why you thought that you saw anything. There—try that."

"There is another kind of seeing."

"There is not."

"Yes, I saw it."

"You mean you wanted it and thought about your want till you saw?"

"I did not want. I did not think."

"I can believe that, little beauty. Well, what was the angel like?"

"He shone."

"Are your people pleased? Oh, the boy said they're marrying you. Do they want the Romans to go? You don't know about that? Run off, boy, and talk to Psellus. He's been to Alexandria. Were you brought up to expect this?" There, I am schoolmastering again, he thought, and said:

"Let's sit over the fire."

She sat down on a stone, straight up, the night passing behind her head. By the centurion's hard fire there was another arrangement of life, like a bass scale played firmly. A long time ago she had seen brightness in a dark room.

She sat slackly.

"Well, little lady?"—is she really a virgin?—"Have you heard of Rome?"

"Yes!"

"It was founded by the son of a mother like you."

"What happened to her?"

"She was numbered among the immortals. A she-wolf looked after her baby. There were two of them. One killed the other, and founded the city."

"What are the immortals?"

"The Gods who are supposed to look after us. Like the one you have at Jerusalem. Dionysos-of-the-vine."

"We have only one God."

"So I have heard. Anyhow, Rhea Silvia became a goddess. Would you like that?"

"No."

"What would you like?"

She thought. The interesting tranquillity in whose circle she sat. Not to marry Joseph. Things to wear and eat. She said:

"Not to go home. Not to go back."

"No one goes back."

"Then I shall be the mother of God."

"What do you think of what I have told you, that every country has its heroes, and most heroes have had for a mother a girl like yourself?"

"What happened to them?"

"Some die: some are married to kings: some join the stars."

"Is God ever good to them?"

"Well, I don't know quite what you expect of God. They had what God gives when he comes personally. Good reveries they must have had.... God is like undiluted wine. We'll have a cup, but not like that."—Jove, she's a pretty girl.—"Of one of them, it was said: *and she bore a blameless child.* Do you know what a man is? Was it a bird? You'll sit on my knee and I'll tell you the story of stories, of Leda who bore two men, saviours of men, and two women who were their enemies, who was married to a swan."

He rocked her but she stared. On a great breath she sailed out on his knee, her sight on the blue hangings above the world. The pool of hot wood rose with them and the next seat was the moon.

"Have I made you familiar with these ladies?"

"Yes."

She began to cry to herself, slid off his knees and squatted by the fire.

"I forgot. This was all for my satisfaction, not yours. But tell me, after all this, do you insist that you saw anything at all?"

"Yes." She plaited her hair.

"Don't you know that the thing which cannot be said is the thing that is not true?"

"No."

"So you'll take your chance with God and man?"

"How do you know I want to have it?"

"How would you like me for its father?"

"Not now."

She became the peasant girl running home to a community of theological peasants. She had come to the point of her cycle when their nature was expressed in hers, and she was ashamed to be where she was. She saw the map of her cycle, the blind round of nature and emotion, fear, a little blessedness, ennui and shame.

"Tell me what will happen to me."

"I think anything may happen, and I don't suppose your people are up to good." He thought: She would have her God in peace, or else no God. That is exactly what will not happen. Life is not like that. There never will be a clear run. If something remarkable gets born, it will be more and less than a man. The fire wants making up. And when she is old she will be lucky if she can look back and notice a coherency. She won't want to. It will either have happened or not. Or another set of events will be insisting. She is ready to run away.

He looked round for wood. The moon had set. That ended it. She hung on quiet, holding herself. He made a sign for wood. And to herself she said: *Let it go, my beauty, let it go.* A new word. A blessing. She saw only the grey tent and its gilt bird. Not even that. She got up.

"Nico!"

"We march at dawn," said Panthera.

"I have to take her back," said Nico. "I don't want to. I want to come to Alexandria with you."

"You can't do both."

He scowled at her. "Come along."

"Cheer up, little lady, you'll be the mother of a hero."

They went away.

* * * * *

"They would never have taken me to Alexandria."

"Panthera would have."

"It is your fault."

"It's not. Cowardy. No, no, no—you can go when you're older."

The sky, emptied of the moon, had the night to itself. It covered them, a witch's mantle, untender, observant.

"It's lucky Joseph will have you."

"His luck you mean."

"No, yours. I wouldn't. If it is the Messiah, no one will know till it's grown up. You don't suppose there will be any more angels?"

"Why not? Yes. I do."

"Bet you there won't be."

"Why won't you let me have anything?"

"You spoilt my chance of going to Alexandria."

"You were afraid to go."

"I shall say how you got your baby. I shall say it's the soldiers. I shall say it's Captain Panthera. They'll believe that."

It seemed that there was no more room in space for her to occupy. Every inch, a spear-point turned. She sighed, the malice gone out of her, the baby pride, the amusement, valour, grace.

"They mustn't say that. He must have his chance."

"You sing all the way back, then, while I'm pinching your arm. It'll get you into practice to sing old Nathaniel's song."

"If I do, you will not keep your promise."

"God isn't the only person who can keep a promise."

"Then you believe in my angel?"

"You might do it, if those old brutes don't spoil it. But I don't let you off, either. You sing, or I tell."

She drew two heavy sobs and, as his finger and thumb tightened, stared with running cheeks and cried: *"I will think upon Rahab and Babylon, Tyre and the Morians also, lo, there was he born. The Lord shall rehearse it when he writeth up*

the peoples that he was born there. The singers also and the trum-
peters shall he rehearse. ..."

His hand went on pinching. The sky went on watching.
The centurian's fire had gone out and the moon. Near
home he stopped pinching and sang after her. "*All my fresh*
springs are in thee."

* * * * *

He led her in, his finger on his lips.

"She went out among the olives to pray. I watched over
her and have brought her back."

Nathaniel followed her into the store-room. Presently
he came out.

"She has learned my psalm. The third verse is her
own. She will come out now."

Joseph rose to fetch her.

"My dear. Speak to me. I believe. I will worship him
and take care of you." She turned from him.

"When you smile like that. I cannot bear it—I am ex-
alted. There is so much pain about. Go through, Mother
of God."

The old faces turned to her.

And Mary said.

A NOTE ON THIS EDITION

Mary Butts's thirty stories were published in three volumes. *Speed the Plough and Other Stories* was issued in 1923 by Chapman & Hall, London, and includes "In Bayswater," "The Saint," and "Madonna of the Magnificat." *Several Occasions* appeared from Wishart, London, in 1932, from which "Widdershins," "Brightness Falls," "In Bloomsbury," "Friendship's Garland," "Green," and "The House-party" have been selected. *Last Stories* was issued posthumously in 1938 by Brendin Publishing Co., London, and includes "The Warning," "Mappa Mundi," "From Altar to Chimney-piece," "With and Without Buttons," "Lettres Imaginaires," "A Lover," and "The House." Discrepancies in punctuation, capitalization, and spelling among those editions naturally are extensive, and original proofsheets were unavailable for inspection. As with the Recovered Classics edition of *The Taverner Novels*, punctuation has been changed when necessary to conform with the Wishart edition of *Armed with Madness* (1928). Obvious spelling and other typographical errors have been corrected, but authorial idiosyncrasies in spelling and style have been largely maintained. The publisher wishes to thank Kathleen Peifer for serving as copy editor and proofreader, and Alexandra Langley for keyboarding the manuscript and for copy editing assistance. The publisher also gratefully acknowledges Kenneth Irby for consulting in the selection, and for copies of several elusive stories; Camilla Bagg for her generous cooperation in behalf of the Mary Butts estate; Christopher Wagstaff for providing copies of most of the stories; and Robert Kelly, Edouard Roditi, and John Ashbery for their encouragement and advice.

The text of this book has been set in a Mergenthaler Linotron version of Baskerville. The design is by Bruce McPherson. William Kalvin at Delmas Type, Ann Arbor, performed the text typography. Of this first printing, there are 1700 copies bound in paper covers and jackets, and 300 copies bound in cloth over boards with mylar jackets.